This novel is a work of fiction. Names, characters, places and incidents are either products of the author's imagination or used fictitiously. Any resemblance to actual events, locales, or persons, living, dead, or undead, is entirely coincidental.

www.wispvine.com

978-1-939997-96-8

1st Edition

BOOKS BY OLIVIA ASH

Dragon Dojo Brotherhood

Reign of Dragons

Fate of Dragons

Blood of Dragons

Age of Dragons

Fall of Dragons

Death of Dragons

War of Dragons

Queen of Dragons

Myths of Dragons

Vessel of Dragons

Gods of Dragons

A Legend Among Dragons

Blackbriar Academy

The Trials of Blackbriar Academy

The Shadows of Blackbriar Academy

The Hex of Blackbriar Academy

The Blood Oath of Blackbriar Academy

The Battle of Blackbriar Academy

The Nighthelm Guardian Series

City of the Sleeping Gods

City of Fractured Souls

City of the Enchanted Queen

Demon Queen Saga

Princes of the Underworld

Wars of the Underworld

Sentinel Saga

By Dahlia Leigh and Olivia Ash

The Shadow Shifter

STAY CONNECTED

Join the exclusive group where all the cool kids hang out... Olivia's secret club for cool ladies! Consider this your formal invitation to a world of hot guys, fun people, and your fellow book lovers. Olivia hangs out in this group all the time. She made the group specifically for readers like you to come together and share their lives and interests, especially regarding the hot guys from her novels.

Check it out! Everyone in there is amazing, and you'll fit right in.

https://www.facebook.com/groups/LilaJeanOliviaAsh/

Sign up for email alerts of new releases AND an

exclusive bonus novella from the Nighthelm Guardian series, *City of the Rebel Runes,* the prequel to *City of Sleeping Gods* only available to subscribers.

https://wispvine.com/newsletter/olivia-ash-email-signup/

Enjoying the series? Awesome! Help others discover the Dragon Dojo Brotherhood by leaving a review at Amazon.

DEATH OF DRAGONS

Book Six of the Dragon Dojo Brotherhood

OLIVIA ASH

BOOK DESCRIPTION

DRAGON DOJO BROTHERHOOD BOOK SIX: DEATH OF DRAGONS

Death is in the air.

It always seems to be, lately. Blood. Mayhem. Destruction.

It just follows me.

The people after me—they're relentless. They've hunted me from the moment I stepped into this new power. They say it's not mine. That it belongs to the dragon Bosses. Hell, maybe even to the gods themselves.

Well, anyone who wants my magic can *fight* me for it.

I'm a diamond dragon, and the only one of my kind. Though I've been able to keep that a secret while my dragon and I get to know each other, we can't hide the truth much longer.

Sooner or later, we'll come across a battle I can't protect her from. We'll have to go into the ring together, and once we do, there's no turning back.

Because there's only one thing the Bosses want more than my magic.

They want *me*.

Vengeance, justice, honor—whatever the powerful dragons of this world try to take from me, I'll get back three-fold.

Good luck to the fools who try me.

CONTENTS

Important Characters & Terms xiii

Chapter One 1
Chapter Two 17
Chapter Three 27
Chapter Four 43
Chapter Five 62
Chapter Six 73
Chapter Seven 88
Chapter Eight 101
Chapter Nine 123
Chapter Ten 140
Chapter Eleven 153
Chapter Twelve 172
Chapter Thirteen 184
Chapter Fourteen 196
Chapter Fifteen 210
Chapter Sixteen 227
Chapter Seventeen 243
Chapter Eighteen 255
Chapter Nineteen 267
Chapter Twenty 280
Chapter Twenty-One 291
Chapter Twenty-Two 318
Chapter Twenty-Three 326
Chapter Twenty-Four 347
Chapter Twenty-Five 362
Chapter Twenty-Six 381
Chapter Twenty-Seven 389
Chapter Twenty-Eight 399

Chapter Twenty-Nine 410
Chapter Thirty 428
Chapter Thirty-One 435
Chapter Thirty-Two 444
Chapter Thirty-Three 459
Chapter Thirty-Four 469
Chapter Thirty-Five 485
Chapter Thirty-Six 495
Chapter Thirty-Seven 503

Author Notes 509
Books by Olivia Ash 515
About the Author 517

IMPORTANT CHARACTERS & TERMS

Characters

Rory Quinn: a former Spectre and the current dragon vessel. Rory was raised as a brutal assassin by her mentor Zurie, but escaped that life. When Zurie tried to force Rory to return, Rory was forced to kill her former mentor. Rory's newfound magic is constantly evolving and changing, and now that she has shifted, her magic continues to defy all known limits. Her diamond dragon is the only one of its kind, and the only other diamond dragons known to exist were the fabled dragon gods themselves. But Rory was born a human, so she can't be a *goddess*… can she?

Andrew Darrington (Drew): a fire dragon shifter. Drew is one of the heirs to the Darrington dragon family. With no real regard for rules or the law in general, Drew tends to know things he shouldn't and isn't fond of sharing that intel with just anyone. Though he originally intended to kidnap Rory and use her power for his own means, her tenacity and strength enchanted him. They have a pact: if he doesn't try to control her, she won't try to control him. Drew sees her as an equal in a world where he's stronger, smarter, and faster than nearly everyone else.

Tucker Chase: a weapons expert and former Knight. Tucker's a loveable goofball who treats every day like it's his last—because it very well might be. He was forced to kill his father, the General of the now-defunct Knights anti-dragon terrorist organization, when the man brought a war to Rory's door. Tucker was originally assigned to hunt Rory down and turn her in to his father, but as he spent more time with her, she became the true family he'd never had. To protect her, Tucker fed his father false intel about her abilities—and gave up his old life to stay at her side.

Levi Sloane: an ice dragon shifter and former Vaer soldier who went feral when his commander killed his very ill little sister. When he was feral, Rory saved him from a snare trap on the edge of the Vaer lands, and he has been by her side ever since. Feral dragons slowly lose touch with their human selves, but Rory helped bring him back from the brink. Though all dragons can communicate telepathically when they touch, Levi and Rory can also communicate this way in human form. To save Rory's life, he and his dragon healed their relationship, and Levi can once again shift and retain full control. He's the only dragon to ever come back from being feral.

Jace Goodwin: a thunderbird dragon shifter and former Master of the Fairfax Dragon Dojo. Jace grew up in high society and has the vast network to prove it. A warrior, he used to operate as the General of the Fairfax army—and his only soft spot is for Rory. He gave up his position at the dojo to take her as his mate, and now his full attention is devoted to her. As Rory's mate, he is deeply connected to her and her magic, and he's the only person who can soothe her wild power. If she dies, his dragon will go feral, so he has quite a bit at stake if one of Rory's many enemies comes after her.

Irena Quinn: Rory's sister and former heir to the Spectre organization. She betrayed Zurie when she discovered her former mentor wanted to sell Rory as an assassin-for-hire, which would mean they would never see each other again. A brutal fighter, Irena's only purpose in life is to keep her sister safe and destroy the Spectres organization that almost killed them both. A powerful bio-weapon created by the Vaer gave Irena strange super-strength and bright green eyes that are eerily similar to Kinsley Vaer. Irena might develop magic or even a dragon of her own, though no one knows for sure what Kinsley's experiments have done to her.

Zurie Bronwen (deceased): former leader of the Spectres and former mentor to Rory and Irena. Zurie was a brutal assassin and held the title of the Ghost. Cold-hearted, calculating, and clever, Zurie considered both Rory and Irena as failed experiments—and she was determined to kill them both. The war she started between the Fairfax family, the Vaer family, and the Knights will have lasting consequences, and it's unclear if Zurie realized just how terrible the outcome would be.

Diesel Richards: a former Knight turned Spectre.

With Zurie dead, Rory out of the picture, and Irena excommunicated for her betrayal, Diesel is now the Ghost. His incentive is to kill both Irena and Rory to ensure no one threatens his rule. He's helped Rory once and tried to kill her on other occasions, so Rory isn't sure what Diesel really wants or what game he's playing with her life.

Harper Fairfax: a thunderbird, the Boss of the Fairfax dragon family, and Jace's cousin. Harper is friendly and bubbly, full of life and joy, but Rory knows a fighter when she sees one. The young woman is smart and cunning. As Rory's first friend, Harper has a special place in Rory's life. She will do anything to protect her friend—including going to war to protect her.

Russell Kane: a thunderbird and new Master of the Fairfax Dojo now that Jace has stepped down. He endured brutal trials to earn his place as the new dojo master. He grew up with Jace and Harper in the dojo and has a deep love for both the castle itself and the people within it. He will do anything to protect the Fairfax dragons—and Harper, for whom he seems to have a soft spot.

Eric Dunn (deceased): a fire dragon and part of the Fairfax family, Eric was the one man Irena was beginning to let herself love. After a betrayal by someone she adored, Irena had shut down. Eric's death broke her, and she left Rory's side shortly after.

Brett Clarke: a former Knight and once the General's second-in-command. With the General still out of commission after his last run-in with Rory, Brett led the Knights' charge against the Fairfax Dojo. When the Knights lost, Brett was captured, and he realized everything he knew about dragons was wrong. He helped Rory defeat the Knights, but they're still not sure if he's trustworthy.

William Chase (deceased): mostly referred to as the General. William is a former military man who was discharged from the army in disgrace for his terrorist connections to the Knights. He now runs them in a brutal regime that kills defectors, and he now has his sights set on his son Tucker.

Guy Durand (deceased): an ice dragon and former second-in-command to Jace Goodwin at the dragon dojo. Guy always wanted power. When he lost the challenge to Jace for control of the dojo, he joined the Vaer and gave over top-secret intel about Rory and the dojo itself. He was killed by Jace after he tried to kidnap Rory and return her to Kinsley.

Ian Rixer (deceased): a fire dragon, Kinsley Vaer's half-brother, and a master manipulator. Ian was smarmy, elitist, and arrogant. He was often referred to as honey-coated evil for his ability to speak so calmly and kindly, even while torturing his prey. He treated everything like a game, and playing that game with Rory cost him his life. He tried to control her and Jace's magic with specially designed iron cuffs to block their power, but Rory's magic can't be contained. She destroyed the cuffs—and him.

Mason Greene (deceased): a fire dragon and sadistic Vaer lord tasked with dismantling the Spectre organization. Irena gave him access to their sensitive Spectre intel in exchange for giving her and Rory a fresh start, but he betrayed them both. His attempt to kill Rory backfired massively and ultimately cost him his life.

Kinsley Vaer: an ice dragon shifter and the Boss of the Vaer family. Her power and cruelty make most grown men tremble in fear. She's utterly ruthless, cruel, vindictive, and vengeful... the sort to kill the messenger just because she's angry. She's increasingly frustrated that Rory has slipped through her fingers so often, and she's done giving her minions chances to redeem themselves. Now, it's personal—and Kinsley is coming after everything Rory loves.

Jett Darrington: a fire dragon, the Boss of the Darrington family, and Drew's father. He wants Rory for reasons not even Drew fully knows, but everyone's certain it can't be good. He disowned his son when Drew wouldn't hand Rory over, but he promised Drew everything he could ever dream of—including ruling the Darrington family—if he betrays her.

Milo Darrington: a fire dragon, Drew's brother, and current heir to the Darrington family line purely because he's older than Drew. Not much of a fighter, but an excellent politician and master manipulator. He's been growing increasingly resentful of his younger brother's skill and charm. When he tried to kidnap Rory and blackmail Drew into doing his bidding, she shifted into her dragon to beat him into submission. He knows her secret, but he's too terrified of her to tell a soul. Probably.

Isaac Palarne: a fire dragon and the Boss of the Palarne family. A skilled warrior and empowering speaker, Isaac can rally almost anyone to his cause. He's a deeply noble man, but there's something unnerving about his eagerness to get Rory to come to the Palarne capital.

Elizabeth Andusk: a golden fire dragon and Boss of the Andusk family. Vain and materialistic, Elizabeth can command attention without even a word. She exudes power mainly through her beauty and has a knack for getting people to share secrets they wouldn't have shared otherwise. She's determined to obtain Rory and considers the girl to be nothing more than another object to control and display.

Victor Bane: a fire dragon and Boss of the Bane family. He's a brutal fighter, excellent negotiator, and never gets caught in his many illicit dealings. With his hot temper, he picks fights whenever he can. He has very little direction and purpose, as he is merely looking for the next thing—or person—he can steal.

Natasha Bane: a fire dragon and Victor's sister, Natasha has almost as much influence and control over the Bane family as her brother does. She's smart, clever, and cunning. A sultry temptress, she enjoys bending men to her whims. Though both demanding and entitled, she knows when to keep her mouth shut to get her way.

Aki Nabal: an ice dragon and Boss of the Nabal family. He's excellent with money and can always see three moves ahead in any dealings—both financial and political. Clever and observant, he can pinpoint a fighter's weaknesses fairly quickly, though he's not an exceptional fighter himself. He believes money is power—and that you can never have enough of either.

Jade Nabal: an ice dragon and Aki's daughter, Jade is young and not much one for words. As a silent observer who prefers to watch rather than engage, little is known about Jade. She and Rory have met once, only briefly, and Rory knows there's far more to Jade than meets the eye.

Other Terms

The Dragon Gods: the origin of all dragon power. The three Dragon Gods are mostly just lore, nowadays. No one even remembers their names. But with the dragon vessel showing up in the world, everyone is beginning to wonder if perhaps they're a bit more than legend…

Dragon Vessel: According to myth, the dragon vessel is the one living creature powerful and worthy enough to possess the magic of the dragon gods. Rory Quinn was kicked into an ancient ceremony pit—the one Mason Greene didn't know was used to judge the worthiness of those who entered. With that ritual, Rory unknowingly brought the immense power of legend back to the world.

Castle Ashgrave: the legendary home of the dragon gods, said to be nothing more than ruin and myth. Drew believes he's found the location, but he's not yet sure.

Mate-bond: the connection only thunderbirds can share that connects two souls. The mate-bond is not finalized until the pair make love for the first time.

Even before it's finalized, however, the mate-bond is powerful. The duo can vaguely feel each other's whereabouts and, if one should die, the other would go feral.

Magical cuffs: complex handcuffs that cover the entirety of a shifter's hands when they're in human form. These cuffs are designed to keep thunderbird magic at bay. The Vaer have designed special cuffs just for Rory, with the ability to block her magic. These cuffs come with a remote that allows the captor to electrocute their captive to help subdue them, as thunderbirds are notoriously powerful.

Spectres: a cruel and heartless organization that raises brutal assassins and hates dragonkind. The Spectres specialize in killing dragons and are known as some of the fiercest murderers on the planet, in part thanks to their highly advanced tech that no one else has yet to duplicate. They're a spider web network that spans the globe, all run by the Ghost. Often, Spectres are raised from birth within the organization and are never given the choice to join. Once a Spectre, always a Spectre—quitting comes with a death sentence.

Override Device: Spectre tech. Very frail and easy to break, it fits into USB ports and can grant access to sensitive files. Though imperfect and obscenely expensive to create, it *usually* works.

Voids: Spectre tech. Fired from a gun with special attachments, a void can force a camera to loop the last 10 seconds and allow for unseen access to secured locations.

The Knights: an international anti-dragon terrorist organization bent on eradicating dragons from the world. Run by General William Chase, they'll do anything and kill anyone it takes to further their mission. There are some rebel Knights organizations that think the current General is too soft, despite his brutal rampage against dragons and his willingness to kill his own family should the need arise.

Fire Dragons: the most common type of dragon shifter. Fire dragons breathe fire and smoke in their dragon forms. They're found in a wide array of colors.

Ice Dragons: uncommon dragons that can freeze others on contact and breathe icy blasts. Usually, ice dragons are white, pale blue, or royal blue. The only known black ice dragons belong to the Vaer family.

Thunderbirds: dragon shifters that glow in their dragon forms and possess the magic of electricity and lightning in both their dragon and human forms. They're the most feared dragons in the world, and also the rarest.

The Seven Dragon Families: the seven dragon organizations that are run like the mob. Each family values different things, from wealth to power to adrenaline. Usually, a dragon is born into a dragon family and never leaves, but there are some who betray their family of origin for the promise of a better life.

Andusk Family: sun dragons who prefer warm climates, almost all of which are golden or orange fire dragons. They're notoriously vain, focused on beauty and being adored. Fairly materialistic, the Andusk dragons hoard wealth and gems and exploit those in less favorable positions.

Bane Family: ambitious fire dragons who deal mainly in illegal activities. They view laws as guidelines that hold others back, while they aren't stupid enough to follow others' rules. They like to see what they can get away with and push the limits.

Darrington Family: the oldest and most powerful family. Darringtons are mostly fire dragons, and angering them is considered a death sentence. They're well situated financially, with a vast network of natural resources, governments, and businesses across the globe. They're notorious for thinking they're above the rules and can get away with anything… because they usually do.

Fairfax Family: a magical family known as the only one to have thunderbird dragons. They have innate magic and talent, but sometimes lack the drive it takes to use those abilities to obtain greater power. They prefer to think of life as a game, and the only winners are those who have fun. To the Fairfax dragons, adrenaline is more important than money, but protecting each other is most important of all.

Nabal Family: wealthy fire and ice dragons. Money and information are most important to the Nabal, and they have an eerie ability to get access to even the most secured intel. Calculating and cunning, the Nabal weigh every risk before taking any action.

Palarne Family: noble fire and ice dragons known for their honor and war skill. Ruled by their ancient dragon code of ethics, the Palarne family operate as a cohesive military unit. Their skills in war are unparalleled by any other family.

Vaer Family: a secretive family of fire and ice dragons, they're known to be behind many conspiracies and dirty dealings in the world. Some see them as brutal savages, but most fear them because they have no ethics or morals, even among themselves.

CHAPTER ONE

He won't get away from *me*.

Not this time.

Biting wind tears past my face as I fly, my dragon and I soaring through the air as one, as fast as we can. My heart thuds in my chest with every beat of my wings. The cold mountain air washes over my glittering scales like a cascade of frigid water, and I love every second of my time in the sky.

And the chase is on.

It takes everything in me just to keep up with the black dragon ahead of me, much less catch him, but I refuse to give up. I won't.

I'm too damn stubborn.

As the stunning dragon blasts through the mountains, the blue magic burning beneath his skin leaves streaks of dazzling light in the air after him.

Jace.

I have one task. Only one mission as I weave through the snow-capped mountains around Ashgrave.

Catch him.

Up ahead, Jace banks to the right, a hard and tight maneuver that he knows I can't do yet.

Asshole.

Instead of following him into the growing shadows of the mountains around us, I bank to the left in a graceful arc around a tall peak. This gives me height, letting me get a lay of the land below me, and honestly it puts me in a better position. Tense and ready to dive, I scan the ground below to see where he went and—more importantly—where he's going.

As the snow-capped trees and the rocky, white mountains whiz past me, he disappears into the darkness of the many ravines, and I huff with frustration. A flurry of dazzling white sparks shoot through my nose as I growl in annoyance, and I try my best to curb my irritation.

After all, that's the whole point of this little exercise.

Flying.

Shifting.

Evading.

I need to master them all. A dragon is vulnerable if she can't shift on a whim, and focusing on the connection with my dragon only makes me a target until the shift actually happens.

And after I shift, I must be able to fly out of any situation. Through tight quarters. Past experienced, expert flyers who have done this their whole lives.

You know, no pressure.

Being a dragon is still so new to me, but I don't have much time to learn.

A red streak barrels through the white, snow-capped mountains—Drew. It looks like he finally caught up with us despite our head start. Even though this game just got twice as hard for me, I growl happily at the challenge.

I'll give them a run for their money.

Our little game has one simple rule—don't get caught. If you get tackled to the ground, you lose.

Simple, but not easy.

Drew barrels toward me, not even bothering to mask his approach. After all, subtle isn't really his style.

I dive, my dazzling scales glittering in the sun

and giving away my position as I dart into a fog that's slowly building along the slope of a nearby mountain. The mist rolls through the ravines and valleys between the mountain peaks, getting thicker as the day draws to a close.

Down here, I need to rely on intuition more than my sight. My heart pangs in warning, and I bank to the left as a mountain slope looms suddenly in the fog. The tip of my wing clips the rock, and though it briefly stings, I grit my teeth through the pain.

I'm tuned into my dragon, listening to her guidance, but she's as new to this as I am.

When we first found Ashgrave, we were able to do flying maneuvers I'd never even dreamed of, but all of that ran on instinct—and not even hers. It was like Ashgrave was telling us what to do.

But I can't rely on him forever. Now that we've rescued him, we need to figure this flying thing out for ourselves.

Through the fog, a shadow appears—just a silhouette at first. I stiffen, wondering which of my men this is and what his game is. As he nears, the royal blue scales of my ice dragon come slowly into focus.

As we fly side by side, we hit a small break in the

fog—and, briefly, I can see his face. His cool blue eyes are trained on me. Focused. Calm.

The hunter.

It would seem Levi has joined our little game as well.

I dart upward, trying to give myself an advantage. After all, it's easier to attack someone from above than below.

He follows effortlessly, and I know that he's probably going easy on me even if Jace and Drew aren't. This is Levi's element, and he could ground me instantly if he wanted.

It hurts my ego a bit to admit that, but it's one of the many reasons I love him—he's one of the greatest fighters I've ever seen.

Let's be real. The only reason I even saw him was because he wanted me to. Drew and Tucker are easy for me to track, and Jace a little less so. But Levi—he's always been impossible to find.

Too silent. Too stealthy.

The perfect predator.

As I break through the fog and into the sun, I take a deep and glorious breath. Despite the game, I let myself enjoy a fleeting moment of the brilliant rush that comes with being a dragon—with flying, with the adrenaline and ecstasy that pumps through my veins with every wing beat and every breath.

It's heaven.

It's where I'm meant to be. *Who* I'm meant to be.

A flicker of warning burns in my chest, and my eyes snap open as a black streak hurls through the air toward me.

Jace.

I dive, not wanting him to catch me, needing to win this if only to prove to myself that I'm a better flier than I give myself credit for.

With my mate hot on my tail, the two of us dive into the ravine, back through the fog.

My goal is to lose him in it.

Easier said than done, probably. But hell, it's worth a try.

I bank and weave my way through the ravine, cutting through the mist as it reduces my line of sight. Down here in the dank and darkness, I have to rely mostly on intuition and instinct to take me through the rocky obstacle course. I push myself harder, trying to think of a way to get behind him, to tackle him to the ground instead of giving him the chance to do that to me.

Another flicker of warning hits me hard in the

chest, but this time there's something up ahead. I just can't see it.

Well, I *do* see it—but only when it's too late to do a damn thing about it.

Out of the thick mist, a cliff rises in front of me with only a thin gap for me to fly through.

Too thin.

It's the sort of maneuver only a master flier can handle, and I'm just not there yet.

Shit.

I have two options—try to go through, or try to bank upward and likely smash against the cliff.

Both are pretty awful options.

A bubbling surge of magic hits me hard as the towering cliff looms closer, and in that moment, my defenses go down.

I growl, the sound building in my throat as I run out of options.

And I have to choose—rein in my magic, or maneuver my way through a tight situation.

I choose flying.

As my focus shifts to my wings, to my breath, to my body, my magic breaks free.

Damn it all.

The surging power within me breaks loose, blasting its way through the mountain. Dust rolls over me. Boulders and rocks soar through the sky from the force of my magic. There's no choice but to fly into it, and as pebbles hit me hard along my spine, I grit my teeth to fight through the pain.

Up ahead, the thin gap has become a slightly larger hole.

I snarl in victory. Talk about *lucky.*

It's only just large enough to fly through—honestly, I'd like it a little wider, but I think I can make this work.

At the last possible second, I tilt ever so slightly to the left, trying to make sure I don't clip my wing on my way through. I hold my breath as I race through the opening, almost wishing I could scrunch in my wings to protect them.

It doesn't work.

Though most of me sails through harmlessly, my wing hits the edge of the rock. I roar in pain as bones break, and I go down. I can't help it. Even though just the tip of my wing is broken, I can't keep my altitude.

I hit a snowy slope hard, and the mountain rumbles beneath me as I tumble downward. The ominous thunder of a building avalanche echoes through the valley as I roll and crash down the mountain.

My world spins, and I feel like I might throw up. I didn't even know dragons *could* feel nauseous.

This *sucks.*

After what feels like eons, I eventually slide to a stop, buried in a thick layer of snow. A searing pain ripples through my wing as I try to stretch it out, huffing in frustration from the fall. Buried in the avalanche, only my head and wings stick above the snow.

Though I want to stand, I can't bring myself to get to my feet. Not yet. A blistering headache burns through my brain, and my entire body hurts. I'll heal quickly, thanks to my dragon magic, but it's going to suck the whole time.

I growl, aggravated and annoyed with myself, and I look over my shoulder as Jace lands behind me. His eyes scan my body, his gaze resting on my wing, and only then do I notice the tear along my beautiful scales.

I slam my claws into the ground hard, trying to vent my frustration with an earth-shaking snarl.

Two blurs, one red and one blue, streak around the corner of the mountain as Drew and Levi approach. They land roughly, the ground shaking beneath them as they race toward me, but Jace snaps at them. They snarl in annoyance, but my mate takes steady steps across the snow toward me and gently brushes his wing along my spine. The gesture opens a connection between us, and a flurry of emotions burn through from him.

Concern. Doubt. Caution.

Are you all right? he asks.

I'm fine, I lie.

Levi gently nuzzles my wounded wing as Drew presses his forehead against mine. In an instant, a mental connection between the four of us opens, and their varying emotions battle for supremacy through our link.

It's a bit overwhelming, but I push through it. In the end, I'm grateful for their devotion and concern —I'm not about to take out my anger on them.

You're supposed to let us *tackle you,* Drew says, a few huffs of laughter escaping him. *You're not supposed to take yourself out.*

Har-har. I roll my eyes and stand, shaking out my body as I try to ignore the blistering ache in my wing.

Rory, you should rest, Levi chides, his blue eyes narrowing as he dares me to disagree.

Deep within, my dragon curls with anger. She's as pissed as I am, and she wants to get this right as much as I do.

We're a team, and we need to master this stupid flying thing once and for all.

I'm fine, I lie again, scanning the mountains around me as I try to ignore the burn in my wing. *Let's try again.*

Rory, Jace chides.

Again, I interrupt.

I don't give any of them a chance to argue. I simply take to the sky, trying to relish the rush of adrenaline that burns through me and block out the agony in my wing.

Every wing beat hurts like hell. It burns and stings, and my body begs me to stop. To pause. To rest.

It's a familiar feeling, one I've experienced all too much as a Spectre. Every time Zurie pushed me too far. Every time we trained for days on end with almost no rest. Every time she broke me, brought me to my knees, and yet forced me to keep going.

It's a brutal and unforgiving way to train, but it's all I know.

As I take to the air, the hunt resumes, and the guys begrudgingly disperse into the foggy ravine around us.

In moments, it's quiet.

Too quiet.

I coast through the air, compromising a bit and letting the wind take me instead of furiously beating my wings against the sky. It's the closest thing to a break I'll give myself—at least for the moment.

I keep low, my claws dragging through the edge of the fog and kicking up little swirls of cloud as I scan the world around me, looking for one of my men. If I can tackle even one of them before they get me, I'll consider this a win.

But in the howling wind of this valley between two mountains, there's nothing.

Tension builds in my back and neck as I survey the world around me, my jaw tense and tight as I prepare for war. To chase. To dive.

Even though adrenaline buzzes through me, nothing happens—and that's almost worse. To know that, at any moment, the tension could break, but to not know when.

To not know what will happen next.

Deep in my chest, there's another flicker of warning, but this time I don't know where the danger is coming from.

It's so strange. So foreign.

It feels like it's coming from all over. From above and below, ahead of and behind me. But I can't see a damn thing.

I growl, my voice like thunder in my chest as I flex my claws, ready for anything, ready for this little drill to become something so much more.

Because that's what this feels like—danger in the mist.

Like something unknown is about to attack.

Out of nowhere, a silhouette breaks through the fog below me.

Too sudden.

Too close.

Yet again, magic blisters over my skin. The ribbons of white light take over, surging in their attempt to protect me. I do my best to rein it in as the impulse takes over, rolling out of reach of the looming figure as my magic builds in surprise.

Too late, I recognize Levi.

The surge of magic becomes too much to control, and even though I grit my teeth to hold it at bay, I can't.

In a fleeting moment, his gaze goes from narrowed and focused on the hunt to wide and caught off guard as my magic carves its way out of me.

Oh gods.

No.

Not Levi.

To my utter and absolute relief, his instinct kicks in. At the last possible second, he darts out of the line of fire.

Thank the *gods* because I couldn't hold that back any longer.

White light bursts from me like an explosion that rattles the mountains around me. It tears through me like it's been dying to claw its way out for ages, hitting every mountain nearby, and blasting holes clear through the rock. The trees around me tremble, shaking loose their snow as an avalanche clamors down every slope, rattling and rumbling through the mountain.

And I'm smack dab in the middle of the mountain's warpath.

I beat my wings hard to escape the thundering snow, but it's not enough.

The avalanche catches me and takes me down the mountain with it as logs and leaves mix with the snow around me. We tumble for a good few minutes, nature and I, until the snow finally comes to a rest at the base of the mountain—with me buried deep within it.

Damn it all.

Even though the snow is heavy against my back, I shake and shimmy until I can at least stick my head out and take a deep breath. As I do, Jace and Drew land beside Levi, each of them looking at me, studying my face like they don't quite know what to say.

I growl in annoyance, shaking off the snow and spreading my wings as I try to figure out what fresh hell is happening now. The surges have been bad, sure, but never like *that.*

Levi is lucky to be *alive.*

The moment I shake loose the snow, however, each of my men freezes. Wide-eyed, their gazes locked on my back, all they can do is stare and gape.

I tilt my head in confusion as I glare at them, trying to figure out what the hell is wrong as each of them walks slowly near with an odd sort of reverence in their expressions. They fan out, surrounding me, looking at something on my back that I can't see.

Curious, I look behind me. A golden glint catches the corner of my eye, and it takes me a moment to register what it is.

A glittering golden stripe covers my spine, running the length of my body, all the way down to my tail.

Well, *that's* new.

Drew's wing brushes against my good one, opening our connection instantly. *Rory, look at this.*

He summons his fire into his throat and burns away just enough of the snow nearby to melt it. The second the small puddle becomes water, it begins to instantly freeze again in the frigid cold of the mountains, creating a sleek mirror in the snow.

As I peer at my reflection, I notice the golden stripe goes all the way to my snout, between my eyes and through the horns on my head.

My body is—well, it's *changing.*

Deep in my core, my dragon curls with delight, and I have to agree. Something tells me this change has to do with the magic growing in my soul. My bones. My blood. It feels like the final stage, the final evolution in my power, but I need to find a way to fully understand this.

I need to understand why I'm changing and what it means—because if I don't, my magic could become *too* powerful to control.

Even for *me.*

CHAPTER TWO

Don't get me wrong, I'm stubborn as hell. But after breaking the tip of my wing, getting swept up in two avalanches, and having a wild magic fluctuation, even I know when to call it a day.

As I gently fly toward Ashgrave, the biting sting of my clipped wing begins to fade.

Gods above, I love dragon magic—and, in this instance, dragon *healing.*

A familiar crescent moon castle appears before me as I lead my men around a bend in the mountains—my little Eden in the snow. The rolling green fields surrounding the castle cast a sharp contrast against the blinding white snow that surrounds it.

I can't help myself—every time I see Ashgrave, my heart swells with pride.

My haven. My home.

My beautiful, evil butler.

The moment we pass through the invisible barrier that keeps the land around Ashgrave green, it feels suddenly warmer. For me, the shift is subtle—something about Ashgrave makes me feel at home here, even in the cold. Drew, however, lets out a sigh of relief as we pass into the warmth, and he shakes his body ever so slightly with delight.

I chuckle. My poor fire dragon just can't handle the cold.

Drew brushes his wing gently against mine as he flies by, and though he doesn't say a thing, a quick rush of affection bleeds through from him as our connection briefly opens. He winks mischievously and veers off toward his tower, where he's setting up his surveillance equipment.

Before I can even react, Levi rolls underneath me, flying upside-down below me as he shows off his raw talent. With an affectionate growl, he brushes his nose against mine, our connection opening briefly as I feel his surge of adrenaline. Wordlessly, he dives, rolling as he catches himself effortlessly mere inches above the grass below. In a fluid, brilliant maneuver, he soars just above the ground for awhile before banking off toward Drew, and the two of them head toward the surveillance tower together.

I can only wonder what kind of trouble they're getting into, and if I'm being honest, I probably don't even want to know.

I half expect Jace to join them, but he splits off in the opposite direction without so much as a goodbye. He heads toward one of the more decrepit towers along the edge of Ashgrave, and I can practically feel his anger radiating from him.

That's odd.

Usually, if I hurt myself, Levi is the one who gets angry—not Jace. Jace knows I can take it, so all I can wonder is what's up with him.

I should check.

I angle after him to see what's going on when I notice Tucker burst through the main doors of the castle and run out onto the field, urgently waving at me with both hands to get my attention.

All right, one thing at a time.

Let's handle this emergency first.

I readjust and fly toward my weapons master, beating the air hard with my wings as I try to gracefully land. I teeter slightly once my claws hit the dirt, but compared to previous landings—especially the ones from today—that was pretty damn graceful.

"Rory, are you okay?" Tucker runs toward me at full bore, his brows knit with concern. He wraps his arms around my face, pressing his forehead against mine as the connection opens between us. A surge of worry and frustration burn into me from him.

I'm fine, I say, admittedly confused at why he's so concerned—after all, he had no way of seeing my crash.

"You *crashed*?!" he snaps, glaring at me as he reads my thoughts.

I groan, scrunching my eyes together in annoyance. In my exhaustion, I must have let him read my thoughts.

I need a nap.

"I *knew* something happened, damn it," he mutters, shaking his head as he scans my face. "I saw a power surge, and—wait, what the hell is that?" He runs his fingers over the gold stripe across my face, his head tilting quizzically as he studies me. After a moment, he takes a step back as he surveys my body, no doubt looking for injuries. "What the hell happened out there, Rory? After the surge, I couldn't do anything to help, and it broke me to think of you in danger while I was stuck in some damn castle."

Despite his concern, I chuckle, curling my wings tight against my body as I look at my former Knight.

It was just a surge, I tell him as he presses his palm against my side, opening the connection once again. *Everything's—*

"This is gorgeous, babe," Tucker interrupts again, running his fingers along the golden line that trails along my spine. As his fingertips brush along the stripe, I shiver with delight. It's a sensational feeling, like having someone caress your soul, and my eyes practically roll back in my head with the ecstasy of it.

"Where did you get this?" Tucker asks. "How did this happen?"

I don't know, I admit, rustling my wings as I try—and, honestly, *fail*—to shrug in dragon form. *I had a surge of magic and then got caught in an avalanche and—*

"You got caught in an avalanche?" Tucker asks, furious. "Did you get buried? Could you breathe? What happened?"

I'm fine, I say again, pressing my head against his with enough force to make him take a few steps back. *Tucker, I'm fine. You can always ask Ashgrave—*

"I did," Tucker interrupts, yet again.

And what did he say? I ask, admittedly curious.

"THE GREAT QUEEN IS SAFE!" Tucker shouts, doing a rather spot-on impersonation of the castle's voice as he wags his finger at me. "SHE IS AND

WILL ALWAYS REMAIN IN PERFECT HEALTH, FRAIL LITTLE HUMAN!"

I chuckle, puffs of air rolling through my nose.

Sounds about right.

"YOU HARDLY EVEN MIMICKED MY VOICE CORRECTLY, LITTLE HUMAN," Ashgrave interjects, an annoyed tone to his voice.

I laugh harder.

Tucker grimaces, rubbing his eyes as he shakes his head. "I hate not being able to join you, Rory," he says. "I hate that when you go off, I can't at least be there to look out for you."

Right, sure, I say sarcastically, tilting my head in mild annoyance. *And how are you going to do that?*

"I need a plane," he says, entirely serious. "A jet. With guns the size of my body."

I roll my eyes. *Oh, of course, my darling. Let me just head to the plane store real quick, and I'll be right back with a big old jet.*

"Rory, I'm serious!" Tucker snaps. "I'm the best damn pilot the Knights ever had, no matter what Brett tries to claim about his ability." My former Knight rolls his eyes with disdain. "Babe, I can fly anything, and I can keep up with you guys. Hell, I'll probably be *faster.*"

I hesitate, not entirely sure if I like this idea.

After all, I destroyed several jets in the fight to bring Ashgrave back to life—every one of those men died in fiery explosions.

If Tucker crashed, I don't think I could save him from that.

These are deadly mountains, and I can't risk losing him.

"Rory," Tucker says, his voice tense with warning, and I figure he probably caught some—if not all—of those thoughts.

I growl with annoyance. *I'll see what I can do.*

He frowns, watching me out of the corner of his eye as if he doesn't quite believe me.

I promise, I say sincerely.

Out of the corner of my eye, I notice the flutter of black wings as Jace readjusts and flies into a large covered platform on one of the towers. I can see his silhouette against the sun as he stares out over the mountains, still as a statue.

I nuzzle Tucker affectionately, reassuring him through our connection as I do my best to send him calm energy and good vibes. *I'm going to check on Jace.*

"Fine," Tucker says, still annoyed. "I'll go vent some of this anger by beating the shit out of Brett."

I narrow my eyes in annoyance.

"I'm joking," Tucker says, shrugging as he backs

toward the castle. “Maybe,” he adds, grinning. “It depends on how fast Brett's feeling today.”

With that, my weapons expert jogs off before I can get another word in edgewise. I hesitate, wondering if I should go after him—but he probably won't do anything.

Probably.

I launch into the air, my wings hitting the sky as I fly toward my mate. My dragon stirs with desire the closer we get to him, and as I near, I land on the shattered tiles of the roof by the decrepit tower he chose to brood in. I walk closer, tucking my wings in beside me as I sit beside him.

To my surprise, he doesn't look over. My dragon curls with longing, pushing me to lean toward him, and I indulge her. I brush my wing against his, and as the connection opens, I feel a torrent of his anger and frustration.

I can't help but wonder if I’ve done something without realizing it. Something to piss him off. Since I’m not sure what to say, we simply sit there in silence as the wind howls past us, watching the beautiful landscape as a waterfall tumbles down a mountain nearby.

I miss the dojo, he admits through our connection.

I sigh. *I do too.*

No, Rory, he says, shaking his head. *It was my purpose. My meaning. My identity.*

A little pang of hurt hits me hard in the chest, but I don't respond.

No, you're worth it, he says, his nose briefly nudging my neck as he no doubt feels my emotion through the connection. *But I need direction, too. I need to sink my teeth into something and have meaning outside the mate bond, same as you do.*

I sigh. *That's fair.*

But I feel like all I'm good for is war, he admits, shaking his head. *Training soldiers. War strategy. Killing. It's all I know.*

I understand where he's coming from, but I just don't have an answer for him.

With a soft little laugh, I nudge him playfully in the side. *You can just bug the hell out of me. Train me to control this newfound magic.*

I guess. He chuckles, and I'm grateful to feel a clear shift in his mood as he really chews on the idea. *What new powers have you noticed?*

Puffs of air roll through my nose as a sarcastic little snort escapes me. *What isn't new? Wild fluctuations. Blue fire. Solidifying weapons from pure magic. Visions. Golden dust shaking off my scales. You name it, Jace.*

Follow me, he says simply, nudging me gently with his head before he flies off into the sky.

For a moment, I simply watch him fly off. I'm the dragon vessel, keeper of the gods' magic, maybe even a goddess myself, and yet—for some reason—I choose to surround myself with the bossiest men on the damn planet.

With a small sigh and a tiny smile, I fly after him.

CHAPTER THREE

Roughly twenty minutes after returning to Ashgrave, I stand yet again on a hilltop overlooking the castle. As the wind whips by me, the new flowing gown Ashgrave gave me dances in the wind, hugging every curve in the breeze.

I'm far enough away that no one will get hurt if I lose control and my magic goes wild.

Again.

Jace clears his throat, and I look over my shoulder at the former dojo master as he clasps his hands together. His black leather jacket and jeans make him look slightly out of place against the snowy backdrop, but the grassy knoll we stand on is warm and comfortable.

I think only Levi would want to train in the snow.

"All right," Jace says, glancing me over. "Let's take an inventory of these new powers you have."

I frown, setting my hands on my hips as I wait for him to continue. Even though we're far enough away to protect the others from a magical fluctuation, I can't help but wonder if Jace is in the line of fire right now, or if he's immune to my magic as well.

He seems to have sway and control over the fluctuations—always has—but they could still kill him.

It's a risk I don't really want to take.

"Are you sure about this?" I ask, tilting my head doubtfully.

After all, so far Drew is the only one who can resist a direct hit from the magic. His whole family can, much to my disappointment, but none survive as well as him.

"It's fine, Rory," Jace says with a cocky grin. "I've been burned by plenty of fledgling thunderbirds. Trust me. I've got this."

I chuckle. "I'm not exactly a fledgling thunderbird, Jace."

"Yeah, that's true," he admits with a small shrug. "But trust me, I'll be fine."

"All right," I say dubiously, tucking a bit of my hair behind one ear and not entirely sure I agree. "Where do we start?"

"Tell me what you can do," he says, crossing his arms and lifting his chin slightly as he looks down at me. "What's new since you shifted? Tell me everything."

"Where do I start?" I whistle softly, my eyes glazing over as I think through the question. I absently scratch my head as I think through everything that's hit me recently—all of the new surges and powers. Everything I don't understand.

Jace seems to get the hint that my question was rhetorical, and I'm grateful for the silence. I need a moment to think through everything. To figure out what feels most important.

I look at my palms, my mind racing through the dangerous journey I had to take to get to Ashgrave. The memories hit me hard. Nearly dying in the heart of the castle. Of being just seconds from losing Ashgrave forever. Of the cold stone floor as I nearly bled out after my duel with the General.

Of Ashgrave's strange fire that burns in the hallway sconces—and how similar it is to my own.

My eyes snap back into focus, and the lines in my palm become clearer as the memory fades.

"I can summon blue fire," I admit without looking up. "I have since Zurie outed me."

"You can?" Jace asks, a twinge of confusion and surprise in his voice. "How come I've never seen it?"

"Because I can't control it," I say with a laugh, shrugging slightly as I look up at my mate. "The only time I did it was…"

I trail off, remembering the dark forest as I leaned my naked body against the trunk of a tree and stared up at the moon. It was such a powerful moment, and the fresh, numb fury that burned through me was still so strong. After Zurie revealed my secrets to the world, the sense of isolation and not knowing was almost too much to bear.

I always hate not knowing what—or who—is coming for me.

I close my eyes, taking myself back to the place where I summoned the magic into my palm, trying to see if I can do this yet again.

My intuition flares and I hastily study the shadows of the dark forest. Someone's nearby, and it's not Jace.

Effortlessly, I summon my magic into my hands, and this time it burns along my fingers like blue fire fueled by my anger. The cool blue light shines against my skin and casts a soft glow against the grass beneath me.

Well, that's new.

Even though there's someone in the shadows, I take a second to simply look at the blue fire flickering over my fingers. I wish I could control this—all this new power. I wish I knew what I was, or what this magic can do.

With a twinge in my fingers and a little snap in my palm, flickering blue fire envelops my hand. I open my eyes to see the blue flames race over my fingers, my hand acting like a torch even though I can't feel a thing. Nothing on me burns, even as the magic crackles across my skin.

The corner of my mouth curves into a small smile, one of delight and surprise. I'll never get tired of magic.

It's too beautiful.

"Whoa," Jace says softly, his boots crunching along the grass as he nears me. He leans toward the blue flame in my palm, the light reflecting slightly in his steely gray eyes as he studies it.

"Can anyone else do this?" I ask. "Tell me this is a thing and not just me."

"It's just you," he says, quirking one brow as he watches me with an impressed expression. "Thunderbirds can use a bit of their power in human form, but not fire or ice dragons. I've never seen something like this. Can you control it?"

"Let's find out," I say with a shrug.

I shake my hand, extinguishing the flame with a few quick flicks, and take a steadying breath. I ball my hand into a fist, summoning the fire yet again, and even though shimmering white light burns along my skin as I manipulate the magic, blue flames burst to light across my fingers once more.

"Huh," I say, grinning, impressed and a little proud of myself. I extinguish it with another few waves of my hand only to summon it again and again each time I try.

Finally, something about my magic came to me easily.

That's a delightful first.

"Throw it," Jace says, tilting his head slightly as he watches me.

"*Throw* it?" I ask, lifting one brow in confusion. "What the hell does that mean?"

"Treat it like your other magic," he says, gesturing toward the fire in my hand. "Manipulate it and use it as a weapon."

For a moment, I simply stare at him, wondering if some wires in his brain have finally crossed, or if I'm really just not understanding what he's saying. The way the flame covers my hand looks more like a torch than something I could throw, so what he's saying doesn't really make any sense.

Though I wait for clarification, he simply watches me—of course—and waits for me to figure it out on my own.

Ass.

I study the fire covering my fingers, tilting my hand every which way as I try to decide what I want to do with this. My white light just kind of erupts from me, but this is sitting happily on my fingertips. I frown, eyeing a stretch of grass in the distance, and curl my fingers as if I'm holding a baseball. The flames tilt and swirl, moving with my fingertips, and I throw my arm like I'm trying to strike out a batter.

To be honest, I expect absolutely nothing to happen.

If anything, I expect to light the grass beneath my feet on fire.

Instead, a blue fireball sails through the air and hits the ground where I was aiming. Instantly, a small blue fire erupts in the grass, eating the green blades like it's ravenous and starved.

I flinch. Oops, I really didn't think that one through—and now I might've set my home on fire.

Yay me.

Before I can so much as take a step toward the ravenous flames, the ground shakes. Instantly, metal hands fly out of the grass and pat the fire out. In mere moments, Ashgrave's mechanical fingers extinguish the flames and disappear once again into the charred dirt.

I chuckle. "Thanks, Ashgrave."

"YOU ARE MOST WELCOME," he says, his voice booming through the air.

"Good," Jace says with a grin and a nod. "What else can you do?"

I rub the back of my neck as I survey the castle in front of me. "Well, I have visions," I admit, recalling all the times I saw these walls before we even got here. "But those just come and go as they please."

"YOU ARE CORRECT, MY QUEEN," Ashgrave interjects. "THE VISIONS ARE YOUR MAGIC SPEAKING TO YOU, AND MAGIC SPEAKS ONLY WHEN IT DEIGNS TO DO SO."

"Uh-huh," Jace says, frowning as he absently scans the sky, no doubt wondering where Ashgrave's voice is even coming from. "Fine. What else?"

"The golden dust on my scales," I say with a small nod, rubbing my neck as I remember. "I don't even know when it started, but it feels very new."

My mate begins to pace around me in a small, slow circle as he rubs the stubble on his jaw. His eyes glaze over, and he seems to lose himself in thought. "I think that's just another change, Rory."

"Thanks, Sherlock," I mutter sarcastically. "Of *course* it's a change. It's new. It's *all* so new—"

"No, that's not what I mean," he interrupts. "Your body changed today after that surge of magic. Your power is growing, and your body is changing with it." His stormy eyes rest on me, stirring my heart with their intensity as he pieces the clues together. "The dust is beautiful, and I think it simply represents your soul."

I smirk. "Sweet talker."

He chuckles, waving away my compliment with a flick of his thick, strong fingers. "What else?"

"Well, there's the solidifying weapons from pure magic." I casually shrug, as if it's nothing, but I can't quite hide the small, proud smile that plays on the edge of my lips.

"Right," he says, his eyes narrowing playfully as he studies my face. "I wonder if you can do more than the dagger."

"Maybe." I curl my fingers and summon the dagger easily into my palm, the white light glittering in the sun as the concentrated power swirls within the form of the small blade. I study it briefly, wondering what other weapons I could bring to life this way.

An axe maybe, or even a bow and arrow.

Now *those* sound *fun*.

The dagger flickers with each thought, the form blurring in blips and pops before the dagger fades out of existence completely.

Ugh.

I frown. "I have to admit, I was kind of hoping that would be easier."

Jace laughs. "It's something to work on, definitely. But I'm not sure it's a top priority since you have the dagger at a minimum."

"Fine," I admit, crossing my arms in disappointment.

"So, that leaves the fluctuations," Jace says, rubbing the back of his head as he watches me.

I nod. "That leaves the fluctuations," I echo, agreeing as disappointment weighs down my shoulders.

With a heavy sigh, he sets his hands in his pockets and leans his head backward as he looks up at the sky. "I've been thinking about this, Rory. When you first came to the dojo, your magic was wild and untamed. No matter what I did, no matter what we tried, it couldn't be refined for ages. It took a while for it to settle before you and I made any progress. So, maybe this is the same."

"The same?" I ask with a baffled laugh. "I wasn't blowing open mountains before."

"You kind of were," he says, tilting his head as he grins.

I laugh. "Look, it was *one* mountain, and it was a very small hole."

He laughs, shaking his head like he can't believe how much I'm downplaying this. "It's a new level, Rory. With new magic comes new challenges." He looks me dead in the eye, daring me to disagree.

I don't, but I don't reply, either. I'm used to conquering things at my own pace, so I don't really want to consider that option.

I mean—*waiting*? Being *patient*?

Bleck.

Jokes aside, the idea that everyone around me is at risk for however long it takes for my magic to settle out on its own leaves me on edge.

"What about shifting?" Jace asks. "And flying, of course. You crashed pretty hard today."

"Thanks for reminding me," I say dryly, rolling my eyes.

"A dragon needs to know two things," Jace says, crossing his arms as he slowly paces around me. "How to shift in the blink of an eye, and how to fly through tight spaces. You have to be able to get out of absolutely any situation."

Ah, here it comes.

The lecture.

"Shift," Jace demands.

I frown, admittedly surprised he skipped the lecture and is going straight to the lesson. I'm not sure where he's going with this little test of his, but I'm always up for a challenge.

I close my eyes, half wondering what his game is as I give in to the shift. I lean into the dragon in my core, doing my best to give her control, but this process is slow. It has been ever since the first shift. It takes time.

Time I wouldn't have in a fight.

There's a change in the air, followed by the flare of warning that something is headed straight for my face. I open my eyes to find Jace's fists headed straight for my nose, and I duck out of the way seconds before it hits.

That sexy *jackass.*

I roll, my dress billowing slightly in the wind as I get my bearings and put some distance between us. I settle into a fighting stance as Jace does the same, his fists lifted toward his chin as he prepares to throw another punch.

"Shift," he demands, tilting his head slightly, daring me to fail.

He throws another punch, this time at my side, and I block with seconds to spare. The powerful blow throws me off balance, but I recover in time to put another few feet between us.

Every block, every attack steals precious focus away from me, and I can't pay attention to both shifting and defending myself.

"SHALL I INTERVENE, MISTRESS?" Ashgrave asks, his voice echoing across the fields.

I debate saying yes, just to watch Jace's expression as mechanical hands bat at him like they did the fire, but I resist the impulse and just chuckle silently to myself as the image flashes through my mind.

"I've got this," I say as I duck another punch from my mate in this impromptu sparring session. "Thanks."

"No one's going to give you an inch in a fight," Jace says as he throws three jabs back-to-back.

Ah, *there* it is. I knew he couldn't resist lecturing me for very long.

I duck each of his blows, more and more of my precious focus slipping away from the shift as our match continues.

"Get out of your head," Jace snaps. "Stop questioning this. Stop trying to control it and let it simply *be*. If you need to shift to get out of a situation, you can't waste time going inward. You and your dragon need to have a perfect connection. Your entire shift should take seconds, not minutes. Now, *shift*."

As I duck and dodge his blows, I try my best to reach the dragon in my core. She curls and twists, eager to give in, eager to prove him wrong, aching to impress him. To impress *me*.

We have to shift, I tell her.

I know, she says.

Even though I'm expecting her to answer, I can't help but freeze at the beautiful melody of her voice. The sound is like sunshine and joy, echoing through me, giving me more power to push through.

She's beautiful. She truly is.

My body begins to vibrate as I duck another blow, and it hums with warmth and life. She wants to take over, and I want to give in. But each time I try, another fist comes at my face, and I have to duck out of the way—which breaks our connection.

Over, and over, and *over*.

It's pissing me off.

The sensation grows, becoming nearly impossible to ignore, and I wonder if that's all it'll take. Just a brief moment where my defenses are down. Just one second to give in—and give *over*—to the shift.

After all, it doesn't matter if he hits me—not if my scales block the blow.

For the briefest moment, I pause, giving myself enough space to buy myself a few seconds of precious time, and I lean into her.

I give in.

My body hums and vibrates, stronger now as the shift finally begins to take over.

But I'm not fast enough.

A blow hits me hard in the side, and I fall to the ground, grimacing as I hold the tender area he hit.

"Damn it," I mutter through gritted teeth.

"You'll get it," Jace says comfortingly.

I open my eyes to find him leaning over me, his hand outstretched as he offers me help getting to my feet. I take it, wrapping my fingers around his as he pulls me toward him.

"You're such a hard ass," I say as my chest hits his, but I can't hide the grin pulling at the edge of my lips.

"Yeah," he says with a cocky shrug. "But that's why you love me."

I chuckle.

"This is what we're going to work on, Rory," he

says, squaring his shoulders as my tall thunderbird looks down at me. “Quick shifts and tight flying.”

“Isn't that my decision?” I ask, smirking at his audacity.

So *bossy.*

Instead of answering, my mate flashes me a mischievous grin. His body shimmers, and in seconds, he shifts into his beautiful black dragon. It’s so dazzlingly fast that I almost don’t even see his body change—and just like that, he takes off into the sky. A gust of wind tears through my hair as his wings cut through the air above my head.

I set my hands on my hips, watching my beautiful dragon as he flies away.

Show off.

CHAPTER FOUR

Deep in the many corridors and rooms that make up Ashgrave's inner workings, I sit at a dining table in a massive room covered with floor-to-ceiling windows. I stare up at the stained glass windows in the roof as they let in dappled light, and as I do, I can't help but lean back in the elaborate chair inlaid with gold and ancient carvings. Several layers of silk cover the seat and backrest, and as I settle into the thick silk cushion, I'm instantly comfortable. It's so thick with fluff that I could easily be sitting on a cloud.

Ah—*bliss*.

Conversation bubbles around me as my men laugh and poke fun at each other, but I'm only half-listening. I lean forward, setting my elbows on the elaborate dining table deep in the heart of Ashgrave, the smell of roasted game and root vegetables wafting through the air.

My plate is empty, though.

All I can do is stare at the orb in my fingertips.

The chatter of my men's conversation fades to a soft murmur as I gaze deep into the swirling fog of the second orb—the one we stole from the Knights when we raided their treasury.

The one *they* stole from the gods.

A crack of lightning tears through the stormy clouds deep within the orb, and I frown, wondering where this should go and what it could possibly do.

Ashgrave defeated everything the Knights had, and all I had to do was plug in a single orb. These things possess immense power, and to think there are more than just these two is almost baffling.

More abilities. More powers.

More devastating magic.

And it all obeys me because *Ashgrave* obeys me.

The thought is still fairly surreal.

"What do you eat per day, Drew?" Tucker asks loudly, laughing. "Like, three deer? Maybe four?"

Jace and Levi chuckle as Drew just shakes his head, their banter snapping me from my brooding thoughts. I smile as I watch them laugh and jab at each other, the four of them like brothers.

It's a dream come true—one I wasn't sure I would ever get to see made real.

Levi's cool blue gaze darts toward me, roving briefly over my face as he tilts his head. He's no doubt studying me and probably reading my thoughts from afar.

"You need to eat, Rory," he says gently.

The others turn toward me, their conversation briefly hitting a lull.

I roll my eyes. "Yes, ma."

The guys chuckle as I set the orb gently on the table and reach for a bit of the sliced meat, heaving the venison and a few cooked carrots onto my plate. Deer meat and carrots—it's about all we've been able to eat since we got here, likely because that's all Ashgrave can find nearby.

"I'd kill for a steak," Drew says, leaning back in his chair as he stares at his half-eaten venison.

"You are so damn spoiled," Jace says, grinning.

"Yeah," Drew says with a cocky grin. "We've been over this, and I thought you accepted it."

I laugh and take a bite of the meat, savoring the hit of flavor. I won't lie, I'm pretty sick of game too, but I'm not about to say anything about it.

Food is food.

"I APOLOGIZE," Ashgrave says, his voice booming through the room. "I WISH I COULD CREATE A PROPER FEAST FOR YOU ALL, BUT ALAS, THIS IS ALL I AM ABLE TO ACQUIRE. WE ARE IN NEED OF SUPPLIES."

"What do you need?" I ask as I take another bite.

"TRIBUTE, MY QUEEN," the castle says casually.

I laugh as the guys shake their heads, already knowing what I'm about to say. "No, make me a shopping list. We'll get you what you need."

There's a brief pause.

"A… A SHOPPING LIST, MISTRESS?" Ashgrave asks, as if the words are foreign and strange. "I DO NOT KNOW WHAT THAT IS, MY QUEEN."

I chuckle, rubbing my eyes. "Never mind, Ashgrave. We'll figure it out later."

"Just make sure you give Brett the crappy cuts," Tucker says, leaning back in his chair as he pops another carrot into his mouth. "All fat. You hear me? Fat and gristle."

"Tucker," I chide quietly.

"What?" Tucker says, shrugging. "He's not one of us."

My smile fades, and I absently stab at the meat on my plate as I consider what Tucker just said.

He's right, of course. Brett isn't and never will be one of us. He'll never be one of my men. He's done too many horrible things for me to forgive, and I certainly don't find him attractive.

These four gorgeous creatures at my table—*these* men are my family. *These* are my lovers. *These* are the people I would die for.

But Brett? No, absolutely not.

I sigh, leaning back in my chair. I had food sent to Brett separately because I need to talk to Ashgrave and my men about something I don't trust him with yet, but maybe I'm being too harsh.

He did help us *get* the orb, after all.

My eyes dart toward the magical glass ball in front of me.

There's a lingering question, however, about his intentions. Perhaps he only helped us steal it because, secretly, he wants it for *himself*. It's something I've considered, and something I won't allow to happen.

I just don't trust him yet, and maybe I never will.

Of course, the longer I leave the orb out in the open, the more chances someone has to steal it.

I think it's time to give this magic a proper home.

"Ashgrave," I say, resting my fingers against my jaw as I stare at the orb. "What are our options for this? Where does it go, and what does it do?"

Around the table, my men quiet down, apparently just as curious to know the answer as I am.

"OF COURSE, MY QUEEN," the castle says. "I AGREE THAT IT IS TIME."

"Time for what?" Tucker asks with an inquisitive frown as he stares up at the ceiling.

It's weird, not having a face to look at while Ashgrave talks to us, but something tells me any face he might have would be more on the terrifying side than anything else.

Gold light dances across the table, only brief flickers of dusty magic at first, but they quickly solidify into figures that march across the polished wooden surface before us all. They flit by, nothing more than brief moments in time, only giving us the barest glimpse into the past.

A woman in a gown.

A dragon flying through the air.

In a flash, the snippets of movement are gone, and the magical hologram of a quite familiar-looking, crescent-shaped castle stretches across the full width of the table. Castle Ashgrave appears before us as we know him—imperfect, with decrepit towers along the northern edge, but my stunning castle nonetheless. The golden arcs of his towers and walls cuts through the half-eaten plate of venison in the center of the table.

I reach for the meat to clear it away, but the booming echo of Ashgrave's voice interrupts me.

"ALLOW ME TO CLEAR THE TABLE, MY QUEEN," he says.

A blinding, golden flash blinds me momentarily, and I shut my eyes on impulse to shield them. When I look again at the table, however, everything is gone —the venison, the carrots, our plates.

"Hey!" Tucker says. "I wasn't done, buddy!"

"YOU ARE QUITE LOUD," my castle chides Tucker in his booming voice.

Drew, Jace, Levi, and I all laugh as Tucker silently shakes his fist at the ceiling, and I can't help but pinch the bridge of my nose as I watch Tucker screw with a vengeful, smiting *castle* of all things.

He *would.*

"Let's focus," I say with a nod toward the table. I briefly stretch my fingers through the magic, and an electric tingle shimmies through my skin anywhere I touch the golden light. It's delightful and feels almost like a tickle, making me shiver with joy.

"WITH MY POWERS RETURNED, I CAN

REMEMBER," Ashgrave says. "I CAN REMEMBER IT ALL."

In a flash, the castle changes, towers resurrecting themselves as bricks lift from the ground and soar to where they're supposed to be. The decrepit ruins quickly become a full castle as smaller buildings stretch out from the road, and the ruins once more become a thriving city.

"THERE ARE FOUR ORBS. THOUGH EACH GOD CONTRIBUTED AT LEAST ONE, EACH HAS EQUAL POWER," Ashgrave says, his voice booming with pride. "EACH ORB EXPANDS MY REACH AND THE GREEN AREAS OF OUR BORDERS, AND GIVES ME ENOUGH POWER TO REBUILD ANOTHER SECTION OF YOUR HOME."

As he finishes speaking, the final tower resurrects, and the beautiful moon-shaped curve of Ashgrave's glorious self stretches into the sky in miniature, all thanks to the golden hologram before us.

"YOU HAVE ALREADY FOUND MY HEART," he says. "THE ORB NEEDED TO FUEL THE PRIMARY FUNCTIONS AND FULL DEFENSES I POSSESS. THIS ONE, I'M AFRAID, IS REQUIRED ABOVE ALL OTHERS

FOR ME TO FUNCTION AT MINIMAL CAPACITY."

Tucker snorts derisively. "By 'minimal capacity,' do you mean the giant mechanical hands that can drag entire tanks and planes into the ground are just your baseline defense?"

"YES," the castle says simply.

In unison, Tucker and Jace burst out laughing.

I grin. Gods, I love this castle.

"WITH THIS, I NOW HAVE COMPLETE CONTROL OVER ALL ENCHANTMENTS IN THE MOUNTAINS. EVERYTHING WILL BOW TO YOUR WHIM."

I quirk one eyebrow, admittedly enticed. To have control over the wisps and the other enchantments of the mountains—now *that* is useful.

"YOU NOW HAVE THE ABILITY TO SEE THROUGH THE MOUNTAINS LIKE I DO. IT WILL ALSO ALLOW ME TO SEE BEYOND MY BORDERS INTO THE LANDS BEYOND, AND GIVE US ACCESS TO TERRAFORMING. YOU CAN BUILD ANYTHING, JUST AS THE FIRST QUEEN BUILT ME."

"And I already have access to all of this?" I ask.

"YES, MY QUEEN," he says. "IT CANNOT BE TAUGHT, BUT COMES NATURALLY WITH

TIME. YOU WILL BEGIN TO FEEL MORE CONNECTED WITH THESE POWERS THE LONGER YOU ARE HERE."

"That's impressive," Levi says with a wry smile.

"Indeed it is," I admit. "What else is there, Ashgrave?"

"THERE ARE THREE OTHER DOMAINS," the castle says. "AND WHEN AN ORB IS PLACED IN EACH OF THESE DOMAINS, ANOTHER ASPECT OF MY MAGIC BECOMES AVAILABLE TO YOU ONCE AGAIN."

"What are they?" I ask, leaning my elbows on the table as I study the golden images before me. "Tell me all of them and everything they do."

"OF COURSE, MY QUEEN," Ashgrave says. "EACH OF THESE DOMAINS IS PROTECTED BY A SERIES OF TUNNELS AND DOORS THAT ONLY I CAN ACCESS. OF COURSE, HISTORICALLY, ONLY THE GODS WERE PERMITTED INSIDE."

"Of course," Drew says, his dark gaze drifting toward me as he grins.

I smile at my smartass fire dragon.

"I WILL TELL YOU EACH IN THE ORDER THEY WERE CREATED," Ashgrave says. "TO

BEGIN—DEEP IN THE HEART OF THE TUNNELS, THERE IS A TREE."

At the center of the moon-shaped curve of the castle, a bright white light blinks into existence. It shines like a small star deep in the bowels of the castle, but there's no other detail.

"THIS WAS CALLED THE MIND'S EYE," Ashgrave says. "A DOMAINABLE CONNECTION TO ME AND THE ABILITY TO ACCESS SOME OF MY MAGIC AT A DISTANCE, REGARDLESS OF WHERE YOU ARE."

I sit with that for a moment, trying to make sure I fully understand. "Explain."

"IT ALLOWS ME TO HAVE A BODY, OF SORTS," my evil butler says, elaborating. "I WOULD BE ABLE TO JOIN YOU ANYWHERE YOU GO. THE FIRST QUEEN CREATED THIS BODY FOR ME TO TRAVEL WITH HER AS NEEDED, SO THAT I COULD MONITOR EVERYTHING HERE AND RELAY ANY ISSUES TO HER IMMEDIATELY."

My heart pangs with delight, and my impulse is to simply say *yes,* that this is it. To have unlimited connection to our home base, regardless of where we go—now *that* is *power.*

"That's impressive," I admit, leaning back in the chair. "It's going to be hard to top that, Ashgrave."

"It shouldn't be necessary," Levi says, tapping his finger on the table. "Seeing as we won't be leaving here, much. That was the whole point of *finding* Ashgrave, wasn't it? To have a home base where you can be protected."

"Levi, we need to hear him out," I say quietly, watching my ice dragon out of the corner of my eye.

He frowns and jumps to his feet, pacing along the far wall as he listens with his hands in his pockets.

"AT THE EAST END OF THE CASTLE," Ashgrave continues, "THERE IS THE ARMY."

"An army?" Jace asks, leaning forward. "An army of what?"

"VIRTUALLY IMPENETRABLE METAL DRAGONS," Ashgrave answers. "WARRIORS YOU CAN TAKE BEYOND THE CASTLE. THEY CAN CHANNEL YOUR MAGIC, MY QUEEN, THOUGH THEY WILL NEVER BE AS POWERFUL AS YOU, AND THEY CAN ALSO CHANNEL MY THOUGHTS AND VOICE."

"If they get destroyed, can you make more?" I ask.

"OF COURSE," he answers. "IN ADDITION, YOU WILL HAVE SPIES—LITTLE BEES THAT FLY

EVERYWHERE AND ACT AS YOUR EYES AND EARS. YOU WILL HAVE THE ABILITY TO MAKE MAGICALLY CHARGED WEAPONS FOR ANY HUMAN AND DRAGON ARMIES YOU HAVE."

"Will that drain me?" I ask.

"NOT AT ALL, MY QUEEN," the castle assures me. "THAT WOULD BE QUITE USELESS IF IT DID. ALL MAGIC CHANNELS THROUGH THE ORBS THEMSELVES."

"That's fascinating," I admit. "I can't believe there's one more—what else could we need?"

"Well, the army gets my vote," Jace says, slamming his fists happily on the table as he grins and leans back in his chair. "Rory, you need a military."

Frowning, I tilt my head, watching him skeptically without saying a word.

I don't know about that.

He's hurting, that much is clear. He wants warriors. He wants purpose. I know how badly he wants to lead an army again, but to create one now might simply make the world fear me even more.

I can't really afford that.

"YOUR FINAL DOMAIN WILL ALLOW YOU TO CREATE YOUR LORDS," Ashgrave says calmly and a bright white light blips into existence somewhere deep in the hallways of Ashgrave along the east end.

"Whoa, whoa, whoa," Tucker says, lifting his hands to make the castle stop. "She already *has* her lords, mister castle man."

I chuckle. "He has a point, Ashgrave. What do you mean by 'creating my lords'?"

"THERE IS A MACHINE DEEP WITHIN THE CASTLE THAT ALLOWS YOU TO FUSE WITH THOSE YOU ARE CLOSEST TO AND TRUST MOST DEEPLY, THEREBY GIVING THEM A PIECE OF YOUR MAGIC."

The castle pauses briefly as if he's not sure he wants to continue, but he ultimately does.

"IT GIVES THEM A PIECE OF YOUR SOUL, MY QUEEN. THEY ACQUIRE SOME OF YOUR POWER, WHICH FUSES WITH THEM IN A UNIQUE WAY AND GIVES THEM UNIQUE ABILITIES. IT WILL ALSO MAKE THEM IMMORTAL."

"Oh, wow. Done," Tucker says, drumming his hands on the table excitedly. "My vote."

I laugh, rubbing my eyes. "And why is that your vote, Tucker?"

"*Hello,*" he says shrugging. "Immortality."

I just laugh. "And what if it makes you a dragon?"

"Oh," he says, frowning. "I hadn't considered that."

"What's wrong with being a dragon?" Drew asks, lifting his chin as if daring Tucker to insult him.

"Hey, someone has to represent humans at this little table of ours," Tucker says, shrugging. "I'm the last one left."

Jace and I laugh, shaking our heads in unison.

Oh, Tucker.

"WHAT WOULD YOU LIKE TO DO, MY QUEEN?" Ashgrave asks. "WHERE SHALL THIS ORB GO?"

"I can use any of the orbs in any of the domains?" I ask, trying to make sure I understand.

"YOU CAN," the castle assures me. "EVERY ORB CONTAINS EQUAL POWER TO THE OTHERS. IT IS MERELY A MATTER OF PREFERENCE, AS MORGANA CREATED ONLY TWO OF THE ORBS. CAELAN AND RAZORUS EACH MADE ONE AS WELL."

I frown, wondering if that's why my dragon wanted me to place a specific orb in Ashgrave's heart —it must have been Morgana's magic. After all, I seem connected to her most of all.

"Well, this is easy." Levi pauses mid-stride and crosses his arms, his cool blue eyes locked on me.

"Make us your lords. Give us additional magic to protect you. Let us do whatever we can to keep you safe."

"I disagree," Drew says, leaning back in his chair. "The Mind's Eye may prove useful, especially if we find ourselves traveling to and from Ashgrave. We don't know what's waiting for us out there."

"Drew you're missing the point," Jace says with a frown. "We only have one orb, and we don't know if or when we'll find any others. This one needs to be used for something truly urgent. That's the army, hands down."

"*Hello,* children!" Tucker says sarcastically. "Immortality, guys. Come *on.*"

I can't help myself. I grin. "Focus, Tucker."

"I am!" he insists. "Let's do this. I'll take Immortality for dessert, please."

"I think we may have more pressing matters to consider," I gently chide my weapons expert.

"Exactly," Jace says with a nod. "And with an army…" he quirks one eyebrow playfully, his gaze drifting toward me as he lets the thought linger in the air.

I frown.

An *army*. Gods, no. Given the current political climate, that seems like an absolute *mistake*.

"Jace has a point," Drew admits.

"Oh don't you start," I chide him.

"What?" Drew asks, baffled. "You don't want an army? What queen doesn't want an *army,* woman?"

"I'm not a queen," I say, my heart not in this argument right now.

"This is moot," Levi interjects. "Kinsley is coming for her, and the four of us need to be able to keep her safe!"

"Don't get on this again," Drew says, rolling his eyes. "I think I'm with Jace on this one."

"*Thank* you," Jace says, gesturing toward the ceiling with exasperated flair. "At least someone here sees reason."

Even as the conversation continues, I pause to admire the two of them—Jace and Drew. Once enemies, and now friends. Really, though, they're even more than friends. They're *brothers.* It used to physically hurt them if they actually agreed on something, and now they can do it without so much as a second thought.

It's beautiful, and I'm proud of them—though I would never *tell* them that.

"I just don't agree," I interrupt their bickering with a shake of my head. "An army? Seriously? No, guys. I just think that's a mistake."

"Think about it," Drew says, frowning. "You could help Harper. You could save hundreds, maybe even thousands of Fairfax lives in the war against the Vaer."

I sigh in momentary defeat.

That *does* sound appealing.

"But if I do that, think of the ramifications," I point out. "Think of how many others it would sway against us? How many would join Kinsley out of *fear*?" I counter. "When the dragon vessel—who is *not* a Boss, nor does she have any diplomatic immunity or power—amasses her own army, how many are going to actually stay and fight at the Fairfax's side? Or will it be us and the Fairfax against the rest of the world?"

For several minutes, no one speaks. The silence stretches on seemingly forever as everyone considers what I said.

I have a point, and none of them can deny it.

Frustratingly, however, so do *they.* Everyone wants something different, and their opinions matter to me.

I'd like for us to be on the same page.

Funny enough, I disagree with them all. Being able to leave the castle and know that it's safe while I'm gone—now *that's* appealing.

I lean back in my chair, frowning as I consider our options.

"Ashgrave, where are the other orbs?" I ask.

"I CAN FEEL THEM, BUT ONLY A FEW. I WORRY ONE HAS BEEN DESTROYED."

I frown. That's really bad.

"How can I find them?" I ask the castle.

"I CAN ONLY FEEL THEIR EXISTENCE. THEIR POWER," Ashgrave says. "I DO NOT KNOW THEIR EXACT LOCATIONS, BUT I HAVE SOMETHING THAT MIGHT HELP."

Beside Levi, a door opens where there was nothing but stone before. Steps carve through the floor, leading into the darkness. Blue fire flares to life in the sconces along the wall, the soft blue glow leading the way into the depths of the castle.

For a moment, none of us stand. An ominous feeling settles into the air as we simply look at the stairs and wonder where they could lead.

This castle is a labyrinth, and even though it's my home, it contains so much darkness. There's so much in here that I know nothing about, and I can't help but wonder what's in its depths.

I can't help but wonder if I'll ever uncover all of the secrets the gods left within these walls—or, honestly, if I even *want* to.

CHAPTER FIVE

The crackle of the soft blue fire in the sconces is the only sound as we walk down the stairs into the darkness and the unknown.

"Where are you taking us?" I ask Ashgrave. "Where does this lead?"

"TO THE TREASURY," Ashgrave answers, his voice booming in the small space. "THIS IS A SECRET STAIRWELL THAT WILL APPEAR ONLY WHEN REQUESTED OR RELEVANT. I CAN SUMMON IT FOR YOU AT ANY POINT, IN ANY PLACE WITHIN THE CASTLE. ONLY THE QUEEN MAY ACCESS THESE CHAMBERS," he adds with a hint of disdain.

"Ashgrave," I say warningly, but I can't hide my grin.

He's just being protective.

"I APOLOGIZE, MY QUEEN," he says as a giant set of double doors appears at the end of the stairs.

As we reach the end of the stairwell, the giant door opens on its own. Light instantly blinds us, and I briefly lift my hand to block the glow as my eyes adjust.

Gold.

This room is filled with *gold*—and a *shitload* of it.

As I walk through the open doors, I find piles of gold coins and bars covering most of the floor around me. Only a small walkway has been left through the glimmering piles, which glisten ever brighter as sunlight streams through tall windows set along the wall.

I pause briefly, surveying the room and not quite processing what I'm seeing. I've been in rooms with this much money in it before, but the money has never belonged to *me*.

It's surreal.

Three suits of dragon armor line the far wall, the metal plates detailed with elegant carvings inlaid with gold as they sit atop three stone dragons. Glass cases with jewels and delicate vases line the shelves that cover the other walls, and several treasure chests filled with pearls and diamonds sit amongst the piles of coins.

"Holy shit," Tucker says under his breath, pausing beside me as we hover by the entrance.

"Yeah," I admit, not quite sure where to start.

I scan the room again, this time noticing two doorways that lead to other chambers within the treasury.

"There's more?" Tucker asks, his eyes landing on the doorways at the same time as mine do.

"I guess so," I admit with a small sigh as a grin breaks across my face.

"MY QUEEN," Ashgrave says with a twinge of pride in his voice. "I FOUND YOUR CROWN."

In the center of the room, a pedestal raises from the cobblestone floor, with an ornate golden crown laid on a black cushion. Diamonds cover every surface, and eight delicate gold points rise from the crown in equal spaces around the entire thing. Each golden point is crowned with an additional diamond as large as my thumb.

I don't think I've ever seen more diamonds on *anything* before. I walk to it, my fingers hovering along the edge, not quite willing to even touch it.

Drew nudges me playfully, and I look up to find

him grinning. He flashes me a knowing look out of the corner of his eye as he passes.

I roll my eyes and step away from the crown. After all, what the hell am I going to do with it? It's just going to sit down here forever.

Levi darts into one of the archways while Tucker runs into the other, and both men pause to peek around the edge of the doorframe as they survey the various rooms.

"There are weapons in this one!" Levi says with a broad grin as he looks at me over his shoulder.

"Ooh," Jace says in an excited tone, jogging after Levi as the two of them explore the chamber together.

Drew and I chuckle, and I just cross my arms as I shake my head.

I walk toward the armor, studying the three sets as they tower above me. It seems odd to think of dragons needing armor, and I wonder if this was more ceremonial than anything else. Drew stands beside me, his smile fading the longer he stares at the war-torn metal.

Two of the suits are sharp, the lines hard and rough with very little detail on the surface—only a few carvings here and there along the edges. I suspect these belonged to practical dragons who weren't fond of pomp and pretense. Deep gouges from past battles cover them, and I wonder how many wars this armor has seen.

But the third set—it *glistens,* polished and beautiful, clearly well-kept and adored. Ornate white and gold filigree covers the entirety of it, right down to the faceplate that would have covered a dragon's forehead.

This armor was *loved*. It was a source of pride to whomever owned it, and they wore it with pride.

I stand beneath it, looking up at the armor as if I'm facing down a dragon. The statue glares at me with dead eyes, and the longer I look, the more scratches I see across its surface. More and more gouges appear, though they're expertly hidden by polish and care.

The other two suits of armor weren't adored like this one, but this one faced just as many wars.

I brush my finger along the edge of the white and gold armor, my fingertip barely touching the piece of metal that would have gone over the dragon's nose.

The moment my finger touches the armor, however, the world around me changes.

In an instant, I face a dragon king, a fearsome red warrior decked out in black armor. A long gouge covers his eye, a silver line through the armor showing the route a talon had taken when it scarred him.

But I feel nothing.

He doesn't scare *me.*

The dragon king snarls at me, and I impulsively step back to put some space between us—only to find myself suspended in the air over a battlefield.

Everything moves in slow motion, as if time itself has nearly come to a stop.

And then I look behind me.

A beautiful and absolutely *stunning* green dragon snarls at the king. The armor I just touched covers her entire body. In the low light, her body shimmers like dark diamonds, catching every color of the rainbow as brilliant white light burns within her mouth.

She's about to deal the final blow in this war against a king—using magic that is all too familiar to me.

The vision ends, and I fall to the ground, gasping with my hand on my chest as I try to process what I've just seen.

Drew is instantly beside me, lifting me into his arms as he watches my face with concern.

"I'm fine," I say before he can even speak. "I'm fine."

"What happened?" Jace asks as he runs into the room with Levi hot on his heels.

"Nothing," I say absently, not really thinking through my words before I say them. "Just a vision."

"Oh, just a vision," Levi says sarcastically, rubbing his eyes. "A vision of what?"

I look back at the armor, frowning. "Of Morgana."

The room is silent, and Drew gently sets me on my feet, his hands on my shoulders as he subtly gives me support in case I fall again.

"The longer you're here, the more you connect to your power," Jace says, his hands balling into fists as he nervously surveys the room. "The more you connect to the gods."

"Yeah," I say wistfully, nodding a little as I process what just happened. "The only problem is I'm connecting with gods who aren't dead. I can *feel* it."

The moment I say the words, I'm hit with two strange sensations.

One, I know I'm absolutely right—even though I have very little in the way of proof.

Two, I wonder if I shouldn't have said that where Ashgrave could hear me. I have to wonder, if Morgana and I both demanded loyalty of him, who he would obey.

"Babe, you need to see this," Tucker says from the other room.

His words snap me from my daze, and I roll out my shoulders, eager to put some distance between me and the armor. As I walk into the room after him, I cast one wary glance back over my shoulder to the beautiful armor and the crown, both of which belonged to the goddess who originally built this place.

But Ashgrave keeps trying to say they belong to me, now—and I have the feeling a time will come when I have to wear them both.

As I enter the second chamber, I'm surprised to find it mostly bare—except for three pedestals in the center of the room, set in a small circle. They face outward, away from each other, and Tucker stands by the only one with something on it.

A small book with a lock sewn deep into the binding. Truth be told, it feels oddly familiar.

Without so much as a word, I lift the book into my fingers, and my dragon *sings*.

Holding this book, she's just *happy*. It's a flurry of

joy and delight, a sense of all being right with the world.

This book *has* to be about us.

I look again at the other two pedestals, wondering what should be on them and why they're empty.

Can't worry too much about that now, I guess.

I lift the book into the air, examining it from every angle as I tenderly run my finger over the lock and the binding. As my skin touches the metal, however, the lock unravels itself and disappears into the leather of the book's cover.

"Ashgrave, what is this?" I ask.

"THESE PEDESTALS ARE FOR THE ASTOR DIARIES, THOUGH TWO OF THEM WERE STOLEN."

"So, they *are* real," I say under my breath.

"THEY ARE," Ashgrave answers. "OR RATHER, THEY WERE. THE ASTOR SISTERS WERE THE HEAD ORACLES, BORN OF A FAMILY SAID TO BE DESCENDED OF THE GODS THEMSELVES."

I look again at the two empty pedestals, wondering what information could possibly be in those books—and knowing I absolutely have to find them.

But at least I have one.

I open the cover, and the first page of the diary has elegant handwriting scrawled across its pages. For a moment, I can't read it—but the longer I stare at the letters, the more I begin to recognize. It's like they're reorganizing themselves into something my brain can understand, and before long, I can read the first sentence.

A handwritten account of the magicks and lore of Clara Astor, High Priestess of the Dragon Oracles.

Well, all right, then.

I thumb through the pages, easily a thousand of them, eager to know what information is locked away in here.

"Let me see," Drew insists, reaching for the book.

The cover instantly snaps closed and the lock reappears, all within the blink of an eye. I laugh in surprise, as I was most certainly *not* expecting that to happen.

"Fine," he says, frowning. "I didn't want to read it anyway."

"*Sure,* you didn't." I chuckle. "I guess I'm the only one who can read it."

"It would seem so," Jace says, crossing his arms as he smirks.

Yet another bit of magic we don't fully understand, but hell, at least this one will be easy enough to master.

It looks like I have a book report to write.

CHAPTER SIX

As the bright and brilliant moon shines through the open doors of my balcony, I take a deep breath and turn another page of the diary we found in the treasury.

Every page has something new—something earth-shattering—and even though my eyelids begin to droop, I fight the exhaustion and power through.

I have to.

These pages—they're about *me.*

This diary was written thousands of years ago, and yet everything I read resonates with something I've experienced.

It's *insane.*

Beside me, Drew adjusts in his sleep. As the soft rustle of sheets on skin filters through the quiet night, my fire dragon weaves his warm fingers around my waist. His palm presses against my bare skin beneath the comforter, his strong grip a tantalizing reminder of the fun we had just hours ago.

But even when I'm tempted to curl up beside him and drift off in his arms, I can't bring myself to put the book down.

The soft pink glow of an approaching dawn breaks across the horizon, casting a soft lightshow behind the mountains, and I figure I'm not doing myself any favors by staying up all night.

I just can't help it. The High Priestess Clara Astor had many secrets, and I absolutely *have* to memorize them all.

My life may depend on it.

I turn to the last page of Clara's diary, my eyes skimming the elegant handwriting as it begins to tighten. The flourishes are weaker now, the handwriting more hurried, and it seems as though this was scribbled on the final page at the last moment, as if someone was coming for her, and she didn't have much time left.

I have begun to suspect terrible things, dreadful things that I do not even want to admit in writing. Things I do not even want to think about, much less acknowledge, but I must.

For the gods, and for my family.

I have begun to suspect that Brigid and Esmeralda are no longer loyal to our masters. In subtle ways over the last several weeks, they have begun to ask me odd questions, and now I believe they are trying to cover their tracks and hide their intentions.

I, however, see what they are doing.

They will betray the gods. Me. Our family. Our legacy. And I am torn; do I warn my masters and sentence my sisters to death, or do I betray my own sacred duty?

I do not have much time to decide. I see their betrayal. It looms. It is coming, and I fear I have discovered it far too late to change the tides. They try to tempt me each time I see them, tempt me away from our masters, from the gods who not only created us, but who can destroy us as well.

I love my sisters, and I have from the day they were born sworn to protect them. But every oracle knows the gods come first, above all else—even family. I find myself admittedly torn between my duty and my blood. Perhaps I am simply weak and undeserving of my post.

I fear this will destroy not just my home, but the world as well. I feel myself getting swept away in the tides of what is coming, and I doubt I will survive for much longer.

Even as they stray, I do my best to remain true. I must, for I am the High Priestess, and I carry weight on my shoulders my sisters do not even know exist. I carry secrets they were never permitted to hear. Those secrets are preserved here in these pages, and I'm locking this diary to protect that knowledge. As extra precaution, I will create many fakes that will be charmed and cursed with dangerous traps, all to protect this one and discourage anyone from ever finding it.

This knowledge is for the gods alone, and should my masters ever read these pages, I ask only this.

Please forgive me.

"Whoa," I mutter under my breath as I skim the final page once more. "That's brutal."

I let out a slow breath and lean my head against the headboard as I stare off into the mountains and the encroaching dawn. There was so much information in these pages that even I feel the need to read through it a dozen more times to absorb it all. There were references to so many things I've never even heard of, and memorization can only take me so far.

This feels like the kind of book I'll need to read

again and again, just to absorb every nuance and every detail.

As exhaustion drags my eyes closed, I have to wonder what could possibly be in those other diaries. Clara implied that her diary contained the most precious secrets, but I figure that's hubris talking—a bit of arrogance stemming from the fact that she was the High Priestess. In thinking she was the one with all the answers.

For the other two books to be gone, I have to assume the information they hold is indeed precious.

And possibly damaging to me.

At my side, Drew stirs, rubbing his eyes as he looks up at me. His gaze slowly meanders from me to the book in my hands. He sits up, weaving his arm around my shoulders as he looks down at the open pages, not-so-subtly looming over me to get a peek.

The diary abruptly shuts as his eyes scan the page, the violent little snap shaking me with surprise.

"Stop doing that, damn it," I mutter, grinning as I rub my eyes.

He groans in annoyance. "Stupid enchantment."

I chuckle and yawn, the exhaustion so thick I can feel it burning the back of my eyes. A headache burrows into my brain, the dull ache getting stronger every second I remain awake. "I should stop anyway. I'm starting to see double."

"What did you find?"

"What *didn't* I find?" I counter, shaking my head as I wonder where I even start. "She talks a lot about how the gods were firm but fair. How they dealt brutal punishments, but only to those who deserved it."

Drew snorts derisively. "Sounds like making excuses for her bosses."

"Oh, absolutely," I say with a little eye roll. "It's pretty clear it's a prettified version from someone who didn't suffer their wrath, at least not as much as most people. She was definitely a favorite. But Drew…" I shake my head as I trail off, thinking over the pages I just read. "Even she was afraid of them."

He lifts his eyebrows briefly in surprise. "Even the High Priestess feared them?"

I nod. "I get the feeling these were really bad dragons," I admit. "Not just mean or cruel, but something more. They were something else, Drew. Maybe too powerful for their own good."

I chew the inside of my lip, wondering what that means about *me*. At least they split their magic in three.

But I have it *all*.

Drew clears his throat uncomfortably, his beautiful bare chest distracting me as he sets his hands behind his head and looks up at the ceiling.

"What else did you get?" he asks in a blatant attempt to change the subject.

I shrug, grateful for the diversion. "Little tidbits of random information. I'm not sure how it all intersects yet or what it all means."

"Like what?"

"Like how dragon magic reacts to some natural elements," I say, picking out the bit of the diary that made me raise my eyebrows the most. "Apparently, there's some ore and metals that act like a conductor for dragon magic, but there wasn't any explanation of how or why."

"Really?" Drew asks, tilting his head toward me in surprise. "Ore, as in metal?"

I let out a frustrated sigh and flip through the pages yet again, trying and failing to find the section where she briefly mentioned this. "She didn't go into too much detail, Drew, and I don't even know what the metal is called. She just referred to it as the ore." I roll my eyes, shrugging. "Not very helpful, for a magic diary."

"Yeah," Drew admits, frowning.

"What gets me the most is the demands they made of people," I admit, chewing my lip. "The tributes they collected regularly were grueling. Sometimes it wiped out entire stores of food. People starved while the grain they needed to live on was stacked up in the storage here in case the gods wanted cake." I roll my eyes.

"What happened if they didn't pay?" Drew asks, his voice tense and tight.

I tilt my head toward him, and we share a brief and heavy glance. Truth be told, I don't want to tell him because while Clara didn't go into detail on some things, that was one thing she discussed at length.

The blood. The chaos. The destruction.

If the gods didn't get their way, they left only fire and rubble in their wake.

In the end, I just shake my head, looking once more out into the balcony and over the mountains as the sun begins to peek through the clouds.

"Did it say anything about the orbs?" Drew asks tactfully, once more changing the subject.

"Quite a lot," I admit. "She talks at length about Ashgrave's weaknesses and strengths, about how all of the orbs need to be active for him to be truly optimal. I have to confess though," I add with a shake of my head. "She made it sound like he was impenetrable and undefeatable as long as he had all his orbs, but we know that's not true. If the Knights were able to steal the gods away like they did and lay siege enough to force him out of commission, then something there doesn't add up."

"What's your gut telling you?" Drew asks.

"Well, there are two options," I say, listing them off on my fingers as I speak. "Either the traitors each took an orb and weakened his defenses or…" I hesitate, not entirely sure I want to say this within his walls. "Maybe he wasn't as impenetrable as they thought."

Maybe we're not as safe here as we think.

Drew lets out a slow breath, rubbing his jaw as he processes everything I've said. "We have to get those orbs, Rory."

"Yeah," I say quietly, running my hand through my hair as I collapse backward into the pillows and stare up at the ceiling with the book on my chest. "Thankfully, that was another thing Clara gave us some insight on."

"What do you mean?" Drew asks, his head tilting toward me with a bit of reserved surprise on his face, like he didn't dare hope too hard.

"We have the locations of some of the orbs," I say,

a smile tugging at the corners of my lips. "Some of the pages are torn out, but I have the location for one of them."

"That's promising, if it's actually still there," he says, his grin widening.

I nod. "It's a start. Will you look into it?" I ask him, tapping my fingers on the diary. "I'll write some notes for you once I can go through it again. See what this place has become, and if the orb might still be there."

"Of course," Drew says with a nod.

It's just a start, but it *is* a solid lead.

It's been so long that I doubt either of the orbs are still in the original locations where the oracles hid them. But a start is better than nothing at all, and this is what I do best.

As long as I have a lead—as long as I have *something* to go on—I can move mountains.

My eyes slowly sink closed, and I feel my breathing starting to even out as the weight of the book on my chest soothes me.

"What do we do with the orb we have?" Drew asks. "We have to be smart about this."

"Uh huh." My words slur a little from exhaustion, and I can't help but feel more and more tired with each passing second.

"With Ashgrave's baseline defenses, no one can get close," Drew continues, far more rested than me and apparently not getting my *let me sleep* hints. "But he could possibly still be overwhelmed with a prolonged raid. The Knights were caught off guard when Ashgrave came back online, but dragons wouldn't be." He pauses, and I hear the subtle clink of a fingernail on teeth as he absently loses himself in thought. "A lot of the buildings are in ruins, and it's clear he's still rebuilding a lot of his power."

"Mm-hmm," I say quietly, taking a deep breath as the book rises and falls on my chest with every breath.

Drew chuckles. "You already know what you're going to do, don't you?"

I grin, my eyes still closed. "I think so. I want to sleep on it first."

The rustle of fabric on skin fills the air as he adjusts once more, and the mattress dips beneath him as he rolls toward me. He plants a rough kiss on my lips, like I'm Sleeping Beauty, and weaves his fingers through my hair.

In an instant, he's on top of me, and the kiss only gets rougher as he weaves his fingers through my loose and messy curls.

It's sudden and hot and *fierce*, and I can't help but

chuckle beneath his mouth as his chest presses the book against mine.

All right, then.

I set the book on the end table beside me as I indulge him and open my eyes. He leans back, watching me with that intensely dark gaze, his eyes darting between mine as he simply admires me, and I can't help but smile wider.

"You're such a Boss," he says, grinning.

I laugh. "Was that another queen reference?"

He chuckles, shrugging. "You got me."

Drew leans in to kiss me once again, but as his lips brush against mine, the chime of his phone interrupts us. He groans in annoyance and crawls back to his side of the bed, grabbing the device off the end table as the sheets fall from him, exposing his gorgeously naked body. My eyes drift to his ass as his head tilts toward his phone, and I grin mischievously.

Hmm—do I want to sleep, or *play*?

"That's weird," Drew says.

"What is it?" I ask. I inch toward him, coming up behind him and wrapping my hands around his waist as I press my naked body against his. The warm sensation of his skin on mine is tantalizing, teasing me with all the fun we could have if I stave off the need to sleep.

"It looks like we nearly got hacked," he says, rubbing the stubble along his jaw as he passes his thumb over the screen, reading through something too quickly for me to follow. "They were trying to get intelligence on where some of our supply sites are for the Spectre tech."

"Well, that's not good," I admit, frowning.

"Definitely not," he agrees with a quick look over his shoulder at me. "We need those metals and materials to make the voids and bugs, along with several of the other pieces of tech Irena stole for us."

"Hmm." I press my forehead into Drew's back, my mind racing with who this could be. Sure, it could be just anyone trying to get information they don't realize belongs to us, but I can't help but wonder if this is Diesel.

If he's onto us. If he not only knows what we stole, but that we're manufacturing everything we possibly can.

My arms tighten around Drew. The world is after me, and I wonder if that will ever change. I know I can't hide my dragon for much longer, and this only cements for me what I already know. I need to learn how to shift quickly and master my flying, because there's no telling when I'll be in a terrible situation. I need both.

Jace might be a bit pushy, but on this, at least, he's right.

I still have a little more time, though, because the only two weak links who know about the fact that I can shift are Milo and Brett.

Milo has been strong-armed into silence, and Brett—well, it seems as though he's most likely on our side, which should keep my secret safe.

Probably.

"Have you heard anything from Milo?" I ask.

Instantly, Drew stiffens. "No, just silence."

I frown, pressing my cheek against Drew's warm back. "That's not good."

"No, it's not," Drew admits with a small sigh." It's incredibly odd, actually, because we usually hear at least some chatter. They might have switched channels again."

"What are the Fairfax going to do?" I prod. "Now that they know Milo killed Jace's brother? That it wasn't you?"

Drew rubs his eyes and shakes his head as he looks at me over his shoulder. "They're not a forgiving bunch."

"No, I guess not," I admit.

Drew plops down on the mattress once again and pulls me tightly to his chest. "Every time I ask Jace, he gets all dark and quiet. He won't tell me much, just that it's better I don't know what happens next."

"Oh, I bet you love that," I say with a wry smile.

"Yeah, he should know better," Drew says, chuckling. "I've been trying to figure out what their plans are, but they're being remarkably tight-lipped." He hums with frustration. "They know I'm trying to listen in, and they don't want me to hear a damn thing."

We sit there in silence as the morning stretches on, and I can't help but wonder if Jace is right about this. If, perhaps, Drew should simply stay out of it and let the Fairfax handle it on their own.

Even worse, I have to wonder if Drew would try to save Milo one more time. If he does, he would steal precious revenge from the Fairfax—from our only allies. From Jace's family.

I can't even fathom what the repercussions might be. Not just for him or me, but for the brotherhood he and Jace have built.

With no idea what else to say, I simply hold my fire dragon tight and hope it never comes to that.

But, deep down, I know better.

It will, and when it does, there will be *blood.*

CHAPTER SEVEN

"DRAGONS DARE TO SHIFT AT YOUR BORDERS, MY QUEEN."

I gasp at the sudden voice that tears me from my sleep, twisting in the sheets and cocking one arm as I prepare to punch someone in the face.

The voice is like an air horn in my ear, and even though I would never admit this out loud, it scares the shit out of me.

In my surprised stupor, I fall off the damn bed.

I hit the ground hard, my head banging against the stone floor, and I groan in pain as my world briefly spins around me.

"Damn it, Ashgrave," I mutter, rubbing my temples as a small headache flares in the back of my skull.

"I APOLOGIZE, MY QUEEN," the castle says, his voice booming through my room. "I DETECT DRAGONS IN ONE OF THE HUMAN VILLAGES JUST BEYOND MY BORDERS, AND I ASSUMED YOU WOULD WANT TO KNOW IMMEDIATELY. WAS I WRONG?"

I frown, grimacing as I sit upright, and briefly survey the room. Drew's gone, a small dent on his side of the bed and the covers thrown aside, and I figure he must have let me sleep in.

My eyes drift to the Astor Diary sitting at my bedside table, and I rub my eyes as I slowly force myself awake.

Ashgrave's words echo in my mind, and it takes me a few moments to really process them. "There are dragons at the border?"

"YES, MY QUEEN."

"How many have shifted? Can you tell?"

"I KNOW ONLY THAT THERE ARE DRAGONS. IF THEY WERE WITHIN MY BORDERS, I COULD TELL YOU MORE. I AM SO SORRY, MY QUEEN."

"No, it's fine. It's fine," I say, waving away his apology. It strikes me as odd that there would be dragons so close to my home, but the fact that they specifically chose a human village concerns me the most. It could be a trap of some kind.

After all, dragons aren't supposed to shift in human zones.

Hell, I didn't even know there were human zones nearby until now.

The Fairfax would tell me they were coming, so I know for sure that whoever this is, they're not friends. I need to investigate, but I also need to make sure they're not just trying to lead me away from Ashgrave.

I can't leave my castle vulnerable. I need to know what's going on, even when I'm away.

I look again at the Astor Diary, my mind racing as I think about what to do, and in that moment, something clicks into place for me.

I know exactly what to do with the second orb.

"Ashgrave, get the guys together and tell them to meet me in the heart of the castle."

"JUST YOUR LORDS, MA'AM?"

I chuckle as I stand, rolling out my shoulders. "Yes, Ashgrave. Brett's not one of my men."

"AT ONCE, MY QUEEN."

It only takes me a few moments to dress, and even though I want to indulge myself with another one of Ashgrave's brilliant gowns, I tug on some jeans and a light jacket instead. There's no telling what's going waiting for us in this village, and I need to be ready for a fight.

It's a bit harder to fight in a dress than in jeans.

I jog down the labyrinth of stairs and hallways that run through Ashgrave, and I'm grateful to know that I'm beginning to memorize the route through this place after all. Sometimes I wonder if Ashgrave helps me out without telling me, changing the hallways and stairs to take me effortlessly to where I want to go, but I like to believe I'm just a quick learner.

Before long, I stand in the heart of the castle, sun shining through the brilliant windows along the walls as I jog toward the pulsing blue light of Ashgrave's heart. Drew, Jace and Levi are already waiting for me, and my men smile as I near them.

"I'm coming!" Tucker shouts from a nearby stairwell, a bit out of breath. "What did I miss?" he adds as he runs into the room with a grin on his face. "Whose ass are we going to kick?"

I chuckle. "There's something we need to do first."

"Ashgrave said there are dragons at the border?" Jace asks, squaring his shoulders as he watches me with a tense expression. "Do we have any information?"

"None," I admit, shaking my head.

"I'm telling you, Rory, we need the defense network up first," Levi says with a frown. "We do that, and we could have drones that go out and check this sort of thing for us before we even show up."

"It's a fair point," I admit. "But it's not what we're going to do."

Drew laughs, and that only makes Levi's scowl deeper.

"Then you're going to build the army?" Jace asks, lifting his chin slightly, as if daring me to disagree.

"Nope."

Drew laughs harder.

"Score," Tucker says, pumping his fist into the air. "Immortality it is."

I shake my head, trying to make them see reason, here. "No, you guys. We need to be able to leave Ashgrave and know he's not vulnerable without us here. We need a line of communication between him and us anytime we're gone, and with everything at stake, I think we're going to be gone a bit more often than we anticipated," I add with a brief glance toward Levi. He frowns, but I persevere and continue on. "Ashgrave, can you bring me the orb from the treasury?"

"OF COURSE, MY QUEEN," the castle answers.

"Rory, are you sure about this?" Levi asks, frowning. "A defense network would

be—"

"Helpful, yes," I finish for him, nodding slightly. "But we have to think about what we need the *most* right now. We're not hiding out here, and the defense network is only useful if we never leave."

Jace scoffs. "That's why an army—"

"Babe, I know," I interrupt. "But I don't think the world is ready for that. I don't think it would work in our favor. At least not yet."

He grimaces, shaking his head, clearly disagreeing.

"HERE YOU ARE, MY QUEEN," the castle interjects.

The ground briefly trembles, and I look behind me as a pedestal rises from the cobblestone floor with the blisteringly bright orb sitting on the pedestal. I lift it, the glass sphere filling the fingers in both my hands as I delicately hold it up and examine the storm brewing inside.

The gods' magic, trapped in a crystal ball.

"Ashgrave, we're going to enable the Mind's Eye," I tell him. "Take us there."

"AT ONCE," the castle answers, a twinge of excitement in his voice.

I smirk. It seems that, perhaps, my evil butler is excited he gets to join our expeditions beyond his walls.

One of the many corridors along the far wall lights up, sconces flaring to life as they lead down a dark hallway and cut into the shadows.

"You guys ready for this?" I ask, looking over my shoulder as I head into the hallway.

Levi and Jace frown, on opposite sides of this debate, and neither of them look all that happy. Tucker jogs ahead into the darkness, passing me and flashing me a quick wink as he races to the lead. Drew follows at a leisurely pace, and as our eyes briefly meet, he simply gestures for me to continue.

Get on with it, then, the motion seems to say.

He's such a charming ass.

As we pass into the fire-lit hallway, a dreamlike sensation overtakes me. Without any view of the sky, I lose track of time, and I can't tell if we've been in the hallway for seconds, minutes, or hours.

It's surreal and strange, and I don't like it at *all.*

As the growing unease burns between my

shoulder blades, I notice a blip of white light appears at the end of the corridor.

The way out.

Finally.

In moments, the white light grows until it becomes a doorway that opens out into an aviary. As we walk into the courtyard, I can't help but look skyward. Instead of a ceiling arching far overhead, there are clouds. Sunlight.

It's almost like we stepped outside, even though we most certainly didn't. Everything in here feels contained, like we're in an enchanted little bubble of sunlight and beauty.

Trees fill most of the courtyard, and it stretches beyond what I can even see, though walls stretch above the canopy. The contrast between stone and the sparse forest makes me feel like I've stepped into a dream, where everything is breathtaking but not quite right.

Not quite *real.*

The bubbling of a brook filters through the air, giving the courtyard a serene and silent ambiance. Sure enough, a small river cuts along the grassy floor nearby.

"Wow," I mutter under my breath, spinning slightly as I take in the beautiful garden.

Though much of the garden is green, a massive oak tree at its center dominates the space, its bark gray and ashy—like all the life was drained from it, leaving only a husk behind.

A massive hole sits in the middle of the trunk, carved into the tree ages ago. It reminds me of a little knoll that an owl might live in. My boots crunch along the grass as I near it, and I jump over the small brook as it cuts through the dirt between me and the oak.

As I near, the orb hums with even more power and light.

It knows this place.

Deep within the carved out hole of the tree, a soft green glow begins to pulse just like the blue pedestal in Ashgrave's heart.

It would seem as though we found one of the domains.

"This is it," I say softly.

"Are you sure about this, Rory?" Jace asks, frowning.

I pause, but only to watch him over my shoulder. I smile softly to reassure him and gently nod.

He sighs in defeat.

Time to get to it, then.

I delicately set the orb into the trunk, resting the crystal ball gently on a small pedestal within the tree.

And the very *moment* the orb touches the domain, the oak flares to life. It's as though all of its energy, all of its magic, is returned in a rush. Its bark glows softly green, like there's enchanted moss covering the entirety of the oak. The gray ashy leaves brighten, stiffening with pride and vigor.

In an instant, the tree comes back to life, and the sun above us shines brighter.

A pulse of energy radiates from the tree, shooting through my hair as it passes me. Everything around us becomes even more vibrant as the blast rolls through it, the courtyard somehow becoming even more beautiful. The water flows faster, bluer now, almost glimmering with light. A few butterflies wander by, spiraling into the air above us.

Around us, the castle sighs with pleasure and delight.

"NOW THAT FEELS LOVELY," he booms.

In the canopy above, the leaves rustle, and I take a cautious step back, frowning as I study the branches that move and shiver overhead. A few leaves cascade around us, spiraling to the ground as I prepare for the unknown.

Something darts out of the tree, flying through

the air above us too far away to see. It dives, light glinting off its body, and I instantly summon my magic into my hands.

Just because it's in Ashgrave, that doesn't mean it won't try to kill me.

But as the odd little thing gets nearer, my lips part in awe.

A mechanized dragon about the size of a cat barrels through the air toward me, slowing ever so slightly as he nears. The cogs and wheels along his wings and face—they remind me so much of the gears within the heart of the castle.

This must be Ashgrave's "body," as it were.

A little puff of steam escapes its mouth as it comes to a stop in front of me, loudly flapping its mechanized wings as it hovers just in front of my face. Its nose briefly brushes mine, and it lands on my shoulder, far heavier than I would have expected. I groan in surprise as I take the creature's weight, but I'm able to stand upright thanks to my enhanced dragon strength.

"What the *hell* is that?" Tucker asks, pointing to the dragon on my shoulder.

"THAT IS THE CLOSEST THING TO A BODY I HAVE," Ashgrave says. "ANY TIME YOU LEAVE, I WILL BE WITH YOU THROUGH THE DRAGON.

YOU WILL EVEN BE ABLE TO ACCESS SOME OF MY MAGIC THROUGH THE CREATURE, THOUGH NOT ALL, AND I WILL BE ABLE TO COMMUNICATE WITH YOU EVEN WHILE YOU ARE AWAY."

I arch my back, a flurry of delightful pride burning within me as I look at the mechanized dragon on my shoulder. "Well, I think we can make that work just fine."

"So, we're really going to do this?" Jace asks, rubbing his temples. "We're just going to waltz into a human zone and ask these dragons what they're doing?"

"We're just going to check, Jace," I remind him. "That's all we're doing. Hopefully, it's nothing, but I'm not just going to ignore dragons at the border. There's no reason for them to be there, and you know it."

"Yeah," he admits, frowning. "But, Rory, no matter what happens…" He trails off with a frustrated groan. "You can't shift, Rory."

"I know." I cross my arms, annoyed with the situation, but he's right. "No one can know about—"

"No," Jace interjects. "*None* of us can. We cannot shift in a human zone even if there are other dragons doing it." He briefly scans all of our faces before his gaze once again rests on me. “There's so much at stake if we do. We cannot break these treaties. It’ll make everything so much worse.”

“Don’t start a war,” Levi says, rolling his eyes. “Got it.”

“All right then,” Tucker says, clapping his hands together and rubbing them. “I'll get the chopper fired up.”

“I guess it's settled then,” I say, cracking my knuckles and grinning. “Let's go see whose asses we need to beat.”

CHAPTER EIGHT

I hold tight to the handle nearest the door as the thunder of the helicopter blades above us rattles the metal frame of our chopper. Cold air whips through the open door, and from here, I have a full view of the mountains as we whiz past.

"Only about ten seconds out now," Tucker says through the shared connection on our headsets, his voice muffled slightly through the channel. With one hand on the controls and his other hovering across the dozens of knobs and buttons on the dashboard, he flips a few switches from his place in the pilot's seat.

With the effortless balance of a warrior, Jace walks up behind me even as the chopper jostles. His thick hand grabs the handhold next to mine as his arm brushes against me. He stares out at the snow as it passes, and I can't help but study his stony expression. His stormy gray eyes dart toward me, and we share a tense look as we prepare for the worst.

I would love for this to be nothing. To be some fluke, or even an error on Ashgrave's part, but I know deep in my bones that it's not.

I know this is going to be bad.

Behind Jace, Drew and Levi roll out their shoulders, both of them just as on edge as I am. We all know we're about to walk right into a fight—we just don't know *why*.

Why dragons would shift on my borders.

Why dragons would risk the treaties that keep our world from war.

All we know is that this violation is at my borders, and if it's this close to home, it probably has something to do with me.

I sigh in disappointment. It always *seems* to, lately.

"What did you say this town's called again?" I ask into the headset.

"*Pepel Derevnya*," Drew answers, nailing the Russian accent as he speaks.

"Gesundheit," Tucker says sarcastically. "Do you need a tissue back there, or were those words?"

Drew just groans in annoyance. "It's Russian. It means the town of ashes."

"Yeah, I'm going to call it Ash Town, then," Tucker says, expertly navigating the chopper through the blistering wind.

Yeah, I won't lie—Ash Town is easier to remember.

Disconnected from it all and fascinated by the rivets holding the helicopter together, Ashgrave hops around the floor of the chopper. The little mechanized dragon seems oddly out of place with the advanced tech of our ride, but he doesn't seem to care. His head tilts inquisitively to the side as he studies a seatbelt as it dangles off one of the few seats along the back of the helicopter, his nose following the buckle as it swings back and forth.

I smirk—it's been fun to introduce him to modern times. He still can't quite wrap his head around the televisions.

He calls them noise boxes, and quite frankly, the irony is too funny. *I'm* not going to correct him.

As we round the mountain, a small village comes into view. Buildings litter both sides of a wide river, and a tangle of snow-dusted roads connect them.

More to the point, at least two dozen dragons

roam between the buildings, smack dab in the middle of it all.

Smoke barrels upward from a few of the buildings as their roofs burn, and small dots race through the streets as dragons corral the humans into huddling circles in the snow. The dark silhouettes of green and black dragons dart through the streets, and my grip tightens on the handle as my worst fears are made true.

I *burn.*

With fury.

With rage.

With the godsdamn *audacity* of these assholes.

And it clicks for me, then—these dragons are abusing their power because they think such an isolated village won't do anything about it.

The humans may not be able to, but I sure as hell *will.*

Though they're still distant, a few of the dragons look our way, their heads turning toward the chopper as they roar to the others in warning. The thunder of their voices reaches us at a slight delay, given how far away they are.

"Oh, this should be fun," Tucker says sarcastically as he takes us in.

"It looks like we're going to have to shift," I say to Jace, casting a wary eye toward him.

He groans, pinching his nose in frustration. "Fine. Drew, Levi and I will. But Rory—"

"I won't," I say softly, not letting him finish.

Unless I *have* to, but I don't tell *him* that.

The longer my dragon remains a secret, the better my chances that she and I will learn to act as a single, cohesive unit before all of hell comes after us.

Whoever these dragons are, I don't want them to know my secret.

Not yet.

"Tucker, you should land away from the village," Drew says into the headset. "I would rather them not destroy our only ride."

"You and me both," Tucker says with an indignant little huff as he takes us down to a small patch of gravel on the outskirts of town.

The black rocks are the only break in the endless snow, and it's far enough away to give us a few moments to put some distance between us and the helicopter.

But only a few.

The moment we land, four dragons on the edge of the village charge toward us.

All right—guess we won't have much time to talk, then.

Time to kick ass instead.

I dart out into the snow, summoning my magic as my men jump out behind me. Ashgrave flies overhead, getting a bit of a lead on us as we race toward the village.

The wind kicks up a dusting of snow, casting a thin fog between us and the encroaching dragons. The mist blends in with the black smoke from the fires burning in the distance, and a smoky haze weaves through the sky.

Far away—too far for me to do a damn thing about it—a woman screams. The shrill sound ends abruptly, and for a moment, all I can hear is the crunch of splintering wood.

My magic burns hotter with my hatred.

These *bastards*.

The air behind me becomes suddenly electric, the energy in every breath changing, becoming charged with magic. It's a subtle shift in the air, like a scent rolling by on a breeze, and I peek briefly over my shoulder to find three dragons behind me.

My men.

Drew's red fire dragon. Levi's blue ice dragon. Jace's stunning black thunderbird.

They growl, their heads low as our opponents approach, my brilliant fighters ready for war.

Tucker jogs up beside me, four guns thrown over his shoulders as he cocks an anti-dragon rifle and nestles the butt of the gun against his shoulder. Without so much as a word, my weapons expert takes aim at the nearest dragon.

The four enemy dragons near, and I wonder if I'm going to have to kill someone today.

Because I damn well will, if they make me.

The mist breaks, and in a sudden rush, three humans appear between us and the dragons. The villagers huddle together, their panicked faces looking back and forth between the black dragons and me, at the white sparks dancing across my skin.

They're scared.

Terrified.

Of *me.*

As we near them, their faces become clearer—a man, a woman, and a child. The man watches me warily, his arms around the woman and a small boy. As he holds them close, death closing in on both sides, the panic he must feel clear on his face.

"Go past us," I tell him, nodding behind me. "We won't stop you."

The man's brows furrow with suspicion and a

hint of confusion, like he doesn't understand. At this point, he can barely contain the terror on his face.

But he doesn't move.

If he knows what I'm saying, he doesn't believe me.

I nod again toward my men, and they open up a path. I simply point to it, silently ushering him through.

The man hesitates, casting one more wary glance over his shoulder at the approaching black dragons before ushering who I assume are his wife and son through the opening.

"Thank you," he says in a thick accent as he passes, casting one last glance over his shoulder at me as they take cover.

So he *did* understand me.

I don't answer. Instead, I turn my back to him as he and his family retreat, choosing instead to stare down the approaching dragons as they begin to circle us one after another after another, leaving the town burning behind them.

Tucker sweeps his anti-dragon rifle across the crowd, no doubt already taking aim and choosing the order he will kill them in.

Drew and Jace growl, the thunder of their voices shaking the ground. Levi, ever the subtle one, merely snarls, his teeth beginning to frost as he summons his magic.

Ashgrave swirls overhead, the mechanical whir of his gears overpowering the howl of the wind, and he lands on the snow beside me. His head turns every which way as he takes in the world around us, assessing the threat.

More and more dragons join us, until it's fairly clear none remain in the village anymore. As they crowd around us, no doubt thinking they'll win simply because we're outnumbered, a sleek and beautiful dragon breaks through the ranks. The others step aside to let her through as she arches her neck gracefully and stares down at me. She pauses briefly, her eyes scanning the five of us.

And in the silence, I decide to let her act first.

Whatever she does next, it will be the deciding factor in whether or not she dies today.

To my surprise, she shifts back to her human form. Her body hums, ribbons of light snaking briefly over her skin as she shrinks, and it takes only a few moments to recognize those sultry eyes.

Natasha Bane.

She grins, setting her hands on her naked hips as she flaunts her exposed body, gorgeous as ever. Her eyes rove over my men, like she's trying to see if they're interested.

Spoiler alert—they're not, and she's just pissing me off.

Not a great start.

I ball my hands into tight fists. I haven't seen Natasha since the meeting at Reggie's place, and this isn't boding well for her thus far.

I hated her then, and I somehow hate her even more now.

"What the hell do you think you're doing?" I snap.

She shrugs. "Going shopping. What else?"

"This is a human zone, and you can't shift here," I remind her as I take a few threatening steps closer. The dragons behind her tense and snarl, but she doesn't so much as blink.

She nods to the men behind me. "Bit of a hypocrite, aren't you?"

"We're here to *stop* you," I say, my eyes narrowing. "It's different."

She takes a few graceful steps toward me, staring me down, her smirk widening as she sizes me up. "And what are you going to do about it, little human? How do you plan to stop me?"

I'm tempted to punch her in the face.

Very tempted.

However, I don't act rashly. She's here to do more than "shop," that much is obvious, and I think it's time I fish a bit of the truth out of this lying scum of a woman.

Instead of answering—or punching her in the face, much to my deep disappointment—I summon the white light into my palm and unleash a quick burst of its raw energy at the snow by her feet. A few bolts of electricity arc from the blast, hitting her, and she shrieks in pain as she takes a few wary steps backward.

Even though killing her is probably the smartest move in the long run, for now I just want to make her mad.

"You *bitch*!" she snaps, shaking out her legs as she glares at me. In seconds, she shifts back into her dragon form, growling and furious as she stares me down.

Good. This is exactly what I wanted—and it's a little disappointing how easy she is to manipulate.

At least Jett is a challenge.

Here's the thing—I *want* her in dragon form. To get her mad. And now that she's pissed, her guard is down.

In her dragon form, I can access her mind. And, angry, her defenses are weaker.

Now that she's angry, I want to see if I can do to *her* what Isaac did to *me*. I'm going to steal her memories and find out why she's really here, even if I have to pin her to the ground to do it.

Behind me, my dragons roar in warning, daring any of Natasha's soldiers to interfere.

"Back up!" Tucker yells over the roars and snarls, cocking his gun as a red dot appears on the nearest dragon's forehead.

Good, they'll keep her minions at bay, and that lets me focus on *her.*

She snarls and snaps at the air, charging me, and I unleash another blast. I'm not sure if she thinks I won't kill her, that she's immune to a brutal attack because she's related to a Boss, but she acts as though I don't have the power to turn her to dust.

I can't tell if she's an idiot, or just cocky as hell.

Both work in my favor, though.

My thundering bolt of magic hits the ground, shaking the earth with the raw force of my power, and another few bits of lightning arch off. These sear her skin, burning her, and leaving little smoking marks on her flawless, regal scales.

Natasha roars with pain, stretching her wings as she tries to stabilize herself, her body sizzling and simmering with pain and rage.

It would seem the Bane are not as immune to my magic as the Darringtons are.

Thank *goodness.*

Truth be told, she does have a *bit* of immunity here. However much I want to wring her arrogant little neck, it would be foolish to kill the Bane Boss's sister. It would give the Bane—and probably every Boss worldwide—license to come after me.

I do *not* need that right now, and she probably knows that.

But only a fool would bet her life on it.

Natasha charges once again, and I raise my hands to summon the final blow. Ashgrave takes to the sky, and as he does, he summons white light into his mouth, preparing to give me support should the need arise.

Time to end this.

The Bane dragon snarls, summoning fire in her throat, and I confess I'm a bit surprised. I didn't think she was a fire dragon. With how comfortable she was, standing naked in the snow, I assumed she was an ice dragon.

But that just works in my favor.

If she's a fire dragon, then she hates being in the snow; and if she hates being in the snow, she's going to be weaker out here in the cold. It'll be easier to catch her off guard when she's this out of her element.

I summon my magic, mostly to deter her, to distract her, and to allow her to think she knows what's coming next. As she nears, however, I race toward her, extinguishing the magic in my palm with a few flicks of my wrist.

And I bolt directly toward her face.

It's a move too fast, too sudden to even follow. As my hands hit her forehead, her eyes widen in surprise. She jerks her head backward to get away, to pull herself out of reach, but I'm faster.

I duck under her claws as she swipes at me, and with every ounce of my power, I punch her hard at the base of the neck in one of the weak points closest to the belly. It's an old Spectre trick, something I learned to disarm opponents long ago, and she goes down.

Hard.

She roars with pain, but before she can so much as react, I nail her again in the side, jabbing her by the heart. The force knocks her clear onto her back, and she coils, snarling as her eyes squeeze shut from the agony of it all.

Natasha is no fighter.

She's merely used to getting her way.

As she writhes on the snow, I set my palm on her side. The connection between us opens to a string of curse words ripping through her, but I don't give her a moment to so much as breathe.

I lean into the connection, searching for what I want—for the reason she's here. As I lean into her, thoughts and emotions swim to the surface. There are no images, no fully formed memories—just darkness and the fleeting sounds of conversation. I wade through her mind, trying to find the most relevant one before she breaks the connection.

Don't, she seethes. *Don't you dare—*

Shut up, Natasha, I demand.

After everything she's done, she's going to give me what I want, whether she likes it or not.

As I wade through her thoughts, I finally find what I'm looking for.

Get to the village, I hear Victor's voice say as I touch a memory. *Be discreet, and don't let that damn dragon vessel know you're there. We need a home base near her if we're going to capture her alive, and we need her alive to sell her.* He pauses. *Don't screw this up, Natasha. You're running out of chances.*

With a snarl, Natasha rolls away from me—and as my fingers leave her scales, the connection breaks.

Damn it.

She backs away, baring her teeth as she lowers her head near my face. She growls, but she doesn't dare touch me. She doesn't want me to know any more than I already do.

It doesn't matter.

I got what I needed.

Fire burns in her throat as she silently threatens me. As her dragons and my men face off, growling and yelling at each other, she and I simply stare each other down, daring the other to act first.

She snarls, her growl rumbling in her throat as her fire burns in her body. Without so much as flinching, I summon the white light into my hands, daring her to mess with me.

And that crazy bitch—she *does*.

She fires.

In the split second that follows, my men charge toward me. Tucker takes aim. Everyone is on edge, rushing to my side—to help, even though I don't need it.

I've got this.

But before I can so much as lift my hands, Ashgrave soars between us and fires a burst of blue flame. The mechanized dragon lands in front of me as he overpowers Natasha's fire.

The entire confrontation lasts only a few seconds, but everyone goes instantly silent.

Her flames disperse, but Ashgrave doesn't slow down or stop. The blast of his blue fire hits her hard in the face, and she careens backward, snarling, more furious than ever as smoke rises from her beautiful scales.

"HOW DARE YOU INSULT, MY QUEEN!" Ashgrave shouts, his voice booming through the cold air despite the small dragon he inhabits. "YOU ARE A FOOL AND A COWARD FOR DARING TO SO MUCH AS TOUCH HER!"

I take a deep breath, briefly glancing at the portable Ashgrave. He stole my thunder, but I can't lie—my little evil butler is too adorable for me to stay angry for long.

Natasha's body shimmers and hums as she shifts back into human form, and though she's naked in the snow, she glares at me with all the fire of a princess. "This isn't over," she seethes, pointing her finger at me. "You just signed your death warrant."

"Really?" I say, setting my hands on my hips as I laugh at her. "I thought you needed me alive, Natasha? You are out of second chances, after all." I wink, just to piss her off.

It works. Her nose wrinkles in disgust, and she opens her mouth to speak.

I don't let her get so much as a word out.

"If you come here again," I interrupt, my voice dropping to a dangerous octave. "I *will* kill you. I don't give a shit about the consequences."

Her mouth snaps shut, and her hands ball into fists as she barely contains her rage.

I know what she wants to do. She wants to attack me. She wants to beat me to a pulp and burn me, and I think for the first time in her life, she found someone she can't control. She can't charm me. She can't seduce me. She can't even hurt me.

For once, she's out of her depth, and I don't think she knows how to handle that.

Without so much as a word, Natasha shifts back into her dragon form and flies off, the small army of other dragons taking to the air as they chase after her. It isn't long before they're merely dots against the foggy sky, and then they disappear completely.

Thank the gods—because I was pretty close to killing someone.

When they're finally gone, I let out a slow breath and rub my eyes as I think again about the memory I stole from Natasha.

This is bad. Victor wants a home base that's close

to me—someplace he can spy on me where he thinks I can't see.

Yet again, my enemies underestimated me, and quite frankly, I'm just lucky Ashgrave's reach is so far. They were counting on me not knowing they were even here, and I suspect they attacked the village to ensure they were too terrified to say anything to me. The Bane were counting on the villagers to simply cower and bow to their whim. To give them whatever they wanted.

Including me.

A soft murmur breaks through the blistering snow, and the small and gentle howl of the wind begins to settle into a soft breeze as a dusting of snow slowly falls across the village. A plume of black smoke begins to turn gray as the fires are put out. One by one, doors begin to open as the humans of the village slowly walk into the street.

"Levi, do you think you can put out any lingering fires?" I ask my blue dragon.

He nods and flies off into the air, blowing a soft mist of ice over the nearest fire.

Slowly, faces in the growing crowds begin to turn toward me, and I wonder if I should go. I don't like the thought that they think I'm some invader, someone coming to take and destroy what's theirs—what little they have.

But to my surprise, they begin to applaud.

A few of them even whistle, and the cheer grows to happy shouts as they walk toward me.

Clapping.

I was expecting anger or even threats, but kindness?

It's—it's just *weird.*

I suppose I should feel grateful or even flattered, but mostly I just feel strange at the thought of these people thinking I'm some sort of hero. My cheeks burn a little with the attention, and I don't like it at all.

"That's enough," I say awkwardly, lifting my hands in an effort to get them to stop. "Guys, let's go."

Behind me, Jace and Drew just laugh, shaking their heads as they force me to endure the applause. Tucker leans on the butt of his gun, smirking at my discomfort.

I groan in annoyance.

They *would.*

One woman pushes through the crowd with a small jewelry box in her hands. She lifts it toward me, her eyes wide and pleading, as if asking me to take it. I frown, confused, and when I don't take the box, she opens it to reveal a small chest of rubies and sapphires, with a small diamond in the middle of them all.

"Take," she says in broken English, pushing the chest toward me again. "Is what you want, yes?"

I shake my head, taking a step back as she still tries to give me the chest. "No, thank you."

The woman frowns, a clear look of confusion on her face as she looks between the chest and me, as if she simply doesn't understand.

I scan their homes, and though the charred holes in a few of the roofs are in obvious need of repair, I begin to notice other signs that this town is in desperate need of love. Boards cover a few of the windows. A few stones are missing from the stairs leading to the front doors on several nearby houses.

With a meager box of jewels that's barely a quarter full, it's clear that these are some of the last nice things these folks even have.

The woman again offers the box to me, and I simply smile and close the lid. "Keep it," I tell her, not entirely sure she can understand me. "I'm not here to steal from you."

For some reason, that only makes her look more bewildered.

"If they come back, tell me," I say, scanning the faces around me as I point in the direction Natasha took. If that man in the mist knew what I was saying, maybe more of the folks here know English as well. "You're under my protection now."

With that, I head back to the chopper, Ashgrave flying through the air overhead as my men take to the air. Tucker races beside me, effortlessly keeping pace despite the four guns strapped to his chest.

Yes, I need to make sure the Bane don't set up shop here, but I also want to do right by the people who are just in harm's way. It's not right that they're in the line of fire simply because they live here. It's not fair.

And though I don't need a mole so close to my home, it would seem as though I have my first subjects.

Drew must be elated—bit by bit, the world is proving him right. The world is giving me a kingdom, and I'm not sure how I feel about that.

I never wanted to be a queen. I want to thrive. To protect the men and family I love.

But, without intending it to, it seems as though my *family* is slowly growing.

CHAPTER NINE

I sit at an ornate table in one of the many war rooms of the castle, facing an entire wall of windows that gives me a stunning view of the grassy knolls below that bleed into the snow-capped mountains beyond.

I settle into my chair with the deep sigh as Drew fiddles with the television on the wall to my left, cursing under his breath as he maneuvers the wires and cables connecting the screen to the outside world.

He tried to make me help, but I told him Spectres don't do grunt work.

I smirk at the memory, setting a little deeper into my seat as a new string of curse words escapes him.

The door behind me opens, and footsteps

thunder into the room—three men, and I recognize all of their gaits.

Well, honestly, I can only recognize two: Tucker's adorable shuffle and Jace's confident stride. The silence means Levi probably came in with them, but I'll never be able to detect that man.

Truth be told, I've stopped trying. He will forever be my master of stealth.

Chairs scrape along the wooden floor, and as I open my eyes, I sure enough find all three men sitting around me. Levi flashes me a small smile, and I sometimes wonder if he does that on purpose—just to mess with me.

Yeah, who am I kidding?

He *definitely* does.

"I can't believe the Bane could be so brazen," Jace says, shaking his head as he leans back into his chair and drapes his arm over the seat beside him. "A full-on attack on a human village, in *dragon form* no less? Did they think they were immune?"

"The world is changing," I admit with a small shrug, my smile fading. "And not in a good way."

"Well, yeah," Tucker says, gesturing toward me like it's obvious. "They all want you, and they're racing each other at this point. To them, time is running out."

I scoff. "I'm pretty sure Natasha wants all of *you* from the way she was practically drooling over you back there."

Tucker contemptuously snorts, like there isn't a snowball's chance in hell of that happening. "I'm flattered and whatever, but 'homicidal bitch' isn't really my type."

Everyone in the room breaks into laughter—except for Drew of course. He's still cussing under his breath as he messes with the damn television.

"Up until now, they've been laying low," Levi points out, his smile slowly fading as he leans his elbows on the table. "We can only guess what they have in store for you."

"Yeah," I admit, chewing my lip as I think it over. "Poor bastards don't know what's coming for them."

Jace grins mischievously, leaning his head on his fist as he watches me with a hint of admiration.

"Got it," Drew says, grinning in victory as the television turns on.

The low chatter of a news station buzzes through the room as a red banner flashes underneath a man talking about financial markets.

"Finally," I say, leaning forward.

My fire dragon frowns, casting a brief glare over his shoulder at my apparent audacity.

“Drew, you know I didn’t mean it that way,” I say, dismissing his irritation with a wave of my hand. “I just mean it's nice to have a connection out here. I feel so detached from everything going on, like it’s a world away and I have no idea what’s really happening.”

“Yeah,” Drew admits, flipping through a couple of the channels. “Don't worry though, Rory. Soon we'll have a full surveillance setup going on and a full connection to everything outside. Now that we have a home base, I can actually set up a proper system.”

I cross my arms and lean back in my chair, watching my fire dragon as I sift through the reality of what he just said.

It's impressive what the man can do with only a cell phone, and the intel he's managed to gather even without having his ideal setup is astounding. I can't wait to see what kind of intel he can get me now that we have a home base.

“What have we missed?” I ask with a nod toward the television.

“This, for starters,” Drew says, flipping through a few more channels.

I catch a few images here and there—a company’s stock price graph, with the arrow pointing downward; a panel of men discussing something around a table; the rubble of an earthquake.

Eventually, Drew lands on a beautiful woman with silky dark hair and mocha-colored skin as she stares intently into the camera from behind a news desk.

"...the march continues for the fourth day," the woman finishes as we come in on the middle of her broadcast. "And the turnout is record-breaking. Here's a view from one of the marches in the Capital, broadcasting live."

The red ticker below her flashes my name.

Dozens of Rory Quinn marches happening around the world.

I groan, rubbing my eyes as I lean back in my chair, frustrated. "Maybe we should just leave the television off."

"No, Rory, look," Jace says gently, reaching over to softly tap me on the shoulder.

I indulge him as the screen flashes to the image of men and women alike walking down a street lined with elegant stone buildings. They wave their signs, chanting something I can't quite make out. I briefly scan the boards as they sway in the air, trying to figure out what they say.

Even after I read them, it takes me a moment to process what I'm seeing.

The disbelief is too strong, and I don't want to hope too hard.

We love you, Rory.

Let her be.

We're all the dragon vessel.

"She's done nothing wrong!" the marchers chant, waving their signs. "Leave her be! She's done nothing wrong! Leave her *be!*"

"Whoa," I say, leaning forward as I quirk an eyebrow in surprise. "A pro-me march? That's a first."

"*Marches,*" Jace corrects with a cocky smirk. "*Plural,* woman. There's forty happening worldwide at the same time."

"What?" I squint at the television, half-wondering if this is just a dream.

If this could possibly be real.

Jace gestures toward the screen. "Since your broadcast revealing the truth about the Knights and Zurie, public opinion has changed dramatically in our favor." Jace leans back in his chair as he looks pointedly at Levi.

"Yes, I know," Levi says with a groan, rolling his eyes. "I made a big deal of it, and I was wrong. Can we move on?"

Jace chuckles.

"This is the world now," Drew adds, tapping the television as he looks at me. "This is what I always knew you could do. What I always knew you could *be*."

"It's just the start," Jace says with a cautious frown. "Don't get too comfortable, Drew."

"What does *that* mean?" Tucker asks.

"It means if we shift in any more human zones, all of this could go away." Jace points at the screen. "We cannot take those risks. Not again."

"What else were we going to do against twenty dragons?" I ask, gesturing out the window in the vague direction of Ash Town.

"It was probably worth the risk this time," Jace admits with a shrug. "But it cannot become a habit. It would be too easy for everyone who hates us to spin it against us. Think of how Brett would have twisted that if he were still a Knight."

With that simple comment, something deliciously devious clicks in my brain.

Oh.

Oh, *my*.

That gives me an idea. A terrible, brilliant idea.

I pinch the bridge of my nose as I stare out the window, wondering if I'm really going to do this—or if, maybe, it's all a giant mistake.

"Ashgrave, bring in Brett."

"OF COURSE, MY QUEEN," the castle answers immediately.

"What?" Jace and Drew say in unison, their noses wrinkled slightly in disgust.

"But *why*, babe?" Tucker demands, grimacing. "He doesn't need to be in on these conversations."

"Most of them, no," I admit. "However, he *is* a master strategist," I add, getting to my feet as I slowly pace the length of the table. "Brett knows publicity and public relations. He knows how to warp public opinion. He's a brilliant guy who's been sitting on his ass, twiddling his thumbs and waiting for something to do." I pause, setting my hands on my hips, more sure now than ever before. "Well, this is it."

"Babe, no," Tucker says, groaning as he rubs his face. "Can't we just kill him?"

"Tucker," I chide, glaring at my weapons expert.

"But *why?*" Tucker whines exaggeratingly,

drooping backward over his chair in what has to be a painfully uncomfortable position.

"Well, don't get your panties in a twist," I say, rolling my eyes. "We don't even know if he's going to do it."

"We don't even know why he's still *here*," Jace points out, his eyes narrowing in suspicion.

"Fair point," I admit, pacing once again as I tenderly bite my lip, lost in thought.

There are so many chess pieces on the metaphorical board—so many players in this game of life and death I've found myself in.

I think again about everything ahead of us.

The Vaer.

The war.

The Spectres.

The Bosses.

The *gods*.

"Brett might be useful," I say quietly, my gaze drifting toward Drew. "In the meantime, we need to find the other orbs."

"I haven't found anything yet," he admits, shoving his hands in his pockets with a frustrated sigh. "I'll keep looking."

"Damn," I mutter under my breath, rubbing my thumb over my lip as I once more lose myself in thought. I want to get those functional, but I'm not sure we'll have time before the war hits.

"We need to stop Kinsley before she amasses any more power," I say as I pace the length of the room. "Jace, does Harper still want me to meet with the Bosses?"

"Of course," he says, leaning his elbows on the table. "You have a lot of sway in this world, Rory."

It's still too weird to acknowledge the last half of what he said, so I just kind of ignore it. "I'll meet with whoever she wants—except for the Palarne."

Jace sighs, tapping his finger absently on the table. "He's a good guy, Rory. I promise."

Drew snorts derisively, and the two men briefly glare at each other—instantly, and thankfully momentarily, at odds.

Jace apparently knows a side of Isaac that neither Drew nor I have experienced.

"Isaac wants something from me," I point out, shaking my head. "Same as all the others. He may be noble, but that doesn't mean he's acting in my best interest, Jace."

"That's a fair point," the former dojo master admits as he leans back in his chair.

"MY QUEEN, BRETT HAS ARRIVED," Ashgrave announces.

"Let him in," I tell the castle.

The door opens to Brett standing in the hallway with his hands in his pockets. All of us look at him, pausing mid-stride or mid-sentence, and an uncomfortable silence settles on the room as we all stare at him—and as he stares at us.

"Hey," Brett says awkwardly, his gaze drifting across every face in the room as he no doubt wonders if he should bother walking inside.

"Hi. 'Kay. Bye," Tucker says, waving Brett off as if that was the extent of the conversation.

"I didn't come here to see *you*," Brett snaps, frowning as he enters anyway.

"That's enough," I chide them both, shutting the door behind him and leaning against it.

I cross my arms, resting the back of my head on the wooden door and lifting my chin slightly as I stare down the former Knight who tried to kill me on several occasions, and *save* me on many others.

He swallows hard, barely able to contain his nerves, but he manages to keep my gaze and square his shoulders. I get the feeling that he's preparing for the worst.

My imagination gets away with me as I wonder what his version of worst-case looks like.

"What do you want?" I ask casually. "Why are you still here?"

He sucks in a deep breath, as if his lungs suddenly deflated and he can't get enough air, and his gaze drifts briefly to the floor. "I need a purpose, Rory. I need a reason to exist."

"You had one," I point out. "You were going to lead the Knights."

"And then I saw the truth," Brett says dejectedly, unable to hold my gaze any longer. "I saw what the Knights really are, and I couldn't stay. I realized I was wrong and that I had been living a lie." He runs a hand through his hair. "I have nothing left. No reason to keep breathing. No purpose to drive me. Nothing."

With that, his gaze drifts finally toward me, and I can see the deep-set sadness in his eyes.

I've seen it a couple times in my life—this look. It's a precipice. An edge. A moment of change that's almost impossible to come back from. He's losing hope, and if he doesn't find what he's looking for soon, only one of two things can happen—either he will become so depressed that he loses himself in his misery, or he'll latch onto something dark and apply his brilliant mind toward the first thing that floats by him.

And that very well may not be in my best interest.

I frown, still debating my options. But if I'm being honest with myself, I've already made up my mind.

"I want you to look at the news and public opinion," I say, absently rubbing my jaw as I watch him, studying him for any tells, any signs that he's up to something devious. But there's nothing, so I continue. "See how people might be manipulating the tides against me and come up with ways to combat it."

This next moment defines who Brett is now, and I watch him *very* carefully. The seconds pass like hours as I study his face and wait to see who this man really is.

What his time with us has done to him.

To my surprise, he lights up with excitement. "Yes. Absolutely," he says, grinning, the first hint of life coming back into his face. "I haven't had much access to the outside world since coming here, but what I have heard is good." He lifts his finger excitedly, like he's asking for a few moments of my time. "Look, see this?" he adds, pointing to the television. "Your broadcast worked wonders. And do you know why?"

As I assume the question is rhetorical, I don't answer.

"It humanized you," he finishes, stretching his fingers with a small flourish, like he's miming *ta-da.*

At that, all of the dragons in the room except for me bristle with indignation, but Brett doesn't seem to notice. He's too snared in his excitement even as Drew, Jace, and Levi all glare at him with a bit more disdain than before.

"There are several key countries that are still indifferent and neutral to you," Brett continues, looking at me with an excited grin. "And that's where we go and help. We give aid, we make appearances, you name it."

"This isn't the time to be going out and kissing babies," Levi snaps. "Too many people want her. They could use any goodwill mission as a trap."

"Maybe," Brett admits with a frustrated nod, as if acknowledging Levi is a chore. "But this is also the *perfect* time. It's a tipping point, and if she does a few strategic things, we can turn the tide in her favor. *Globally*, guys."

"He has a point," Drew admits with a frustrated scowl.

Tucker just sighs in anger, sinking deeper in his chair as he glares daggers at Brett.

Jace and I, however, share a fleeting look that confirms everything I've been thinking so far. This has potential, and even Jace can admit Brett is good at what he does. Jace is a general through and through, and that means seeing strength even in his enemies—and those he's not altogether too fond of.

I don't love the idea of making a lot of rounds, but if I'm already visiting the Bosses, I'm already leaving Ashgrave. There's minimal additional risk, especially if we keep visits short.

With a pensive sigh, I kick off the wall and sit once more in my chair as I stare out at the beautiful mountains beyond my castle.

"I'll think about it, Brett," I eventually tell the former Knight. "Give me solid plans and several actions, and we'll pick what we feel works."

"Yes, of course," Brett says, clapping his hands together excitedly. "I'll start right now." With that, the former Knight darts back into the hallway and jogs down the stairs, apparently eager to get started.

All he needed was a bit of direction.

"Well, at least he's keeping busy," Tucker says, scowling after Brett.

I shrug. "Yeah, well—"

The chime of my phone interrupts me, and I look down to see a text from an unknown number.

There's another in the works, it says.

That's it.

No context. No clues.

Nothing but an ominous warning from an unknown number.

I impulsively stiffen, and though Diesel has messed with me before, something tells me this is Irena.

Something tells me this is legit.

I frown, trying to figure out what she means—if this is in fact her, of course. This isn't one of our codes. This is entirely new and unplanned, without even an attempt at filtering the meaning beyond being vague.

This is something hasty, something thrown together and urgent, sent to me the moment the sender had a second to do so.

There's another in the works.

That could mean so many things. Another battle? Another onslaught? Another kidnapping attempt?

The phone chimes again, and I look down to see a picture of a familiar crystal, one so very much like the crystal Zurie used to drain me of my magic not so long ago.

My heart skips a beat, and for a moment, I simply stare at the picture in disbelief. My lips part in surprise, and all I can do is gape in disgust. In horror.

In dread.

Someone else is trying to steal my magic yet again, using the very crystal that nearly killed my dragon.

Deep in my chest, she curls with anxiety, clinging to me for dear life as we both cringe.

I just can't catch a damn break.

CHAPTER TEN

"Damn it all, are you sure?" Harper asks through the audio line connected to my headset as the helicopter whirs around us.

I nod at the video feed of her on the tablet in my hand, rubbing my eyes as an ocean races by the window to my left.

I adjust the headset on my head as Drew and Jace lean over a shared laptop, the two of them talking in hushed tones through another channel on their headsets. I'm not sure what they're doing, but I assume they're up to mischief.

They usually are.

Ashgrave—bless him, he's been staring out of the window, immobile, for a good hour, fascinated by the world beyond the castle.

It's been awhile since he's had a chance to see the world, and something about the endless ocean snares his heart.

Tucker and Levi, however, talk with furrowed brows and deep-set frowns in the pilot and copilot chairs, and the only words I've been able to catch from them are from Levi as he turns his head—momentarily, here and there, I can read his lips. As far as I can tell, they're talking about Brett on a private channel, and it doesn't seem to be good.

I sigh, trying to focus on one devastating change at a time.

Through the video feed on the tablet in my hands, Harper groans and rubs her face, glaring off camera for a moment as she thinks through what I shared about another crystal in the works.

Irena hasn't contacted me since the text—again, if that even was her—which sets my nerves on fire. I adjust the tablet so that I don't have to crane my neck and look down at her. "I feel the same way, Harper. If another crystal is in the works, that's bad news for all of us."

"How is that even possible?" She shakes her head, rubbing her temples as if she can't quite believe it.

Hell, I don't really believe it either.

Irena and I haven't had a chance to talk about this

yet, and whatever she's doing, however she discovered this, it seems like she's in deep. I'm itching to call the number she texted me from, but there's no telling if it's secure, and I'm not taking that chance.

Not with something this important.

"Rory, I don't know," Harper says, shaking her head. "Maybe you shouldn't do these meetings with the Bosses. Maybe you need to go back to Ashgrave. Maybe you need to—"

"Hide?"

She pauses, frowning, but she glares at me with a knowing expression—like, yeah, that's exactly what she thinks I should do.

"Harper, stop it," I say, leaning toward the tablet and wishing I could shake her out of this.

She lets out a slow breath, clearly centering herself as she gently nods. "You're right. We don't exactly have the luxury of time."

"There's always going to be someone after me," I say with a shrug. "I can't spend my life hiding from the world."

Harper grins, looking playfully at the camera. "Then I guess let's make an example of them, huh?"

"Damn right," I say, grinning.

She chuckles, her shoulders relaxing slightly. "Do you know who it could be?"

"Hell, who can we even rule out?" I say with a frustrated wave of my hand. "Everyone we know seems to have means, motive, or both—Diesel. Natasha. Her brother Victor. Kinsley. The Oracles themselves."

I roll my eyes. There's just too many people who want me dead.

Yay, me.

"Aki Nabal?" Harper asks cautiously, lifting one eyebrow as if she can't quite bring herself to believe it.

"The man I'm going to talk to right now?" I ask sarcastically. "Is there something you haven't told me, Harper?"

She lets out a slow breath, like she isn't even sure where to start—like this is a subject she wasn't even sure if she should bring up. "You know by now that the world is changing, Rory. It gets worse every time I come home from a meeting or mission. Aki has been acting… I don't know." Harper shrugs. "Odd. Unusual, even for him. He seems thrown off his game by something. More focused than usual. I've offered him things he's begged me for in the past, and he won't bite."

"Do you think Kinsley has her claws in him?" I ask, frowning.

"I think she's close," Harper admits quietly, rubbing her eyes again. "I think she's really close."

"What have you noticed?" I prod. "Give me details."

"It's more what I *haven't* noticed," Harper admits. "His daughter has been missing for months, and usually she's with him at every function. Every meeting." Harper shakes her head. "Something's wrong, Rory. No one has seen her, and I'm a little worried that Aki…"

She trails off, like she can't even bring herself to finish the thought.

"What?" I press.

"I'm worried he did something," Harper admits. "I'm worried he's trying to cover it up."

"Not to be rude," Drew interjects, leaning into the frame beside me as he looks at Harper. "But I don't see how that's our problem."

"Shush you," I say, pushing him playfully out of the camera shot. "Go spy on someone over there," I add, gesturing toward Tucker.

Jace chuckles. "We'll switch off your channel, Rory."

"The one you shouldn't have been on in the first place, you mean?" I ask, quirking one eyebrow as I pretend to be angry.

I can't help it. It's impossible to be irritated with them for very long.

"Yeah, exactly," Jace says with a smirk as he and Drew both tap the channels on their headsets.

Harper chuckles, shaking her head. "You must have your hands full all the time."

"You have no idea." I laugh, rubbing the back of my neck as I lean back against the plush seat in the chopper.

"He does have a point, though," Harper admits.

I shake my head. Something about this is not sitting right with me. "I don't know, Harper. If something happened to Jade, we can't let him sweep this under the rug. She seemed sweet enough the last time I met her."

"You mean the last time you were at Reggie's?" Harper asks.

"Yeah," I say, nodding. "I didn't really talk to her much, though. She seems really young. She's what? Eighteen?"

"Yeah, I think so," Harper says. "Honestly, there's always been tension between her and her dad, but no one knows why."

"I can take a couple guesses," I admit dryly, frowning as I think about the Nabal Boss and the vast stores of information he seems to have access to. "Honestly, he reminds me of Zurie a little bit."

"Oh, well, that's great," Harper says sarcastically.

"Yeah, exactly." I rub my jaw, thinking through the two of them and comparing the similarities. "Access to incredible stores of information and wealth? Check." I tick off the list I'm starting with my fingers. "Secret agenda? Check. Vendetta against yours truly?" I chuckle. "Check."

"It may not be that bad," Harper says, lifting one hand to slow me down.

"Maybe not, but I don't trust him worth a damn."

"And you shouldn't," Harper agrees. "You shouldn't trust any of these Bosses. They all want you, Rory, for one reason or another. It's just a matter of time before they try to take what they think is theirs."

"Yeah, I know." I absently study my fingernails as I try not to think too hard about what she just said.

"Hey, Rory," Tucker's voice comes in through the channel on my headset. "Make sure to ask for a plane."

I chuckle, shaking my head, but Harper laughs as she overhears him.

"A *plane*?" she asks, one eyebrow quirked in skeptical surprise.

"Yeah," Tucker says. "Rory said she'd get me a plane."

"I did *not,*" I correct him, looking up from the tablet as Levi shakes his head, chuckling.

Tucker, however, is peering over his shoulder at me with an excited, almost breathless look on his face. He gestures toward the tablet, urging me to get on with it already and egging me on like a kid in high school.

"I thought this was a private channel," I say, glaring between Tucker, Levi, Jace, and Drew.

"Nothing's private with Drew around," Harper says, rolling her eyes.

"Hey," Drew says, frowning—after already promising to get off the channel.

We all burst into laughter, and I just shake my head, grateful I have men I can trust enough to know that even if they're listening in, nothing bad will come of it.

"Harper," I say, rubbing my temples, almost unable to believe I'm about to do this. "Will you please buy Tucker a plane?"

"A jet!" Tucker interjects. "With big-ass guns!"

"Oh, yeah," she says dryly. "Let me go to the plane store."

I grin, lifting one eyebrow as I playfully glare at

my weapons expert. "Yeah, that's what I said."

"Oh, come on," he says, pouting. "You all get to fly. Why can't I?"

"For real though, Harper," I say, grinning as I look at the Boss. "Think you can wrangle that and an attack helicopter?"

"Yeah, I'll see what I can do," she says with a shrug.

"Yes!" Tucker says, pumping his fist in victory.

I chuckle, shaking my head. "Make sure it's totally decked out please. Enough firepower to put on a fireworks show."

"Well, duh," she says, rolling her eyes. "The finest weapons money can buy, right?"

"Damn right," Tucker says, chiming in.

"You'll need them," Harper says, her smile fading.

And mine fades with it.

"What do you mean?" I ask.

"You know my magic is…" Harper frowns, waving her hands around a little as she tries to come up with the word. "Hard to control, at least some of it. Sometimes I get intuitive hits, an impulsive understanding that comes out of nowhere like a bolt of lightning, and I just know. I don't know how I know, but I just know."

"What are you trying to say, Harper?" I ask,

admittedly confused.

She groans in frustration, like words aren't her friend right now. "There's something about Aki that you need to keep an eye on," Harper says. "Something about him feels wrong, and I don't know what it is. It's been eating me up for the past several days." Harper throws her hands in the air, frustrated. "Our intelligence has picked up a few things. It's clear he wants to get information out of you about the gods and your magic. He wants to know how it all works. He will probably try to test you."

"Yeah, well, let him try," I say, crossing my arms. "I've grown a lot since I last fought him."

"Yeah. But, Rory, the neutral zones are becoming less safe," Harper says, her brows twisting upward in worry. "Be careful."

"I will, I promise. I have no intention of getting killed or captured anytime soon."

"Yeah, well, I'd worry about you if you did," Harper says, chuckling. "Speaking of…"

"Yeah?" I ask wearily.

"Of all of our potential allies," Harper says hesitantly, "the Bane have been most likely to join us."

"I don't trust them at all," I say, leaning forward, furious she would even consider it.

"Duh," Harper says with a frustrated shrug. "Neither do I, but we don't have a lot of choices. If we have a potential ally, we just need to test them. See if they're legit."

"Oh," I say, grinning as it slowly dawns on me what she's doing. "You set up a meeting with them, didn't you?"

"Guilty," she says, looking at me hopefully.

I sigh. "When?"

"After Aki. You'll have a gap between meetings."

Oh, Harper.

So devious.

"That's why you want me to talk to them, isn't it? I'm the bait."

"What?" Jace and Levi shout in unison, their tone furious as they glare at the tablet.

"Yeah," Harper says, grimacing a little as she watches my expression. "But you don't have to. That's why I'm telling you ahead of time."

"Of course I'll do it," I say, rolling my eyes as I wave the thought away.

"*What*!?" Jace and Levi say in unison again, this time glaring at me.

"Guys, come on," I chide, my gaze darting between the two of them.

They frown, looking at each other and shaking their heads, and I'm sure they're going to come up with some sort of contingency plan in case this all goes south.

Hell, I already have three.

“Look, Reggie has the place on lockdown,” Harper says. “He'll be watching every room. Every hallway. Every bathroom.”

“Eww,” Tucker says.

“Not like *that*,” Harper snaps, her gaze darting to the edge of the frame as if she's waiting for Tucker to pop into view any second.

“He’s piloting the chopper,” I tell her.

“Oh.”

“Who else do you have lined up?” I ask her, wondering how far she plans to take this.

“What do you mean?” Harper asks.

“Don’t be coy,” I chide her. “I'm sure you're going to want me to talk to others,” I point out. “The Palarne. The Darringtons.”

At the mention of the Darringtons, Harper's expression changes. She goes from warm and bubbly to cold, stiffening almost instantly, and she just stares at me as if daring me to continue.

Huh, I guess now we know how the Fairfax feel, now that they know who really killed Jace's brother, Garrett.

“Are you going to put that aside?” I ask quietly,

watching her expression for an answer since I'm starting to think she won't tell me. "Are you going to connect with the Darringtons even though—"

"It's better if you don't know," Harper says, a small spark of electricity burning in her eyes as she stares me down. "You're almost to Reggie's place according to the GPS tracker. Be safe, Rory."

"Harper, don't—"

With that, the screen goes black.

I sigh, rubbing my eyes. "That's not good."

"No, it's not," Jace admits through the line, the four of them still listening in even though they shouldn't be.

"What's she going to do, Jace?" I ask.

Jace stiffens, his gaze darting between me and Drew. "It's better if—"

"We don't know," Drew and I finish for him.

The thing is, I'm not sure I agree with that. I think the Fairfax know exactly what they want to do, and they know exactly what could happen if they try to kill Milo.

The problem is they want their revenge, and that bloodlust is blinding them to what they really need—forgiveness.

Especially in this world where we have so few allies at *all*.

CHAPTER ELEVEN

As the chopper lands on an asphalt circle with Reggie's castle in the distance, Reggie himself is standing at the edge of the walkway with a big smile on his chubby face, his bald head shining in the sun. Before the whirring blades above us even turn off, he jogs over to us and opens the door. His eyes sweep us all and land on me, and his smile somehow gets wider.

"Rory," he says as I hop out of the helicopter. In true fashionista form, he lightly taps his mouth against each of my cheeks, making an exaggerated *kiss-kiss* noise with each movement.

I can't help but grin at this guy—in an ocean of crazy, his over-the-top welcome is a fun little flourish, especially considering how tense everything was the last time I was here.

Hell, he greets me like an old friend, and I don't have many of those.

I've got to say, I like this guy.

Ashgrave flies toward us from the chopper as Tucker powers down the helicopter. Levi is the first to join me, since Drew and Jace are leaning toward Tucker in the pilot seat—the three of them probably plotting something when they think I can't hear.

The mechanical dragon lands on my shoulder. As my body briefly sways from his surprising weight, the little dragon gives Reggie a once-over.

"WHAT SORT OF KING ARE YOU?" Ashgrave demands from my shoulder, tilting his mechanical head as he examines Reggie and his dark suit. "YOU ARE AN ODD LITTLE MAN, BUT IF MY QUEEN LIKES YOU, THEN SO DO I."

"Holy *crackers*! What was that?!" Reggie asks, flinching as he leans exaggeratedly away from me.

His gaze drifts to Ashgrave, and his mouth goes wide.

"Ashgrave, be nice," I chide my castle-butler.

"APOLOGIES, MY QUEEN," the castle answers as Jace and Drew jump out of the chopper to join me.

"It seems that we have quite a lot to catch up on," Reggie says with a small smile as he studies the mechanical dragon on my shoulder.

"You have no idea, Reggie," I say dryly, shaking my head as Levi and Tucker join us.

When Jace, Drew, and Tucker are finally done plotting their silent mischief, the six of us walk toward the castle, and it's almost strange to not see dragons on every surface. The last time I was here, they were everywhere—in the woods, overhead, on the roofs.

I could barely turn my head without seeing a dozen of them and now…

…nothing.

It's unnerving.

"The castle's not as busy as it was when you were last here," Reggie says, and I figure he's picking up on a bit of my unease. "But I have made sure that all the finest comforts are provided for you."

"Thank you, Reggie," I say with a grateful nod.

"Unfortunately, there's been a slight hiccup," the castle master continues, his gaze anxiously darting toward me. "It would seem the Nabal Boss has arrived a full twelve hours early, and he wants to speak with you immediately."

In unison, Tucker, Jace, and I groan, and I can't resist the impulse to roll my eyes.

Of course he did.

Aki is trying to trip me up, and I debate making him wait just out of spite. But I'm trying to put this guy in a good mood, so in the end, I decide to indulge him.

This time, anyway.

"Take us there, Reggie," I say.

"Good call, Rory," Jace says, giving me an approving little nod.

I can't help but smile with a little hint of pride—maybe I'm starting to make sense of this whole diplomacy thing after all.

As we enter the magnificent palace, Reggie leads us silently through the hallways, and I slowly tune the world around me out.

I'm on the hunt. It's instinct, and no amount of time away from Zurie can squelch it.

My Spectre training has me looking in every crevice and corner for ways out. For cameras. For any hint of danger, but it's mostly unconscious. Impulse.

Camera up there in the corner, by the ceiling.

Four windows to my right, each leading to a bed of greenery that would soften a fall.

It’s habit.

Rule 12 of the Spectres—always know when and how to escape.

Even from a friend’s home—or in this case, castle.

With my four men at my back, I know I'm safe—at least as safe as the dragon vessel can be in a space that's not her own.

My mind buzzes with what lies ahead—Aki, and whatever little game he’s playing. It’s unclear to me, however, what he's trying to do. What information he's trying to get out of me.

That's how he works. He deals in information like bankers deal in money, and he has more of it than anyone else on the planet.

The question simply is, what does he want from *me*?

As we near a set of double doors, Reggie hesitates and takes a deep breath, centering himself before the introduction. Seconds later, he throws them open with a flourish and gestures for the five of us—and Ashgrave—to enter ahead of him.

Though the weight of Ashgrave on my shoulder weighs me down, I force myself to stand a little taller as I enter the room.

On the plus side, I'm not trying to impress

anyone. There are no gowns. No formalities. No bullshit.

Just the way I like it.

On the other hand, we've been traveling for a solid eight hours, and we're exhausted. Some time to myself and possibly a nap would have been nice, but I suspect Aki knows that.

He wants us tired—an exhausted person is easier to wring for information.

As we enter the room, I briefly sweep the space to find the Nabal Boss sitting at the head of the table on the opposite end of the room.

Alone.

Between him and me is the table I shot lightning through the last time I was here, and boy, has Reggie done it up. Gold foil inlay coats the scar I left in his rich mahogany table, each and every divot lined with glittering gold. A thick layer of resin encases the entire thing to protect it, and I resist the impulse to smirk.

Giving him that little trinket has basically meant I can stay here, free of charge, for life. According to Drew, it's quadrupled Reggie's business. If he wants me to destroy anything else, I'm happy to oblige.

Especially if I get free stuff for doing it.

I sit at the opposite end of the table, and my men take the chairs beside me. To my surprise, there's no one else in the room—just the six of us as Reggie closes the doors behind him and leaves us alone. I suspected Aki would bring soldiers. A general, maybe, or even Jade. To my disappointment, she's nowhere in sight either.

Secretly, I had hoped she would show up today and prove Harper wrong.

I'm still new to negotiation, and quite frankly, I don't really know what to do. As silence stretches along the room, Aki doesn't seem bothered at all. In fact, he weaves his fingers together in front of his face as he watches me without a sound, clearly waiting for me to speak first.

"You're the one who wanted to have our little meeting twelve hours early," I say dryly, quirking one eyebrow as I wait for him to start the conversation.

Aki chuckles, leaning forward as he nods to my four men. "I was under the impression we would speak alone. I don't like being outnumbered, Rory.

"Then you shouldn't make assumptions," I counter, tilting my head a little as I dare him to keep gaslighting me.

His smile briefly falters, but he recovers. "If I recall, you and Harper were the ones who wanted to speak to me. So, speak."

I frown briefly at his tone, and beside me, so do Jace and Drew. They know what he's doing, and they recognize a power play when they see one. Both of them have been in these situations before, and neither of them wants to be here now.

"You already know what this is about," I say, lifting Ashgrave off my shoulder and setting him on the table beside me. Aki's eyes linger on the mechanical dragon, no doubt curious, but he somehow resists the impulse to ask questions.

"You want me to join you and Harper against the Vaer," Aki says with a bored tone, waving his hand dismissively, as if it's a silly request.

"It's only a matter of time, Aki," I say, leaning my elbows on the table as I try to drive home my point. "It's only a matter of time before this gets so bad that you're dragged into it anyway. We have a chance to stop this now, and it's our duty to end this before it gets ugly."

"Don't talk to me about duty," Aki interrupts, leaning his elbows on the table as he matches my posture. "The Nabal don't give a shit about duty. We care about survival, and we are not interested in fighting the Vaer so that Harper can win this little grudge match."

"It's not a grudge match," I snap, my nose crinkling with disdain as I dare him to disagree. "This isn't about the dojo. It's not about pride. It's not about being right. It's about stopping Kinsley before—"

"Before what?" Aki says flippantly, leaning back in his chair again. "Before she kidnaps you? Before she drains your blood and does who knows what with it?" He runs his hand through his hair as he shakes his head. "Rory, not all of us are willing to put our armies on the line for you."

"This is not about me!" I snap, slamming my hand against the table. The wooden surface shivers beneath my fist, and Aki's gaze briefly sweeps along the table before it returns to my face.

"Are you sure?" he asks, his eyes narrowing.

"This is not about me," I repeat more calmly. "This is about what Kinsley will do now that she has nothing to lose."

"It has always been about you," he says quietly, an almost eerie serenity in his voice as he glares at me.

And as he studies me, I can almost see the cogs turning in his devious little brain.

"Fine," I say, narrowing my eyes as I dare him to

take this too far. "Let's say this *is* about me, Aki. She's been after me since the start, and you have to ask yourself why. What does she want with me, and how is that going to affect you if she succeeds?"

The Nabal Boss frowns, his gaze drifting to the table as his eyes slip out of focus. For the first time since I entered this room, he's actually considering what I said—and that shows progress.

"We keep ourselves away from trouble," he says finally, shaking his head. "Thanks for the offer."

I scoff in irritation. "Then why did you come here? It's clear you're not really willing to consider this."

"I wanted to have a chat," he admits, tilting his head slightly as he watches me.

Baiting me.

"That's a long trip for something we could handle with a phone call," I say, calling out his bullshit.

He smirks a little, and I catch a hint of satisfaction. I figure he's impressed that I can see through him, but I'm not sure why. By now, he should know that his tricks don't work on me.

"I have some questions for you," he confesses.

"Of course you do," I say, not bothering to hide a small eye roll.

"Tell me about your magic," he demands. "What new abilities have you discovered? What—"

I click my tongue in disappointment, like I caught a child stealing cookies. I don't care that I interrupted one of the most influential men on the planet—if anything, that just works in my favor.

He tried *his* power move, and now it's time for him to see mine.

I lean back in my chair and cross my arms. In the silence that stretches on between us, I simply smile and watch him, knowing that every passing second makes him more uncomfortable. His eyebrows scrunch in annoyance, and it's clear he's trying not to show his irritation.

But I can see it.

"How about this?" I ask, tilting my head as I study his face. "A question for a question."

Beside me, Drew and Tucker shift in their seats, each of them looking at me with an unnerved expression. Only Levi and Jace remain calm. I know none of them like where this is going, but I know what I'm doing, and they trust me.

"Interesting," Aki says, grinning as he sits back in his chair. "Alright. I'll go first. What's that thing?" he asks, nodding briefly toward the mechanized dragon beside me.

"Introduce yourself, Ashgrave," I say, weaving my fingers together as I rest my chin on the backs of my hands.

"I AM THE CASTLE ASHGRAVE," the tiny dragon announces in a voice far too loud for his little body.

His voice tears through the room, and sparks dart along his metal body as he flares to life.

"I OBEY THE ONE QUEEN AND SMITE ALL SHE DEIGNS ME TO DESTROY. DARE NOT DEFY HER, PEASANT, OR YOU WILL FACE MY WRATH."

I subtly bite the inside of my cheek to keep myself from laughing.

Ashgrave just called the Nabal Boss a *peasant.*

Aki's eyes go wide as he leans back in his chair, gripping the armrests as the shock and surprise of the moment get the better of him. But it only lasts for a second, and almost instantly, he forces his shoulders to relax. Even as his body relaxes, however, his eyes never leave the mechanized dragon beside me.

"My turn," I say, not bothering to mask the hint of delight in my voice at seeing him caught so off-guard. "Why won't you join Harper? Give me the real reason why you won't, now. Are you scared?"

The Nabal Boss laughs humorlessly. "Hardly. I have secrets that could cripple the Vaer and the Fairfax both, child. I weigh every option before I make any choices, and right now there's just no benefit to joining either side."

As he speaks, I study his face for the signs of a tell. I want to know if he's lying, and I figure this is why he wanted to speak to me in person—to do the same to me. He, however, seems to be telling the truth. He really believes he has secrets that could cripple both armies, and deep down I find it hard to believe if that's true. If it is, why hasn't he done it? Why would he withhold that information at all?

I suspect he believes he's above the law. In his heart, he likely believes he's above all of this. Above these petty squabbles.

Though I maintain my stony, impenetrable mask that doesn't betray a hint of emotion, his heartless answer bothers me.

It also tells me everything I need to know.

He is never going to join us. He just wanted to lure me out in the open and see what information he could bleed from me.

That just pisses me off.

"My turn," he says. "What abilities have you mastered since we last met?"

Oh, man. I don't want to tell him that, but I do want to keep him talking.

Time for a bit of a loophole.

"My magic is getting stronger," I say vaguely, my gaze drifting toward Jace as he and I share a knowing look. "For starters, I can do this."

On command, a surge of heat rushes through me, and blue flame flares over my fingertips as the fire crackles. I turn my hands every which way, examining them as the flames lick my fingers.

"Fascinating," Aki says, leaning forward as his eyes narrow, clearly studying the magic in my fingers. "What else?"

I frown at his dismissive tone and shake out my hands as the fire dissolves. I debate telling him about my pure magic dagger, but I think that should remain a secret.

For now.

After all, asking me what skills I've mastered is a bit too unclear. I'm not about to show all of my cards, especially not to him.

"That's it," I say, treading the line between truth and lie as I walk the tightrope of my loophole.

He frowns, his eyes narrowing in suspicion, and it's clear he knows I'm holding back. "This game of ours only works if both parties play, Rory."

"I agree," I say, resting one elbow on the table. "But you asked what powers I mastered, not what powers I have. It's a loophole. Spectres are great at those."

At the mention of my previous life, Aki goes suddenly still. It's strange to see the flicker of terror that comes with the mention of my past life, especially such fear on a man like him. It's that sudden burst of panic, to know he's in the room with an assassin and has been many times over.

It shuts him up.

"My turn," I say, smiling warmly. "Where's your daughter? It seems odd that no one's seen her in a while."

In an instant, his entire mood shifts. He goes from still and slightly fearful to disgusted at the mere mention of her. The sudden, almost *violent* shift catches even me off guard, and I lean slightly back as I study his face.

Something *clearly* happened.

And I very much doubt she's alive—not after a look of such deep loathing at the mere mention of her name.

My heart pangs for her—she was just a girl, and she may well have been killed by her own father.

I grit my teeth, trying to quell the rising rage in

my chest. I don't know what happened, and I have no proof.

Not yet.

For several moments, no one says anything, and I'm not going to be the one to break the silence. Though it seems like he's not going to answer me, this is one question I suddenly very much want the answer to.

"Is our little game over already, Aki?" I taunt him, my eyes narrowing as I dare him to say yes.

I have so much information he wants. That's the whole reason he came all this way—to try to wring me of everything he could gather.

For this one question to set him this off-guard—well, now, I absolutely *have* to know what he's going to say next. This is a man who keeps his cool in any situation, and for the first time, it would seem as though he's lost it.

"Our game is indeed over," Aki says, standing abruptly. His chair scrapes along the floor, and his shoulders slowly rise as his breath quickens.

"What did you do to her?" I demand, my fingers curling into a fist.

He glares at me—technically, our game has ended, and he may never answer me. But after a moment, he simply shakes his head. "I don't allow for failure."

The words hit me hard in my chest, and for a few moments, I can't breathe.

They hit home, and they sound far too familiar.

Zurie's voice echoes suddenly in my head, and it's like she's back from the grave.

I don't allow failure, Rory.

I can't count all the times Zurie said the exact same thing to me down in the pits below her unassuming fortress. In the pitch-black tunnels of the mountain where she trained me and Irena, I heard her voice over and over.

I don't allow for failure.

Those who fail me die.

I swallow hard, snapping myself from the memory. Sweat slicks my palms as I press them against the table, trying my best to keep my calm even as ribbons of white light burn along my arms. Jace watches me warily, and I can tell he wants to reach out, to soothe me, to hold me tight—even as Drew glares at me to *fix this.* Levi and Tucker look at each other, like they're not sure what to do or what the hell is happening.

Even though Aki's words weren't about me, what

he said hurt far more than I would ever dare to admit.

Without so much as another word, the thumping stomp of Aki's footsteps trace toward the door. The edges of my vision go black as I fight the flashback, as I fight the memory and try to stay in the moment.

If the Nabal Boss is walking away from the chance to learn more about me, this must really hurt for him, too. Whatever happened between him and Jade is dark.

Very, *very* dark.

As the door opens, I can't help but wonder what this guy did and who he really is. I thought he was some tycoon, some rich guy with secrets, but he seems far too willing to disown his own daughter. To possibly even kill her.

"From what I know about you," I say darkly, not bothering to look at Aki to see if he's even listening, "I think *you* failed *her*."

With that, I look him dead in the eye, and he knows exactly what I mean.

Whatever happened between him and Jade is his fault.

And, deep down, he *knows* it.

Aki scoffs in disgust, but he doesn't say another

word. With that, he stalks off into the hallway and leaves the silent room behind.

CHAPTER TWELVE

As I walk through the hallways of Reggie's castle with Jace and Drew in tow, I can't help but lose myself in thought. Levi and Tucker left to secure the perimeter, and I ordered Ashgrave to join them.

Though I trust Reggie, I trust my men more. They're more skilled, more experienced, and I'll sleep better when they secure the area.

"In here," Drew says, his voice cutting into my thoughts.

I snap out of my daze as he grabs my arm and drags me into a dark room while Jace briefly scans the hallway, no doubt to see if somebody is following us.

"What the hell?" I mutter.

"Is it clear?" Drew asks tensely, ignoring me, his gaze focused on Jace.

"Clear," the former dojo master says with a nod. With that, Jace shuts the door behind us, the only light streaming in from the open windows of the living room suite. The forest is visible through the glass, clouds streaming by the sun.

The two of them look at me, their eyes narrowing in anger, and they square their shoulders. Drew crosses his arms while Jace sets his hands on his hips, and for a moment, the two of them just watch me like they're expecting me to say something.

"What?" I ask again, shrugging in my confusion at what the hell I've done *now* to piss them off.

"You have to be more careful," Drew chides, shaking his head. "You didn't handle that well at all."

"I handled that just fine, thank you," I say, setting my hands on my hips as I stare down the two of them. "What the hell are you talking about?"

"Aki is far more dangerous than he lets on," Jace warns, his voice dark and tense.

"So am I," I point out, my gaze darting between the two of them.

Jace groans. "Yeah, but bringing up his daughter? Rory, what were you—"

"He could very well have killed his own daughter for all we know!" I snap, gesturing out the window. "Maybe he's about to!"

"Rory," Drew says softly as he pinches the bridge of his nose. "You have to be delicate with the Bosses."

"No," I interrupt, not even letting him finish the thought. "I'm *not* delicate, Drew. I'm fierce. I'm smart. I'm careful, but I'm not dainty and that won't ever change. One thing I won't do is ignore my intuition, and that man is up to something. Something bad." I hesitate, studying both of their faces and daring them to disagree with me. "He's up to something that could hurt us, and he needs to know what he's up against."

"Yes, Rory," Jace concedes, lifting one hand in surrender to appease me. "But that's not everything."

My phone buzzes in my pocket, interrupting us. Though the last thing I want to do is talk to someone else right now, I whip it out to check, just in case this is Irena.

It's a number I don't recognize.

"Take it," Drew says, shaking his head. "Jace and I will try to run damage control."

Damage control.

I grit my teeth in anger, my grip tightening on the phone. It creaks a little beneath my enhanced dragon strength, and I let out a small breath to calm myself as Drew stalks toward the door.

Jace, however, doesn't move. With his gaze trained on me, he studies my face with a stony expression I can barely read.

After a moment, he sighs and sets one hand on my shoulder before kissing my forehead. With that gentle moment of unexpected tenderness, he follows Drew out the door and leaves me alone in the room.

Well, alone-ish.

They're probably not far, and for all I know, Drew probably planted some kind of surveillance device on me. It wouldn't surprise me at all, even though I would tear him a new asshole for it.

Even though I'm irritated and the last thing I want to do is talk to someone, I let out an impatient sigh and answer the phone.

By now, I have a protocol for these occasions. After I answer, I don't say anything. I wait for the other person to speak.

I'm not in the mood for games.

"What fresh hell are you getting yourself into *now*?" Irena asks.

Even though I'm angry, I can't help but grin a little at the sound of my sister's voice. "Glad you're not dead."

"And a merry good morning to you, too," she says sarcastically, and I can almost imagine her flourishing her hand as she says it.

I doubt we have long, and we need to get down to business. As I think through the many things I want to share with her, my smile begins to fade. "How did you find out about the crystal?"

Irena lets out a long, slow sigh, and I can feel the heaviness in it. I've heard that sigh before, and I can imagine her rubbing her eyes as she figures out how she wants to word what she's about to say. "You know I'd do anything for you, right?"

"Of course," I say without pausing. "It's mutual."

"I know," she says softly, and I can hear the smile in her voice. "Rory, don't be mad, okay?"

Oh, gods.

I rub my eyes. I'm probably going to be mad.

"Just say it," I tell her.

"When you told me about the orbs, I went hunting. I wanted to find you something, anything at all to help you out. I need to know you're safe, and the best thing to do is to get Ashgrave fully-operational."

I swallow hard, and my breath quickens as I wonder where this is going. I start to piece it together, and I try not to let myself hope too hard, but I find myself gripping the phone a little tighter regardless. "And?"

"My first thought was Diesel, of course," Irena admits. "The Spectres are an ancient organization—not as old as the Knights, but we still go back centuries. I figured that if anyone hates dragons as much as us, we're bound to have found something along the way."

I begin to pace the elaborate room, wondering why she's dragging this out and at what point I'm supposed to get mad.

"We raided Diesel's fortress," she says, her voice strained as she finally confesses.

"You did what?!" I snap, almost unwilling to believe she would be that foolish. "Irena, what were you thinking? He has all of the Spectres at his command. He knows that you're after him. He—"

"Will you shut up?" Irena says, laughing. "I know what I'm doing, and I have quite a few Spectres of my own, thanks."

I hesitate, caught off-guard by her admission. It's strange to think of her as having an army of her own, but I saw as much back when she joined us in the battle for Ashgrave. There are those who want out of the Spectres, and she's the only way for them to get it. Of course, she has an army of her own.

"So, what did you find?" I finally ask.

"No orbs," she confesses, and my heart sinks a little despite trying not to hope too hard. "But I did find communication between him and a strange third party talking about the crystal." She hesitates. "This mysterious third party promised Diesel certain, well, *rights*," she says, hesitating. "The things he wants to do to you, Rory…" Irena trails off, her voice getting hard and angry, and I figure I'm never going to know what those messages said. "Basically, this third party wants to drain you of your power, and the deal is Diesel gets you afterward if he helps make it happen."

"Damn it," I mutter, shaking my head as I pace the room. "So, Diesel has allies outside of the Spectres."

"Somehow, despite his personality, it seems so," she admits with an annoyed huff. "We barely got out of there, Rory. He's enhanced the Spectre fortress in unbelievable ways. Made it almost impenetrable, even more so than before. Even turned our old room into a mop closet."

"Of course, he did," I said dryly. "That spiteful jackass."

"I lost several of my best guys," Irena admits, her voice catching.

"I'm sorry," I say, and I mean it. For us to have allies is a rare thing, and it's painful to lose any of them.

"It's official though," Irena continues. "Diesel and I are at war, and to end this, I need to kill him. He'll keep fighting me, but he's the last of the old guard, and so far he hasn't taken on an heir. If I can kill him, I can cripple the Spectres. Rory, he's..." Irena trails off, searching for the word. "He's different than Zurie."

"Well, yeah," I say, wondering where the confusion is on that one.

"No, no, you don't understand," Irena says. "He's not even thinking about an after-death plan, Rory."

"What?" I ask, laughing a little in disbelief.

"He thinks he's smarter than us—combined," Irena says. "He has no doubt in his mind that he'll end us."

"Well, that works in our favor," I admit. "If he's really that cocky."

"Yeah, but we can't be," Irena interjects. "Everything we do has to be carefully planned, and it's hard for me to trust anyone because they could all be a double agent for Diesel. Hell, I have several within his ranks."

I smirk, proud of my sister. Even if she's not

quite capable of processing grief, her revenge is deadly, and I pity anyone stupid enough to anger her.

"You especially need to be careful," she continues. "I've seen a lot of pro-Rory marches, and that's great, but..."

"But?" I prod, waiting for the inevitable lecture that I know is coming.

"There's still a lot of hate for you out there, Rory," Irena warns me. "Clashes. A few terrorist attacks are in the works, some of which the human governments are trying to stop or cover up. And the bounties on your head?" Irena whistles. "They're getting higher and higher every day. There's insane competition to capture you before you get too powerful. Everyone wants to do it while it can still be swept under the rug, and that won't be an option for much longer. Rory..." Irena hesitates, making sure I'm listening.

"Yeah?"

"Do *not* trust the Andusk or the Bane. Do you understand me?"

"Yes," I say, my eyes narrowing in suspicion as I wonder what she's not telling me here. "The Bane is a given, but the Andusk? Why—"

Before I can finish, an idea comes to me. Something Drew mentioned not too long ago. Something I've almost forgotten.

"Irena, do me a favor. See if there are any notifications on any obscure materials being stolen, namely rare ores and metals."

"Oh, that's—that's random." She hesitates, a bit of a baffled tone in her voice, and I can imagine her tapping her finger on her lips as she thinks. "That sounds kind of familiar, but I need to look at my notes. Why?"

"I'm not totally sure," I admit. "Someone's trying to steal resources, namely the resources we're using to make Spectre tech."

"It sounds like Diesel," Irena says.

"Maybe."

But my intuition says it's something else.

"I'll keep looking," Irena says. "In the meantime, I'm sending you a present, and it'll be at Ashgrave when you get home. Tell your castle not to kill any of my men, please."

I chuckle. "You're so *demanding*."

"Har har," she says dryly.

"What are you sending?"

"I managed to get a few overrides together. Only a couple, but they should last you for a little while," Irena answers. "I'm sending lots of voids, of course, and several guns with all the attachments you'll need. Plus, I found some new tech, something that was in development, but Zurie couldn't get it together in time. Drew and I refined it."

"What is it?"

"Bugs actually," Irena says. "Surveillance equipment that's barely detectable. I think you're going to like it."

"Hell yeah," I say, laughing. "Send a little extra of everything, if you can. I want to send some of it to Harper."

For a moment, Irena doesn't say anything, and I wonder if I've lost the connection. I briefly look at the phone, but the line is still active.

Irena sighs. "Do I have to?"

I sigh. "Technically no, but you should."

"She's a dragon, Rory."

"So am I," I point out. "And you, probably."

Irena groans in annoyance, and I can feel the two sides of her fighting. Everything she learned as a Spectre is fighting with everything she knows now and everything she might be.

"Fine," she finally admits. "Just them, though. I don't want you to give this to any other allies you might get. Do you understand?"

I groan. "At this rate, I don't think you'll have to worry about that."

Irena laughs. "What? Your animal magnetism isn't kicking in?"

Despite myself, I laugh. "You're an idiot."

"Yeah, but you love me."

"Eh," I say, feigning indifference even as I chuckle under my breath. "Look, don't die, okay?"

"You too, baby sister."

That's the plan—don't die, and kick the ass of whatever fool tries to mess with me or the people I love.

CHAPTER THIRTEEN

I can't find Drew in the massive expanse of the castle, and I figure he's probably setting up a surveillance system somewhere to spy on people he shouldn't be spying on and getting intel that will be incredibly beneficial.

In my heart, however, I can feel my mate, and I know that Jace isn't far.

So I go to him.

The beacon in my soul takes me upward, and the more stairs I climb, the more I'm beginning to think he's probably sitting on the roof. I'm tempted to simply shift and fly up there, but this isn't Ashgrave. My dragon is still a secret for a little while longer, and I want to keep it that way as long as possible.

Out here, I can't be sure who's watching.

When I feel that I'm standing directly beneath him, I find the nearest window and climb out onto the roof to find him sitting at the peak of the steep slope, staring off into the distance with his back to me.

For a moment, I simply admire his silhouette in the sunlight—his broad shoulders, his strong back, the muscles pressing against his shirt. His dirty blonde hair looks almost brown in the setting sun, and I wonder what's going through his mind.

I climb the shingles and sit beside him without so much as a word, brushing my elbow against his as I get close without looking at him. I stare off into the mountains around us, spotting the high-rise buildings of the nearest city—the same city Carter chased us through the last time we left this place.

Something tells me I won't have as many issues the next time I try to leave. I have never been a helpless damsel, but I'm far less vulnerable than ever before—and all of my enemies know it.

I sneak a glance at my mate to find his brows furrowed in anger as he glares out at the sunset. His shoulders are tense and tight, like he's ready for battle. The longer I look at him, the more I see a man who's holding back, who's biting his tongue for one reason or another, unwilling or unable to share what's on his mind.

"Talk to me, Jace," I say quietly.

My voice seems to break whatever spell he's under, and he blinks rapidly for a few seconds before sighing deeply. He rubs his face and shakes his head. "I don't know, Rory."

"Well, something's clearly wrong," I point out, resting my elbows on my knees as I balance on the angled roof. "You've been so tense, lately."

"I know," he admits, biting the inside of his cheek.

"If it's about Aki—"

"It's not," he interrupts. "Not really. I know you're strong and capable, Rory."

I grin, my heart fluttering a bit with flattery. To receive a compliment like that from a warrior like Jace, well, I won't lie.

It makes me happy.

"You're always ready for a fight," he continues. "But I'm always ready for a full-on war."

My smile fades, and I'm not sure what to say.

"They're different," he adds. "I can see twenty moves ahead, Rory, and you're playing a dangerous game with the Bosses."

"I know," I admit. "Relax. I've got this."

He chuckles. “The only time I can relax is when I’m inside of you.”

I laugh, blushing a little. I hadn't quite been expecting *that* little rated-R comeback. “Are you propositioning me on a rooftop?”

He chuckles, rubbing the stubble on his jaw as he shakes his head. “This honeymoon has been so nice, Rory, but I need purpose again.”

I snort in surprise. “How is attacking a Knights’ fortress, nearly dying in a mountain range, and starting a war a *honeymoon*?”

He laughs. “Well, when you put it like that…”

I shake my head. “You're unbelievable, Jace Goodwin.”

“You like it,” he says with a grin.

Yeah, I really do, but I'll never tell him that.

He looks off wistfully into the horizon. “Training. Teaching. Fighting. It's all I've ever known, Rory. It's what I need.”

And with that, I can finally see where he's taking this.

So, I cut to the chase.

“You want an army,” I say simply.

He pauses, not looking at me, and as the silence searches between us, it confirms what I suspected.

“Don't *you*?” he asks after a while.

"Not really," I admit. "I've never had an army before, but it feels like inviting trouble. I'm really not sure it's the best course of action right now. We went to Ashgrave to have a home base, not to declare ourselves as a kingdom."

"That may not be something you get to choose," Jace says, his tone a bit sad.

"Think about it though," I say, gesturing out toward the city in the distance. "The dragon vessel is already a controversial topic. People don't like the magic I have. They don't like how much power I have," I say, balling my hands into fists. "Just me being me scares them. I have more power than most dragons combined, and I don't even know what to do with all of it. That scares people, and when people are afraid, they do stupid shit. Do we want to stoke that fire?"

"True," Jace admits, his gaze finally drifting toward me as he no doubt pieces together where I'm taking this.

"People already fear me," I say. "If I go around building armies and amassing followers…" I trail off, shaking my head, my eyes dipping out of focus as I consider what that could do. "I just think everything's going to get so much worse. People will think I'm—"

"A Boss?" Jace finishes, hinting for the first time at something Drew has been mentioning for a while.

"Yeah," I admit, shaking my head. "I think I need to tackle one crazy thing at a time, Jace."

"You may not have that luxury, babe," Jace says quietly.

I look at him in surprise, and his stormy gaze snares me, leaving me breathless as the weight of what he said hits me hard.

"I need you to understand something," he adds, leaning toward me. "What happened in Ash Town—that village?" He pauses, shaking his head. "It can't happen again. You cannot get used to shifting in human zones. Do you understand?"

"I heard you the first hundred times," I say, rolling my eyes.

"No, Rory, this is serious," he snaps, his tone getting firm. "I don't think you appreciate the depth of how terrible it will be if we do that again in a populated area. Sure, a small town in the middle of nowhere..." he trails off, shrugging as he flippantly waves his hand as if it doesn't matter. "That's fine, but if you do that in a city, that's war."

"We're already at war," I say, rolling my eyes.

"No, we're not," Jace says, scoffing. "We're

preparing for it, but there hasn't been a single massive battle yet. That's not how dragons fight."

"Enlighten me then," I say, my eyes narrowing as I study his face.

"Dragon war brews," he answers, indulging me. "It's a festering tide of resentment and anger that builds and builds and builds until it snaps." His gaze darts to me when he says the final word, emphasizing the severity of it. "And when a dragon snaps, he's bloodthirsty. He kills everything in sight. He razes cities. He destroys kingdoms. He decimates. And *Kinsley*? She's the queen of bloodthirsty retribution. When she makes her first blow, it devastates her opponent." His gray eyes watch me, daring me to speak even as he steals my breath away. "Every moment she's not actively trying to kill you, Rory, she's looking for your every weakness. She's studying you. This isn't the calm before the storm—it's her actively doing everything she can to rip you to shreds, so that when the moment comes, you won't even have the chance to breathe before she does it."

For a moment, neither of us speaks, and the growing silence of the setting sun fills the void as I consider what he said.

He's right, of course. Spectres know nothing

about war, not really. The few major battles we've had as a unit are reserved for dire circumstances, situations where there's no other recourse. Assassins work best in the dark, alone. Spectres are shadows in the night that operate on fear and not knowing when they'll strike.

It works for us.

But dragons operate differently. They're big and ferocious, and it only makes sense that their wars are the same. It wasn't always relevant for me to know the ins and outs of dragon culture, but what I did know—what I did pick up—was brutal.

There are no prisoners.

There is no mercy.

There's only blood and death. That's the dragon way.

"Because of that," Jace continues after a while, "humans feared us for so long, and they had every right to." He shrugs. "Anytime a human village got caught in the middle of a dragon war, everyone in it died or was taken as a slave and prisoner. Even humans who wanted nothing to do with dragons couldn't get away." He shakes his head. "That's where we came from, Rory. And this peace we have with them, it's fragile." He gestures toward the city in the distance. "All of those people fear us. They fear dragons even as we fascinate them, and if they lose faith in us—"

"Then we lose that peace," I answer for him.

"Exactly," Jace says, nodding. "If they see that the dragon vessel ignores the ordinances and treaties that protect human cities, well…" He trails off, shrugging. "It won't be good for us, Rory. It won't be good for any dragon anywhere. They'll see you as a rogue. Some Bosses will use that to their advantage. They'll use it to corral you and to limit where you can go. Some humans may just outright try to kill you."

"Like the time they already did that?" I ask, rolling my eyes.

"It'll get worse." Jace just shakes his head. "And it won't be limited to just us. Every dragon everywhere suffers if the treaties are violated, because if one dragon family makes their presence known in a city, humans all over the world will unite against us. They outnumber us, Rory. They always have, and they always will. We may be more powerful, but there are just more of them." He hesitates. "Probably enough of them to kill us all if they really unite."

I grit my teeth, considering what he said and not entirely willing to actually believe it.

But it is a risk and a *giant* what-if.

"I guess I'm selfish," I say, shaking my head. "But if it comes down to protecting the people I love, Jace, I'll shift anyway, even with all of that at stake."

My eyes dart toward him, and his stormy gaze snares me once again. I expect him to be angry, but he smiles, his eyes crinkling ever so slightly with delight.

With love.

Without a word, he kisses my forehead, and as his lips brush my skin, tendrils of delight snake through me, stirring my dragon awake. She leans toward him, aching for me to be ever closer.

I indulge her.

Weaving my fingers along his leg and underneath his shirt, my touch traces the hard muscle along his abdomen. I want this moment to last forever—him and me, on the same page. Devoted. Ferocious.

Fighters.

In my periphery, a blue streak buzzes through the air toward us, snapping me from the moment.

Levi.

He angles toward us, landing on the roof delicately, his talons brushing effortlessly against the shingles without so much as scratching even one of them.

"I guess it's my turn to patrol," Jace says, standing. "Try to stay out of trouble, Rory."

"I promise nothing," I say with a wicked little grin.

The former dojo master rolls his eyes, but he can't suppress a chuckle as his body hums and wavers. He shifts, his beautiful black dragon digging its claws into the roof as it takes over, and I can't help but wonder how many times a month Reggie must have to repair the shingles along the various buildings in this neutral zone.

We dragons must break a *lot* of his stuff.

With a quick nod to Levi, Jace launches into the air—a black streak through the growing dusk as he surveys the edges of Reggie's land.

I sigh, watching my mate fly off as Levi nestles up against me. He brushes his forehead along mine, opening the connection between us, and I smile as a rush of love and affection burns through from him.

He loves you, Levi assures me. *We all do.*

I know, I say back. *I love you, too.*

It's a new game for us now, Levi continues. *Bigger board, more players. It's hard to manage all the pieces.*

I don't think that's the problem, I admit, looking after Jace as he weaves along the edge of the forest in the distance. *I think the problem is he knows exactly what he wants to do, exactly how he wants to play this game, but he needs me on board for it to happen.*

Ah, Levi says, and I can't help but wonder if he picks up the hints in my thoughts at the army Jace wants to build.

The chopping whir of a helicopter in the distance catches my attention, and I turn around to find eight of them racing toward the castle.

"It would seem we have an audience," I say, standing.

Levi arches his neck, tenderly brushing his wing against my bare arm to keep our connection open as we both watch the choppers approach.

The Bane are early, he says.

Yeah, well, I'm sensing a pattern, I confess. *Let's go talk to the assholes who tried to extort the people near Ashgrave.*

You know we can't trust them, right? Levi says.

Of course not, I admit. *But hopefully they can still be useful.*

And if they're not?

I smirk. *Then we don't have to play nice anymore, do we?*

CHAPTER FOURTEEN

With Ashgrave on my shoulder and my men at my side, I let Reggie lead the way through the various hallways of his expansive castle. To my surprise, he's not smiling.

So something must be wrong.

"Just say it," I tell him, sticking my hands in my jean pockets since I haven't had the chance to change into any of the stupid dresses Harper made me bring. These Bosses are keeping me on my toes.

Honestly, that's the way I prefer it. Anything else is too boring.

At first, Reggie doesn't answer. In the silence, I cast a brief glance over my shoulder at Jace. My mate frowns, his brows furrowing as his gaze darts between me and the human leading us down the hallway. The moment he saw the Bane on the way, he turned around, his patrol instantly over.

Drew, Levi, and Tucker walk behind him, the five of us taking up the full width of the massive hallway, and I have to confess I'm glad they're all here. Though we should probably have at least one or two of them on patrol, securing the castle in case this is some sort of decoy or trap, I prefer to have my men at my side during a meeting like this.

Mostly to keep me from bashing Natasha's face in. But yes, also for support.

"Reggie," I chide when he still hasn't answered me after a few moments.

"Times are changing," Reggie says wistfully, shaking his head. "I can see it more and more clearly with every Boss who walks through these hallways, but I didn't want to believe it." He pauses, looking over his shoulder at me, his brows tilted slightly upward. "Not until I saw you."

"What does that mean?" I ask, frowning.

"It means my worst fears are confirmed," he confesses, shrugging as he rubs the back of his neck. "I don't have to listen to your conversations to know the gravity of what's being said. To know that they're not going the way that you want them to. To know that with every Boss that comes through these doors we're a little bit closer to a global war."

"Don't think like that," I say, even though he's absolutely right.

"This way," he says, turning left down the hallway instead of heading toward the main meeting room like I was expecting.

"Where are we going?" I ask, hesitating at the crossroads in the hallway.

"I learned the hard way to never have two meetings in the same room back-to-back after the Nabal have been in there," he says with a wry laugh. "I have my team sweeping the room you were just in for wiretaps, and we've already found three."

I sigh and shake my head as I follow Reggie through the maze of corridors.

Before long, he throws open a set of double doors to reveal an elegant room with a fireplace at one end and a long slender table in the middle. A wall of windows lets in light from one side, illuminating the two dragon shifters sitting at the head of the table.

Natasha and Victor Bane.

To my right, the light soft glow coming in the windows from behind them obscures and masks most of Victor's face since he has his back to it entirely. Natasha, however, sits beside him, and the light illuminates half of her devious expression as she watches me silently.

"Take as much time as you need," Reggie says cordially, gesturing to the Bane first before sharing a tense look with me.

I nod to him briefly in thanks and head toward the other end of the table. My men fill the seats beside me, and Ashgrave hops onto the table as he stares down Natasha.

She frowns, her glare shifting to the mechanical dragon beside me, and I smirk at the reminder of our last interaction.

Victor crosses his thick arms, lifting his chin slightly as he watches me, apparently waiting for me to say something. Natasha leans on her elbows, resting her chin on her elegant hands as her dark eyes narrow.

The fact that the Bane are the most likely family to join Harper strikes me as total bullshit, and I'm grateful Harper sees through them.

I don't trust these assholes to so much as make me a cup of tea.

Even though we need allies, I think it would be a mistake to allow them into our inner circle. These are people who only look out for themselves, and I don't think that's suddenly going to change because Kinsley got pissed off.

So, today, I'm going to make them angry—because then I can flush out their true intentions. Throw them off their game, and I'll be able to see all their cards in an instant.

For a moment, I hesitate, remembering the warning Drew and Jace both gave me.

Be delicate with the Bosses.

Diplomacy 101.

I frown as I watch Victor impatiently tap his finger on his bicep as he stares at my men, his frown getting deeper and deeper with every passing second.

"You invited us here. Remember?" Victor snaps, leaning forward as he points at me.

I take a deep and steadying breath as I finalize my game plan.

Yep.

I'm going to do this.

Fuck being *delicate*.

"Maybe, but you're the ones who insisted on showing up early, *remember*?" I shrug, gesturing to the room around us. "What's so urgent that we had to talk *now*, Victor?"

The Bane Boss mumbles under his breath,

shaking his head in irritation, but Natasha sets a comforting hand on his shoulder. "It's fine, big brother. She doesn't know how any of this works. Besides, she's just Harper's little pawn." Natasha hesitates, subtly smirking as her gaze drifts toward me. "Isn't she?"

This girl is obviously baiting me, and I don't bite.

My ego isn't that frail.

Even though she annoys the hell out of me, I won't give her the satisfaction of ever knowing it.

"You can be petty to someone else," I snap, not bothering to mask my disdain for them both as I roll my eyes. "The only reason we're here is to talk about Kinsley. To talk about what she's going to do to you if she gets her way. She's coming for everyone, not just me, and she will devour everything in her path."

"Sing a new song," Victor says dismissively, scoffing. "This is everything Harper has already said. Say something new."

It really irks me how little self-preservation these assholes have, both the Bane and the Nabal.

This should be easy. The big bad Boss lady wants a super-weapon—me. Once she has it, it's pretty obvious she won't exactly go quietly into the night.

She will use it, and she will most likely start with

every single Boss who didn't do her bidding from the start.

It baffles me that none of these people can see this, or if they can, they're just ignoring it.

The Bane are cruel. Vindictive even. Manipulative.

But stupid?

I truly don't think they are.

There's something else at play. Something else must be going on behind the scenes, something sinister and dark that's making all of these people act as though this doesn't apply to them.

And I have to figure out what that is before it destroys everything I love.

"I think we're done," I say with a bored shrug. "My mistake. I called you here because I thought you were smarter than this, but I can see now that you're both a waste of my time."

Beside me, Drew subtly groans and rolls his eyes, as if he can't believe I would say something like that.

Jace, however, doesn't so much as blink. He's here at my side no matter what I say, and he'll wait until afterward to yell at me if he thinks I say something wrong.

Lucky me.

"Excuse me?" Victor says with indignation in his tone.

"I'm wasting my time," I repeat, as if he simply hadn't heard me the first time. I stand and brush off my shirt as if I'm uninterested. "You obviously have no sense of self-preservation, and me trying to appeal to whatever ego-driven arrogance is jostling around in that brain of yours, well—that's just a waste of my time. Ergo, I think we're done." I tilt my head, raising one eyebrow and daring him to disagree with me.

He will, of course.

That's the point.

The only reason any of these guys came here was to talk to me. If I take that carrot away, they're forced to dance for me to make me stay a little longer.

It's not the most graceful negotiation tactic, but hell, it'll work.

"Oh, and for the record," I say, rolling out my shoulders as my gaze drifts toward Natasha, "You are forbidden from the lands near Ashgrave." I hesitate, smirking a little as my eyes dart toward Victor. "If it happens again, I won't be so kind as to let you leave."

The subtle threat is clear.

Threaten my home again, and I will kill you both.

And I mean it.

There's a heavy silence in the room. I can almost imagine Drew's eyes boring daggers into the back of my head, but I don't look. Instead, I hold Victor's gaze, letting him know that I mean every word with absolute certainty.

Victor's stony expression breaks, and he starts to laugh.

That bastard—he's *laughing.*

It takes him over, the kind of full-body event that sends tears down your face, and he shakes his head in astonishment.

I know he's waiting for me to ask him what's so damn funny, but again, I won't give him the satisfaction.

When no one joins him, his laughter slowly starts to fade, and his intense gaze settles on me. "That's tall talk for someone with no army."

Though I don't show it on my face, I inwardly cringe.

Hard.

I know Jace is going to use that against me as argument for everything he's been telling me thus far—and in this sudden, painful moment, I'm not sure I can disagree with him anymore.

"I don't need an army," I say, wrinkling my nose in disgust as I hold Victor's gaze.

But honestly, I'm not entirely sure if I'm right anymore.

Victor scoffs. "You're just a human with some sparks in her hands. You're nothing serious. You're not a threat." He stands, his chair scraping along the floor as he sets his palms against the table, daring me to prove him wrong.

The air in the room gets heavy. Tense. Tight with the promise of a fist fight. Even though they're outnumbered, Victor and Natasha don't look worried. They simply watch me, waiting to see what I'll do next, and I assume they must have soldiers nearby—probably waiting to bash in the windows and outnumber us in the blink of an eye.

At the table, my men stiffen, their gazes darting to each other as they silently make battle plans.

Hell, maybe I'll get to bash Natasha's face in after all.

The thought makes me a little happier, despite the circumstances.

At this point, I refuse to let Harper join with them. We can't trust the Bane, and my little test worked. I got them mad, and it made them show their true colors.

It was a little too easy, to be honest.

I'm a tad disappointed.

In the tense and heavy room, I crack a smile. I watch Victor intensely, my smile getting wider, and his roguish smirk begins to fade as he no doubt wonders what the hell is wrong with me. It unsettles him, just like I wanted it to, and I look at him as if he's a stupid little child who said something funny.

"Are you really enough of an idiot to think I'm no threat?" I ask, my voice purposefully gentle.

"You have nothing," Natasha interjects, standing as she gives me a disdainful once-over. "You have, what? A decrepit old castle and a little bird that shoots sparks?"

"Shut up, Natasha," Victor snaps.

She scoffs with indignation, and she scowls at him. To my surprise, however, she obeys.

"If you're so dangerous," Victor says, his gaze returning to me. "Then tell me what's to stop me from taking you right now. I nearly threw you in a cage last time we were both here, and only the Palarne stopped me. You think you can stop me from doing that again?"

At that, my men jump to their feet, flanking me and putting their thick, muscled bodies between me and the Boss who just threatened me. There's a heavy murmur in the room as everyone talks over each other, daring Victor to do something that stupid, to be truly that brazen in this world that's quickly growing bored of rules.

But I don't move.

I don't so much as flinch as everyone around me prepares to draw blood.

My eyes never leave Victor's, and the two of us glare at each other as he waits for me to answer.

The fool—he truly is waiting. He wants to know what I'll do, and I think deep down he knows that attempting to capture me would be a deadly mistake. I think, deep down, he knows I'm willing to kill him and Natasha. That I don't give a shit about procedure or law.

Not anymore.

And he's waiting to see if he's right.

Without a word, I summon my magic. Electricity crackles across my skin like the buzz of a taser as white light shimmers across my arms. Up my neck. Along my cheeks and jaw.

The room crackles with the raw power in my body. In my blood.

In my soul.

I stare at him as I summon the magic of the gods, as it hums through me at my command, ready to kill with just a thought. And though I don't really want to, I summon the dagger into my palm.

Simply so he can see it for himself.

The heavy weight of the magical weapon fills my hand, assuring me that it'll be there if I need to dig my blade into anyone's chest.

For the briefest of moments, Victor's gaze falls to the blade before it pops back up to my face.

He saw it. He knows it's new, and he doesn't understand it. He probably doesn't understand how I could have all of these abilities, or how my magic could grow like this.

Good.

I lift one hand, my palm flat and pointed to the ceiling, and I gesture for him to come at me. "If you're going to be an idiot and do something stupid, I suggest you act quickly."

He grits his teeth, balling one hand into a fist as he actually considers it. I'm sure he brought a small army, if not the entire thing. They're probably hiding in the woods just out of reach, just far enough away that I could kill him before they get here.

He underestimated me, and he won't do it again.

The feeling is mutual.

I'm prepared to shift if I have to, but I don't want

to blow my secret on these assholes. If I shift now, the world will know.

With a slow breath, Victor breaks the spell in the room, and the tension releases with a huff as he grabs his chair and throws it against the wall. The beautiful white chair shatters into a hundred pieces, the splinters falling to the ground as he stalks toward the door. He storms into the hallway without so much as another word, and Natasha follows slowly in his wake.

As she reaches the door, she rests her elegant fingers on the edge and pauses, looking over her shoulder at me with a depraved little smirk. Her eyes narrow like she has some great secret.

And in that moment, it hits me.

Natasha must be making the crystal.

It just makes sense. She has access to illicit networks, vast wealth, and no morals. If anyone's going to steal something as valuable as my magic, it's *got* to be her.

Her grin broadens, and she walks into the hallway, taking her secret with her.

CHAPTER FIFTEEN

I sit in the back of a helicopter with my men as the chopper races through the night back to my castle. Ashgrave rests against my feet like a dog, his back against my legs as he keeps a silent vigil over me.

Tucker mans the helicopter's controls, but after the blatant threat on our lives, we're all tense. Silent. Prepared at any moment for an attack—in a helicopter with no weapons.

It's fun.

Super fun.

Hopefully, Harper finds Tucker that jet after all. It looks like we will probably need it sooner rather than later.

We all sit in stillness, lost in thought, and I can

only assume they're replaying the moment with the Bane just like I am. How close we came to a fight breaking out in Reggie's castle, in a gorgeous room with a delicate fireplace. So unassuming.

It's clear to me that the neutral zones truly mean nothing nowadays, and that every step I take must be tread with even more caution than before.

I can feel the tension getting worse every day, and it won't be long now before it just snaps. Before something so horrible happens that there's no going back.

And I'm fairly certain Kinsley will be the one to pull that trigger. To break what little peace we have left in this world.

I have to be the one to stop it. I have to stop *her.*

My phone buzzes in my pocket, and I whip it out to see the number we gave Brett show up on my screen. I'm still not entirely sure giving him a phone was the best idea, but Drew's watching it closely. After a brief glance at his own phone—which I assume he set up to alert him to all Brett's activity, he and I share a tense glance.

And to my surprise, Drew just shrugs.

Oh. Well, I guess that's a good sign.

I tug a small cord from my headset and plug it into the phone, connecting Brett to the entire channel. All of my men look at me silently, listening in through their own headsets.

Before I say so much as a word, Brett clears his throat. "There's been another earthquake."

"Okay," I say slowly, not entirely sure why he called to tell us this.

"No, no, you don't get it," he says, his tone excited. "It's in an isolated Pacific Islands region, and the earthquake *just* hit. No governments can get there in time to save the people hit by the first quake, but if you take aid, it'll make you look amazing."

Oh.

Right.

While I was off trying not to start a war with the Bane and trying to figure out if Aki Nabal had killed his own daughter, Brett was doing what I had originally asked him to do.

Look for ways to skew public opinion in my favor.

It's kind of nice to think that I could simply forget about him for a while, and he didn't end up destroying anything or killing anyone.

Bonus.

"Of course," I say, trying to shake the thoughts of the last two meetings from my head and focus on the moment. "So, you're suggesting we make a public appearance?"

"Exactly," he says breathlessly energized. "Save lives. Bring water. The whole nine yards."

It's weird to hear Brett *excited*.

This is a man who's come for me and my men several times. A man who tried to kill us all at one point or another. Who *led* the damn battle against the dojo.

Up until now, he's been such a wildcard—someone I wasn't sure I could trust or even listen to, and in all the time he's been with us, he's barely even smiled.

To hear him eager, like he has his purpose back—it's strange. I almost feel a hint of pride, and I don't really understand it.

Jace and I share a tense glance, and I frown. "I'm not sure this is the best time to be making appearances, Brett."

Especially given everything Natasha, Victor, and Aki just said.

"No, you need to," he says, still breathless. "The death toll is mounting, and if you can get in there, you can actually save lives. You can make a real difference to these people, Rory. It's not just about appearances."

"To him it is," Levi mutters, rolling his eyes.

If Brett heard that, he doesn't reply. It's true, though. Brett is more about the strategy than nobility or morals, but that doesn't make him less right.

He just knows how to push my buttons.

I have to confess, I'm torn. The idea that an isolated region is completely without help in the wake of a natural disaster—that just tweaks my heart in ways I didn't know my heart could even be tweaked. To know that I could save lives, even in such a crazy tumultuous world, well…

It's tempting.

"What's the risk here?" I ask, my gaze drifting toward Drew.

My fire dragon frowns and whips out his tablet, his fingers racing furiously as he does who knows what and accesses networks he probably should not have any access to at all to get me an answer.

"If you go in," Brett interjects, "you can help and get out. If you can get out of there within three hours, you'll be fine."

"You might be on to something here, Brett," Tucker interjects, frowning and looking at the floor as he interrupts us on the shared connection. "But if anything happens to Rory or any of us, Ashgrave will kill you."

Brett groans with annoyance. "Yes. I get it, okay? When will you all stop thinking I'm going to kill you in your sleep?"

"Never, actually," Tucker snaps as he flips a switch from the pilot's seat. "And that was oddly specific, Brett."

"Guys, stop," I interject. "I need to think."

I cross my arms and tap my finger on my bicep, my eyes drifting out of focus as my thoughts furiously race through the possibilities and options.

The risks. The rewards.

In the end, all I can think of is that little village on the edge of Ashgrave. How helpless they were against dragons. They didn't have armies. They didn't have weapons. Hell, they barely had anything.

They needed me.

"Brett, send us the coordinates," I demand.

"Right away," he says, and I can hear the smile in his voice. It's broad and happy, and I just hope this isn't a trick.

Brett has had enough chances to kill us that I don't think this could be a trap, but I can't rule out the possibility entirely.

"Thanks," I add before hanging up.

"Did you just *thank* Brett Clarke?" Tucker says, frowning at me over his shoulder like he can't believe what I just did.

"I guess I did. Have I committed a mortal sin?"

"The worst," Tucker says, clicking his tongue as he shakes his head. "I'll have to punish you severely, preferably while you're naked and tied to my bed."

"Whoa, I have dibs tonight," Jace snaps.

I chuckle, shaking my head and turning my attention toward Drew. "Can you confirm?"

"I already did," he says. "It's legit. No aid is coming for four hours, but my guess is it's probably more like three and a half if they see us."

"Wow," I say, shrugging. "Then Brett's estimate was spot on."

"Yeah," Drew begrudgingly admits, but he can barely hide how impressed he is with Brett's calculations.

"So, what'll it be, Rory?" Jace asks, leaning his elbows on his knees as he looks at me.

I hesitate, making sure that what I'm about to do is the smartest choice, but I slowly nod. "We're going. Drew, can you help Tucker navigate?"

"I've got it," Tucker says. "You just focus on being pretty, Drew."

Drew grins briefly before he turns to me, all

business once more. "I'll call in some choppers with resources. See what I can get together," he says.

With that, my fire dragon switches off to another channel and whips out his phone, his thumb racing across the screen as he dials someone.

"AND WHAT CAN I DO, MY QUEEN?" Ashgrave asks over the din of the chopper.

"As soon as we land, look for the injured. Anyone trapped in the rubble. Once you find them, come get me."

"I AM USED TO CAUSING MAYHEM, NOT SAVING OTHERS FROM IT, BUT I SHALL DO MY BEST, MY QUEEN."

"Uh, thanks," I say, not entirely sure how to respond to that. "Levi, I need you to watch the perimeter," I add, leaning toward my ice dragon.

Without a word, he nods and flashes me a small smile.

I know he'll have it handled.

That leaves me and Jace to hunt for the wounded—and, if possible, stave off death itself for these people.

The trip is quick, and before I know it, we're descending onto a slab of fractured asphalt. In the darkness, I stare out at thick plumes of smoke and fires that rage through the tattered destroyed buildings of what was once a beautiful little village on an island.

It's horrible.

Before the chopper even lands, I rip open the door and hop out, staying low as the whir of the helicopter blades whips my hair into a frenzy. Ashgrave bolts past me, on the hunt for someone to help.

I just assume he's going to be a little confused to start out with, since he's used to doing the smiting and not the rescuing.

People stumble through the rubble, a thick layer of smoke hanging in the air like fog, and I squint as I try to make sense of it all.

In mere seconds, a silhouette is beside me, and I flinch in surprise before I recognize Levi.

"Put this in," he says, handing me a small comm for my ear. As I oblige him, he puts his own in his left ear and darts into the smoke, his form quickly disappearing into the smog.

As the comm springs to life, I hear the soft chatter of Tucker and Drew debating where they can start first. But for me, this isn't as much about strategy as it is about being where I'm needed.

This is about *listening.*

Deep in my core, my dragon stirs, and I look over my shoulder as Jace hops out of the chopper. His eyes narrow as he scans the rubble, just like I did.

The panicked murmur of people talking nearby in a language I don't recognize wafts past me, and I noticed a small huddle of women holding three children close as they sit on the steps of what was once a home. They rock back and forth, the mothers' arms tight around their children as they watch me with wide and fearful eyes.

They look at me like I'm about to eat them.

I frown, trying to ignore their judgmental glares, and I listen for the sound of screams or a fading heartbeat. In the raging crackle of the fires tearing through the rubble, it takes a little while before I can fully lean into my enhanced dragon senses and let them guide the way.

Nearby, I hear a muffled scream. It's distant, almost like it's underwater, and I figure there must be a hell of a lot of rubble between me and whoever this is. I follow it, letting my ear guide me and find myself at the flattened remnants of what was once a single-story home.

The muffled scream gets louder, and I frown as I rummage through the rubble. I carefully lift a large slab of concrete that's resting on several boulders, and the scream gets louder. I grit my teeth as I lift the slab, letting my dragon strength take over, and toss it backward onto a stretch of charred grass.

And there, in the depth of the rubble, I see a little hand slowly curling into a fist.

"I'm here," I say softly, climbing over the rubble toward the small and delicate figure as quickly as I can. "It's going to be okay."

In the wreckage, a little girl sobs.

"It's okay," I say as I reach another slab of concrete and lift it. This time, instead of more rubble, I see a girl, her small pink dress tattered and torn, her hair a mess, her face covered in ash. She looks up at me with eyes unnaturally white in comparison to her soot-covered skin, and she coughs.

Laying there in the debris, her arm sits at an unnatural angle, bent in places it shouldn't bend. Streams of salty tears streak down her face as she watches me. Her brows tilt upward, and I can't tell if she's scared of me, her situation, or if she's just in pain.

Maybe all of the above.

"It's okay," I say softly, resting the slab of concrete on my back as I reach for her. She flinches, leaning impulsively away from me. After all, I'm just a stranger she doesn't know doing the impossible by holding a heavy slab of concrete on my back.

Even though I doubt I could look non-threatening at this point, I try to simply smile and usher her closer.

After a weary moment where she simply studies my face, she tries to sit up. She whimpers but manages to crawl across the rubble toward me. Before long, I lift her into my arms. She wraps her good arm around my neck and shoulders, holding tightly as I use my other hand to lift the slab that had been against my back.

Tenderly, almost too slowly, we make our way out, and after a few moments, I let the concrete slab fall once again against the rubble of what was once her home.

"Is there anyone else in there?" I ask, but she looks at me with wide eyes, and I can tell she doesn't understand what I'm saying.

Through the thick smog, a man's silhouette appears. He walks toward me, and after a few moments, I recognize Jace's confident gait. As his face appears in the smog, our eyes meet, and he jogs toward us.

"We're starting a medic tent over by the chopper," he says, nodding behind him. "Is there anyone else in there?"

"I asked but she can't understand me," I confess.

Jace turns his attention toward the little girl, and he flashes her a dazzling smile as he says something to her in a language I don't understand.

She sniffles and shakes her head, saying something back to him in a sweet little voice.

"Her parents were out," he says. "At the grocery store."

"Good. Okay," I say, admittedly relieved because as far as I can tell, there's no other heartbeats or breaths going on in that pile of rubble, and I would have hated having to tell her that her parents were dead.

I take her through the smog as quickly as I can without running, because every footstep jostles her broken arm a little more. Once I reach the tent, I find Tucker wrapping a thick gash on the arm of an elderly man. The man gasps as I near, his eyes going wide with horror, and I wonder just what these people believe about me that makes them react this way.

It doesn't matter though. As long as I can help.

I carefully set the girl down on a blanket beside Tucker as he finishes wrapping the man's arm and turns his attention toward us.

"Hey there, hun," he says, smiling broadly at the little girl as he kneels beside her. "It's going to be okay. I'm going to fix you up. Promise."

Though her eyes are still wide and it's clear she doesn't understand anything he's saying, a small smile tugs at her lips, and she looks between him and me.

I guess I'm scary, but Tucker is all charm.

Figures.

Ashgrave sails overhead, and I flag him down. "Stay with her," I command him, nodding to the little girl. "Make sure she finds her family."

"OF COURSE, MY QUEEN."

"And Ashgrave, try not to scare her."

He hesitates, as if that's a big ask, but ultimately nods. "I WILL DO MY BEST."

With the little girl taken care of, I ruffle her hair fondly and dart back into the smog, the memory of her small smile lingering on my mind.

It fuels me.

I lose track of how many times I dart in and out of the fog. In fact, we're there so long that the sun begins to rise and disperse the smoke. With every passing moment, I can see a little better. A little farther.

We probably can't stay here much longer.

The whir of choppers through the air catches my attention, and I grimace as six helicopters fly overhead.

"Damn it, who's that?" I ask into my comm, pressing my finger against the little device in my ear as I talk to my men.

"They're with me," Drew answers quickly. "They're here to pass out water and supplies."

I let out a small breath of relief. "How much longer do we have?"

"Only about thirty minutes, Rory," Jace admits.

Damn it, I need to move faster. There's still a lot of people trapped, and every passing second means a little less oxygen for those in the rubble. I lift another concrete slab, and this time a family of four looks up at me from a small cave created by what was once the foundation in their home. We watch each other for a brief moment, the heavy concrete slab still against my back as I gesture toward the open street.

To my relief, they smile widely, their brows tilting upward in gratitude and joy as they limp out into the open air, sucking in deep breaths of the smoke-filled sky. When the last of them is through, I pause and listen once again to the rubble, hoping I can catch a breath or heartbeat.

But there's nothing.

I lower the slab and make my way to the next house. A thick layer of soot has settled on my skin, and I rub my forearm against my brow to wipe away the sweat that's been brewing since I got here. I pause by the rubble and listen, hoping I can catch another heartbeat or a breath, but there's nothing here.

No sign of life.

Deep in my soul, I hope that no one was in here when the earthquake hit. It hurts my soul to think of the dead lying beneath the rubble. To think that I hadn't been fast enough.

The shuffle of footsteps through the soot catches my attention, and I look over my shoulder to find an elderly woman wrapped in what was once a beautiful golden shawl, now stained with soot and blood. Her eyes lock on me as she nears, and I wonder what she needs.

I expect her to ask for water, or to perhaps usher me toward another pile of rubble to help her.

Instead, she reaches for my hand and holds it

tight. A broad smile breaks across her face, and when she looks at me, I feel oddly seen. Recognized. Acknowledged and appreciated, all at once.

"Thank you," she says, her voice tinged with an accent I don't recognize.

I smile. I can't help it. This feels good, though I don't admit that out loud. Helping. Rescuing. Healing.

I feel like I'm doing something meaningful.

Something *right*.

"Time to go, Rory," Drew says into my headset, breaking the beautiful spell of the moment as the woman shuffles off again into the smog. "We have word of a few bounty hunters on the move, and we have less than fifteen minutes to get out."

"Damn it," I mutter.

It's hard to believe that Brett was actually right. I still don't trust that man, but I can't lie to myself.

He's one smart bastard.

CHAPTER SIXTEEN

Back in Ashgrave, I take a deep breath and close my eyes as the gentle wind brushes across my face. I stand just inside of the doors that lead to my balcony. I lean against the doorframe as the sun casts shadows across the stone that protrudes out over my kingdom.

My kingdom of five.

I sigh and pinch the bridge of my nose, my mind racing with everything that just happened with the Nabal and the Bane.

With the earthquake.

With the way that woman thanked me, held my hand so tightly I thought my bones would pop.

She was simply so grateful they weren't alone.

"MY QUEEN," Ashgrave announces, cutting

through the serenity with his booming voice.

I flinch in surprise, but only a little. Bit by bit, I'm getting used to his constant—and painfully loud —interruptions.

"Yes?"

"THE STRANGER YOU DON'T FULLY TRUST IS BEING AGGRESSIVE AND THREATENING."

I frown, a little confused. "You mean Brett?"

"INDEED, MY QUEEN. HE'S THROWING THINGS. WOULD YOU LIKE ME TO SMITE THE FOOL FOR—"

"Don't kill him, damn it," I interrupt. "Let me see what's going on."

I walk toward my door, but as I do, another opens in the wall. The hinges of this second door creak as it swings inward, revealing a passage I've never noticed before.

"What's this?" I ask the castle.

"I CAN TAKE YOU THROUGH MY WALLS AT WILL SO THAT YOU DO NOT WASTE TIME WALKING AROUND THE LABYRINTH."

"Oh, isn't that nice," I say, grinning as I set my hands on my hips and I admire this new little development.

"THIS PASSAGE WILL TAKE YOU DIRECTLY TO HIM," the castle assures me.

I walk inside, taking the passage and its identical walls for only a short way before I reach another door. Before I can even touch it, it swings open, and once again sunlight streams across the floor ahead of me. I step through the doorway into another hallway, casting a brief glance around to get my bearings.

Based on the position of the sun, I'm at the north end of the castle, all in a few seconds.

"Now I like *that* a lot," I admit, looking over my shoulder as the door closes on its own.

The grunt of a man exerting effort catches my ear, and I follow the huffing groans a short way before I reach an open archway. As I near, the thunk of a dagger hitting wood catches my attention, and I frown in confusion.

Silently, I peek through the door frame to find Brett with his back to me, facing a makeshift wooden target he hung on the far wall. The room is mostly empty, with only a table beside him. He holds seven dinner knives in his hand, the hodgepodge of blades clearly taken from the kitchen as he hoists one over his shoulder and aims at the target.

With another grunt, he effortlessly throws it and hits the little white circle he painted in the center.

Huh.

Not bad at all.

I squint at the ceiling, wondering if there's a screw loose in my castle's brain. That my evil butler would think this was aggression is kind of adorable, but I have to say I'm grateful he let me know.

I don't know where Brett stands with us, though I have to admit I'm starting to hate him less.

It's an odd feeling, but until I figure out whether or not I trust him, I need to keep a close eye on him.

He hoists another blade over his shoulder, his focus trained on the target.

"What are you doing?" I ask, just as he's about to throw it.

He flinches, jumping at the sound of my voice, and it screws up his aim. The blade digs into the grout in the stone wall as he looks over his shoulder at me with wide eyes.

Though his left hand still holds the blades, he sets the right hand on his heart and takes a deep breath. "You scared me shitless."

I chuckle. "It's what I do."

"Care to join me?" he asks, waving the hodge-podge of daggers in the air as if it's enticing.

"Polite pass," I say, crossing my arms.

He tugs out another kitchen knife from the small clump in his left hand. "Since no one will give me a gun, I have to resort to throwing steak knives to stay sharp." He throws it, missing the center target by an inch, and growls softly in disappointment.

He was trying to show off—but honestly, he was better when he thought no one was watching.

"Why would we give you a gun?" I ask, laughing.

He scoffs. "When are you going to trust me?"

"When you've fully earned it."

For a brief moment, he looks over his shoulder at me in frustration, but in the end, he doesn't say anything and doesn't push the matter.

Smart man.

I rub my neck absently. "I have to admit, the lead on the earthquake was a good one. Thank you."

"Of course," he says, pulling out another knife as he focuses on the target. "As soon as others crop up, I'll let you know."

"I'm impressed," I admit. "You did good."

He pauses, about to throw a knife, and once again looks at me. But this time it's different. It's—well, affectionate, and it throws me entirely off guard.

His lips part slightly, as if he's debating carefully on what he wants to say next, and he lets the knives in his hands drop to the floor. As they clatter, he takes a few steps toward me, his gaze never leaving mine and growing more intense by the second.

Oh, *hell* no.

The moment he gets too close, I grab his wrist and twist it hard, pinning him against the nearest wall. He groans in pain. Though his cheek flattens against the stone, he smirks slightly, like he's biting back laughter.

"What the hell are you doing?" I demand.

"I'm sorry, Rory," he says, chuckling even as he winces in pain from my grip.

"You are *never* getting laid. You got it?" I demand. "At least not by me. You can be my PR guy and you can stay, but you are never going to be one of my men."

He grins. "I accepted that a while ago. I just thought I would try."

"Well, stop trying."

"Yes, ma'am."

"And stop calling me ma'am," I add as I let him go with an angry flourish.

He rolls out his shoulder and sets his hand around his wrist, flexing out his fingers to get the blood moving again. "Then what should I call you?"

"THE GREAT QUEEN OF CHAOS," answers Ashgrave. "GODDESS OF THESE MOUNTAINS AND MISTRESS OF THE VALLEY OF THE GODS."

I groan, rubbing my eyes at my ludicrous castle.

"I AM SORRY TO INTERJECT, MY QUEEN," the castle says. "BUT A HUMAN IS MAKING THE TREK HERE BY HIMSELF THROUGH THE MOUNTAINS."

I frown in confusion, my gaze drifting briefly toward Brett. "Why would a human try to kill themselves?"

Brett shrugs.

"Ashgrave, bring him here safely," I demand. "I want to know what he has to say before I decide what to do with him."

"OF COURSE, MY QUEEN. SHALL I ALERT YOUR LORDS?"

"Yes."

I *definitely* want to get their take on whatever fresh hell is about to spring up in our midst.

Behind me, a door opens in the wall, leading into a staircase that ascends toward another door in the distance. Sconces flare to life, leading the way through the darkness.

"Uh, that's new," Brett says, tilting his head as he sets his hands on his hips and studies it.

"You have no idea," I say, grinning as I jog inside.

The door shuts behind me as I take the stairs two at a time, the blue light of the flame casting a soft glow against my skin as I race toward the door ahead. Before I can even reach the door, it opens, leading me into the all-too familiar throne room.

Five chairs sit on a pedestal to my right, a short staircase leading up to them. Light cuts through the open windows all around me, and as I walk into the room, the door shuts behind me.

I guess this is where Ashgrave will bring the stranger.

Seconds later, the great doors to my left swing open, and both Levi and Drew walk in. Jace and Tucker jog through seconds later, and in mere moments, we're all assembled.

"Somebody's coming through the mountain pass?" Jace asks me, incredulously.

I shrug. "I'm just as baffled as you are. How could he even hope to survive the trek?"

"Maybe he's not planning to," Jace says, frowning as his eyes narrow in suspicion.

"So, what's the game plan?" Tucker asks, clapping his hands together as he rubs them, his gaze on me.

"We figure out what the hell he wants, I guess?" I shrug. "He's human, which means he probably isn't carrying enough weapons to hurt us. So, you know, plus."

"Always a plus," Levi adds, smirking.

I grin. "If he were a shifter, I would probably meet him out there. But a human? I'm okay with Ashgrave bringing him here."

"It's probably for the best," Jace agrees. "In here, we have full control. Strategically, it makes the most sense."

I cross my arms as I scan their faces. "How should we take this?"

"You're going to sit up there, and you're going to be a queen," Drew says, nodding toward the throne. "Intimidate the fuck out of him."

I roll my eyes. "No, seriously. What are we doing?"

For a moment, no one says anything, and I scan their faces as I wait for the punch line.

Because this has to be a joke.

"Rory, the people around here see you as a ruler," Drew says, nodding again to the throne. "So, go rule."

"Don't be ridiculous," I say, shaking my head. "We're the only ones here. Who do I rule?"

"Every kingdom has a beginning," Jace says, setting his hands on my shoulders as he grins down at me.

"Nope." I shake my head. "Don't you start too, Jace."

He just chuckles.

"Go on," Drew says, setting his hand between my shoulder blades and ushering me up the stairs.

"So pushy. Geez," I mutter, trying not to trip over the steps as he ushers me toward the throne. "Fine. I'll indulge you, but just this once. Do you understand?"

"Uh-huh," he mutters, grinning, knowing damn well that this won't be the last time, either.

I plop into the seat, trying hard to get comfortable in the stiff chair made of stone. I shift my weight a little too much as I try to find a position that doesn't hurt my tailbone.

A distant yell catches my attention, and it reminds me of the screams you hear on a roller-coaster—distant and prolonged, like someone's endlessly falling with no idea whether or not anything will catch them before they hit the ground. I frown, looking briefly at Jace, who simply shrugs in just as much confusion as me.

Seconds later, a door opens in the wall across from us, and a man tumbles out onto the stone. He slides across the ground, landing on his back as he stares up into the ceiling, clearly dazed. Spider webs cover his hair, like he's been falling through a tunnel that hasn't seen activity in a very long time.

I rub my eyes. Damn it, Ashgrave.

For a few seconds, he doesn't move, but I do see his chest breathing, so at least my evil butler didn't kill him.

After a moment, he sits up, his hand on his head as he tries to get his bearings. He sways slightly as the room no doubt spins for him, and he stumbles to his feet.

I'm tempted to apologize for my castle's means in getting him here, but I don't. I don't know who this man is. I don't know what he wants. I don't know why he's here. And for those reasons, I maintain a stony expression that betrays nothing.

He won't get a hint of compassion until I know he won't hurt the people I love or the world I'm creating.

His eyes scan the massive room, slowly drifting over everything before settling on me, and the moment our eyes meet, he gasps in surprise and takes a wary step backward.

"My queen," he says, kneeling instantly. Though he still sways slightly, he manages to keep his balance as his gaze drifts respectfully to the floor.

I frown, not comfortable with this at all, and look over my shoulder toward Drew.

The ass just chuckles.

"You can stand up," I say dryly, hoping to the gods this guy does.

I don't want to have a conversation with someone kneeling before me. That's just weird.

"Who are you?" I ask, setting my elbow on the armrest beside me and doing my best to look relaxed and maybe even a little bored.

It's hard to do in a chair like this.

"My name is Edgar, my queen," he says, standing even though his head remains bowed. "I'm the mayor of *Pepel Derevnya*."

Ah. Ash Town.

I stiffen impulsively at the name of the little village on the outskirts of Ashgrave's boundaries, the one I saved from Natasha. "Is everything all right?" I ask, concerned. "Are the Bane back?"

My mind begins to instantly race as I wonder what could have happened. If they came back, I need to figure out how on earth Ashgrave didn't notice.

"Everything's fine," he says, apparently catching a hint of my concern. He smiles gently, as though my apprehension is endearing. "We're safe and everything is well, all thanks to you."

"Oh," I say, relaxing my shoulders. "You're quite welcome."

"Truly," he presses, taking a few steps forward.

"We are forever in your debt. My father was the mayor before me, and for as long as either of us could remember, the Bane have taken from us. Every year, they come to us demanding things we don't have, and they burn our village when we can't provide it. We do our best, but it's never enough."

My instinct is to get angry. I want to slam my fist against the throne. I want to break something at the thought that these dragons have been abusing these people for so long.

But I don't.

I don't betray a hint of emotion. I simply watch him, setting my finger on my chin as I let him speak.

"When you arrived, we thought it would end in fire," he continues, his gaze drifting once again to the floor. "We thought for certain that this would be it. That it would be the day our little village finally perished, the day there was nothing left—not even us." His shoulders droop, and his eyes briefly glaze over as he relives that moment of intense fear. "But then you saved us." His brows knit in confusion. "And you wouldn't even let us pay you for it."

I frown as I remember the little box of trinkets and gems, the few things the people in this town even have. The things they tried to give me when I sent Natasha packing.

"We never expected a dragon to show kindness," Edgar confesses.

At that, both Drew and Jace grunt in annoyance, and I can't help but feel the same bubble of irritation snake through me at the lack of confidence in us.

But if I lived in a village that was attacked every year by dragons who stole everything of value we had, I would probably feel the same way.

"You don't have to worry about the Bane anymore," I promise Edgar. "I'll take care of them if they try to do anything to you, to anyone in the village."

For a moment, Edgar doesn't speak. He simply smiles at me, his grin broadening with every passing second, like I passed some kind of test he desperately hoped I would pass. "We thank you, my queen."

"You don't have to call me—"

"You're welcome," Drew interrupts me, casting a sideways glance to me in warning.

I frown at him, thoroughly irritated that he would interrupt me, much less demand I be called a queen.

But he knows ever so slightly more about this than I do, and for now, I let him have this. After all, I can always tell them to stop calling me queen later, probably when he's not around.

I'm an assassin. A dragon.

But a queen? I don't even know where to start with *that* nonsense. It sounds heavy, like the sort of thing that seems fun until you're faced with the reality of it all.

"We would like to invite you back to the village for celebration," Edgar says, interrupting my thoughts. "It is our way of saying thank you for protecting us. Please, will you come?"

At first, I don't answer, and my gaze drifts toward Jace. This isn't really the time to be throwing a party, and I can't help but wonder if it's all a tad frivolous given everything that's coming our way.

I expect Jace to frown. To subtly shake his head in disagreement, or to express in some way that this is a terrible idea.

But he doesn't. He just smiles, the gentle tug of his smirk getting ever so wider as I look his way.

"We have also brought you this," Edgar says, lifting a small black box toward me. He opens it with a flourish, and a glittering diamond rests on a thin gold chain against the black velvet pillow. "It's not much, my queen, but we would very much be honored if you would wear it or at least accept it as a token of our gratitude."

"That's not necessary," I say, waving away the thought. "You don't owe me anything."

"Please," he says, his brows tilting upward. "We don't have much, but we do have our pride. We cannot accept anything for free. It's not our way."

I sigh gently in defeat because I know that look. It's the expression of a man who just wants to do right by his family and his people. Who's trying so hard in a world that makes it difficult to be good and honorable.

"All right," I concede, not entirely loving this. "Thank you."

A broad smile cuts across his face, and he nods, setting the little black box at the base of the stairs, all while keeping a respectful distance.

I'm not foolish enough to accept a gift without checking it, and as soon as he's gone, I'll look for any signs of a bug or tracker. But in my heart, I doubt I'll find any. Everything about this man seems genuine, and after everything my men and I have endured lately, kindness is a bit refreshing.

I look at the little black box, the first bit of tribute anyone has brought me, and a poignant thought strikes me.

I guess I am starting to become a bit queen-ish—whether I like it or not.

CHAPTER SEVENTEEN

The crinkle of paper cuts through the otherwise silent room as I spread out one of a dozen maps across the war room table. I lean my palms against the surface, taking a deep breath as I scan the various supposed locations for where Kinsley is currently living.

The soft murmur of the quiet television mounted to the wall behind me hums through the room, and it feels kind of strange to be alone. I'm so used to having one of my men with me most of the time that this feels so foreign, so alien, even though it was once my life to live alone like this. I don't know if I could ever go back to it.

But this—this I have to do alone.

I eye the open box of Spectre tech on the table—

it's smaller than I had hoped, with only eight guns, twenty attachments, some voids, a few overrides, and two bugs.

Only two.

I pick up one of the bugs, turning over the flat disc as I lift it into the air to study its edges. Eight thin spikes poke out from it in sharp angles, like the legs of a spider, and I figure that's more of a cosmetic touch than anything else.

However much she denied it, Zurie always had a flair for theatrical touches.

As I turn it in the light, I marvel at how thin it is—like paper. According to the specs, it has a camouflage mode that would render it utterly undetectable.

If it works, that is.

I've never had the chance to use these, which sets me on edge. When it comes to my tech, I don't like the unfamiliar. The new. When you're in the middle of a heist, you don't want your tech to fail you.

That's why, half the time, I hate those damn overrides. They're magical, sure—but only if you can get one to work.

I set the bug back in its delicate little box.

There's a thought that's been in the back of my head for a while now. What if I take the fight to

Kinsley? What if I stop her before this gets out of hand?

Because let's face it, the moment she starts this war, it's going to be a snowball that engulfs everything. She said so herself. No one is safe, not from her wrath, and she'll use anyone against me if she can. She brazenly attacked the dojo, and the only reason she didn't burn everything to the ground is because the Fairfax are fierce warriors—and because the Knights and the Spectres got in the way.

I can only imagine what would have happened if I had truly faced Kinsley's wrath at the dojo.

If I had faced *her.*

I didn't know about my dragon then, not really, not enough to fight someone as strong and influential as her.

As devastating as that battle was, we got lucky. We got lucky that she chose to stay on the sidelines. That she prefers not to get her delicate little fingers dirty.

But she has a lot of blood on her hands, and she's more than willing to douse them with more.

I sigh deeply as I wade through the dozens of pages on the table, and nothing stands out to me. Nothing seems right, and my gut says going after her now isn't a good move. I've walked into her fortresses before, but this time it's different. Instead of going for one of her cronies—instead of having all of the details I need ahead of time—I would be going in blind.

It's just not a smart move, and I'm not willing to take the risk.

I groan in frustration and sit in the nearest chair, draping my arm across the back of the one beside me as I stare up at the ceiling. I rub my eyes, the exhausted sting of a couple days' poor sleep giving me a headache, but I fight through.

I always fight through it.

My phone buzzes, and I whip it out to see a text from Harper.

Headed your way with a present.

I quirk one eyebrow—this should be fun.

"MY QUEEN," says the castle. "INTRUDERS ARE APPROACHING. SHALL I DESTROY THEM?"

"Why is that always your go-to?" I ask under my breath, not really serious about getting an answer. "Is it Harper?"

"I AM NOT CERTAIN."

"Maybe don't kill them yet, then," I say, standing. "Let me have a look first."

"VERY WELL, MY QUEEN."

In the wall nearby, a door springs open from nothing, leading to a spiral staircase that winds upward. I take the stairs two at a time as I race toward what I'm hoping will be a viewing platform, and sure enough, before long, wind kicks down the tunnel and sunlight warms the wall ahead. I round the next bend to find an open platform covered with a small roof that lets me see perfectly in all directions.

The wind kicks up my hair as I step out onto the platform and survey the world around me. Mountains circle us on all sides, their peaks capped with thick layers of snow, and only a small circle of Ashgrave's influence keeps the grass around me green. A sharp line between grass and snow shows the limits of Ashgrave's magic, and I wonder how much longer until we can get him fully operational.

That's a long road ahead of us, and I think for now it's time to take things one at a time.

In the distance, three black dots scream toward us, approaching fast. For a moment, I can't tell what they are. As the seconds pass, however, two helicopters come into view alongside a jet that streaks quickly past them. The jet approaches blindingly fast, and I impulsively summon magic into my hands in case I need to blow it out of the sky.

I fish out my phone and shoot Harper a quick text.

Two choppers and a jet—that's all you?

The jet circles the castle in a smooth and steady arc, and I wonder if the pilot is looking for a place to touch down. There aren't a lot of runways in Ashgrave, but I'm not making anything happen until I know for sure who this is.

Yeah, it's me, Harper texts back.

I let out a small sigh of relief.

Time to see what's going on—and what Harper needs.

The jet lands on a large strip of stone along the outskirts of Ashgrave, and I figure we're going to need to make some sort of landing pad if this is going to become a regular thing.

Thanks to a strategic stairwell Ashgrave conjured for me, I appear to be the first one to greet our visitors. As I step out into the sunlight, the cool air gently caresses my face, and I suck in a deep breath.

It's nice to have a bit of a distraction amongst all the war planning.

The jet's cockpit pops open, and the pilot stands, taking off his helmet. I see a familiar face, and the moment our eyes connect, Russell smiles broadly at me.

"Long time no see," he says, grinning.

"I didn't know you could fly jets," I admit, laughing. "Isn't that kind of a pointless skill when you're a dragon shifter?"

"It's fun," he says, shrugging as he climbs out. "Harper's on the way in the chopper."

I look over the jet and into the sky as the helicopters approach, grinning as the thunder of footsteps on the grass echoes behind me. Without looking over my shoulder, I can recognize Jace, Drew and—

"That's a hell of a jet!" Tucker says, running up, the familiar shuffle of his gait like a song to my heart.

I laugh as I look over my shoulder, all four of my men coming closer, and I'm not at all surprised that I still can't detect Levi's silent gait. Our eyes meet, and he smiles gently.

"To what do we owe the pleasure?" I ask Russell as he walks over and gives me a hug.

"A gift from us to you," Russell says, gesturing back at the jet. "Well, I guess technically to Tucker."

"That's for *me*?" Tucker says, his eyebrows shooting up his face. "Are you serious?"

"The chopper is, too," Russell adds as the whir of the blades get closer. "Well, one of them is. We're using the other to get back home, since Harper is easy to spot when she flies."

"Oh, Russell!" Tucker says not bothering to mask his playfully sarcastic tone. "You've made me the happiest girl in the world!"

We all laugh as the choppers near, setting down beside the jet. Seconds later, Harper jumps out, and a few dojo soldiers follow. Jace's face lights up, and he jogs over to greet them. They clasp hands and laugh, talking about something I can't hear over the whir of the blades.

Harper jogs toward me and smiles, gesturing back at them. "What do you think?"

"I think you're the best damn friend I've ever had," I admit, laughing. "This is far too generous, Harper. When I asked you—"

"Yeah, yeah," she interrupts with a wave of her hand. "I know that you were joking, but I could tell

Tucker wasn't. I get it," she adds, her eyes darting toward him. "You want to fly with the rest of them."

"Yeah," he says, uncharacteristically serious as his eyes dart toward me.

"You want to take it for a spin?" I ask with a nod toward the jet.

"Hell yeah, I do." He grabs the helmet from Russell's hands as he races toward the plane.

"Don't you want a tutorial first?" Russell shouts.

"Nah," Tucker says with a shrug. "I stole a couple of these from you guys back when I was a Knight."

"Oh, gods," Harper says, rubbing her face with her hands as she shakes her head.

"You guys are the best," I say, hugging them both at once as I race off to an empty patch of field beside the jet. "You're welcome to stay the night!" I add, shouting over my shoulder.

"We plan to! We're starving," Harper shouts back, waving me off to have my fun as she heads inside.

Ugh—hope she likes venison and carrots, then, because that's still all we've got.

Tucker tugs on his helmet and hops into the cockpit, the glass pod closing over his head as he fiddles with a couple of the switches. The engine roars to life, and I close my eyes, letting my dragon take over.

After all, he doesn't get to have *all* the fun.

My body shifts and hums, and several precious moments pass before the shift takes hold—precious moments where Jace would have knocked me on my ass if he'd gotten a chance.

I'm getting better, but I'm still not good enough.

As the shift takes hold, an exhilarating rush of adrenaline pumps through me. My body stretches and pops, wings sprouting from my back as my claws dig into the dirt. I shake out my body as the shift finishes, gold dust falling off my scales as I sink into my dragon form.

The jet engine roars louder, and before I know it, Tucker is racing off down the makeshift runway. The plane takes to the air, angling sideways as he banks effortlessly in front of a mountain. In seconds, he's airborne, and I roar with excitement as I take to the sky to join him.

We sail through the beautiful mountains, and in mere seconds, the castle disappears behind the snow-capped peaks. A soft flurry of snow rushes past us, and I catch up to Tucker after a few moments of furiously pumping my wings. I suspect he's making the jet go slowly, and even now it's a struggle to keep up. Dragons are fast—sure—but a jet is unparalleled. It's one of the few things faster than us, and the fact that I'm able to keep up at all gives me an exhilarating little ego boost.

We weave through the mountains, banking gently as we fly. To my surprise, Tucker begins to push me. He takes sharper curves, angling through gaps in the mountains that he really shouldn't angle through.

I bet Jace put him up to this.

With a quick boost, his engines flare, and he tilts perfectly sideways as he angles toward a small gap in the mountains that no sane pilot would go through.

Ever.

But that's Tucker. He lives with dragons and abandoned his old life for me.

He's a little crazy, and I love it.

Tucker soars through, and I feel a burst of adrenaline and excitement for him as he effortlessly passes through the gap.

I follow, angling myself sideways. My wings stretch as tight as they can as I try to follow.

The last time I tried to do something like this, I clipped my wing and crashed *hard*. I'm tempted to go around since this is supposed to just be a fun little expedition for the two of us, but I'm never going to get better if I don't try, if I don't push myself.

As the gap nears, I stiffen, hoping that I'm able to pull this off.

Hoping I can get better in time for whatever is coming our way.

The gap nears, and in seconds, I'm through. Only the tip of my wing clips the mountain, and though it stings, I know it will fade. I right myself on the other side, shaking slightly as Tucker's jet circles me. As he passes, our eyes briefly meet, and he pumps his fist in victory.

That adorable jerk.

He *was* testing me.

We race through the mountains, my weapons master showing off as he does a barrel roll through the sky. Even with the threat of war and Kinsley's rage looming on the horizon, I let myself celebrate with him. It's nice to know I'm getting the hang of this whole dragon thing.

The only downside is I'm not sure I'll learn fast enough to face what's coming for us.

Because it is coming. And soon.

And when Kinsley unleashes hell on us all, the whole world will burn unless I stop her.

CHAPTER EIGHTEEN

I wake to the pounding thud of a fist against my door.

I snap upright, holding the blanket to my bare chest as I scan the room. It irks me that someone could get close enough to knock on my door without me waking up. Part of me wonders if I'm getting soft. If I'm getting used to other people looking out for me.

In the haze of being suddenly and violently awoken, I briefly doubt the trust I've put in the castle around me.

But it quickly fades.

"What the hell is that?" I snap as somebody bangs again on my door.

Beside me, Tucker stirs in his sleep, grabbing one

of the pillows and putting it over his head to muffle the noise. He groans, mumbling something unintelligible.

"What?" I ask.

"It's got to be Brett," Tucker says again in an irritated tone.

"What makes you say that?"

"No one else knocks."

I chuckle. He has a point.

"Ashgrave, get me some clothes please," I say as I get out of bed.

In an instant, light glimmers through the cracks in the stone beneath me, crawling up my legs as I walk toward the door and instantly becoming fabric that weaves itself around me in a gentle white robe.

In the hallway, someone breathes hard, and I throw open the door just as a dark silhouette lifts his hand to knock again.

In the shadows, it's difficult to see his features, but I recognize Brett right away.

"You better have a damn good reason for this," I warn him.

Before he can speak, the shuffle of footsteps running down the hallway catches my attention, and I look up as Jace and Drew both round the corner. They race toward me with furrowed brows and deep frowns, and the mood in the hallway shifts.

If they're all gathered without Levi, then my ice dragon must be on patrol.

Old habits die hard, even when you live in an enchanted, all-smiting castle.

"What happened?" I ask, wary.

"*This* happened," Brett says, charging into the room as he pulls out his phone.

"Get out," Tucker says, throwing a pillow at the former Knight.

Brett easily dodges the pillow, and Tucker follows it up with a second one.

"Can you be serious for two seconds?" Brett snaps as he hands me the phone.

"No," Tucker and I say in unison as I take the phone.

It's a video, paused on a shot of a dark cavern. Drew and Jace come up behind me, looking over my shoulder, and without a word, Drew taps the screen to play it.

A low growl fills the cavern, echoing through the phone's speakers as a dragon appears from the shadows. His dark orange scales look oddly familiar, and I don't know why. I feel like I've seen this dragon before, but looking at him feels like a dream.

Like a nightmare.

He snarls, fire brewing in his throat as he looks past the camera, and a familiar patter of footsteps echoes through the speakers. His eyes trail something off-screen, and before long, a silhouette appears in the dark cave. It's a woman's figure, and she faces the dragon with her back to the camera, like she doesn't even know it's there.

The dragon snarls, and he begins to circle her. Though anyone else would be scared, she seems calm, her shoulders relaxed, and a long blade fills her left hand. She keeps her distance from the dragon, eyeing him and sizing him up as she keeps an even pace.

As she steps into a beam of moonlight trailing through an opening in the ceiling above, her face is finally visible.

It's me.

I stiffen with dread. In a rush, I remember.

This was ages ago, deep in Zurie's tunnels. I was given a mission—a brutal mission I didn't want to complete.

And I know exactly how this video ends.

The dragon roars, baring his teeth as he spews fire against the cave wall. In the video, I roll effortlessly out of the way, every movement controlled and fluid, like a dancer defying death. This was easily a decade ago, and you can see it in my features —mainly in the hard and heartless expression on my face.

Like this means nothing to me.

Like facing down a dragon is normal.

Back then, I didn't know I could live another life. Back then, every day was a struggle, and every breath was a cliffhanger. I hadn't even earned the right to go on missions, much less be left alone, and this was one of the only things I had to fill my days.

Life as Zurie's executioner.

The dragon and I dance a deadly waltz, and the end of the video nears. He roars again, and in the video, I race toward the walls, using my momentum to scale the sheer stone before leaping toward his neck.

Before making the kill.

As the blade glints in the low light in the video, I look away. There's the slice of a dagger through skin, and the meaty thud of the dragon's head hitting the ground. I scrunch my eyes together, disgusted by my old life, but I had no choice.

Not back then.

"Oh my gods," I mutter under my breath, at a loss for words.

"This is everywhere," Brett says, his voice terrified. "There's no context, no evidence of who released it, nothing. It was just released to the world, and everyone is talking about it. You're on every news station worldwide. I've never seen you trend so much on the social media sites."

He grabs the phone back, flipping through a dozen apps, one after the other as he rattles them off, but I tune him out. I don't even know what half of those websites and apps even *are.*

Brett runs a hand through his short hair, exasperated and breathlessly worried. "I swear everyone in the world has already seen this, Rory, multiple times, and nothing about this is good."

"Well, don't *panic,*" Jace snaps, glaring at the former Knight.

"We just have to figure out who released it," Drew adds calmly, his shoulder squaring as he scowls at the phone. "Tell me whose ass I need to kick."

"Diesel," I say quietly.

All four men in the room go silent, staring at me in silent horror.

"What makes you think it's Diesel?" Jace asks, taking a curious step toward me.

"There's only one place this could have come from," I answer. "The Spectres. And only two people have access to that information. Irena would never release this to the public. Ergo…"

"Diesel," Jace finishes for me, nodding.

"Yeah," I say quietly, my eyes glossing over as I stare at the back of Brett's phone, reliving the video over and over again in my mind.

Diesel is trying to ruin the good I've been doing. He's trying to take away everything I love and dismantle it brick by brick, just as Zurie did.

He wants to use my past to ruin my future.

One by one, the men in the room begin to talk, their voices overlapping as they try to come up with a plan. As they try to follow up with what they could possibly do at this point for damage control.

Without a word, I step out onto my balcony, their voices fading as I climb onto the roof. I need to be alone, and as the shingles scrape against my bare feet, I climb higher and higher until the chatter of their voices fades.

I know they saw me leave, but I'm grateful they didn't try to follow.

As the wind cuts past me, I sit in the darkness and rub my eyes. I'm usually such a fighter, the one to respond in an instant and make a plan. But this…

This was a low blow.

I take a deep breath and wrap my arms around my

knees, setting my forehead against the soft fabric covering my legs as I try to think through everything that's going on. I could just come out with a video and explain what happened, but so much damage has been done. I don't want to let Diesel put me on the defensive, but honestly, I can't even think about this strategically.

Not right now.

I killed so many dragons when I was a Spectre, and I hated every single kill order. I hated Zurie for making me do it. I hated the life I had been trapped in and the lack of choice I was given.

Kill or be killed.

Become a murderer or face the firing squad.

The soft clatter of skin on shingles catches my attention, and I look up, half expecting to find Jace or Drew climbing onto the roof. But in the darkness, I spot two delicate hands and long slender fingers holding tight to the edge of the roof. There's a soft, feminine grunt, and seconds later, Harper pulls herself onto the roof with me.

As soon as she catches her balance, our eyes meet, and I can tell she's deciding whether or not to come over.

Whether or not to leave me alone.

In the end, she climbs toward me and sits at my

side for several moments in silence. We simply watch the darkness and the moon as it hangs low in the sky, the wind whipping past us and kicking up our hair.

Here we are—two dragons, both the only ones of our kind, alone in the darkness.

"Are you okay?" Harper asks, not even looking at me.

"No," I answer honestly.

I was tempted to lie. Tempted to tell her that everything's fine and that I'll figure it out because I always do. But that's the funny thing about friends—you don't have to lie. You can be raw and real and not okay, and a real friend will sit with you in that discomfort.

It's kind of nice to have a friend.

"What was that?" she asks finally, turning her soft gaze toward me. "The video?"

My jaw tenses, and I debate whether or not I want to answer that question. I rub my eyes, sighing. "Years ago, Zurie gave me a kill order. Someone had tried to hunt her down and kill her, an assassin who also happened to be a dragon shifter—someone working for the Darringtons. He was good, but not good enough."

I shake my head, biting the inside of my cheek as the execution plays yet again in my mind.

"Zurie caught him," I continue. "She found him out and threw him in her dungeons, but I had to kill him. I *hate* that." I shake my head, squeezing my eyes shut. "I hate myself for doing it, but I had to back then. It was kill or be killed, Harper. I did what I had to in order to survive, and I hated myself a little bit more every day for it. I feel the weight of all the people I've had to kill, and I hate Diesel for bringing that memory back."

I suck in a deep breath and look up into the sky, into the deep stars that seem to go on forever, and the soft white clouds that pass by the moon.

"Even if that was all I had left, I would never go back," I confess. "I wouldn't go back to that life or the person I was, even if my only other choice was death. I just can't, not knowing what I know now."

There's a soft beep—almost inaudible—and I look over to find Harper lowering her phone. She catches my eye, and we share a brief glance before she returns her attention to the device in her hands.

I wait, trying to figure out what's happening and what she just did, and it takes me a moment to realize she recorded it.

She recorded that.

She recorded all of it.

"Harper, what are you doing?" I ask, my heart panging with dread in my chest.

"This is who you are, Rory," she says, showing me the screen.

There I am on the recording, looking up into the sky with an expression of utter agony. Of utter torment.

Of regret.

"What are you—"

"The world needs to see this," Harper says quietly. "I forgave you the moment I saw the video, Rory, because I know who you are. But they need to know too."

For a moment, I simply watch her, barely able to breathe as I debate whether or not this is a good idea. I don't want to show this weakness. I don't want to show this side of myself.

But I don't get the chance to stop her.

With a gentle brush of her thumb on the screen, a little arrow icon appears, and the video fades to black.

Sent.

Without another word, she climbs back down the roof and toward the balcony below, and I just watch her go.

I can't even move. I'm kind of numb.

This new life is tough. It's brutal. There are so many people after me, I can't even keep count of them all. I don't even know all the people who want me dead, and that's wearing on me. With each passing day, I care a little less about the names and the faces of the assassins coming after me.

That's part of stepping into the light, I guess.

And as much as I want to forget my old life, it happened. There are things I need to atone for. Things I can't run from.

And people who want to kill me for it regardless of who I am now.

I gently bite my lip as I think about what Jace said about building an army. About having a general.

I'm really starting to wonder if he's right.

I'm also starting to wonder how much he'll rub it in my face if I admit it to him, but I have to at least be honest with myself.

With everyone and everything after me, maybe having warriors fight for me isn't such a terrible idea after all.

Just *maybe*.

CHAPTER NINETEEN

When dawn breaks the next morning, everyone currently breathing within Ashgrave Castle is in a little war room one floor beneath my bedroom. Russell and his soldiers left this morning, but Harper wanted to stay with me to help us figure this out.

And we're all brainstorming—rather loudly, I might add.

"We need to figure out who released that, and we need to do it now," Drew snaps as he rifles through dozens of pages from his seat at the head of the table.

Every chair is filled, and everyone has something in front of them. Brett furiously scrolls through a tablet while Jace and Levi pour over dozens of documents that Drew managed to procure from various illicit sources.

The more I learn about Drew's information-gathering tactics, the less I want to know.

Harper paces the far side of the room, her eyes slipping out of focus and her arms crossed as she walks back and forth, back and forth, lost in thought.

Tucker sits beside me, furiously typing on a laptop as websites and screens flash in front of him. He bites on the cap of a pen absently as he walks through the information on the screen, occasionally pausing to roll the pen to the other side of his mouth before continuing.

But all I can do is think.

Like Harper, I'm lost in thought. In memory. The dull thunk of the dragon's head hitting the floor echoes again and again in my mind.

It's something I want to atone for, but I have no idea how. I've spent so many years killing dragons—unwillingly but still—that I have no way to repent for what I've done.

At least that's how it feels.

"Okay, I've got some ideas," Brett interjects, grabbing the remote as he mutes the TV behind him. The flashing images of various news stations still distract me, and it's hard to focus on him instead of the bright red banner underneath the newscaster that has my name in all caps.

"This is *not* the time to be making appearances," Jace interjects before Brett can even get his idea out.

"I strongly disagree," Brett says, setting down his tablet as he shoves it across the table.

It slides toward Jace, who catches it and briefly scans the screen before frowning and looking again at Brett. "You want her in Monaco?"

"It has the highest per capita rate of millionaires in the world."

"And?" Drew asks dryly, waiting for Brett to get to the point.

Brett groans with irritation, as if this is obvious and no one else seems to get it. "People with that much money have influence, and people with influence can turn the tides in our favor. We go out there, we rub some elbows, and we show them who she really is. If we have these people championing for us—"

"No," I interject, shaking my head.

"What?" he asks, clearly baffled. It seems like he was expecting pushback from everyone but me.

"I said no," I repeat calmly, standing and setting

my palms on the table. "I'm not a politician. I'm not going to go around schmoozing people in the hopes that I can tug the strings of their influence in my favor." I scowl, glaring at the television. "All of this seems forced, and I don't want to do anything unless it feels real."

"But…" Brett groans, rubbing his face as he turns his back to us for a moment.

"Look, the damage is contained," Drew says, interjecting. "Harper's video helped immensely."

Harper pauses mid-stride, scanning the room and nodding briefly before she continues her pacing.

She knew exactly what it would do, and that's why she did it. To help me.

To maybe even save me.

Damn, I love that girl.

"Maybe, but we can't afford any more videos coming out," Brett says. "We're on thin ice, here."

"Gods, your voice is so annoying," Tucker says under his breath.

I chuckle.

If Brett heard Tucker's little jibe, he ignores it and points at the television as he scans all of our faces. "If another video comes out, we are screwed. Let's be real, guys. We all know Diesel has access to plenty more."

For a moment, the room goes quiet, and every gaze turns toward me. The weight of their stares feels like a boulder on my back, and but I refuse to look away. I simply watch the television, trying to ignore the brewing guilt of what I've done.

He's right, of course. There are probably many more videos where that one came from. I now realize Zurie was recording me at all times, and she forced me to do many horrible things.

I didn't even know they were filming when I killed that dragon. Who knows what else Zurie filmed without my knowledge, all to use against me if she ever needed it.

I let out a long, slow breath, but it doesn't make me feel any better.

"That's not who I am," I say, straightening my back and rolling out my shoulders. "This isn't who I am," I add with a small gesture toward Brett. "I don't go around schmoozing people. I don't play the games people try to force on me. I do things my way, and I never surrender." My gaze darts toward Brett to make sure he understands. My eyes narrow to emphasize my point. "I don't run. I don't react. I simply act, and when I do, it's decisive, it's final, and it's fierce."

Out of the corner of my eye, Jace smiles broadly.

Our eyes meet, and his are filled with pride. For a moment, he forgets the papers in his hands, and he seems to forget everything else in the room as well.

For a moment, it's just him and me. Partners in crime and with each other to the end, through everything.

It's comforting to know he'll always have my back, and I'll always have his.

"We have to make sure that no other videos are released," Drew says, standing as he takes a deep breath and runs his hand through his hair. "That means we have to figure out for *sure* who's releasing these."

"It's Diesel," I say flatly.

"It could be another Spectre," Drew says, shrugging. "It could be someone else with access to either his or Irena's data. It could be anyone."

"That's doubtful," Jace says, shaking his head. "At a minimum, we should start with the person we think is behind this and go from there."

"And, luckily, now we have his tech," I add, setting my hands on my hips. "Irena sent over everything."

"Exactly," Jace says, nodding. "Everything we have in production, at least so far. Getting the materials for everything that we have plans for was rough, but the guns, voids, overrides, and bugs are going to be useful."

"At least for those who know how to use it," Harper interjects, finally breaking her silence.

We pause, turning our attention toward her.

"Well, you know how to use it," Harper says, looking at me. "And I assume Drew figured it out because, you know, he's Drew," she adds, gesturing toward the fire dragon as he smirks with pride. "But the rest of us need training, and before I can send it to any of my soldiers, they need *extensive* training. They've never worked with anything like this before."

"And you don't think we have time," I finish for her.

"I don't," she confesses, shaking her head. "This video was strategic, and I know there are going to be more."

"Well, one thing's for certain," I say, cracking my knuckles absently as my eyes gloss over. "Diesel is working with the person creating the crystal—and this could very well be part of their joint strategy to snare me, for all we know. We need to find whoever is making the crystal before they get any further with it. What Zurie brought back there in the Knights' fortress…" I trail off and shudder at the memory. "All she had to do was open a box, and I was practically disarmed. I could barely do anything, and all the crystal did was exist. I can't let that happen again."

"We won't," Levi says, breaking his silence and sharing an intense glance with me.

"There's a problem though," Tucker points out. "We don't know who it is, or how to even stop them."

"We set a trap," I say.

Everyone pauses, and I can practically feel the breathless reaction in the room. I've set traps before, and they all know how it's going to go.

They all know who's going to be the bait.

"Rory," Levi says in warning as he frowns at me.

"Oh, come on," I say, throwing my hands out as I look at everyone around me. "We have to set a trap for them. They've been so careful, so cautious this entire time, and the only reason we know about them is because they're getting desperate. Desperate people fall for traps."

"Unless they bait *you* into one," Drew points out.

"I'm smarter than that," I remind him. "We all are."

"It would be nice if we knew who we were setting the trap for," Harper points out as she shakes her head in frustration. "There's so many people it could be."

"Diesel," I suggest. "Or Natasha," I add, wrinkling my nose in disgust.

"The Andusk," Drew suggests.

"Aki Nabal," Harper interjects.

"Kinsley," Levi says with disdain.

"What about the Oracles?" Jace offers. "If they're still around, and they know you have the gods' magic…"

"And that the gods are still alive," I add, tilting my head as I consider his suggestion.

Oh, man, I have more enemies than I even thought.

Freaking fantastic.

"We need help," Brett says, collapsing in his chair with a defeated sigh.

I open my mouth to speak, but I hesitate because I don't quite know how I want to say what I'm about to say or if it's even a good idea.

"What about the Darringtons?" I suggest, my gaze darting between Harper and Drew. "If we can get them on our side, it could change everything. The Darringtons have the most fearsome army of any kingdom, even more so than the Palarnes. If we can get them to join us, maybe we can squash this once and for all."

Harper tenses, her intense glare trained on me. Her shoulders freeze, and I can tell that for this moment at least she isn't breathing. She simply watches me, suspended in her anger and resentment and hatred for the Darrington family.

"I can't even bring myself to look at them," she confesses, her voice tense and quiet before her gaze darts toward Drew. "Present company excluded of course."

Jace chuckles. "Drew's basically a Fairfax now, so it's fine."

My fire dragon scoffs, playfully rolling his eyes. "How dare you, heathen."

The quiet murmur of conversation continues, but there's a soft ring in my ear as I unconsciously tune them out. My thoughts are racing, and I just got a wicked little idea, one that's either going to work brilliantly or fail spectacularly.

Those are usually where I do my best work—those all-or-nothing sort of plans.

"Look," I interject, and the room quiets down. "Here's the reality of it all. Someone released a video, purposefully trying to destroy my image.

That person may or may not be working to build a crystal that could drain me of my magic using ancient and powerful spells, and who knows what else. We absolutely have to capture these people, and to stop this—to stop Kinsley—we need to do something a little crazy." I hesitate, my gaze drifting across the room before it settles on Drew. "I think we need to go to the Darringtons, to their capital to see if they'll join us, and if not, to plant a bug and that way we can spy on them, get intel and see if they're behind this or at least know who might be."

I go still, and silence settles across the room as I gauge everyone's reactions.

To no one's surprise, Drew looks furious. His brows scrunch up as he scowls, as if I went too far.

Maybe I did, but that doesn't make me wrong.

I quickly scan the other expressions. Jace is frighteningly still, has a guarded expression almost impossible to read as he stares at me, his fingers woven together in front of his face.

Beside him, Levi's cool blue gaze is like ice, and I know he's none too fond of this either, because the longer I look at him, the deeper his frown goes.

Tucker's head is in his hands as he shakes his head in surprise, and Brett is watching the TV with his eyes glazed over, a curious expression on his face.

But Harper—surprisingly—looks intrigued, and I doubt it's because she wants them as an ally. Her eyes narrow, and she looks out the window, lost in thought, a mischievous little smirk on her face. It's so subtle that I almost miss it, but I've known her long enough to realize when she gets a devious little idea.

She's definitely up to something.

"You, outside. Now!" Drew snaps, his chair scraping along the floor as he stands and thunders toward me.

"*Excuse* me?" I demand, lifting an eyebrow at his audacity.

He doesn't answer. Instead, he grabs my bicep and drags me through the room toward the door. Everyone watches us leave, and I'm half tempted to knock Drew on his ass.

Right, like that'll ever happen.

He's built like a tank, and he's one of the only dragons who can leave me utterly at his mercy. If I hit him, I would probably barely knock him off balance. I can decapitate a dragon and take on a dozen men at once, but Drew is something else entirely, more of a demigod than a man, and damn it all, I can't so much as wriggle from his grip as he throws open the door and drags me into the hallway.

I don't care if I love him deeply. I don't care if he means the world to me—and he absolutely does.

This is entirely out of line.

And I'm about to tear him a new asshole.

CHAPTER TWENTY

As Drew drags me down the hallway toward his bedroom, my bicep begins to hurt from his intense grip.

This has to stop.

Now.

Gritting my teeth, I throw the full weight of my new and enhanced dragon strength into his side, pinning him against the wall. To my utter astonishment, he actually wavers instead of acting like a giant boulder, immovable and untouchable by everything around him.

He actually bends beneath my strength.

He hits the wall hard, grunting as his grip loosens ever so slightly around my bicep. Most likely from surprise, because I know I'm surprised as hell myself.

I take the opportunity and twist my arm, wrenching it free before I shove him hard in the chest, pushing him against the wall as I glare up at the beautiful fire dragon that has captured my heart from the moment I saw him.

And as much as I love him, I am freaking pissed.

"Don't you ever drag me out of a room like that again!" I snap, glaring daggers at him, at his handsome face as he stares down at me.

His eyes narrow, and his jaw tenses as he grabs my shoulders. In a lightning-fast move, he spins me around and pins me against the opposite wall. "Then don't make such a wild and dangerous suggestion again!"

"It's not wild," I say, smacking his hand away.

Yet again, to my utter astonishment, his hand moves. I must be getting stronger. The magic within me must be enhancing everything about me even more than I realize.

The longer I'm in Ashgrave, the more of my magic I connect to, and the less I understand it.

But for now, I need to focus on Drew.

"Rory, going to the capital isn't like going to a neutral zone," he snaps, getting close to me, his towering and muscled body blocking out the light around me as he basically sandwiches me against the wall.

My dragon stirs with delight and desire, and it takes everything in me not to roll my eyes in annoyance. I'm trying to have a serious moment here, and she can't help but be turned on.

The little hussy.

“Neutral zones don’t even matter anymore, Drew,” I remind him, narrowing my eyes and trying to seem angrier than I am, even as my dragon aches for him.

Horny little traitor.

He glowers down at me, but he doesn’t disagree.

Because he knows I’m right.

“Neutral zones don’t have any weight anymore, not in these increasingly lawless times,” I snap, gesturing back toward the war room. “It doesn’t make sense to go to a neutral zone to meet with the Darringtons, especially when we can use the meeting as an opportunity to bug them in their own damn home!”

“It’s not *safe,*” he says, ignoring me.

“Do you think I'm an idiot?” I ask, lifting my chin and daring him to answer.

“Of course you're not an idiot,” he says, shaking his head. But that doesn't wipe the angry expression from his face. "I just think you don't understand the depths of what you're suggesting."

"Then enlighten me," I retort sarcastically.

I already know what's coming. Everything he's about to say I can pretty much guarantee will not be a surprise.

But he needs to get this out, and we won't get anywhere until he feels heard.

"They could attack at any moment," he says, echoing what I already knew. "And who's going to rescue us if they do? My father has already put a bounty on you that pretty much dwarfs any other in terms of reward. Do you know how many dozens of bounty hunters out there are just trying to get you so they can turn you over to him? And we don't even know why."

Drew groans in frustration, running his hands through his hair as he walks a little down the hallway, pacing back and forth in front of me.

"We don't know what he wants to do to you," my fire dragon continues. "Or why he's been trying so desperately to get his hands on you. And you want to just walk into his house? What's going to stop him from taking you the moment we set foot in the Darrington capital? We will be outnumbered, and there's not a damn thing anyone can do to help us."

My impulse is to jump in and tell him that I know almost all of that already. Admittedly, the bit about the bounty hunters is new to me, but that's the only bit I wasn't prepared for—even though it's entirely unsurprising.

But I don't say anything.

I wait.

I cross my arms and lean against the hallway, lifting one eyebrow as if I'm waiting for him to continue.

As if I'm waiting for more.

"Damn it, Rory, say something." He sets his hands on the back of his head, his thick biceps flexing with the movement as he watches me intensely.

Another shiver of delight sneaks through me at his solid muscle, and a ribbon of warmth shoots between my thighs as my dragon yet again burns with desire for this guy.

He's so damn hot, especially when he's angry, and I have to confess I agree with her.

I'm just a little bit better at focusing than she is.

"I know full well what I suggested," I tell him. "I know the risks. I know the dangers. I know what we're facing. And you know I wouldn't have even said it if I didn't think the risk was worth taking."

"But why?" he says, shrugging violently. "You

don't know him like I do. You don't know what he'll do to—"

"I think I do," I say calmly. Quietly.

Something in my voice seems to disarm him. His expression calms ever so slightly, his shoulders relaxing as his eyes dart back and forth between mine.

He's searching for an answer, and I feel like he's finally calm enough to hear it.

"The world doesn't know I'm a diamond dragon," I remind him. "In my dragon form, my magic is wild and destructive. I've turned grown dragons to ash in seconds with just a breath, and even though I can't fully control this magic yet, it's destructive enough to leave the capital as nothing but a crater when I'm done with it if they dare try to contain me. I'm not going to go into this blind, Drew. We know all of the ways people can contain and restrict my magic, and we'll prepare. And if your father tries anything, then that proves to me he can't be trusted as an ally, and I will never bring this up again."

I take a few steps toward him, until our chests are practically touching, and I lift my hand to delicately trace my fingers along his jawline.

"I'm never going to jeopardize what I love, Drew," I promise. "I'm never going to throw myself in the line of fire unless there's a good reason. If we can show your father that we're not to be messed with, that we're a force to be reckoned with and worthy of an alliance, then maybe we can finally stop this brewing chaos once and for all." I pause, looking deep into my fire dragon's eyes. "Maybe you can finally feel safe going home."

At that, he practically deflates. His shoulders droop, and his head tilts slightly, his lips parting as if he's at a loss for words. As if I pinpointed the one thing he's wanted all this time, but never found himself able to ask for, even from himself.

As powerful as we all are, there's still a human bit to us that needs a family. Though the five of us will always be family to each other, there's still a part of us that aches for home. For the family we were born into.

Tucker and I will never have that again, and though I have Irena, Tucker has no one. Levi has no one. Only Jace and Drew still have their family, and Drew has a chance, here, to reconnect with them.

And maybe I'm wrong. Maybe the Darringtons are irredeemable.

But for Drew, I want to try.

With my hands still by his face, Drew tenderly wraps his hands around my wrists, his massive fingers engulfing me as he tugs me closer. I rub my thumb along the stubble on his jaw, and he sighs deeply, pressing his forehead against mine.

He doesn't say a word, but he doesn't need to. This little moment of tenderness is all I needed to confirm what I had thought.

"If we walk in there, we may not walk out," he says quietly. "If you have to use your magic, you could hurt one of us. It's still too wild, Rory."

"That's why I go in with you," I tell him. "Only you. You're resistant to it. Immune to it. And though I think Jace might be as well, we don't know for sure, and it's not something I'm willing to test."

Drew snorts humorlessly, and a little ribbon of black smoke snakes out of his nose. "You know they're never going to go for that."

"They don't have to like it," I admit with a wry grin. "But I'm not willing to risk their lives, and we need a way out. Me blowing everything to shit is our best bet."

"If it comes down to it, you are actually willing to show your diamond dragon?" Drew asks, catching my eye. "Because once you show Jett, there's no going back."

"I know," I say. "I hope it doesn't come to that, but

yes, if that's what we have to do, it's what we have to do."

Whether or not Jett knows I'm a diamond dragon, both scenarios play in my favor.

It's rare that things work out so well for me, but this time, I'll take it as one of the few lucky breaks I'll get.

Either he knows he's out of his league, with a dragon as powerful as the gods, or he'll be caught off guard when a diamond dragon shifts in his palace and destroys everything. I'll either have his respect, or the element of surprise.

"I don't like it," Drew admits. "He doesn't have any reason to think we're a threat, not really. At least not yet. We don't have an army. We don't have anything."

"That's not true, and you know it," I chide him. "We've allied with the Fairfax, so that means fighting us is fighting them."

It strikes me again that it would be beneficial to have our own army, something to perhaps even circle the Darrington capital and remind Jett of the wrath he'll face if he does anything.

Damn it, Jace was right, wasn't he? I really do need an army.

"So, we bluff," I say out loud, still lost in my thoughts.

"What?" Drew asks.

"We bluff," I repeat myself. "We tell Jett I have an army. That Ashgrave has one, and that if he dares threaten me, he'll get to see it for himself. That anyone who sees the army knows it'll be the last thing they ever see."

"Damn," Drew says under his breath, smirking. "You're brutal."

I chuckle. "You love it."

"I really do," he admits, lifting my chin with his finger and rubbing his thumb along my lips as he looks down at me.

His touch smolders against my skin, and my body aches for him. My gaze drifts to his mouth, and I get hungry for him. Hungry for more. Yet again, my dragon coils with delight.

She loves it when he gets forceful, and hell, I can't deny it. So do I.

Drew sighs with frustration, setting his hands on either side of my head as he leans his forehead against mine, pressing me against the wall behind me. Even through his irritation, he inhales my scent like it's intoxicating and rubs his nose against mine.

"Fine, woman. You get your way. But before we leave, I need to make at least twenty contingency plans, because I will not let him harm one hair on your head."

I grin. I had expected as much. Relied on it even. I have a solid plan or three for how I want us to get out, but Drew knows the Darrington capital better than I do, and I could always use his backup plans.

It makes me feel a little more certain that this crazy plan of mine might actually work.

"And once I'm done," Drew continues, brushing his lips teasingly against mine, "I'm going to come back and fuck you until all of my anger is gone."

I grin under his mouth, loving the way he teases me. "I think that's going to take a while, Drew."

And I'm going to love every minute of it.

CHAPTER TWENTY-ONE

The chop of a helicopter blade on the air above us rattles through the helicopter as we tear through the sky toward the Darrington capital. The headset muffles most of the blaring noise around me, and it's strange to sit in a helicopter with only Drew beside me.

Everyone hated my plan, of course, at least at first. Levi and Jace had yelled over each other—which was new to me—and Tucker had let loose such a colorful string of curse words so impressive and varied that I swear I learned a few new ones myself.

But in the end, they all saw reason, and to my surprise, Drew backed me up. He knows how important this is, and with the right contingency plans, we won't be trapped in the Darrington capital today.

I have no intention of becoming a prisoner, and I would rather blow this place to hell than be trapped within its walls. Jett knows that, and I have that to my advantage.

The man has no idea what he's really up against.

The primary contingency plan has Tucker, Jace, and Levi on standby, ready to infiltrate this place should they lose contact with us. My mate recruited a few of his old dojo buddies—the best of the best, his elite—to prepare for a stealth infiltration should the need arise. Drew gave them several entrances to choose from and a host of maps thick enough to keep them busy for a little while memorizing them all.

Harper insisted on having her armies nearby, and I wasn't about to say no to *that.*

I just hope it doesn't come down to a bloody confrontation with the Darringtons.

As we near the Darrington capital, two dozen red fire dragons swarm the helicopter flying alongside us, their wings almost touching the chopper blades. The soldiers around us fly too close, purposefully trying to set our nerves on edge as their wings brush the side of the helicopter. The Darrington pilot that picked us up doesn't seem the least bit worried, and in fact, he pretty much ignored us the entire trip.

Assholes.

Beside me, Drew sits tense and upright. Earlier, he gave me a play-by-play of everything that was going to happen. All the ways they would try to intimidate us. So far, he's been spot on.

Overwhelming escort with too many dragons on the way in? Check.

Silent helicopter pilot who makes us feel like we aren't even there? Check.

When we land, I suspect we'll face a militant formation of most if not all of the army gathered in a courtyard to remind us that, in the scheme of things, we're actually quite small and insignificant.

Truth be told, I'm on edge, but at this point, there's nothing we can do and no way we can stop this. I set the snowball rolling, and I just hope it doesn't come to bite me in the ass.

I'm fairly sure it won't, but we'll just have to see. If I have to fight my way out of this, at least I'm not doing it alone.

The more I see, the more I begin to doubt that this is going to work exactly the way I wanted. In a perfect world, we would walk in, cut to the chase, and make this right. I want Drew to have his family connection, but I'm beginning to lose what little hope I had that that's even possible anymore. I want to get Harper an ally, but I know she won't even really consider it. She hasn't gone to the Darringtons at all despite their obvious military might.

It's said that anyone who goes up against the Darrington army is a fool and destined to die. That's the kind of reputation that wins wars before they even start, and it's what has allowed the Darringtons to get away with so much through the centuries. If we had that on our side, Kinsley wouldn't stand a chance.

It concerns me that Harper won't look past her resentment of Milo, and Jace, to his credit, won't talk to me about it but at least he won't refuse it all together.

In fact, Harper wasn't even there this morning when I got up. Ashgrave told me she'd left in the night without so much as a note.

I frown, sinking into my seat as I stare out the window at the dozens of dragons to my left. That girl is up to something, and I can't help but suspect it has something to do with the Darringtons, something that could destroy what precarious peace we even have with them.

The fact is if nothing else, we'll at least plant the

bug today. Either way, we win. No matter what happens, this is worth every ounce of risk we take.

On the horizon, the capital appears through the mountains, and a towering palace cuts through the center of a string of red shingles and golden tiles that cover the roofs of this beautiful capital. I can't help but suck in a breath of surprise as I look at the stunning sight—monuments, elaborate cobblestone roads that weave through the buildings. This place is breathtaking.

And Drew gave it all up, just to be with me.

I weave my hand in his, the subtle movement impossible to detect. I have so much I want to share with him, but I don't trust the connection is secure. We have to assume the Darringtons are listening to everything we say even if we take off the headsets, and from here until we leave, we can't say anything we don't want Jett to hear.

In fact, we're not even wearing comms. It puts us at a disadvantage, not being able to talk to Jace, Tucker, and Levi on the outskirts, but Jett will have them removed anyway and I can't really blame him.

This is supposed to be a secure, confidential conversation, and if we walk in wearing transmitters and radios, that's going to look a bit suspect.

That doesn't mean I don't have a few of them

hidden on my body anyway, just in case. It just means I'm going to pretend to play along.

For now.

The helicopter passes over a long stretch of an elegant golden walkway that leads into the palace, and sure enough, dragons line the edge. Three lines of red and orange dragons fill the courtyard below, standing in militant formation with only a small circle left for the helicopter to land.

Oh, this is going to be fun.

As the helicopter lands, one of the soldiers rushes up and opens the door for us, and I doubt it's an act of chivalry. From here on out, the Darringtons want to be in control of every single moment and every single movement.

This is Jett's way of telling us to get out of the damn helicopter.

I jump onto the pavement, and with every step I take, I remind myself that I'm the one in control here. That I am the one with the ace up my sleeve and twenty contingency plans.

No matter what happens today, I will not end it as a prisoner.

And if Jett tries anything, I will burn his home to the ground. I don't give a shit how beautiful it is or who's in my way.

As we walk down the elegant path, Drew scans the dragons around me, his eyes occasionally narrowing in recognition as his gaze scans the faces nearby. These are people he grew up with. People he fought with.

And yet he comes here today as an outsider. No longer one of them.

I can only imagine what this feels like for him.

None of the dragons so much as looks at us though as we walk toward the palace, and before long we're crossing into the beautiful golden doors as butlers in white gloves hold them open.

As we enter, an elderly man in a suit bows to us and gestures for us to follow him. Without so much as a word, he turns his back to us and walks down the hallway, and I suppose that's that.

Time to meet with the Boss.

As we walk noiselessly down the hallways, the only sound is our footsteps echoing through the massive corridors. Everything seems unnecessarily large here, as if this entire palace was built for dragons and humans alike to walk through. The windows are easily three stories tall, with floor-to-ceiling curtains that must weigh hundreds of pounds held open with elegant golden ties. Light streams through the windows, casting warm beams of light that are interrupted only by the occasional stretch of wall between each one. Ornate doors line the wall on the other side, their elegant handles curved and the doors closed.

To my surprise, the Darrington mansion is far more regal than I expected. I suspected we would be surrounded by Jett's military. That everything would be Spartan, themed around war and blood, but there's an almost elegant softness to this place that catches me off guard.

The butler leads us around a corner, and down this stretch of hallway, the windows disappear. Skylights let in a soft glow that fills the entirety of the space. On either side of us, massive suits of dragon armor line the walls, leaving only enough room for four men to walk side by side.

Ah.

This is more in line with what I was expecting.

The hallway ends in a massive set of double doors. Ten soldiers stand between us and what I assume is a type of war room. As we near them, the butler steps aside and gestures for us to go forward.

One of the soldiers steps between us and the entry, however, greeting us with a curt nod as he scans our faces. As his gaze wanders over Drew, he frowns.

"Richard," Drew says with a curt nod.

"Drew," the man says in an equally dry tone, the two of them apparently welcoming each other in the curt and slightly dismissive fashion of the Darringtons.

"Are you going to step aside?" Drew asks, maintaining his stony glare.

"You know we have to search you first," Richard says, shaking his head slightly. "Protocol."

Drew rolls his eyes and stretches out his arms without so much as another word, inviting them to get this the hell over with.

The soldiers surround us, slightly inching us apart, and I figure this is nothing more than another intimidation tactic to make us feel isolated and separated.

I don't fight it. I simply set my hands on the back of my head as three soldiers quickly pat down my arms, waist, and legs.

"A comm, Drew? Really?" Richard asks as he holds it up to the light.

Drew just grins. "I had to try."

Richard shakes his head, pocketing the decoy comm we planted specifically for them to find. The two real ones are in my cleavage, and I dare them to even try to grab *that*.

The soldier's hands are a little too comfortable with my body, exploring the same spots two or three times, and for the moment, I simply allow it. I want to pick my battles here, and if they get a little handsy, there's not really any harm done.

It's just annoying.

One of the soldiers feels his way up my waist as he checks for weapons. His path is heading toward my chest, and as his fingers graze my bra, I roughly smack his hand away.

In an instant, the room becomes tense. I expected as much—this is the battle worth fighting, after all.

They don't get to find what's hidden in my bra. It's too important.

All of the soldiers stand, talking over each other as I interfere with their inspection.

"What are you doing?" Richard snaps at me, glaring as if I just shot one of his soldiers in the face instead of smacking away a hand.

"I think you've explored enough," Drew interjects, shoving one of the soldiers aside as he takes his spot beside me.

"We need to check her."

"You've checked me plenty," I interrupt, glaring at the soldier who was getting a little too handsy for my liking.

I can still feel the comms tucked safely into my cleavage, and it's quite a comfort to know they're there. To know that if we do have to leave here, we'll have instant connection with the outside. To know that Jett's attempt to disarm us failed.

I'm not about to let them find those *now*.

"Enough," Richard interjects, waving his soldiers aside. "Let them through."

Though the soldiers around us scowl, pausing for the briefest moment as if they might disobey their Captain, they finally comply and step aside. The two closest to the doors grab the handles, swinging open the entry so that we can walk inside.

As the doors open, the first thing I notice is the massive fireplace at the far end of the room, easily large enough for me to step into. My boots clack against the marble tile, and I quickly scan the elegant space. Everything, to my surprise, is white and trimmed with gold—right down to the massive windows on either side of us that let in enough light to make the room seem like it's glowing.

And there, sitting at a white marble table in the middle of the room, with his back to the fireplace, is Jett. Milo stands beside him with his hands behind his back. As we enter, he tenses, his chin lifted slightly as if he's trying not to show his fear.

Well, he's doing a shit job of it.

As we near, I can more clearly see the thin, silver scar that covers Jett's left eye—a memento from our last battle. It's healed, but clearly visible.

I can't help but wonder how much resentment he still has for that.

Time to find out, I guess.

This is it—the main war room where Jett meets with all of his important guests. According to Drew, he has many of his military meetings in here as well.

It seemed like a weakness, to be honest, when Drew first told me that. It puts him at risk for bugs, but now that I'm in the room, I can see why he likes it. Sure, it's breathtaking, but it's more so how it makes his company feel.

Small.

It's an imposing room with a towering ceiling that makes you feel insignificant, and that's likely what he wants to do to everyone who enters.

Make them think they don't stand a chance against him, because most people don't.

But I'm not most people.

Without so much as a word or an invitation, I sit across from Jett, and the large table makes me feel as though I might have to shout to be heard. Drew sits beside me.

This is it, the moment where we plant our bug.

We don't know how long we'll be here. He might move us to another room, or send us packing within seconds. If we're going to plant our surveillance device, we have to do it immediately—and totally undetected.

So much depends on this moment.

No pressure.

The doors shut behind us, and I suspect that's yet another intimidation tactic. To have my back to an exit puts me at a disadvantage. Soldiers could come streaming through and shoot me for all I know. I have no control over the situation—at least that's what Jett thinks, and that's what I'm going to let him believe.

I cross my legs, making a little bit of a show of it, letting my skirts hike up ever so slightly past my knee. The point is to distract them, to make sure that all eyes are on me.

Because I'm not the one with the bug.

Drew is.

"That was quite a show, Jett," I say, crossing my arms carefully, setting my forearms beneath my chest to enhance my cleavage and draw even more attention.

It's all to enhance the distraction, of course. To

make sure all eyes are on me. Luckily, it's just the four of us in the room.

Fewer eyes to fight for.

Both Milo and Jett watch me with guarded expressions as Drew leans forward, setting his elbows on his knees with his hands beneath the table. It's not the most natural position or posture, but it's what Drew needs to do to plant the bug. He glares at his father, and Jett only looks at him for the briefest of moments—like he's insignificant and hardly worthy of a Boss's time.

I fight a twinge of anger at Jett's flagrant dismissal of his own son, but that's not really why we're here.

The little device is paper-thin, and by now, he should have it on the edge of his finger, ready to subtly tap underneath the table. The moment it touches the marble, it will stick, and ideally, if the technology works, the camouflage will kick in. To the undiscerning eye, it will be indistinguishable from the table itself, camouflaging its tiny surface to blend in with everything around it.

Ideally.

This is new untested tech, and I hate that we are putting so much faith on mere specs and blueprints

Zurie designed, but we have to. This is all we have, and we have to make it work.

"What's the matter, Rory?" Jett asks, smirking. "You don't feel welcomed?"

He's baiting me, and I'm not going to indulge him. "I'm surprised you agreed to meet with us."

"You shouldn't be," he says dryly, setting his elbows on the table as he leans forward. "You asked to come to my capital, where I have complete control, just to have a conversation. Am I surprised?" He hesitates, shrugging. "Yes, a little bit. But I'm intrigued as well. So, to what do I owe the pleasure?"

"I think you know why we're here," I say as Drew leans in toward the table a little more.

I adjust my body to make sure their attention stays on me. We want to get the bug as far under the table as possible, since anything close to the edge might be more easily noticed.

"You want me to put my armies at Harper's command," he says with a sarcastic little flourish of his hand. "Is that right?"

"You're close," I confess.

"I must admit I'm surprised she hasn't come herself," Jett says, leaning his head on one fist as he looks at me. "She's asked everyone else, but not us. Would you happen to know why?"

"I might," I admit, lifting my chin slightly as I flaunt the fact that I know something he doesn't.

It's fun, actually, to lord something over Jett Darrington. I don't get to do it often enough.

This is banter, and usually I hate wasting time like this. It's a back and forth, nothing but a boring little tennis match that achieves nothing except perhaps to make Jett feel smart and witty for a few seconds, but the point is to keep his attention away from Drew. Thankfully, it's working. I see the slightest twitch of Drew's arm, just the subtlest movement, almost like he was pressing his hand against the bottom of the table.

As he leans back, I know for sure it's done.

My impulse is to let out a slow breath of relief, but I don't want to give anything away. I sit a little taller, relaxing my arms against my cleavage so that it's not so pronounced.

I'm not trying to give these guys a show, not now that the distraction is over.

Time to get down to business.

Jett opens his mouth to speak, to continue our little banter, but I've more than had my fill.

"Tell me what you really want," I demand, arching my back like a queen as I glare at the Darrington Boss in front of me. "Out of all of this, what do you want to get? This war with Kinsley, this nonsense with you trying to capture me—just get to the point."

He chuckles, rubbing his thumb along his jaw as he looks at me with a guarded expression. Whatever he's thinking, he doesn't want me to know about it, and I don't like that look at all.

It reminds me of Diesel, to be honest. It's a face I can't trust, an expression that tells me there's so much more going on than I know.

That makes me uneasy.

"You want to know why I've been trying to get you here?" he says, clarifying. "Why I told Drew I would give him everything if he brought you to me?"

"Obviously," I say dryly.

"And what makes you think I'm just going to tell you?" Jett asks, gesturing toward me. "And for that matter, what makes you think you're leaving today?"

I'm sure he expected me to frown. To get tense. To maybe even look nervous.

But that just confirms for me that Jett has no idea *what* I am, *who* I am, or what I'm capable of.

I smirk, and it throws him a little off his game. His cocky little smile falls, and for a brief moment, I see the real Jett. Confused. Uncertain.

Wary.

"I won't be staying here," I tell him. "Nothing you

can do can keep me in your city, and if you try, I'll destroy everything. When I'm done, there won't even be rubble. All I will leave you with, Jett Darrington, is ash."

There's a spellbinding moment of silence that settles on the room as the gravity of my threat weighs against all of us. Beside me, Drew tenses, ready to fight his own family to make sure we get out of here alive today.

Behind Jett, Milo stiffens, his gaze locked on me and his brows twisted slightly with fear. It's subtle, only barely noticeable, but I see it, and he knows what would happen if Jett tried to keep me here today. He knows exactly what I would do to this entire palace and everyone in it.

And he knows exactly how much it would hurt.

Jett laughs, and it's a hearty, real, full-bodied laugh. It catches me off guard and breaks the spell in the room. He squeezes his eyes shut, pinching the bridge of his nose as he shakes his head in astonishment.

"You never cease to amaze me, girl. You're full of surprises. I assume you have something up your sleeve if you're willing to walk in here, because I know you're not that stupid." He sets his elbows on the table and looks at me. "The question is what is it, and are you really a threat?"

I hold his gaze for a tense moment and smile. "Would you like to find out?"

Jett chuckles again, shaking his head as if this entire thing is just too damn hilarious. "A little bit, I admit, yes," he says, crossing his arms as he leans back in his chair. "But for the moment, we can be civil. Tell me what you want, and I'll make you an offer."

Interesting.

"All right," I say, leaning my elbows on the table and weaving my fingers together as I glare at him over my hands. "I would like a truce between you and me. I would like us to be allies, at least with this war against Kinsley. You may not even need to fight her. If you just show up and threaten her—"

"Look, kid," Jett says, cutting me off with the wave of his hand. "You're new to this world, and you don't know how crazy Kinsley is. That woman is bat shit insane."

"I'm well aware," I say, annoyed that he interrupted me.

"No," Jett says, shaking his head. "You're not. You don't know about the heads she's put on stakes around her palaces. You don't know about the people who have disappeared into the tunnels beneath her many fortresses and homes." Jett leans slowly forward, snaring me with his intense gaze as he relays secrets I wonder if Drew even knows. "You haven't heard the screams from her place, or heard the things her people call her when they think they're alone." The Darrington Boss frowns, shaking his head. "That woman is insane, and me showing up with my armies isn't going to stop her."

"Is that a hint of fear I detect?" I ask, legitimately curious.

Jett snorts derisively. "Not fear, girl. It's called wisdom, and I know better than to think I won't have to fight in this little war of yours. My people's lives will be on the line if I join you, and I have to look at this the same way every other Boss does. Who's likely to join her, and who's likely to join you?" He pauses, quirking one eyebrow as if waiting for me to answer the question.

He probably knows exactly how lucky we've been thus far, how absolutely no one has joined us yet and how thus far it appears to be just me and Harper against an evil ice queen.

"This war is not tipping in your favor," Jett says, leaning forward. "And I will give you this freebie—

consider it a friendly warning. She's not alone anymore."

I stiffen impulsively, not quite sure I like the sound of that.

Jett smirks, nodding. "That's right, little girl. Kinsley has an ally, and she knows that her bio-weapon is worthless. They're already in production to make one resistant to the antidote you created."

"How do you know that?" Drew snaps. "How could you possibly—"

"Everything you know," Jett interjects as he glares at his son, "you learned from me. Remember that, boy."

Drew's nose wrinkles in disdain, but he doesn't respond.

He doesn't have to.

"Is it you?" I ask, shining a light on the elephant in the room—on what we're all wondering.

"No," Jett says, leaning back in his chair, and I study his face for tells of a lie. But as far as I can tell, he's speaking the truth. "I don't know who it is, either. Just that she's aware of the bio-weapon, and if she's aware of the bio-weapon..." He trails off, gesturing vaguely toward the window as he waits for us to piece everything together.

"Then a Boss must have told her," Drew finishes,

shaking his head in frustration. "Because only the Bosses knew."

"Exactly," Jett says with a slight nod of his head.

"Why are you telling us this?" I ask, suspicious.

"Because I want you to know what you're getting yourself into," Jett says, leaning his elbows on the table as his glare focuses on me. "And that I'm the only one who can save you from it."

Oh, gods.

Here we go.

"And this is the part where you tell me what you want," I say, tilting my head as I cross my arms, waiting for him to get on with it—and knowing I won't like this one bit.

"You're a smart girl," he says with a little shrug. "And all of this can go away easily. All you have to do is bow to me and do everything I tell you." He pauses, smirking, and his gaze drifts toward my chest.

It's not hard to guess that his condition that I obey him would apply to every moment of the rest of my life. Jett seems like the kind of guy who likes to lord his power over the women in his life, and I figure this is just his elaborate way of getting back at Drew for leaving.

Jett wants me to give myself to him and only him.

You have *got* to be fucking kidding me.

Beside me, Drew sets his hand on my knee, his grip tightening possessively around my leg as he glares at his father.

"That's never going to happen," I say as calmly as I can.

What I really want to do is set his table on fire and maybe punch Jett Darrington in the face. My dragon curls with rage at his demands, aching to push free and put this man in his place. To show him who's boss.

And I can't lie, I would love to fight Jett one-on-one. Dragon to dragon.

But him being a cocky douchebag isn't reason enough for me to give away my secret.

Not yet.

"Those are my terms," he says, clasping his hands together as he leans his elbows on the table. "If you don't like it, you can leave here today as a failure with no treaty."

"I'm not the failure here," I point out. "I'm not the one putting my people in the line of fire just to get a mistress and make your son angry. You said you could make all of this go away, right? So make it go away, Jett, for *them.* For your people. Not to get back at your son. You're dangling their safety—"

"They're fine," Jett interjects.

"They won't be for long," I snap.

The room sizzles with tension as my words hang in the air. It sounds like a threat, but it's just a warning. Kinsley has been preparing for her opening move in our little game, and I can feel in my bones that she won't stay silent for much longer.

She's going to do something horrible, and once she does, there's not going to be any turning back.

"You're being a stubborn ass," I say, glaring at Jett.

I expect him to get angry, to maybe even flip me off. But he just laughs again, shaking his head. "I see why you like her, Drew."

"Focus," Drew chides. "This is serious."

But it's too late. The way Jett's laughing, the way he's taking a threat like Kinsley so lightly—now everything about this screams of arrogance.

He's not going to join us, and I think the reason he gave me such an obscene offer is because he knew I would never take it. He wanted to see my power for himself, to see if I was coming into his den foolishly or if I legitimately had something up my sleeve.

And he sees now that I do.

So, he just wants me gone.

I knew this was a long shot. To think I could convince Jett to not be a stubborn asshole, well, perhaps it was a bit too hopeful. I'm striking out with the Bosses and it's getting frustrating, but at least there is a silver lining to all of this.

We now have a live bug camouflaged and hidden in the central war room of the Darrington stronghold.

And they're never going to find it.

The fact is the Bosses don't fear me, yet. Not really. All of them think they can still control me, and I need them to realize that's never going to happen.

But that's probably not going to get through their thick skulls until my dragon is public.

"I think we're done," I say, standing.

For a moment, no one else moves—even Drew. He looks between me and Jett like he still wants to try to convince his father to see reason. I hesitate, watching my fire dragon and wondering if maybe there is a glimmer of hope after all. If he thinks we can stay here.

If he thinks a few more conversations can fix this, I'll indulge him.

But in the end, he stands, too.

In the end, he has given up as well.

"Thank you for your time," I say to Jett, squaring my shoulders as I turn toward the door.

As we leave, I catch Milo's eye briefly and smirk in silent warning to keep his mouth shut about what he knows. He swallows hard, his eyes a little wide as he watches me, and it's clear he's afraid.

He should be. The coward.

To his credit, it seems like he's kept my secret, but I know I won't be able to keep it for much longer. If Jett knew what I could do, he would have dangled it in my face.

As I reach the doors, they open, and twenty guards block our way into the hall. Richard stands at the front of them, his broad shoulders squared as he dares us to try to break through his soldiers' ranks.

Drew and I pause, and I look silently over my shoulder at Jett, wondering if this is going to be like escaping Mr. Viet.

I wonder if I'm going to need to rely on the armies and contingency plans we set up around the palace, thanks to Drew's moles and contacts on the border.

Jett and I make eye contact, and he frowns when he realizes I'm not afraid. I'm not nervous.

I'm simply waiting to see what he does next.

If anything, I'm begging him to try so that I can show him what I am and what I can do.

I'm almost salivating for an excuse to whip his ass.

With a frustrated sigh, he waves the guards to step aside. To my surprise, they oblige and open up a path into the hallway. The butler stands midway down the hall and gestures for us to follow him as he turns his back to us yet again without so much as a word.

And just like that, we're allowed to leave.

I was expecting at least some trouble, and Jett didn't give us any. Not really.

It's a surprise, and I'm not entirely sure if it's a welcome one. I have to wonder if Jett is starting to realize I'm not some damsel for him to corral into submission or—more likely—if he has something else up his sleeve entirely.

Something I'm not going to like.

But I'm a diamond dragon, and if Jett comes for me, I'll break him.

CHAPTER TWENTY-TWO

Back at Ashgrave, I stand on my balcony in the growing night, my palms resting against the railing as I stare up at the moon. It peeks through thin whispers of clouds, casting a soft blue glow across Ashgrave, across my castle.

Across my snowy realm.

When we got home, Ashgrave told me the nearby village wants me to swing by in a few days for that party.

A *party.*

It feels weird, and I'm tempted to not go. Even after becoming more comfortable in the spotlight, I don't like the idea of being the guest of honor at a celebration. I don't feel like I really did anything to deserve it, not really. Everything I did was just the right thing to do, and I can't deny that it benefits me as well.

But it'll make them happy.

I don't want to let them down, and there doesn't seem to be any danger in going as far as I can tell. It's just weird to think that they're genuinely grateful.

I'm so used to people trying to kill me that people being nice is just strange.

In my pocket, my phone buzzes. When I fish out the phone, I don't recognize the number at all. My instinct is to think it's Irena, but I can't be too careful anymore—especially not after Diesel got ahold of my number before.

He has his hands in many pots, and I wouldn't be at all surprised if he found my new number as well.

I answer, holding the phone to my ear without saying a word, and I wait for whoever this is to speak first.

"Your little speech on the rooftop won't stop me," Diesel says.

Impulsively, I close my eyes in disappointment. It takes everything in me to not sigh in annoyance, to not let any sound escape me. Even though I knew this could be him, I desperately wanted it to be someone else.

Almost anyone else.

This man is chasing me. Hunting me.

The longer this goes on, the more risk there is of him winning.

"I know where you are," he continues. "And I'll find my way in."

"Stop stalling then," I say darkly, and with that, I hang up.

I look at my phone, and the rage within me burns bright. It's hot and fierce and *furious*, and I want nothing more than to wring his neck. To break it.

To break *him*.

In my anger, I crush the phone in my hand, and I don't for even one moment regret it. There are always more phones to be had, and in my life, I've always treated these devices as disposable because there's no knowing when someone will find out how to reach me or track me. I need to be able to throw one away on a whim.

He knows where I am because the world knows where I am. The world knows about Ashgrave at this point. Everyone with even remote access to a satellite has pinpointed the location, and they're probably just waiting. Wondering. Watching to see what I'll do with it. The world wants to know what other powers this magical castle has, and for the moment, I want them to dream big.

I need them to dream big until my threats aren't a bluff anymore.

With a grunt of rage and frustration, I throw my phone into the air. It soars through the sky toward the mountains, flying so far that I lose sight of it. I cuss under my breath, leaning my elbows on the balcony as I shake my head in frustration.

Diesel has to die. His time is up, and I'm the one who has to stop him.

I take a deep breath, my rage gently subsiding as I get a strange sort of clarity. It's a calmness about something I've been so unsure of, so certain it was a mistake that I wouldn't even really consider it, not entirely.

But now I know.

I look up again at the moon, and I wish that I felt as calm as the world around me. But I need to find Jace.

I need to find my general.

I close my eyes and take a deep and steadying breath as I search for him. Deep within me, my dragon twists and churns with knowing. The beacon in my chest leads me to him, since my dragon already knows exactly where he is. She keeps tabs on him always—our mate.

He's off to my right, most likely somewhere

along the roofline based on my intuitive hit, and I listen to it.

I hoist myself on to the edge of the balcony and close my eyes as the wind rips past me, tussling my hair and cooling the last lingering rage ever so slightly. As I exhale, I step off the balcony, and on my way down, I shift.

My body hums and changes as I push myself further, aching to hurry my shift, and become more in control of this process. As the ground nears, I spread my arms, and they slowly become wings. They catch me, and I fly low over the ground as I recover, my claws digging into the dirt as I push off and fly into the sky.

It wasn't the most graceful shift, and I got a little too close to the ground there for my liking, but hey —I didn't die.

Always a plus.

I follow the beacon in my heart that takes me to Jace, tilting slightly as I wobble on the wind. I grit my teeth in frustration and annoyance, wishing this was easier, not knowing why I'm not picking it up faster. I'm always a quick learner—always have been —yet this just feels so foreign.

The beacon gets brighter as I get nearer, and

soon enough I see a silhouette lounging on a rooftop at the far end of the castle. I angle myself toward him, and even though he doesn't look over, he knows I'm near.

I angle downward and shift on my way toward the roof. My body hums once again, and it takes too long for me to become a human form. Well, at least longer than I'd like it to. When I'm about five feet from the rooftop—fully human and stark-naked once again—I drop to the roof, sliding a little as I catch my balance.

He finally looks over his shoulder, a mere ten feet away from me now, and his gaze wanders over my naked body as he mischievously grins.

Before he can say anything, I take a deep breath and close my eyes, bracing myself for what I'm about to say. "Be my general, Jace."

He doesn't respond, and I open my eyes to find him watching me intensely. His body stiffens, and every muscle in his body seems to flex—like he's bracing himself or doesn't quite believe me. Like he's worried he's dreaming.

"We need an army," I concede, scanning the mountains around me as I confess to being wrong. "And we need the most capable dragon alive to lead it. I need you, Jace. I need you to push me to the max. To make me strong. Hell is coming for me, and I won't let it destroy what we've built."

Without a word, he stands and crosses toward me. Though I know he's tempted to let his eyes rove my body, he somehow manages to keep his gaze locked on my face. His jaw tenses, his brows tilt ever so slightly upward as he studies me.

He rests his finger underneath my jaw and gently rubs his thumb along my cheek. "You're already strong, Rory."

I can't help it. I smile, and my heart flutters with the compliment.

"But I can make you stronger," he adds.

I nod, slowly at first, but it seems we've reached an agreement the way we usually do—without much in the way of talking.

"You trust me, Rory," he says. "Don't you?"

"Of course," I say.

"Then stay here," he says.

With that, he jumps off the roof, shifting on his way down as he angles elegantly and gracefully over the grass below. He flies off without even so much as a glance backward, and I can't help but grin. I know when one of my men is up to mischief, and Jace most certainly is.

I'm just wondering what the hell he has up his sleeve—and if I'm going to love it or hate it completely.

CHAPTER TWENTY-THREE

In the soft chilly wind, there is only silence.

I stand on the roof of Ashgrave, listening to the night, and I hear nothing. The white moon illuminates a bit of the world around me, but most of everything is shrouded in shadow and stands out against the horizon as nothing but a silhouette, only a shade or two darker than the world behind it. The cloud rolls over the moon, shrouding everything in even more darkness, and I strain my ear to listen.

Jace has disappeared into the darkness and won't even tell me what he's doing, which means he's up to mischief.

I listen to the beacon in my heart. My dragon and I narrow in on him. He's nearby, just out of sight, circling me slowly which implies that he's actually fairly far away, and I don't know what his game is.

I have no idea what he's up to.

I narrow my eyes, squinting in the darkness as I try to make out his figure. In my chest, the beacon grows brighter as he gets close, but I still can't see him. He's like a wraith in the night, completely invisible.

Probably until it's too late.

This has to be a test. After all, I just asked him to train me, to make me stronger, and he accepted.

I just don't know what this test could possibly prove.

The beacon in my chest grows ever brighter, and I know he's getting close even though I still can't see him. I tense, impossibly settling into a fighting stance as I prepare for a duel, but I have no idea what he's getting at and I'm not sure what to expect.

Out of nowhere, he appears, the blue glow of his face emerging from the darkness like a bullet, and he's too close for me to even react. In a blisteringly fast second, he grabs me in one claw, his talons wrapping around my waist as he hoists me into the air.

Ribbons of white light dance across my skin as my body is flooded with adrenaline and the impulse to fight. It takes everything in me to keep it at bay, to remind my instinct that this is Jace—that he would never hurt me.

Even if he does confuse the hell out of me sometimes.

I wrap my hands around his talons, and the connection opens up our mental link.

Are you having fun? I chide him, glaring up at the dragon above me.

He chuckles, sparks fluttering out of his nose as he briefly looks down at me and nods.

Care to explain what the hell you're doing?

You trust me? He asks again.

I roll my eyes. *Of course, I trust you.*

You know I would never do anything to hurt you?

Yes, I say hesitantly, not entirely liking where this is going.

Then we're going to do a little exercise I learned at the academy. An exercise we used on fledgling dragons who had just shifted. Are you ready?

I'm not entirely sure, I confess, my body tensing with concern.

He chuckles again. *No one's ever really ready for this.*

You're not really winning me over here, I admit.

You got this, Rory, he says, briefly looking down at

me again, and a surge of pride flows through him into me.

I can't help it. I grin at his confidence in me—but just a little bit.

Get ready, he says.

Ready for what?

Before I can even finish the thought, he lets go.

And I fall.

I tumble into the darkness, my stomach lurching into my throat as my hair whips past my face. I look up at him as he shrinks into the sky, my back to the ground as my body is frozen in disbelief.

He dropped me.

He fucking *dropped* me.

His eyes narrow as he watches me sail toward the ground below, and he hovers, body tensing.

But he doesn't dive.

He doesn't try to rescue me.

He just watches.

My first impulse is to hurl a beam of magic at him in anger. It won't solve much, but it'll feel good for a second.

My second impulse is to save my own ass.

I pivot, looking down at the ground as it rapidly approaches, and the motion makes me spin briefly out of control. I grit my teeth, throwing my arms and legs wide to try to slow the momentum as I look at the rapidly approaching, snow-covered ground.

And just like that, a ribbon of adrenaline shoots through me.

It's like life.

It's joy.

In that moment, I feel connected to everything.

To every breath. To every sensation.

To my dragon.

Take over, I tell her.

I thought you'd never ask, she says in response, her voice like heaven in my ear.

And with that, we shift.

It's instantaneous and perfect. There's no hesitation. No doubt. Not even a flicker of fear or uncertainty. My body hums and pops, the adrenaline shooting through me and filling me with the life-giving joy that I love. But this time it's stronger, faster.

And entirely in my control.

Almost before I can even register it, my wings spread open, catching the air as I stop my fall and instead begin to soar.

My body hums in victory and triumph. I roar into the sky, almost unbelieving of what I just did. Golden dust shimmies from my scales as I soar through the air, and I unleash a massive bolt of white light into the clouds in victory.

I did it.

I freaking *did* it.

Finally.

I curve back toward Jace, and he roars as well. As we reach each other, he does a barrel roll over me in victory, and I can practically feel the satisfaction radiating off him as he watches me.

As we fly, we hit a draft and soar. His wing brushes mine, opening the connection between us.

You clever asshole, I say before he can so much as send an emotion my way.

He chuckles and nods. *I knew you could do it.*

I shake my head, hardly agreeing with his methods, but hell, it worked. *How did you know that would work?*

I didn't, he admits. *I wanted it to work, but there's never any guarantee. It all comes down to you.*

I scoff. *So, you dropped your mate over a mountain range in the hopes she wouldn't fall to her death?*

I would have caught you, he says, rolling his eyes.

I laugh, shaking my head, not quite believing how far this man has come from trying to lock me in a dungeon to keep me out of harm's way.

Shift back, he says. *I'll catch you this time.*

I growl a little in hesitation, not liking this at all, but in the end, I trust him. I briefly look down at the ground below me, at the crags and rocky slopes that would kill me if I hit them. But I decide not to think about it too hard.

After all, as soon as I stopped thinking about it too hard, that's when I made my first instant shift.

I take a deep breath and reach inward, asking my dragon yet again to shift. She hums with disappointment and reluctance, but we trust each other—and Jace.

The process is a little slow, but mid-flight, I fall for the second time tonight—a naked little human streaming through the dark midnight sky.

Before I can even go a dozen feet, Jace swoops in and catches me, his claw delicately wrapping around my body as we swoop over the mountains. I let out a victorious yell as the adrenaline rushes within me.

This is incredible and so damn fun.

Are you ready? He says, and I get the distinct impression he's about to drop me again.

As I'll ever be, I admit.

Tense and ready for the drop, I expect him to immediately let go. For a moment or two, however, nothing changes. I prepare for the inevitable, but nothing happens.

When he hasn't dropped me yet, I peek through one eye, looking up at him to find him already looking down at me. The moment our eyes meet—the moment I so much as relax a little—he lets go.

That gorgeous jackass.

As I fall through the air again, I can't help but holler in excitement as the adrenaline rushes through me, giving me life and energy I didn't have twenty minutes ago. As the ground gets ever closer, I reach inward, and yet again, I shift.

With just a thought.

My wings catch the air, my body humming with delight and adrenaline as I catch a draft over the mountains. I bank toward Jace again, and he roars once more in triumph.

As the hours wear on, I lose track of how many times he catches and drops me again and again. It becomes effortless, like a fluid dance. Every time he tries to catch me off guard by dropping me before or after I expect it, I manage to recover. And before long, there's not even a hint of terror as I fall.

Because I trust her.

My dragon.

I know she'll always catch me, and it was that trust that I was missing. I didn't know it before, but I know it now with absolute certainty.

My dragon will *always* catch me.

As I make my final shift, rolling into my dragon form with effortless grace, I delicately curl my wing and do a barrel roll over Jace. It's effortless and smooth, and I feel in complete control for the entire flight.

I roar with success and triumph as the sun peeks above the mountains. We've been up all night, but I don't even care.

We did it when I was beginning to worry I wouldn't be able to manage it, at least not in time.

Jace roars alongside me, both of us lost in the victory of what we achieved tonight as we bank back toward the castle. He leads the way, and I wonder what else he has up his sleeve.

My wing brushes his, but before I can say anything, a surge of mischievous energy rushes through from him.

Follow me, he says, his eyes narrowing playfully as he races ahead.

I dart after him, pushing myself to my limits to keep up with the seasoned flyer in front of me. To my surprise, I mostly manage to do it. I keep trying to get ahead of him, and here and there I almost get the leg up on him, but he does have quite a bit more experience than me at flying.

Give me a few months, and I'll be faster.

As we approach the castle, he angles toward the center tower—toward my room. He races toward my balcony at breakneck speed, and I wonder if he's about to blow a hole through my bedroom.

Lord, I hope not.

As he nears, his body hums and shifts, and instead of crashing against the stone, he dives into my bedroom. With the ease of a practiced warrior, he rolls effortlessly across the floor and jumps to his feet, his shoulder lightly brushing the far wall as he gets his balance.

Huh.

Challenge accepted.

I dart in after him, closing my eyes briefly as I give into the shift, and my dragon instantly obeys.

I've never taken a dive quite this fast, but I'm always one for a new adventure.

I dart into the bedroom after him, rolling effortlessly across the stone floor before jumping to my feet and landing in his arms. He laughs and holds me tight, swinging me around in a circle as we celebrate.

"I knew you could do it," he says, his hands on either side of my head as he kisses me roughly.

I can't even say anything. I'm laughing, completely out of breath as he kisses me. Even though we're not in dragon form anymore, I can still feel the pride radiating off him.

He pushes me to be better, and I'm so grateful for it.

I'm so grateful for *him.*

As he fiercely kisses me, he takes a few steps closer, his bare torso pressing against mine as he walks me backward through my room. I can't even tell where we're going—and I don't even care. I'm drunk on his kiss, his electrifying touch burning through me like sultry lightning as he leads me wordlessly through my bedroom.

With every step, he gets harder, his thick cock inching its way between my thighs until his shaft presses flat against my entrance. I grin under his mouth, about to make a wise crack about his growing erection when he roughly shoves my shoulders. I fall backward, gasping a little in surprise before my back hits my bed

"Scoundrel." I narrow my eyes at him, grinning playfully as he saunters closer.

"That's a new nickname," he says as he climbs on top of me, roughly shoving my thighs apart. "I like it."

Before I can say a thing, he kisses me roughly again and wraps his fingers around the side of my neck, holding me in place. My hands weave up his arms as my treasonous body surrenders to him—long before I have.

I wanted to make him work for it a little more, but my dragon has other ideas.

She wants her mate, and she wants him *now.*

My hips tilt upward, inviting him in as heat rushes through my navel and down my thighs. Everything in me wants him to take me already.

To make me his.

Jace tilts my head away, exposing my neck, and bites me. His teeth tighten over my skin, only hard enough to send a delightful thrill through me as his hard abdomen sandwiches me against the mattress. He looms over me, powerful and strong, and I can tell from the look in his eye that he's done talking.

In a single night, he did what we couldn't do in weeks. He pushes me to be so much better—and now he wants his reward.

With one hand still around my neck, his other hand traces over my breasts and down my side. He grabs my hip, pinning me to the bed as he sets his knees against mine. His rough fingers pinch me, but the blips of pain are almost electric as the tip of his cock presses against my entrance.

Deep within me, my dragon moans for him. It's

rough and guttural, an ache and longing that can only be fulfilled when *he* fills *me.*

As his cock presses slowly into me, I feel called to open my eyes—only to find him looking down at me with a blurred expression somewhere between love and dominance. His mouth curls into a devious little grin, and with that, he forces the first half of his cock into me.

I moan, gasping as he takes his time with me, stretching me as he has his way with me. His grip on my waist tightens, keeping me in place even though I want to ride him, to drive his cock deeper.

He's toying with me.

Again.

"You're so *mean,*" I manage to say between my breathless gasps.

"Yeah," he says, leaning over me as he nibbles my ear.

Oh, *gods.*

When he does that, I'm just a goner.

I can't help but relax into him as he gently bites my earlobe, the sexy pinch of his hand on my hip blistering its way through my brain. Right now, I'll do absolutely anything this man asks of me—and he damn well knows that.

"Show me what your hips can do," he demands.

"What did you have in mind?" My eyes flutter closed as he gently pulses his cock within me, teasing me mercilessly without giving me everything I want.

Without so much as a word, he leans toward me and grabs both of my hips. With one fluid motion, he rolls us both—with his cock still in me—until he's on his back and I'm sitting on his dick. He holds my hips above him, his cock still only halfway inside as he glares mischievously up at me.

Oh, how devious.

I can work with this.

I spread my thighs wider so that I can take him in, surrendering completely and giving him all of me. His hands relax, trailing along my waist and down to my ass before he grabs me tightly, steering me from behind as I ride him.

I sink lower on him as his cock forces its way into me, going deeper, stretching me with every glorious inch of his dick. When my entrance finally hits the base of his cock, I can't help myself—I grin with delight and arch my back, setting my hands on his hard abs as I relish the sensation of his bare cock inside of me.

It's heaven.

"Have you been taking that birth control tea?" he

asks, pumping his hips to get his cock deeper into me.

I gasp a little with delightful surprise as his cock moves within me. "Every morning, like clockwork."

"Damn," he says, a hint of disappointment in his tone. "I want to put a baby in you."

I laugh. "Now's not really the best time."

"It's never a great time," he counters. "But at least we can practice."

With that, he shoves his hips upward, and I rest both hands on his rock hard abs as he throws me off balance. I moan as he bucks into me, his body rubbing against my clit with the movement.

He grabs my hips again and lifts me as he pulls slowly out. His cock rubs along my entrance, tantalizing, the sensation overwhelming me even as I try to remember that *I'm* the one who should be riding *him.*

I roll my hips, rubbing my clit against his hard body as I take control, and he chuckles as he releases his tight grip on my waist.

He's giving me control—for the moment.

If I know Jace, he'll take it back from me the second he gets lost in his lust—and I won't mind at *all.*

With a slow and graceful rhythm, I roll my hips,

taking the full length of him within me. As his cock slides once more into me, I shiver with utter delight.

In and out, in and out, I ride him, knowing he's only allowing this until he can't take it anymore.

Every twist of my hips, he permits.

Every moment I have control of his cock, he's allowing.

He growls with pleasure, his back arching as he begins to slowly thrust into me, matching my rhythm. He grabs my thighs, his thumbs pressing against my inner leg as he stretches me wider, giving himself better access.

As he slowly begins to take control again.

His grip tightens, and the next time I ride the full length of his cock, taking him in me, he pulls me roughly to the base of his dick. I moan with pleasure as he rides me from below, taking over, unable to hold back anymore.

His pace quickens, and my eyes flutter shut. Even though I'm on top, I'm absolutely not in control.

He bucks into me, harder with every thrust, his hands controlling every movement of my hips as he takes over. He growls with the effort, his body humming with lust as he takes me, as he makes me his over and over.

He said it himself—he wants to get me pregnant,

and he's going to practice as roughly as he can until the day I let him do it.

As he bucks into me, his hands gravitate to my hips. His thumb reaches down to my clit, rubbing against the tender bud with every thrust of his thick cock. I gasp with pleasure as he drives me closer and closer to my climax, always dangling it just out of reach.

I arch my head backward as he rides me hard from below, my hands wandering the length of my body as I lose myself in my bliss. I weave my fingers up my waist, over my breasts, and wrap my hands behind my neck as he takes me. I don't even try to hold back the moans of delight. I lean backward as he rides me harder and harder, arching my back so as to give him even more access to my pussy. I want him to fill every inch of me, to ride me until I can't even think anymore.

Deep within me, my orgasm builds. It's a tsunami of delight that crashes through me, and I moan as it hits me hard.

I ride the waves of pleasure as he continues to buck hard into me, riding me through my climax as I cum on his thick cock.

When my orgasm begins to slowly fade, I sigh with relief and delight and fall onto him. I catch myself, but only barely, and my palms rest against his hard abs, my arms shaking slightly from the exhaustion and adrenaline.

But Jace isn't done with me yet.

He rolls me onto my back in one fluid movement and pulls out of me. Breathing heavily, I look up at him, too blissed out to see more than blurry colors for a second or two, and all I can feel are his hands on my thighs as he readjusts me, scooting me up the bed. The mattress dips beneath his knees as he tugs me close, and I feel his cock against my sensitive entrance once again.

Slowly, almost delicately, he slides his cock into me. Every inch feels like another orgasm. Every second that passes takes me closer to another climax. He knows how over-stimulated I am right now, and he uses it to his advantage to drive me wild. I arch my back as he shoves the full length of his dick into me. When the base of his cock reaches my entrance, he rolls his hips, rubbing his body against my tender clit.

And gods above, it's heaven.

I grab fistfuls of the comforter on either side of me as he brings me to my knees, and I'm utterly lost in him. In his cock. In the masterful way he dominates me from every direction.

I expect him to take it slow, to be tender and delicate.

But I am oh, so delightfully wrong.

Jace pulls out of me and, with his hands pinning my hips to the bed, shoves the full length of his cock into me. He bucks into me, again and again with wild abandon, hammering his dick into me over and over. He rides me harder than he's ever ridden me in my life, and I can't even take it.

I wrap my legs around him as he screws me mercilessly, and I love every minute of it.

A second orgasm builds within me, and I dig my nails into his back as it takes me. I gasp, arching backward as I ride the second wave of my climax, and this time Jace cums with me. He growls with delight, and I feel a hot rush flood deep within me. I arch my back, taking all of him, spreading my legs to let him go as deep as possible.

Jace relaxes, leaning into me, burrowing his face into my neck as he continues to pump his cock into me. He presses the base of his dick against my entrance as the last surge of his orgasm fills me, and I hum with delight, biting my lip as I simply give into the sensation. I wrap my arms around him, holding him close.

He tenderly tucks my hair behind my ear and

kisses my neck. "When you are ready for a kid, I get dibs."

I laugh. "You mean you want my first kid to be yours?"

"Hell yeah I do," he says, rubbing his body against my over-stimulated clit once again.

I gasp with delight and pleasure as he sends ribbons of lust through me. My eyes flutter closed, and though his dick is still in me, I can feel it beginning to harden again already at the mere thought of knocking me up.

I can't help myself—I grin with wicked delight. The thought of my four men competing to see who can get me pregnant first is almost too fun.

Back when I was a Spectre, I never let myself dream of having kids before. Not really. Zurie always insisted I should once I hit twenty-five, but I knew why—she just wanted more soldiers, and every Spectre born into the organization becomes another fighter for the Ghost to control.

But now, I have a real family. Men who love me. Men who will protect any kids we have with their lives, and I have to confess—I like the idea.

As Jace kisses my neck, his hands weaving around my waist as he prepares for another round, I can't help but think of Kinsley. Of Diesel. Of all the people who want me and these precious men dead.

Before I bring any life into this world, I need to destroy the people who would dare hurt them.

And I *intend* to.

CHAPTER TWENTY-FOUR

I sit in the castle's dining room alone as the warm sun cascades through the windows behind me, casting shadows of the windowsill across the table. I lean back in my chair—a throne really—and practically chug a cup of the anti-pregnancy tea. This is the way I start every morning, nowadays, because these men keep me busy—and this is not the time for a baby.

No matter how fervently Jace may want one.

A familiar thunder of footsteps in the hallway catches my attention, and I instantly recognize Drew's gait. Moments later, he walks through the doorway mid-yawn, rubbing his eyes. There are dark lines beneath his gorgeous eyes, and his shoulders droop with exhaustion. He looks like he barely slept.

"What's going on, sleeping beauty?" I ask, grinning over my cup as I look up at him.

He grunts in answer, dragging out the chair across from me so that he can sit and grab one of the rolls on the table. He frowns while he shoves it in his face and grabs another.

Oh, good, Drew's feeling moody.

What a great start to the morning.

"Is the bug working?" I ask, trying to distract him from whatever is making him so damn grumpy.

"Fully functional," he says with a grunt. "Nothing interesting to report, yet. Mostly just Jett being an ass, so nothing new."

"Bummer."

"Is Jace up yet?" Drew clears his throat and briefly looks at me, like he's hiding something.

I frown. "Not yet. Why?"

"No reason." My fire dragon shrugs, trying to play it cool—and failing, which is unusual for him.

"Uh huh."

As far as I'm aware, everyone else is still asleep. I don't know why I've been getting up earlier and earlier, but something about being in Ashgrave just feels right, like sleep is a waste of time. Being here fills me with energy and life.

In my pocket, my phone buzzes, and I fish it out to see a cryptic message from Harper.

Come to the capital.

I frown, and in my periphery, Drew fishes out his own phone and looks at it as well. He pauses mid-bite, frowning as he stares at the screen, and his eyes glaze over as if he's processing what he just read and piecing things together.

"Text from Harper?" I ask, putting my phone away.

He nods, his cheek still protruding a little with the bread. Slowly, almost painfully, he puts his phone away, his gaze drifting out the window. His body tenses, and his breath quickens ever so slightly as he swallows.

I narrow my eyes in suspicion. "You know what this is about, don't you?"

His gaze darts toward me, and he tosses the half-eaten roll on the plate in front of him. He runs his hand through his hair and leans back in his seat. "I got some troubling news last night."

"What is it?" I ask, a sense of dread building in my chest. "Spit it out, Drew. It's obvious you know what's going on."

He just shakes his head. "I don't want to tell you, Rory—mainly because I really hope I'm wrong."

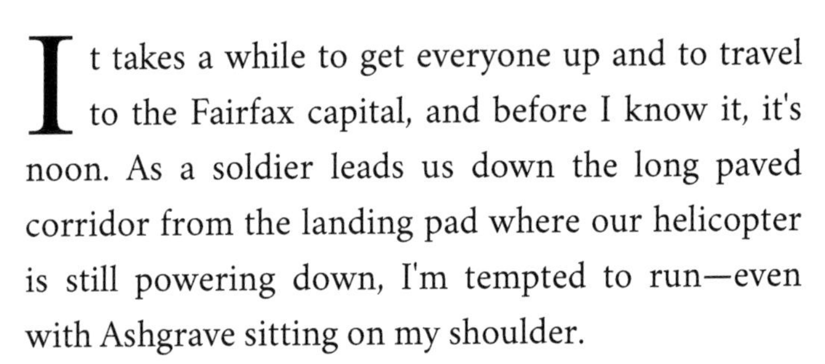

It takes a while to get everyone up and to travel to the Fairfax capital, and before I know it, it's noon. As a soldier leads us down the long paved corridor from the landing pad where our helicopter is still powering down, I'm tempted to run—even with Ashgrave sitting on my shoulder.

Seriously, I don't know how much longer I can let this dragon perch on my shoulder like this. He's damn *heavy,* even for my enhanced dragon strength.

Everything about this seems wrong, and I know that once we figure out what's happened, I'm not going to like it.

The possibilities are racing through my brain like wildfire. Kinsley made a move. Diesel has Irena. Maybe Harper found out who's making this crystal, though my money is still on Natasha. Maybe I'll walk in and find her tied up and gagged, ready for justice.

But something tells me I wouldn't feel this sense of dread if whatever was about to happen was good.

Behind me, my men keep pace easily, and no one

says a word. Everyone is on edge, and yet again, I look warily at Drew. He hasn't said another word since breakfast, and even though he's never exactly been one to share his feelings, this is a new level of reserved. Even Jace doesn't know what's going on, and as we walk silently through the Fairfax palace, he and I share a tense look.

The soldier who greeted us at the landing pad now leads us to a set of double doors guarded by two additional warriors who stand at attention. As we near, they salute and open the doors with a flourish to reveal an ornate throne set on a small platform in the middle. The expansive throne room is as large as a football field, with columns keeping up the ornate domed ceiling above us. Everything is silver and red, and the light in the glass dome overhead plays along the colorful walls like a symphony of light.

It's breathtaking, but it doesn't quell the dread burning in my chest.

As we enter, a secret door on the far wall opens. To my surprise, Russell walks in with his hands behind his back with a big scowl on his face. I expect a smile, or some other great gesture of welcome that puts me at ease, because that's Russell's way.

But when he sees us, his frown only deepens. When his eyes drift toward Drew, he tenses, his stride thrown off ever so slightly—like he's caught off guard.

That's it.

I have had absolutely enough of this.

"Tell me what the hell is going on," I snap, glaring at the new dojo master as he approaches us. "Right now."

"Usually, I would chide you for making demands of a Fairfax officer in the Fairfax capital," Russell says, smirking ever so slightly. "But given the situation, I understand why you're upset."

"Do you?" I ask, not bothering to mask my sarcasm. "Because you called me halfway across the world without so much as a hint of context, Drew won't talk, and none of us has any clue what the hell is going to happen next."

Drew snorts in annoyance, rolling his eyes as he looks away.

"You know, don't you?" Russell asks, his gaze drifting toward my fire dragon.

Even though the rest of us don't know what the hell is happening, that one little line seems to break Drew.

My fire dragon sighs in disappointment, his eyes bunching as if he had hoped against hope that maybe he was wrong, and everything Russell just said only confirmed for him that he was absolutely right.

It's not often that Drew doesn't want to be right.

"Russell," Jace snaps, taking a menacing step forward. "You have two seconds to give us some goddamn answers."

"Let me just show you," Russell says, gesturing for us to follow. With that, he walks back toward the door he entered through, and I assume we're supposed to follow.

With an aggravated huff, I glare briefly at Jace, but I ultimately indulge the Fairfax general. The five of us follow Russell silently, and the only sound through the stone as we take a spiral staircase down into the depths of the palace.

It's dark, the only light coming from the occasional sconce along the wall, and for a while, all I can hear is our footsteps echoing through the narrow space and the occasional drip of water.

But after a while, I start to hear a gentle hum. It's strange and distant, hard to place, and altogether foreign to me. Slowly, it begins to feel familiar. The hum becomes the distant roar of conversation of hundreds—if not *thousands*—of people talking over each other, and that sense of dread in my chest only gets stronger.

The staircase finally ends in an open door, and as we walk through, I squint as we're hit by light. The bright noon sun burns through dozens of narrow windows overhead as we walk into a massive cavern lit by the warm light of a thousand candles hanging from the ceiling in iron chandeliers. The world around us slopes downward, and hundreds of shifters fill the stands, each of them facing a center arena as massive as an airport hangar.

Beneath the Fairfax capital, there's an arena.

A freaking *arena.*

To my shock, there's a solitary man in the center of the ring. From this distance, I can't quite make out his face, but Drew instantly stiffens.

Russell leads us along a pathway that winds through the stands before hitting a staircase encased in stone. For a brief moment, the world around me disappears, and the thunder of voices becomes momentarily muffled by the rock.

As I race down the stairs toward the arena, I can't see a thing, but I think that's the point—to give us access to the ring itself without anyone seeing us until we're close.

The VIP entrance.

As we reach the bottom of the stairs, the world opens up once again, and I once more see the entirety of the arena—this time from the bottom floor. It's even more massive than I thought.

Now that I'm closer, however, I can clearly see the man in the ring.

It's Milo Darrington, clapped in chains—and staring us down.

Beside me, Jace, Levi, and Tucker instantly freeze, and I can barely breathe. Ashgrave's mechanical head darts between us, silently picking up on our alarm, but he's never met Milo before.

He doesn't know how terrible this is.

"What the *fuck* are you thinking?" Jace snaps, glaring at Russell.

"We're thinking we want revenge, Jace," Russell snaps back, turning on his heel to glare at the former dojo master. "And I think you want it, too."

In that moment, Jace freezes. He's furious, his body nearly shaking with rage as his hands ball into fists, but his gaze darts once again to the arena. Jace's hatred and thirst for revenge battle with his ache to do the right thing and not make an enemy of the Darringtons.

And quite frankly, I'm not sure which side is going to win.

"Welcome, Fairfax dragons," Harper's voice booms through the air. "It would seem our guests of honor have arrived, and that means we can finally begin!"

Instantly, a huge roar builds in the audience as everyone hollers in excitement. It sounds more like a sports match than an execution, but this is a death sentence.

Milo isn't Drew.

Milo isn't the kind of fighter who can survive a duel to the death—and that's Fairfax law. Important matters are settled with a duel, and the options are simple—win, concede, or die.

And something tells me Milo won't simply surrender. He's a coward, but he's also a Darrington.

Their pride makes them do stupid things.

It's one of the reasons Drew protected his brother for so long. It's one of the reasons Drew let everyone believe that he was the cause of their pain and suffering. That *he* killed Jace's brother when in fact it was Milo.

"That's why Harper left," I say, it all suddenly coming together for me. "When we told her we were going to the Darringtons, she was preparing."

I glare accusingly at Russell who squares his shoulders and silently watches me, confirming my suspicions without so much as a word.

They used our visit as a distraction to kidnap Milo from his own damn home.

I close my eyes, shaking my head as a wave of betrayal rocks through me. The Fairfax dragons are good and just most of the time, but when they feel wronged, they want revenge, and they'll do terrible things to get it.

"Welcome to the revenge ring," Harper announces again, and I scan the world around me as I try to find her. "For years, we thought wrongly that Drew Darrington killed Garrett Goodwin, the brother of our former dojo master and a legend among our warriors. We have had to live with that pain for years, but now we know the truth. Drew was merely covering for his cowardly brother Milo, and now all with a grievance against this man can have their vengeance."

Around us, the soldiers and dragons filling the stands roar yet again with excitement. They came to see blood, and damn it all, I know they're going to get it.

"I knew this would happen," Drew says, rubbing his eyes. "I just didn't want it to."

"Drew are you okay?" I ask softly, knowing he couldn't possibly be all right but not really sure what else I can say or do in the situation to make it better.

To no one's surprise, he doesn't answer, and I can't blame him.

I quickly scan the faces of my men, trying to figure out what we can do, but we're all shattered and caught off guard.

Levi's eyes are wide as he stares at the arena, and as I look at him, our eyes meet. He just shakes his head in shock. This is too severe. It's too much, and even he doesn't know how to stop this.

I look at Tucker, who has his hand on the gun at his waist, but he knows better than to draw it here. This isn't our domain, and there's not a damn thing we can do to fix this.

But Jace—Jace looks numb.

In an instant, as he glares at Milo, all of his hatred bubbles to the surface. I recognize that expression. It's the embodiment of all the rage he took out on Drew before he knew the truth, and now I see all of that hatred, all of that anger, come back in a rush.

None of it has healed.

All he did was forgive *Drew*. The underlying rage, the underlying pain of losing his brother—that never went away.

"We begin as it ended," Harper's voice announces over the stands. "As is custom, he with the greatest grievance goes in first. He who has the most at stake and the most to heal has the first opportunity to fight."

Around us, the Fairfax dragons roar in anticipation because they already know who's going to be sent in.

"Jace Goodwin," Harper announces. "You may enter."

Russell claps Jace on the back, silently comforting his friend and mentor. Jace squares his shoulders, lifting his chin as he glares at Milo in the center of the ring.

To his credit, Milo doesn't look afraid. He simply stands there with chains around his wrists and ankles, watching us, waiting to see what we'll do.

Jace takes a step toward the ring.

I grab his wrist. "Jace, what are you—"

"I need to do this," he interrupts, his intense and stormy gaze snaring me.

"You really don't," I tell him, trying to talk some sense into him.

Into *all* of them.

But he's lost. He's lost in that hatred. Lost in that rage. There's not a damn thing I can do to stop this.

I've never felt this powerless before.

My mate twists his hand out of mine and walks

again toward the ring. I want to stop him, but I'm not sure how.

Drew grabs Jace's shoulder and spins him around —and I wonder if Drew is going to do it for me.

"Don't get in my way," Jace seethes before Drew can say a word. "If you try, I will break you."

Drew squares his shoulders, glaring at Jace, at one of the few men who has ever gone head-to-head with him and come out on top.

Everyone nearby holds their breath—there's no telling what will happen next.

These are two of the most powerful dragons in the world, and if they fought, they would decimate this entire arena. Hell, their battle over me nearly destroyed the dojo—and *that* ended *well*.

They glare at each other, silently demanding the other step down. I'm not sure how it happened, but this somehow managed to get *worse*.

I always wondered if Drew still considered Milo to be his brother with all the horrible things Milo has done. It's hard to think of him as Drew's blood, much less worthy of his protection. He's tried to capture me, blackmail Drew, and kill us all at some point or another.

I can't lie, a bit of me feels gutted that Drew would still defend a man like that.

"I'm not going to stop you," Drew says quietly. "I just want to go in first."

"What?" Jace frowns, his brows knit in confusion, as he—and all of us, really—is caught entirely off-guard.

"I need this, Jace," Drew says. "I need closure just as much as you do, and if you go in first, I may never get the chance."

Oh, shit.

Jace is tense, and it looks for all the world like they might start throwing punches at any moment. To my surprise, however, he simply nods toward the ring. "Make it quick, Drew."

Oh, *gods*.

Drew rolls his shoulders out and walks toward the ring, shooting one last look back at me before he steps into the arena and faces his brother, possibly for the last time.

I don't know what's going to happen, but I do know this much—this is going to end in blood.

And a *lot* of it.

CHAPTER TWENTY-FIVE

As Drew walks into the arena to thunderous applause and roars, Russell ushers me over to another small staircase that leads to an isolated cluster of seats surrounded on all sides by stone walls.

I figure these are the box seats reserved for those who are granted the best view—and possibly an audience in the ring itself.

I sit in the center seat, my ass perched on the edge of the cushion as I lean forward, still in a state of shock about everything I'm seeing.

It's all too much.

Too sudden.

Too damn *crazy*.

Jace flops into the seat beside me, his legs spread

as he slumps in the seat. His hand rubs the stubble on his jaw as he glares into the ring. He doesn't say a word, and even though I'm tempted to dig into him, to lecture him on the insanity of all of this, I don't bother.

He won't hear it.

None of them will.

For once in my life, I truly cannot stop this—at least not yet.

If I'm going to make any of them see reason, I have to be clever. I have to wait for the opportune moment, and I need to be painfully careful.

Russell sits on my other side, but he leaves an empty seat between us. Levi tries to sit in it, but Russell shakes his head. "That's reserved for Harper."

"Oh, good, she will be joining us?" I ask sarcastically.

Because I'm ready to rip her a new asshole. This is insanity, and she shouldn't allow it.

"Yes, actually," Harper says from behind me.

I look over my shoulder to find her walking up the steps, her intense gaze trained on me as she takes the seat Russell reserved for her. We look out over the arena as two soldiers unshackle Milo, shoving him forward onto his hands and knees before Drew.

The crowd eats it up.

"What the hell are you thinking?" I snap, glaring at her.

She watches me, her eyes narrowing slightly at my audacity as she leans back in her seat, setting her fingertips against each other as she crosses one leg over the other. "I'm thinking I'm finally going to get revenge, Rory."

"That's a Darrington," I say, gesturing toward the ring.

Technically, there are two, but I'm only worried about one of them. And even though he's an asshole that's tried to kidnap me and do who knows what else in the past, I feel like I'm the only one thinking about the ramifications of killing the current heir to the Darrington line.

I hate him, sure.

That doesn't mean letting him die is what's best for any of us.

"I think it's time the Darringtons realized they're not above the law anymore," Harper says, her soft eyes wandering over the arena. "I won't lie to you, Rory. All those years I thought it was Drew, I kept looking for ways to get him down here. I knew better, though, than to try. He really is above the law. But Milo..." she smirks. "He's *not*."

Russell taps the half-wall that separates our seats

from the short gap between us and the arena. As his fingers press against the stone, a hidden panel opens, revealing a series of buttons and knobs—a little control panel. He pushes a little red button, and instantly, the roar of the crowd is almost entirely canceled out.

And all I hear is Drew's voice.

"…and you *deserve* this," he snaps as he circles Milo. "You *asshole.*"

A microphone.

In the ring.

Hell, there's probably a series of them embedded in the arena, and we've just been granted an audience. I doubt Milo and Drew even know we're listening in.

"Are you seriously going to let them do this to me?" Milo says, glaring at his brother as he stands. "You're going to let them kill me?"

"You killed Garrett," Drew says, shrugging lazily even though I know he's putting on a show.

This burns him up. Eats away at him. That's why he didn't sleep last night.

But he's not going to let Milo know that.

I wanted desperately for Drew to have his family back. To help him heal an old wound. To have his father *and* his brother once again.

But tonight, he might lose both.

"Why should I save your ass, Milo?" Drew asks, tilting his head as he glares at the man. "For years, I've been your bodyguard, the one who shoulders the blame and the responsibility when you're not man enough to take it."

"Shut your damn mouth," Milo snaps, his hand balling into a fist. His body hums, and I wonder if he's going to shift before they can actually talk through this.

The crowd roars around them, and I figure Milo and Drew assume they can't be heard. They must assume this is a private conversation, and that only makes this harder to watch.

For once, both of them are baring their souls—this is the *real* them, the bits of themselves they don't share all too often.

Neither man knows anyone else can hear him.

"I won't be quiet anymore." Drew shakes his head. "You're here because you deserve to be here, and whatever happens today, you're on your own. I came in here to tell you that. Don't do anything stupid thinking I'm going to rush in and save your ass at the last minute." Drew pauses, glaring at his brother as he crosses his arms, his thick biceps bulging. "Because I won't."

With that, the color drains from Milo's face. He goes stiff and still. Deep down, Milo must have figured Drew would save the day yet again.

Because Drew always has, over and over, for most of Milo's life. Drew has stepped in to fix what his brother breaks.

And Drew is officially done.

"They're going to kill me, Drew," Milo says quietly, horrified as he gestures toward Harper. "You're just going to let them?"

"For once in your damn life, think about how you got here instead of what you think people owe you," Drew snaps, grabbing Milo's collar and lifting the fire dragon off his feet. "Think about what you did to deserve to be in this room right now. Who *you* killed. Who you treated as disposable. Who you threatened, marginalized, and minimized. Think about all the ways you failed yourself instead of what you're entitled to, you arrogant *asshole*."

With that, Drew throws Milo across the ring. Milo tumbles, sliding the last few feet as he struggles to regain his composure. He teeters but gets his balance and charges Drew.

"You're my *brother*," Milo seethes as he throws a punch at Drew's face. "You *do* owe me. We're blood, you bastard!"

Drew catches Milo's hand in his fist and twists, and I hear the resounding crack of a broken bone as Milo falls to the ground.

"I don't owe you shit," Drew says, glaring down at the man on the ground.

Milo sucks in air between his teeth, flexing his fingers as his misshapen hand begins to already correct itself.

That's the Darrington bloodline in full effect—advanced healing beyond that of a normal dragon, incredible strength that trumps all others, and immense power that burns in their very blood.

That's Drew's birthright—and, unfortunately, also Milo's.

Milo pushes himself to his feet and shakes out his hand, and I wonder how long it takes before the pain goes away. Despite the chaos of everything going on, I can't help but feel a little envious.

Instant healing like that must be absolutely amazing.

"And for the record, you're not my brother." Drew spits on the ground, as if the mere thought is disgusting. "Those men up there?" Drew adds, pointing toward the box. Toward Jace. Toward Levi. Toward Tucker. "Those men are more brothers than you'll ever be."

"Aw, shucks," Tucker says, and I look over my shoulder as he waves his hand flirtatiously at Drew.

Drew doesn't seem to notice, however, as he's entirely focused on Milo. "I can't believe I saved your sorry ass for so long. I can't believe I thought you were family. I can't believe I thought what we had—what Jett forced us to be—was worth defending. You don't deserve my protection just because we were born into the same family, Milo. Those men up there deserve my protection because they *earned* it." He points again at us, and I can't fight the swell of pride that blooms within me.

"You traitorous coward," Milo says, seething as he circles Drew. "When Father finds out about this—"

"You think he will?" Drew interrupts, lifting his chin as if daring Milo to disagree. "You think anyone's going to know what happened to you? You think Jett is going to save you just because I won't?"

Milo growls in anger and frustration. Something in him snaps, and he charges, cocking his fist to throw a devastating blow.

He doesn't get the chance.

Like lightning, Drew punches him hard in the face. With that single hit, Milo crumples to the ground. He tries to push himself up, but he falls again and again, his body teetering as he tries to reorient himself after such a hearty attack.

"If you survive this," Drew says quietly, "if you make it out of here alive, I hope you let it change you. I hope it breaks you, and I hope it makes you see everything you've done wrong. Once you're out of here, I want you to know in no uncertain terms that I will never save your ass again."

With that, Drew turns his back on his brother—well, former brother—as the man rests on his forearms and knees, still trying to push himself to his feet. The guards step aside as Drew barrels out of the ring.

"Finally," Jace says, jumping to his feet.

"Jace, wait," I say, grabbing his hand.

I want him to see reason, but I don't know if it's possible at this point.

Instead of answering, he grabs both sides of my face and kisses me fiercely. It's rough and passionate, raw and dominating, and it silences me completely—mostly because it catches me so off guard.

He pulls away, his nose brushing mine as his stormy gaze snares me. "You can't stop this."

The kiss steals the breath from my lungs, and try as I might, I can't seem to speak. His eyes dart between mine for a few moments before he turns his back on me and jogs down the stairs toward the arena.

I feel like the whole damn world has gone insane, and I rub my temples in aggravation. Harper and Russell just watch me, as if they're waiting to see what I'm going to do.

They're just waiting to see if they need to stop me.

The fact is this is not my domain. I have no control over anything that happens here. All I can do is ask the people around me to see reason, and I have to understand that they may very well not.

It's driving me crazy.

I stand at the top of the stairs as Drew and Jace pass each other. Drew sets his hand on Jace's shoulder, and Jace nods briefly to the fire dragon. The former enemies truly have become brothers, and despite the chaos around us, it's a beautiful thing to witness, to know for certain after all of the trauma and bloodshed we've gone through together, we really are a family.

I just wish Drew didn't have to watch his old family die in the process.

Drew storms down the path that leads past the stairs to our little box seats, and as he blares past me, it becomes suddenly clear that he has no intention of joining us.

"Drew, where are you—"

"Rory," he interrupts, his dark gaze darting toward me as he pauses at the base of the steps. "I love you more than life itself, but right now I need to be alone."

I sigh, and it's the final surrender to the chaos around me.

I can't stop Drew.

I can't stop Jace.

And I may not even be able to stop Harper.

It's agonizing.

I simply nod, and he sighs with relief as he continues on his path out of the arena. I don't know where he's going, but I do know that I can't follow him. That I shouldn't and don't want to.

With a discouraged groan, I lean against the edge of the box seats, crossing my arms as I stare out over the arena.

The crowd roars as Jace enters, and Milo finally gets to his feet. He teeters slightly, his eyes narrowing on Jace as the man enters, and his face falls.

In that moment, I watch Milo shatter.

Jace is a master fighter. A warrior. And in all the

time since Milo killed Garrett, Jace has been training, pushing himself, honing his skills.

He's a greater fighter than the last time they faced each other—far superior to anything Milo could even hope to be.

Milo knows what's coming for him. He has suddenly realized the most probable outcome for today. He knows he's probably going to die in this ring, and truth be told, I don't want to care. Milo really is a coward. He's hidden behind Drew for so long that he's forgotten how to fight. He's forgotten how to lead. He treats the people around him as disposable, and yes, he probably deserves this fate.

But the world isn't fair.

Sooner or later, the Darringtons will find out what happened.

Sooner or later, this feud between the Darringtons and the Fairfax will only escalate until one side forgives the other—or *destroys* them.

And I can't help but feel like I'm the one who's supposed to help them heal this grudge. It started long before I entered the picture, but it's starting to seem like I'm the only one who can stop it.

I just don't know how.

"Jace," Milo says as the man enters. "Have mercy."

"Like you had mercy for Garrett?" Jace counters,

wrinkling his nose in disgust as he circles the Darrington in the center of the ring. "Like you've shown mercy every time you tried to kidnap Rory? Every time you tried to take my mate from me?"

"I was just doing what my father told me to."

"Shut your mouth," Jace snaps. "I can't even stand the sound of your voice."

I rub the back of my neck, dread burning in my chest as I watch this.

"Are you going to kill me?" Milo asks, squaring his shoulders like he's bracing himself for the inevitable.

"I sure as hell want to," Jace says, standing across from him. "Tell me why I shouldn't."

"Because Jett will come for you," Milo says, gesturing toward one of the windows high above us. "He'll figure this out. He'll hunt you down, and he'll gut you."

"You really think he'll manage?" Jace says, smirking. "I'm a thunderbird. Drew has already said he disowns you, and let's be honest, Milo," Jace adds with a quick glance toward me. "You've seen what Rory can do. You've seen what she is. You really think your father can win against *that*?"

To his credit, Milo doesn't answer. He gulps hard and looks at me, and I can see the fear deep in his bones. He's terrified, but not just of the situation.

He's terrified of me.

And he knows that no help is coming. He knows that for the first time, he's entirely on his own, and I think this is far more sobering than Harper even intended this experience to be for him.

Harper wanted revenge, but to Milo, this is a moment of clarity, the sort of moment where life changes and all illusion is stripped away. Where only the truth remains. Where he realizes he's not as strong as he thinks he is.

Now that he's here, with the money and obedient soldiers stripped away from him, he realizes he's just a shifter—and not even an entirely powerful one either.

I suspect Milo hasn't been at the mercy of anyone but Drew or his father before, and he doesn't know the world of hurt that's about to break over his head.

"That's what I thought," Jace says, shaking out his shoulders. "Now try to take this like a man."

With that, Jace's body hums as he shifts, letting his beautiful black dragon take over. Occasional ribbons of blue light shimmy across his stunning scales as his magic burns within him.

Apparently taking Jace's warning to heart, Milo

shifts as well. Within seconds, the red dragon that flew toward me and Drew on that mountaintop what seems like ages ago appears in the ring before me. The two dragons circle each other, snarling, and it's clear that Milo has been backed into a corner. He knows he probably won't win today, but he's not going to take this laying down.

Jace attacks, snarling as he digs his claws into Milo's side. Milo roars in pain, batting Jace away with his tail. But Jace takes the hit like a champ, barely flinching as the spiky tail crashes against his back, drawing blood.

The two dragons are locked in a deadly struggle, snarling us they bite each other. Blood stains the arena floor, but neither man backs down.

It's almost too much to even watch—and, considering what I've endured in the past, that's saying something.

I've seen dragons duel before time and time again. I've watched them kill each other, watched them burn to ash, watched them freeze each other and shatter the icy blocks of what was once a shifter.

But this—this feels too gruesome.

This is a blood match, and I finally understand what the point of the revenge ring really is. This is the Fairfax place of healing. As much as I love the

Fairfax, they don't entirely know how to work through their feelings. By putting the person they hate in an arena and dueling, there are only two options.

Kill the person or forgive them. And, let's be real —I figure that after you've beaten the shit out of someone, it's probably a little easier to forgive them.

Provided they don't take a grudge of their own out of the ring once you do.

I feel like I'm the only one who sees this as the cycle it really is—an endless back-and-forth of revenge that's never satiated, and that's never healed.

As the two dragons snarl in the ring, taking a quick breather as they study each other for weaknesses, I once again look at Harper.

She ignores me completely.

Harper is entirely focused on the arena, leaning forward in her seat as if she's thirsty to get in there herself.

I figure she probably is.

Beside her, Russell leans his head on one fist, and his eyes briefly dart toward me. We share a tense glance, and I realize that he doesn't want to do this either. He probably cautioned Harper against this, but she is the Boss, and she makes the decisions here. He sighs in defeat, locked between duty and obligation and shakes his head in disappointment.

I look at Levi and Tucker, but they're both already watching me, and I can tell they're waiting. They're waiting for me to act. They're waiting for me to stop this.

I need to be clever, and I need to come up with something soon.

In the ring, Jace digs his claws into Milo's hide and flies into the air. Milo twists and growls, spewing fire every which way, but Jace gracefully darts out of the line of attack each time a blaze heads toward his face or wing. He's too fast, too masterful a flyer and fighter to lose against someone like Milo.

When Jace reaches the ceiling, he drags his talons through one of Milo's wings—and that's brutal. It disarms your opponent, rendering them unable to fly. Milo roars in pain, and before the agonizing sound even finishes, Jace drops him.

Milo plummets to the ground, his wing tattered and unable to catch the air. Instead of recovering, he hits the ground hard. A crater forms, and dust billows into the ring.

As the dust slowly settles, Milo is in the center of the crater, breathing heavily, dripping with blood as he tries to claw his way out. He slowly drags himself out of the hole as Jace lands on the other side of it, snarling.

This is it—the final blow or the moment of forgiveness.

Jace roars, stretching his wings wide as he takes a few menacing steps forward, and I recognize that movement. It was what he did when he demanded that Guy Durand submit to him.

It's a command for surrender or death, and whatever Milo does next will decide his fate.

It's an act of kindness really, one I wasn't expecting. I think, to Jace, this isn't really worth it. He wants his revenge, but he's so disgusted by Milo he can't even bring himself to kill the man.

Milo hesitates, breathing heavily, his wing tattered and destroyed. It's probably only a matter of time before it heals, but I figure that's something that will leave a grisly scar—something he'll remember for the rest of his life.

However long that ends up being.

Milo looks around the arena as the crowd jeers at him, and I can see his pride battling with his sense of self-preservation.

If it were Jett, I suspect his pride would win.

But Milo is *not* his father.

Ultimately, Milo bows his head, setting it against

the floor as he closes his eyes and surrenders to Jace.

Jace roars, the ear-splitting sound shaking the very ground as he accepts—perhaps begrudgingly—Milo's surrender. Jace shifts into his human form, glaring at Milo, and that's it.

The fight is done.

Jace exits on the opposite side of the arena from me, and I catch my mate's expression as he shoots one more disgusted glare at the Darrington dragon, still bowing in defeat in the arena.

Jace won. Milo surrendered.

But nothing was healed—and nothing will change.

CHAPTER TWENTY-SIX

With the crowd around me roaring for blood and a beaten Darrington dragon heaving in the middle of the arena, Harper stands.

Apparently, she gets to go next.

My breath catches in my throat as she glares at the arena, and I get the feeling that she wants to end this once and for all. Jace forgiving Milo wasn't enough for her. It wasn't enough for any of the Fairfax dragons around me, judging by the blood-thirsty screams of the crowd.

They came here to see death, and they haven't gotten what they wanted.

Judging from the expression on her face, it seems as though Harper intends to give it to them.

She walks briskly toward the arena, and I set my

hand on her shoulder, stopping her mid-stride as I block her way through to the stairs. She glares at me, and I hold her eye, the two of us locked in a silent struggle, each daring the other to speak first.

Behind her, Russell, Levi, and Tucker watch us breathlessly, each of them on the edge of their seats, ready to interject at a moment's notice.

"This is not a good idea, Harper," I say quietly, watching her intently. My body is rigid as I prepare for the worst.

"You think this is enough?" she asks, her eyes narrowing as she dares me to disagree. "You think that Milo is going to walk out of here a changed man? Jace didn't forgive him, Rory. You saw that. He was just too disgusted to continue, too revolted that Milo surrendered when he should have fought to the death. He gave Milo an out that only a coward would take."

"And you think killing him is any better?" I counter.

"If he survives today, he's going to rule the Darringtons," she says. "Drew has been disowned. He's never going to take over, and Milo has to realize that the world won't pander to him without his baby brother around as his enforcer."

"You and I both know that if you go into that ring, Milo is going to die," I snap.

"And why do you care?" she says, batting my hand aside as she glares at me. "He's tried to kill your men and kidnap you. Why do you give a shit if he lives?"

"I don't want to," I confess. "I despise him, but I feel like I'm the only one who's thinking about the ramifications of what happens if you do kill him. I don't think you've thought this through. You think Jett's never going to figure this out?" I ask, gesturing toward the arena. "You think that nothing's going to happen after you get your revenge? You think this is just the end? This is only going to get worse."

"Rory," she says quietly, her voice deadly and dark as she takes a menacing step toward me.

I lift my chin defiantly, daring her to push me out of the way—because if she does, the fight won't be in the arena.

It'll be right here.

"Rory," she says again, shaking her head. "I love you like the sister I never had, but if you ever question me like this in my own home again, I will be forced to beat your ass." She narrows her eyes in warning. "You're not in charge here. This is not your domain, and I refuse to allow you to doubt me. Jace's brother was like a brother to *me*, too. He and Jace believed in me when no one else did, Rory." She sets her hands on my shoulders, her intense gaze more riveting than ever. "And that bastard killed him over a fucking trade deal. I don't give a shit about policy. I don't give a shit about Jett. The Darringtons took something from me, and I need *revenge*."

Though her grip on my shoulders is painful and I can feel her rage bubbling through her, I tenderly set my hands on her shoulders, mirroring her movement. I tilt my brow slightly upward, hoping she can see beyond her hate for just a moment. "No amount of blood is ever going to solve this pain."

She grits her teeth, shaking her head, and I know what's going through her mind right now. She's so close to revenge, so close to feeling a little bit better about all of the loss and all of the rage.

In her mind, she's inches from closure, and I'm the only thing in her way.

I need a compromise, and I need to come up with it fast.

"Let me go in first," I say quietly.

Her eyes dart toward me, narrowing in suspicion.

"If I can give you closure, will you stop this fight?" I ask.

Her nose crinkles in disdain, and she takes a step

back, knocking my hands off her shoulders as she glares at me. "You want me to give up my one chance of revenge? The one chance I will ever have?"

"Yes," I say softly, trying my best to remain calm even though all I want to do is shake some sense into her.

She scoffs, furious. "And what will you give me?"

Gods above, she is *not* thinking straight.

I've never seen her like this before.

Harper is in Boss Mode and ready to beat someone to shit. She's not going to be happy until she gets that, and whatever price she asks of me is going to be artificially inflated because I'm taking away something she desperately wants.

Fine.

"I'm giving you a chance to not go to war with the Darringtons," I say, gesturing toward the arena. "And it will make the Fairfax happy."

"Darringtons and war go hand-in-hand," she snaps. "That's not enough."

"Then what is?" I ask, shrugging in frustration.

Harper crosses her arms, giving me a brief glance over as she considers my question. She goes suddenly still, and a brief spark flares in her eyes as something clicks for her.

Oh, man, I do *not* like that look.

"I want you to talk to the Palarne again," she says, lifting her chin as she names her price. "It's a fair trade."

The crowd around us roars louder, impatient and thirsty for blood as I stopped their Boss from finishing what they all want to see. I'm running out of time, and I don't like this deal at all.

But I'm trapped between a rock and a hard place.

None of them can think straight, not when they're this close to the vengeance they've been thirsty for, and they're not going to think straight until all of this is over.

By then, it'll be too late, and no one will admit they were wrong.

It pisses me off that in her rage, Harper is asking me to do something that could very well put me in danger, but I know she asked for it because she thought I would say no.

To save my men, to save Harper, and to save the Fairfax dragons, though, I'll do it anyway.

"Fine," I say.

One of her brows briefly twitches in surprise. It proves she was not expecting me to agree, but she quickly dons her mask again, and I once more can't read her expression.

"Then show me what you've got," she says with a nod toward the arena.

I square my shoulders, jogging down the steps on my way toward the ring. The soldiers along the edge part for me as I walk in, and the crowd around me roars with bloodlust.

They want to see a Darrington die, and I wonder what they're going to do when I refuse to give it to them.

With my first steps into the ring, I notice Jace and Drew enter on the opposite side of the arena from the box seats. Jace's bare chest is beautiful and distracting, and he wears only a loose pair of shorts as he and Drew talk in hushed tones.

In the same moment, however, they both look up —and our eyes meet.

Drew freezes midstride. Jace's mouth parts, and the two men stare at me in horror as the crowd cheers around me.

By now, they've both had time to calm down. They know what's at stake, and from the look on their faces, they want me out of the ring.

They don't want their woman to start a war, but I know what I'm doing.

Mostly.

In the center of the ring, beside the crater he

carved into the floor, Milo struggles to breathe. He has barely moved since his fight with Jace, and he looks absolutely beaten. Bruised.

Broken.

As I walk toward him, his eyes widen with fear. His gaze darts around the arena and back to me. He struggles to get to his feet, struggles to prepare for the next fight, like it came too soon.

This man does not want to accept his fate, even though he knows what's coming for him.

If he does what I tell him, maybe he won't have to die today, but the Darringtons are stubborn and prideful.

I want to make this work. I want to do what's best for the world, not just a momentary lapse of bloodlust-fueled judgment.

But I'm not entirely sure how to make this right.

All I can do is try.

CHAPTER TWENTY-SEVEN

As I look at Milo, he growls, black smoke shooting from his nose as he dares me to attack. To his credit, he's at least trying to go down fighting, and he most certainly has not accepted death today even if he did surrender to Jace. I can see the war raging in his eyes between pride and his wounded ego, and just like the rest of them, he's not thinking straight.

They backed him into a corner, and he's just trying to figure a way out.

Everyone in this room knows I can shift. I could easily turn into a dragon now, and my secret would stay safe for another day. But that would go against what I'm trying to do right now.

Milo is afraid of me because he knows I could

kill him. Doing so would give the Fairfax what they want, but I think I know what they actually need.

It's so simple, and yet so hard to ask for—much less give.

And even though Milo is a wounded prisoner trapped in a bloody arena, he has to be the one to give it to them.

He snarls threateningly, still staring at me, fire burning in this throat as he prepares for battle. His eyes scan me with uncertainty, like he doesn't know why I haven't shifted yet.

Like he wonders what I'm up to. What my game is. He wants to know how I'm trying to mess with his head.

I set my hand out, my palm flat as I wait for him to press his nose against it.

Just as Isaac Palarne has almost always done, I wait for an audience, politely asking to speak when anyone else would have simply opened a connection.

He snorts, a huff of black smoke trailing into the air as he takes a wary step back, still looking for the trick. For the trap.

But there isn't one.

He snarls a threatening warning, and his intention is clear—if I try anything, he'll bite my hand off.

I simply roll my eyes. "I just want to talk, you idiot."

He growls again but more softly this time and presses his nose against my palm. In an instant, our connection opens, and there are a couple of reasons I did it this way.

For starters, it's an olive branch. While I could have told him to just shift down and have a conversation, right now our minds are open to each other. It's a sign of trust, however little of it I have for him.

But also, I want the truth, and through the connection, I will be able to more easily feel a lie.

So much rides on this conversation, and it strikes me as odd that only he and I will hear it.

Are you ready for this to end? I ask before he can say anything.

He hesitates, his chest still heaving. He gently tilts his head, looking at his wounded wing without breaking the connection.

Yes, he finally says.

Will you do what I tell you, even if it's difficult? I narrow my eyes, trying to drive home the point. *Even if it wounds your pride?*

He narrows his eyes in suspicion as the crowd jeers around us, demanding blood and battle.

Yes.

And there's no hint of a lie.

He's ready.

Do you know what to do? I ask, quirking one eyebrow, giving him a chance to step up and do what's right before I have to make it obvious.

He tilts his head slightly, obviously confused, and I groan in annoyance at these prideful dragons.

"Apologize," I say out loud, breaking the connection as I take a step back.

He snarls in irritation, shaking his head slightly, like he can't possibly do that.

I just glare at him as the crowd cheers around me.

His gaze wanders the stands around us at the hundreds, if not thousands, of Fairfax dragon shifters who want his head on a spike. He spins slightly as he studies the arena stands around him, his wounded wing dragging along the floor as the webbing slowly knits itself together again, his super-fast healing working at maximum capacity to mend him after his devastating battle with Jace.

As he finishes his circle, he looks at me again. I cross my arms, nodding to the box behind me where Harper is no doubt sitting on the edge of her seat, just waiting for her chance to get into this ring. I look over my shoulder to find her leaning against the half-wall that divides the box seats from the world around, and she glares at Milo as if there's no one else in the arena.

As if she's chomping at the bit for the chance to rip his head off.

And that's when I see it.

That's the moment Milo snaps.

His body hums as he shifts down to a human form, and he falls to his hands and knees, his head hung as he tries his best to stand.

I don't help him. This is something he needs to do for himself, and all I did was stand between him and the firing squad.

But I won't be here for very long, and if he screws this up, I'll step aside.

At this point, it all comes down to him.

He sucks in a deep breath as he stands, tilting his head back as he surveys the world around him—at all the dragons who want him dead. It's a sobering moment to watch him realize how many people hate him for a mistake he made so long ago, but it was a mistake he never accepted as his to bear. It was a mistake he never repented for. There was never an apology. Never an attempt to make things right.

This, right now, is his one and only chance.

He looks over his shoulder at Drew, who stands

at the edge of the arena with his arms crossed. Jace stands at his side, and the two of them glare daggers at Milo. It's like they're both waiting for another chance to get into the arena, even though both know that will never happen.

"I'm sorry," Milo says. Every syllable of the simple phrase seems to gut him, like he's never said those words before and they're foreign on his tongue.

"Shut up, all of you!" Harper shouts, her voice carrying through the arena stands. "Be quiet for a minute, and let him speak!"

Instantly, the crowd goes silent. All eyes are on Milo, who stands naked before them—both literally and figuratively.

"I failed you," he says, his voice booming through the silent arena. "I was selfish. I was just trying to prove my father right, trying to make him see that I deserved to be his heir instead of…"

Milo trails off, looking over his shoulder yet again at Drew, and he doesn't finish the sentence. He shakes his head in disappointment, rubbing his eyes with one hand as he sets the other on his hips.

"I thought I could do anything," he confesses. "I thought I could get away with anything. My whole life, that's what I was told, and I lived as if it were true. I didn't care who I hurt, and I didn't care whose lives I destroyed. I treated other people as disposable." He hesitates, looking back at Harper. "I failed all of you, and I failed myself."

As Milo finishes speaking, the room is still eerily quiet. I scan the stands as I try to figure out if they're going to forgive him.

If *Harper* is going to forgive him.

If Jace and Drew can put aside their disgust and disdain for this man long enough to let there be a real truce.

Long enough for there to be real peace.

I look at them. At my men. At Drew with his arms crossed as he glares at Milo, shaking his head slightly even as the hatred and disgust fade from his expression. At Jace, who runs a hand through his hair as he glares at the man he's hated for so long—but he relaxes. He lets go.

And then I look at Harper.

She still leans against the half wall, glaring at Milo with the full fury of the sun. The longer she stares at him, the longer there's silence, the more her shoulders begin to relax. With a slow and steady sigh, she hangs her head, and it seems like all of a sudden, she's lighter. Calmer.

And that's when I know. They forgave.

They *truly* forgave.

"I pardon you," Harper says, her voice booming through the arena. "I pardon you for the hurt and the damage you have caused us, and I think today you have paid us back in full. I consider your debt repaid, and I want you the hell out of my kingdom."

"Thank you," Milo says, his expression tense.

I expected him to grovel, and I have to admit, he's earned a bit of respect for the fact that he didn't. He simply spoke his truth and waited for judgment—that takes guts.

Harper turns her back to him without another word and disappears into the shadows of the box seats. Several soldiers thunder toward Milo, ushering him out of the arena without so much as a word, but he pauses briefly as he passes me to shake my hand.

We don't need to say anything. The simple act is enough to show his gratitude.

I saved his life, and I get the feeling he won't forget that.

"Are you going to let this be the end?" I ask, gesturing for the soldiers to wait a minute.

The soldiers obey, and I suspect they're as eager to hear the answer as I am. The two dojo soldiers look at him, and we all wait as he takes a steadying breath.

He watches me ominously for a moment before he nods. “This is the end.”

With that, the guards usher him out of the ring, and I follow at a safe distance, not quite sure how I feel about this whole mess even though I’m grateful that it's over.

When I reach the box seats, I take the steps two at a time, only to find Harper standing at the top with her arms crossed.

I hesitate a couple of stairs below her, looking up as she and I share a tense look. After all, I took vengeance from her even if it was the right thing to do.

“You don't have to go talk to the Palarne,” Harper says.

“Why don't we talk about that after?”

“No,” she says, shaking her head. “I asked that of you out of anger, and it wasn't right.”

“Harper, I’m not mad. You were just—”

“Stop,” she says cutting me off again. “You should go.”

I frown, a little gutted at her dismissive behavior, but she charges down the steps and brushes past me. Seconds later, Russell follows, pausing beside me to silently clap me on the shoulder. He lets out a small sigh before following his Boss, and I rub my eyes, wondering if I did, in fact, do the right thing.

Levi leans against the doorframe above me and simply watches them disappear. Moments later, Tucker appears beside him, his hands on his hips as he looks after Russell and Harper.

Tucker whistles in surprise. "She's scary when she's mad."

Levi scoffs. "So is Rory."

I chuckle, running my hand through my hair as I look up at him. "I'll take that as a compliment, Levi."

"Good," he says with a nod. "Because it is. Now let's get the hell out of here."

"Yeah," I concede.

He doesn't have to ask *me* twice—not after all that.

CHAPTER TWENTY-EIGHT

I try for two days to get a hold of Harper.

And I strike out every time.

According to Russell, she disappeared into the mountains. He sent a crew after her to keep an eye on her, but judging by his tense tone every time I spoke with him, I could tell he was itching to get out there, too.

I debate flying back to the capital to check on her, but the party in Ash Town is today, and I'm out of time to check on her.

Honestly, though, I'm just not in the mood.

I fiddle with the little diamond Edgar gave me as I stare out the window. I figured I should wear the gift they gave me as a sign of gratitude, and as I run my fingers over it, I can't deny that I kind of like how dainty it feels.

My men and I sit in the chopper with Tucker silently piloting, and nothing but the chop of the helicopter blades through the air fills the cabin. There's a somber mood across all of us, and there has been ever since the battle in the arena. Milo was escorted to the boundary, but none of us saw him again on the way out.

Ashgrave flies alongside the helicopter, keeping watch on the horizon as we fly.

Drew and Jace sit on opposite ends of the bench across from me, staring out opposite windows. Jace leans forward with his elbows on his knees as he glares out at the rapidly approaching mountains. Drew meanwhile leans back in his seat, arms crossed, legs spread as he glares out into the horizon.

No one's been in much of a talking mood.

I tilt my head toward Levi to check on him, and he's already watching me with a pensive expression. He's guarded and silent, and with a subtle tilt of his head, I can tell what he's thinking.

Are you okay?

I nod, though it's not altogether the truth. This whole experience has been so strange, and I'm still not entirely sure if I did the right thing by saving Milo.

Maybe he should have died back there in the arena. I don't really know anymore.

In my pocket, my phone buzzes, and I fish it out to see yet another unknown number. Part of me wishes Irena would just get a consistent number, damn it, because now I'm never sure if it's going to be her or Diesel.

Ugh, fine.

I'll answer.

I use a small attachment on my headset to connect it to the phone. For a moment, I don't say anything, and I let the whir of the chopper blades above us fill the silence.

"It's good to hear from you, too," Irena says, her voice chipper.

I let out a slow breath of relief. "She lives."

"Not yet anyway," she says casually and chuckles.

I grin, a little caught off guard by her joy. Every time I talk to her, she's a little happier—though, honestly, she *shouldn't* be. After all, she's at war with the Ghost.

But this is her element. She's a total badass and a natural leader. Every day that passes, she probably gathers more and more people to follow her.

"To what do I owe the pleasure?" I ask.

"I found an old file," she says, and the muffled creak of a chair implies that she's leaning backward, probably with her feet up on a table. "Honestly, it's more of just a letter, something that fell between the cracks of a desk in Zurie's old office."

"Interesting," I confess. "And you were in there recently? Just poking around?"

"Maybe," she says mischievously, and I know without a doubt that's a yes.

"What did you find, Irena?" I ask, biting back the urge to lecture her.

"The Ghost before Zurie was named Marcus," Irena says, and I hear the crinkle of a page in the distance.

That name sounds familiar, and for a moment, I'm not sure why. It takes me a minute to remember some of the stories I heard, the ones other Spectres mumbled and whispered through the darkness of Zurie's stronghold whenever people thought she wasn't listening. Stories of a previous Ghost, one who was so fearsome no one even dared speak his name.

Zurie's mentor.

I grip the phone a little tighter on impulse and lean forward. "What did you find out about him?"

"He's the one who recruited Mom," Irena says, her tone softening ever so slightly at the mention of our mother. "He found her when she was just five, an orphan on the streets, and he took her in. Rory, she was his favorite. She was fierce. Dangerous. Smart. No one could beat her in a fight. She was supposed to be the Ghost, not Zurie."

"What the hell?" I ask, admittedly confused. "Then what happened?"

Irena sighs. "She wanted us to have a better life than she did. They caught her trying to sneak us out, but you and I both know that being born into the Spectres is a life sentence."

"They killed her for it?" I ask.

"Yeah." Irena clears her throat. "Marcus was gutted. I found this letter he wrote to her the day she was killed, and I guess this is the closest thing to processing emotion a Spectre has ever come. He was devastated. They all fought, and she stabbed him. He didn't survive long after he wrote this."

"Who killed her?" I ask, gritting my teeth.

"Zurie," Irena says, her tone hard. "She slit Mom's throat—while Diesel held her down."

I grimace, the rage and hatred burning in my chest for this man who just won't die, who just won't leave us alone. Deep within me, my dragon coils with rage. White light blurs across my skin, and both Jace and Drew look up from their brooding thoughts to watch me with concern.

I guess they're not listening in on this call, which surprises me. I always assume they're eavesdropping.

"Thanks for telling me," I say.

Even though it only pissed me off, I'm grateful to know the truth.

"Of course," she says, and she clears her throat again. "I, um, I need to go."

"Yeah," I say, giving her an easy out. I know she probably just wants to be alone, and I can grant her that.

The line cuts out, and for a moment, I just stare down at my phone as it flashes to signal the end of the call.

Mom died in an attempt to give us a better life.

It makes me think about the village people we're heading to see now, about how I told him I would protect them. These are honest people who just want to live, and they got caught in the crossfire of dragons.

It's not fair. It's not right, but it's mine to fix.

I sigh and rub my face, tucking my phone back in my pocket as I stare out the window.

"We're here, ladies," Tucker announces into the

headsets, and I can hear the jovial tone he's forcing into his voice. He's trying to make us laugh and snap us all out of this hazy gloom that settled across us.

It's not working, but it's the thought that counts.

He lowers the helicopter, and I take a deep breath to brace myself to interact with people. If anything, I guess maybe this is the perfect time for a party. We're at our lowest, and we could use a little time off.

As we land, the villagers cheer, and I open the door to smiling faces as the blades of the helicopter slow. They usher me forward, and I oblige them as my men hop out of the helicopter behind me.

The people of Ash Town greet me with strings of pearls that they swing over my head, and I chuckle as they do the same to my men. There's something adorable about seeing Drew with all his bulky muscles wearing three strings of pearls, and I can't help but laugh. Even he chuckles, shaking his head, enduring this for me and kneels to let a little girl put another string around his neck.

Jace, Tucker, and Levi awkwardly stoop as the villagers slide pearl necklaces over their heads, as well, and it’s a joy to see the slow smiles break across my men’s faces.

Ashgrave sails overhead, circling us as we settle

in. He'll keep watch while we relax—though I never really let my guard down for long.

There are bonfires everywhere, and it's nice to see smoke and flame that's not actively destroying everything this time. Warm light shines through the windows in every home, and lanterns are strung between the alleys and down the streets such that the village practically glows with light. The scent of roasting meat wafts by me, and I suck in a deep breath as I savor the spicy sensation on the air.

"I'll say hell yes to that," Tucker says, sniffing the air as he claps his hands together and rubs them.

I grin, and for the moment at least, I leave my worries in the chopper.

Despite myself, I get completely caught up in the festivities.

Before I know it, I'm sitting in the center chair of five makeshift thrones set along the edge of a bonfire pit as five women dance a beautiful and elegant dance around the bonfire in the middle. Around us, people chant and clap to the rhythm, swaying side to side as they lose themselves in the song. Drums and stringed instruments play along the outskirts of the circle, and the sound fills the air for miles.

And through all of this, I'm the guest of honor.

This may be a tiny village, but damn, they know how to party.

A young man brings me another cup of wine, and I nod my head in thanks to him as I take it. I'm on my fourth one, but I don't even feel remotely buzzed. I'm starting to wonder if I even can get drunk at this point.

That might be the *one* downside to dragon magic, apart from all the people actively trying to kill me.

The wine still fills me with a happy warmth that burns down my throat in the cold air.

It still doesn't quite feel real. There's a part of me that's still suspicious, that's still waiting for a trap to spring and refuses to let my guard down, and I don't know if that's the Spectre within me or the woman who's been hunted since she got this dragon magic. And even though my dragon is relaxed and coiling to the rhythm of the music, I can't help but be a little on edge.

Out of the corner of my eye, a silhouette darts toward me. I tense impulsively, ready for battle in an instant.

To my surprise, however, it's just a little girl.

She brings me another string of pearls, pink ones this time, and hesitates when she's about five feet away. She slows to almost standing still, her cheeks red with embarrassment as our eyes meet. Now that she has my attention, she shuffles aimlessly, digging her toe in the dirt as she debates whether or not she wants to actually come forward.

I relax my shoulders, leaning my hands on my elbows and trying not to seem threatening as I gesture for her to come near.

To my delight, she beams at me, smiling broadly as she races over and lifts the pink pearls to go over my head. I let her slide them around my neck, and before I can do a thing, she wraps me in a tight hug.

"You're my hero," she says softly, almost too quietly to hear, her voice tinged with an accent I can't place.

With an impish little giggle, she smiles at me again, and races off toward a man and woman standing on the outskirts of the circle. They kneel as she comes closer and give her a big hug, and the man nods to me briefly as our eyes meet.

That little moment—it weighs on me.

Even though the rhythm and dancers continue to sway and swirl around me, I start to tune it out.

All I can see is that little girl watching the fire,

watching the woman dance and enjoying herself, and I suddenly feel so responsible—somehow even more so than before.

That moment—that little hug—it changed things for me.

What these people are forced to face is not fair. They're caught between dragons, and I knew that. I knew it was my duty to keep them safe. But this is different. I want to make sure that little girl gets a better childhood than I had, just like Mom tried to do it for me.

Mom was a brilliant fighter, and she failed.

But I definitely won't.

I stare into the fire, wondering what I can do differently. How I can change things and make this right. It makes me think again about the Palarne, about how Harper is having a hell of a time getting allies, and yet Kinsley already has a Boss on her side.

I know Harper said I didn't need to go see Isaac, but I think I absolutely do—and not just for myself.

I lift the little string of pink pearls and delicately brush my thumb across one of them, and in that moment, I know.

It's time.

CHAPTER TWENTY-NINE

"Rory, you don't have to do this," Harper says into the connection over my headset.

I've never been one to enjoy travel, mostly because Zurie made me do it so much, and the fact that I'm in the helicopter yet again flying halfway across the world for a meeting is not lost on me. It would be kind of nice to simply stay at Ashgrave for a while, but it's comforting to know I have a home base if I ever need it.

With Levi in the co-pilot seat and Tucker flying the chopper, that leaves Jace, Drew, Ashgrave, and me in the backseat. Ashgrave curls at my side like a little metal, bloodthirsty cat while I talk with the Fairfax Boss.

Knowing my men, they're all listening in on the conversation.

"I'm not doing this for you, Harper," I say, and it's only partially a lie.

For the most part, I'm doing this for everyone because if the Fairfax have an ally, that will encourage others to join us as well.

Especially if Jace gets his way and we build that army.

I look at him out of the corner of my eye, and the moment my gaze hits him, he tenses like he can feel me, and looks my way. He smirks and taps the headset, suggesting I continue the conversation.

"Look, I'm not mad anymore," Harper says. "I wasn't even really mad in the arena. I just needed space."

"I know," I say, a little surprised and very much impressed that we're even talking about this, since the dragon way is to shove our feelings deep down.

"So, why are you going to the Palarne?" she repeats.

"Because we need an ally," I say simply. "And because he's the closest we've got."

"He invaded your memories," Harper reminds me, as if I need the reminder at all. "I don't know if we can trust him, Rory."

I snort derisively. "We can't trust any of them. That's why we're going to plant a bug."

There's a brief pause on the line like she can't quite believe what I just said.

"You sneaky bastard," she eventually says, laughing.

"Yep," I say, nodding. "Guilty."

"So, that's why you're going to the capital instead of a neutral zone," she says, and I can hear everything clicking in place for her as she speaks. "You're going because you want to plant the bug somewhere we can listen in and catch them if they try to betray us."

"Bingo," I say.

"Well, damn," she says, whistling softly under her breath. "I'm impressed."

"Damn right you are," I say, laughing. "I'm quite remarkable."

She chuckles, and it's nice to hear her laughter again. There was a moment there where I was really worried, but now, like magic, everything's fine again.

She just needed some space.

"Well, don't get caught," she says.

"Duh," I mutter.

She laughs. "I mean it, Rory. The Palarne are all about law, and if you break any of them—"

"I know," I say sincerely this time. "We won't get caught."

"In case he tries to pull a fast one on you, we'll assemble nearby," Harper promises. "I'm not going to let anything happen to you. To *any* of you."

"I know," I say, grinning, grateful to have a friend like her.

"All right, all right," she says. "Enough of the mushy nonsense."

Laughing, I hang up and take a deep breath as Tucker angles the chopper past the mountains and into the Palarne capital.

As we round a towering peak, an expansive city opens up beneath us—a modern metropolis unlike any I've ever seen. I was expecting a palace, maybe, but the Palarne have a full-on capital here that fills the small valley between a moon-shaped series of mountains.

"Well, this is going to be a fun little adventure," Tucker says through the headset.

"What is?" I ask.

"We're going to be landing on a skyscraper, guys," Tucker says, chuckling. "Never done that before."

"Oh, that's good," Drew says sarcastically, looking over his shoulder a Tucker. "Try not to kill us, will you?"

"Eh," Tucker says, shrugging. "No promises."

He takes the helicopter in toward the tallest building, carefully lowering it onto a giant circular landing pad. People with orange lights help us navigate, and before long, the helicopter touches down on the roof. A door nearby opens, and four men run out, keeping their heads low as the chopper blades begin to slow, and Tucker turns the helicopter off.

"Now or never," I say as I take off my headset.

We funnel out of the helicopter, and between the rushing gale of the wind and the slowly dying blades of the chopper, nobody bothers speaking because we know we won't hear each other.

Ashgrave angles around us, diving as he lands abruptly on my shoulder. The four men usher us in through the doors, and as soon as we're all through, they shut it. My ear rings in the sudden silence, and the man nearest to me nods in welcome.

"My name's Payton," he says, bowing his head briefly as he sets a hand on his chest. "Brigadier-General."

"You're Isaac's brother," Drew says, a hint of surprise in his voice.

Payton chuckles. "That too, but I feel like Brigadier-General might be a bit more impressive, Mr. Darrington."

I chuckle.

I like this guy.

"Isaac's waiting for you in the throne room," Payton says, gesturing for us to follow. We jog down the stairs after him, and I take note that his three soldiers follow up behind.

As always, they're keeping a careful watch.

They're already far ahead of the Darringtons I have to admit. It's nice to be greeted by only four soldiers instead of a whole army, but I don't for one second believe that the Palarnes can be trusted.

Not yet.

The staircase ends in a broad hallway wide enough for two dragons to pass through side by side, and I figure that's the point. With these massive buildings and their penchant for war, the Palarne probably want to be able to come and go as they please in any shape they desire.

At the end of the expansive hallway lined with red and gold banners are two double doors inlaid with gold. Two soldiers stand guard, and as we walk closer, they grab the handles and open them with a flourish. I know all of this is supposed to feel grand and maybe even threatening, but at this point, it's more of the same. Every time I pass through another kingdom's doors, I begin to see more and more of the show and wonder what's real.

As we enter, the first thing I notice is Isaac sitting on a massive white throne, his legs slightly spread as he leans his elbow on one armrest of the impressive chair. Iron spikes jet out at the top like they were confiscated from their enemies' blades and set behind the Boss as a reminder of what happens to those who defy the Palarne.

Hell, knowing them, that's probably exactly what happened.

I take a brief scan of the world around me, weighing the throne room for exits and threats. There's a camera in every corner and covering every blind spot. No matter what we do in this room, we'll be seen. So, as much as I'd like to, we can't put the bug here.

Damn.

I'll have to get him to take us into a war room, something behind the scenes, and perhaps not observed so closely.

To my surprise, Isaac doesn't say anything as we enter. He merely watches every step we take as we near his throne, his hand covering his mouth as he all but glares at us with suspicion.

Huh, how surprising. He's usually made small talk by now.

As I reach the stairs to the small platform his throne is set on, I set my hands on my hips. "Well, I'm here. This is what you wanted from the start, isn't it?"

"It is," he admits, finally breaking his silence as he leans back in this chair. "Ideally, however, you would have come under different circumstances."

"What's changed?" I quirk one eyebrow, trying to see if he'll give me anything good.

"Kinsley has come to see me already, and she's made both promises and threats." He hesitates, giving me a once-over. "And most of them seem to pertain to you."

"Oh, that's great," Tucker says, rubbing the back of his neck.

Levi subtly smacks him in the side—a wordless warning to shut the hell up.

I'm tempted to suggest we go to another room, mostly because I want to plant the bug somewhere we will overhear something useful, but I know better. If I make a suggestion right now, Isaac is going to be suspicious of it.

So I wait.

"I assume you know why I'm here," I say, crossing my arms. "I assume you know what I want."

"Of course," he says, shrugging. "This isn't a new conversation."

"But these are new circumstances," I point out, using his own words against him.

"That they are," he admits with a small sigh, gesturing for the soldiers in the room to leave.

For a moment, all we hear is the clamor of their footsteps across the marble floor and then the thud of the heavy door slamming, leaving only me, my men, Isaac and Payton in the room.

I'm a little surprised. A warrior like Isaac doesn't strike me as someone cocky enough to leave himself outnumbered in a room, but that's exactly what he just did.

We're technically not allies yet.

I can't tell if he's making a power move or if he legitimately doesn't see me as a threat. But I can still play this to my advantage.

"Isaac," I say quietly. "Let's cut the bullshit. There's something you want from me, right?"

He simply watches me for a moment, his gaze drifting briefly toward Payton before he slowly nods.

"Fine," I say, gesturing toward the two of them. "Then let's barter."

For a moment, Isaac doesn't speak. He simply watches me, and yet again he sets his hand over his mouth as he studies my face like he's reading something in my features that only he can see.

It's unnerving, but I don't let him know that.

I never let my stoic mask falter, and beside me, both Jace and Drew cross their arms in unison, daring Isaac to let the silence go on much longer. Though I don't look behind me, I know that Levi and Tucker are probably doing the same.

In response, Payton sets his hands behind his back, squaring his shoulders and spreading his legs apart slightly to give him a stronger stance. He lifts his chin as he glares at them, and in that one moment, everyone prepares for a fistfight.

I won't let it devolve into that.

"Follow me," Isaac says with a weary sigh, standing as he gestures for us to join him. He trots down the stairs and leads us to a door on the far side of his throne. It opens as we near, and two soldiers salute to him as we pass into a hallway.

Ah, that's why Isaac wasn't afraid. There are probably dozens of soldiers ready at a moment's notice to take out any perceived threat.

Figures.

Within moments, he leads us to another door, and this time he opens it and leads us inside. A wall of glass on the far end of the room lets in the warm sunny light and casts shadows over a long wooden table that fills most of the room. A massive television covers another wall, and Isaac takes his seat at the head of the table across from the television. He leans back in his chair and gestures toward the other seats, silently telling us to sit as well.

Can do.

As we each take our seats, Ashgrave jumps onto the table and sits in front of me like a gargoyle, silently watching everyone in the room. While Isaac's attention is focused on the little mechanical dragon, I subtly glance toward Levi, the stealthiest of us—and the one with the bug.

He nods subtly, almost imperceptibly, waiting for the silent cue for where I want him to plant it. This is a highly sensitive microphone so anywhere will probably do, but to be safe, I'd like him to pick a seat that sees the least traffic.

Levi is supposed to sit across from me so that I can draw attention while he plants the bug. I take the seat with my back to the window, the one I figure most visitors would take—since no one wants their back to a door in a negotiation.

If Levi takes the seat across from me, that means there are fewer chances of someone accidentally knocking their knee against it under the table.

Levi takes the subtle cue and sits across from me, leaning his elbows on his knees as he sticks his hand under the table and slouches. It's hardly the position I'm used to seeing him in since this man typically has perfect posture, but it's what he has to do to hide the bug.

Now, I just need to be the diversion.

"I know you said you don't want to get involved," I say to Isaac, "but it's clear I have something you want. So, what is it?"

Isaac isn't like Jett. Isaac is a man of honor and one of the only Bosses who doesn't stare directly at my cleavage. Even though I played a pretty blatant sex card to get Jett's attention, it won't work with the Boss in front of me now.

Only logic will.

"This mess needs to end," Isaac says, shaking his head as he rubs his temples.

"But it won't," Jace points out as he sits next to me. "You know that, Isaac."

"He's known that for a while," Drew counters,

sitting in the chair opposite Isaac, at the other head of the table.

"That's not quite how you worded it when we first discussed the matter," Isaac says, narrowing his eyes as he glares at the fire dragon.

"That was before..." Drew trails off, his gaze darting briefly toward me before he glares out the window, and I figure this is what he and Isaac talked about before I realized who the red dragon really was back when I first got my magic.

"It doesn't matter now," I point out. "The fact is this is what we have to deal with. Kinsley is on the warpath, and she's going to destroy everything. Everyone. It's just a matter of time."

"That's what everyone keeps saying," Isaac says, shaking his head. "But she hasn't done anything except release a few videos."

"You know that's not true," Drew says, tapping his finger on the table to emphasize his point. "You've seen the signs, same as I have. The resources that are disappearing. The terrorist attacks on a mine here, on a mine there. The subtle and silent change of power as ownership shifts from one nameless organization to another." Drew shakes his head, scoffing. "Kinsley is amassing every resource she needs, and she nearly has everything."

"So, are you going to wait for her to attack?" I ask, leaning back in my chair to further draw attention away from Levi as he reaches further under the table. "Or are you going to help me nip this in the bud?"

Isaac shakes his head. "You won't like my price."

"It can't be worse than Jett's," I counter, smirking.

Isaac chuckles. "No, probably not. But you still won't like it."

"Then tell me," I say, shrugging.

Instead of answering, Isaac looks briefly at his brother, who stands by the door with his arms crossed and his back against the exit. As their eyes meet, his brother squints in mild confusion. Their expressions change, and it's almost like they're having a silent conversation without so much as touching each other to open a mental connection.

Now that is impressive, and I have to admit I'm a little envious.

"I need to think about it," Isaac says, standing, his chair scraping along the floor as he sets his palms against the table. "You'll be staying in our finest suites, of course, and—"

"We're not staying," I interrupt, laughing. "You can give us an answer now or on the phone. But in no way will we be staying more than another twenty minutes."

Isaac glares at me, and it's the first hint of indignation I've seen on his face. He's usually so calm, so poised and unshakeable. But to see this brief rush of anger is almost unsettling.

I'm clearly not doing what he wants me to, and I'm absolutely okay with that.

"Isaac, you don't need to draw this out," Payton interjects, breaking his silence.

We all turn our heads toward him, and as attention turns toward Payton, I briefly catch Levi's eye.

He nods at me subtly to let me know the bug has been planted, and we're done.

I let out a slow breath of relief.

"We've talked in circles about this," Payton says. "Stop playing games, Isaac. We all know what's at stake here. The Vaer have a Boss on their side, and there would be absolute mutiny among the ranks if you were forced to join Kinsley. You *know* that," Payton adds, taking a frustrated step forward as he glares at his brother.

Isaac frowns, scowling at Payton with a silent command to shut the hell up.

It doesn't work.

"You know what we have to do," Payton continues, gesturing toward me as if that's answer enough.

Isaac grunts in annoyance, shaking his head before he turns his attention toward me. "You said you wanted to know my price?"

"I'll hear it." I cross my arms to make it clear that just because he wants something, it doesn't mean he'll get it.

"You wear a tracker," he says simply, his brows rising ever so slightly as if he's daring me to reject his offer.

"What?" Jace and Drew snap, both of them jumping to their feet.

"A tracker?" I ask in disbelief.

"You've got to be joking," Levi says, wrinkling his nose in disgust.

"You're out of your mind," Tucker adds, shaking his head in disappointment.

"Why?" I demand.

Isaac and I share an intense glance, and for a moment, I think he may not answer me. He simply watches me, silently judging my reaction, and I think that this must be the way I look whenever I'm looking at someone's face for tells of a lie.

He's studying me.

He knows I'm a Spectre—or was. He knows my skills. He knows what I'm capable of.

And I think he's afraid.

He wants to know what I'm doing at all times, and that leaves me suspicious yet again of his motivations.

"You have influence, Rory," he says simply, standing as he crosses his arms, and watches me. "You sway minds. I'm not asking to hear everything you say. I'm not asking for video feed or audio. I just want to know where you are."

He didn't answer my question, and right now, I have to decide if I'm going to press that or if I'm going to allow what seems to be a fairly simple compromise to finally get us an ally.

The truth is whatever his motivations, a tracker with no video and no audio is easy enough to overcome, even if he wants me to implant it. It's simple enough to fish out. I'm not afraid of a little blood and a bit of pain.

All this does is confirm for me that Isaac has other plans. He's not like Jett. He doesn't want to lord me over anyone or turn me into a mistress, but he does want my power. I can't help but feel he and the old gods have something to do with each other.

"I won't wear a tracker," I tell him simply. "But I

feel like this is something we can compromise on. You want to know where I am at any given moment, right?"

He simply nods.

"Then I'll give you something better," I say, standing. "Regular phone calls, regular conversation, and you can ask questions to your heart's content."

"And you'll answer them all?" he asks skeptically.

I smirk. "Oh, Isaac, you know me better than that."

He chuckles, shaking his head.

"But I will answer some of them," I add.

We share an intense glance, and I know in that moment that I've won him over. He hesitates, no doubt working through the possibilities and how this could fail. But in the end, he sticks out his hand, and I take it.

And just like that, we have ourselves our first ally. I almost can't believe it, and the bug Levi just planted will help us confirm if this was, in fact, the right choice.

CHAPTER THIRTY

I almost can't believe I'm really here, sitting in a war room with Isaac in the Palarne capital. Even just a couple of weeks ago, I would have thought I'd be in chains, and yet, miraculously, I have free rein of the palace.

Well, mostly.

Jace, Drew, and Payton are brainstorming at the moment in a military meeting across the hall. Levi slipped away unseen in large part thanks to a distraction Tucker made, and he's off to scope the palace to ensure it's safe, to ensure there's nothing we should be worried about right now.

If anyone can find something, it'll be Levi. No one will be able to tell he's even there until it's too late.

He would have made a great Spectre.

Tucker's up on the roof tending to the helicopter —his new baby, which he loves only slightly less than his jet.

That leaves Ashgrave and I alone in a room with Isaac Palarne.

The air is quiet. Tense. The weight of everything we want to say hangs unspoken between us, everything I want to accuse him of to let him know I'm aware of his motivations and intentions—at least what I think they are anyway.

But I don't say a word.

I don't want to ruin this newfound truce we have between us, not this close to a war with Kinsley.

Ashgrave walks along the floor, inspecting the room as he silently makes his rounds to secure the small space.

Unsure of what else to do, I hook my thumbs on my belt loops and slowly pace along the wall of windows, staring out at the beautiful Palarne capital. It's fascinating. I would have suspected the Palarne to be dragons of tradition, to have ancient buildings that were hundreds if not thousands of years old—but to see a metropolis nestled between the crescent moon mountains around them is a pleasant surprise.

I'm starting to think the Palarne will be full of surprises.

"This war is going to happen," Isaacs says, his chair creaking as he leans back. "That's the only reason Payton and I are doing this. Are you prepared for what's coming?"

I don't answer, instead shooting a brief glance over my shoulder at him as he reclines in his chair, his eyes locked on me. Jace was right about how Spectres view confrontation. We aren't used to full-on war. We're used to stopping them before they can even start. We're the grim reapers, the ones that come in the night to do what no one else is willing to.

To his credit, Isaac doesn't wait for me to reply. He simply sighs and shakes his head. "All the signs are there," he continues. "Drew was right, of course. Amassing armies. Missing people. Embassies going empty as public dissent gets stronger. Stolen goods turning up where they shouldn't be, in the hands of people who shouldn't have them." He pauses, those intense eyes nestling on me for a second. "You know the bounties on your head are obscene, right? Do you know how much money people will give up just to have you?"

I smirk. "How much money did you put on the

bounty that you issued for me? How much will you pay?"

He laughs, a hearty chuckle that feels real and shakes his head. "You came to me on your own, girl."

I smirk, deciding to omit the part where I came out of desperation.

There are footsteps in the hallway, and I tilt my head to listen to see if they're familiar. I hear the soft and dainty gait of Harper and relax a little bit, grateful she's finally here. Now that she has a new ally, they need to have a meeting with the Bosses.

I'm just not sure why I'm here or why they both insisted I stay.

The door opens to a white-gloved soldier who nods courteously at her as she enters.

"Sorry, I'm late," she says, shaking her head as she takes the seat nearest to the door, the one next to the bug Levi planted. "I had to deal with an attack on one of our mines."

With that, she briefly looks at me with an ominous expression and so much is left unsaid.

"Which mine?" Isaac asks.

"Nothing major," she says, shaking her head and waving away his question as if it doesn't matter. "Just some obscure ore, one I use for a pet project." With that, she sits back in her chair, and I can almost feel her watching me out of the corner of her eye.

The only pet project of hers I know of is my Spectre tech.

Ah, *hell*.

I hear the hum of Isaac's voice, his words starting to fade into a deep murmur as I slowly tune them out. I lose track of what they're saying as I stare out the window, lost in thought.

That's the third time I've heard of various mines being hit. All of them rare, natural resources, and most of them metal.

It doesn't add up.

We thought it was Diesel before, that he had somehow figured out what we were doing and where our mines were so that he could sabotage what we were building. He knows we're coming for him, and I know he'll do everything he can to hit us where it hurts most.

Our tech.

But the wheels in my head start to turn, and now I'm wondering if I'm even right.

If there might be another party at play here.

If the bounties on my head are getting higher like Isaac said, the thief who's making the second crystal knows they don't have long to corner me.

Not with all that competition.

It seems like—perhaps—they're getting desperate and reckless, which means they're letting more and more of their heists go noticed.

My mind buzzes with options as I slowly piece the puzzle together. I was so quick to assume before that I knew who this was and why they were doing it, but now I'm starting to think I was very, very wrong.

And then it clicks for me.

In a sudden, almost painful rush, I remember an obscure little note in the diary I found in Ashgrave's treasury, an offhand little comment that I disregarded almost as quickly as I read it.

Dragon magic reacts to some natural elements. There are some ores that act as a conductor for magic like mine.

For a moment, I can't breathe. What if the thief needs this ore for the crystal?

My lips part in shock and surprise as the final piece comes together for me, one that was there all along and just went overlooked. The thief thinks no one cares about a few attacks on mines. The thief is making assumptions that they can get away with what they're doing.

The thief doesn't realize I know.

I get out my phone and type out a text to my men because I have a brilliant, awful idea. If the thief wants the ore and me, why not dangle both in front of his or her face at the same time?

Whoever this is, they've been covering their tracks remarkably well, but I still think this is Natasha. She has all the means to make this happen as well as the motivation.

And if this thief wants trouble, I'll bring it to her.

CHAPTER THIRTY-ONE

The trap is set—nothing to do now but wait.

I pace back and forth in my bedroom, chewing my nail as I wait for Drew and Jace to give me answers.

To let me know if this worked.

In the tense silence that seems to stretch on forever, Tucker cleans his guns on the ornate table on the other side of the room, nothing but a few towels between his grease-covered weapons and a table that's older than much of recorded history.

I'm too focused on what Drew and Jace are going to say to stop him.

Levi, meanwhile, leans against the open doorway of the balcony nearby, staring out into the mountains as we wait.

"They're coming back," Levi says as he looks out into the balcony.

I jog toward him, and sure enough, a red and black dragon fly toward the castle. To my relief, Ashgrave's mechanical dragon is not with them.

That means it worked—and Ashgrave is waiting to snare whomever might step into our trap.

Instead of flying to my balcony, however, they arc toward Drew's observation tower, and I wonder what they're up to. I frown, shaking my head as I debate jogging up there to find them.

In the end, I give them a few moments to finish up whatever mischief they're up to.

After only about ten minutes, I hear the thunder of footsteps in the hallway—two familiar gaits.

Drew and Jace.

I stand in front of the door with my arms crossed, waiting for them to open it. Sure enough, it swings open and the two of them enter, their eyes immediately on me.

I stiffen, wondering if my plan worked. To my relief, Jace simply nods.

"We borrowed a bit of the ore from Harper's mine," Drew says as he shuts the door. "A few strategically linked messages on unsecured channels suggest that you're currently there, locking it down in a warehouse not far from here. If the thief comes for the ore, Ashgrave will snare them and keep them in place until we can arrive." He hesitates, clicking his tongue affectionately. "I'm impressed, Rory. That's a hell of a plan."

I let out a slow breath of relief, but I can't allow myself to relax. "Let's not take any chances," I say, shaking my head. "We're going to wait nearby. I don't want to risk letting this person get away."

As I pass Drew on my way to the door, he grabs my arm, rooting me in place. "You're not going anywhere. It's dangerous enough as it is. You don't need to fly into the fire."

I try not to let him see how frustrating it is that his enhanced strength keeps me rooted in place. I try to wrestle out of his grip like I did last time, but he seems prepared for it—and just clamps down tighter.

Ow, damn it.

I smirk up at him like his grip on my bicep doesn't bother me. "I'm pretty sure I'm fireproof."

"I'm not about to test it," he snaps.

"Let her go," Levi demands, and for a moment, the two of them glare at each other.

"Drew, stop being an idiot," Jace says, smacking the fire dragon's arm away. Drew's grip on me slides off, but he simply grabs me with his other arm and holds me to his chest as he glares at the men around him.

"Oh, are we fighting again?" Tucker says, briefly looking up from his guns as he continues to clean them.

"Thanks for your support," I say sarcastically.

He shrugs. "Meh, you've got it handled, honey."

"MY QUEEN," Ashgrave says, his voice is thundering through the room. "FOR WHATEVER IT IS WORTH, THE SITUATION IS CURRENTLY HANDLED, AND NOTHING IS HAPPENING."

"That doesn't mean it won't," I chide him.

Through Drew's grip on me, I can feel his phone vibrate in his pocket. He has one arm wrapped around both of my shoulders, holding me tightly to his chest, so he fishes out the phone with his other hand. I look over my shoulder as he scans the screen—and he instantly stiffens, his grip tightening on me as he reads.

Oh, that's not good.

"What is it?" I ask him.

He doesn't answer, and after a moment, he simply looks at me with an apprehensive expression, his brows twisted slightly upward, like he doesn't want to say.

In the hallway, footsteps race along the cobblestone floor, and there's only one person that could be.

Brett.

Seconds later, he bangs on the door, his fist against the wood as he waits for someone to answer.

Whatever's happening, this is really bad.

“Open it, Ashgrave,” I tell him, rolling my eyes.

The door opens, and Brett immediately charges in, waving his phone in the air. “Kinsley is demanding that you come to her, Rory.”

Drew's grip around my body tightens ever so slightly, and he just glares at Brett as if he hates the man for saying what he couldn’t bring himself to say.

“Give me that,” I say, wrestling my way out of Drew’s grip so that I can grab Brett's phone.

A broadcast plays on the screen, and to my horror, the first thing I see is a beautiful white dragon with piercing green eyes, blasting a skyscraper with ice.

The red banner beneath the broadcast simply says, *‘Kinsley Vaer on warpath. Demands dragon vessel to arrive.’*

For a moment, I can't hear anything but the ringing in my ear. The mumble of my men arguing with Brett is like a soft hum in the back of my mind, but I can't understand anything they're saying. All I can see is a stunning ice dragon destroying the city around her, freezing humans with a breath.

And the swarm of dragons descending on the city behind her.

"That crazy bitch," I say under my breath, still not quite believing what I'm seeing. She's brought a whole army.

"But she's fighting humans," Levi says, grabbing the phone from me as he glares at it. "What is she doing? I knew she was insane, but this—"

"She's forcing us to act," Jace interrupts, grabbing the phone out of Levi's hands as he glares at us. "Kinsley has never been one to care about the treaty with the humans, and now she has an excuse to ignore it." With that, he looks at me, and the unspoken implication weighs heavy on my shoulders.

She's killing all of these people just to get to me.

They're nothing but bait.

"This timing could not be worse." Jace grimaces and gestures out the balcony doors. "We just set the trap and notified the world of where we want them to think you are."

"And you'll notice where Kinsley showed up," Drew says, shaking his phone for emphasis.

"She was listening," I say quietly, piecing it together. "She did this on purpose, the first moment she caught wind that I'd left Ashgrave."

"Precisely," Drew says. "She wanted to catch you off guard."

"And maybe help whomever is trying to steal the ore," Levi adds.

I groan in frustration, rubbing my eyes. This could not get worse.

"Kinsley won't stay for long," Drew says, shaking his head. "The human reserves and armed forces are likely already on their way, but she will be able to kill thousands before she retreats. She's causing enough damage to destroy the reputations of all dragons." He hesitates, looking at me. "Including you, Rory."

"It's genius," Brett says, grinning. "She's put you in a bind because of the brand you've begun to build as a hero. You have to go. If you don't, people will think you've abandoned them, and they'll hate you again."

"Shut up, Brett," Tucker and Drew say in unison.

"I need to think," I say rubbing my temples as I step away, turning my back on all of them.

If I go, I give her what she wants. If I don't, I'll be labeled as a coward who let people die to save her own skin.

It's not much of a choice.

"If you go, you will probably have to shift," Jace says. "We all will, and the ramifications of us fighting in a human zone are obscene."

"Wait, wait, wait," Tucker says, standing as he gestures for us all to calm down. "What are the human armies doing right now? I assume they've already assembled."

"The police force is already on site, but they won't be able to stop a dragon army," Drew says, shrugging. "The casualties are too high already, and it's just getting worse with every passing second. They can't just start firing anti-dragon missiles in the middle of a metropolis."

I lean against the bedpost as I shake my head, resigning to what I'm going to have to do. "The moment reinforcements arrive, that city is going to be a war zone, and even more people will die."

Jace groans in frustration, and I know he's going to say something about the treaty. About regulations. About the ramifications of us going in, of shifting and fighting off dragons as dragons.

But I've already made up my mind.

Everyone has said that Kinsley's first move—her first *real* move—would be a devastating first blow that would cripple most opponents.

Well, this is her first real move, and I'm going to show her that she can't cripple me.

I look again at the phone in Drew's hands, and he stiffens. He walks toward me, tossing the device on the bed and wrapping his hands around my shoulders, silently imploring me to come up with something else. I just shake my head and set my finger on his lips before he can speak.

He can't save me from this. No one can.

It's time for me to step up and become what I never thought I would be—a hero, of all things.

Here goes nothing.

CHAPTER THIRTY-TWO

The world around me is oddly muffled as I walk through the abandoned streets of what was once a thriving metropolis. In the distance, there is screaming, sirens, gunfire—everything you should never hear in a time of peace.

It's blatantly obvious that Kinsley strategically chose this city above all others.

She wanted me—and only me—to show up. She wanted a large population far enough away from military centers that it would take the humans a decent amount of time to mobilize, which gave her enough of a lead to get me out in the open before everything went to hell.

She wanted a city where I would show up before anyone else.

The city's police force lines the streets ahead of me, their guns raised at the sky while they hold military-issue shields to protect them from dragon fire.

It's not enough.

The scream of a jet catches my attention, and I briefly look up as Tucker flies overhead toward the swarming dragons and the black smoke that's quickly approaching. After the roar of the jet disappears into the distance, I hear only my pulse thudding in my ear. I hear the footsteps of my men behind me, ready to shift.

Ready to fight.

Brett insisted on coming, but he's staying with the chopper on the edge of town, keeping by his phone so that he can alert us if the trap we set by the ore goes off. At least, that's what he said, but I know him better to think he'll actually do it.

I think deep down Brett misses war—and we've certainly found ourselves smack-dab in the middle of one.

A policeman up ahead looks over his shoulder, glaring daggers at me as I near. "Get back, woman! Are you crazy?"

"Ray, do you know who that is?" somebody else says under his breath. "That's the dragon vessel."

"Oh, hell," another man says under his breath.

"She's insane—why the hell is she even here? She's going to get us all killed!"

I can practically feel the dread radiating from them. None of them thought I would come.

But here I am.

I walk through them, my attention turned to the sky. I can't deal with them right now. I can't reason with them or persuade them to let me stay. It would just be a waste of my energy when I need to focus entirely on the brutal fight that lays ahead of me.

And I need to finish it all before the trap for our little magic thief goes off.

I simply walk toward the front of the line and watch as the dragons fly overhead. A beam of flame hits the nearest skyscraper, and windows shatter as black smoke billows into the sky. Three of the nearby buildings are frozen solid, encased in ice that slowly begins to melt in the hot sun.

But it won't melt fast enough to save anyone inside.

This has to stop.

"Kinsley!" I shout, my voice carrying farther than it should. My voice echoes through the buildings, bouncing off of every surface as it carries into the sky.

My dragon and I are so *pissed.*

Kinsley must know I'm here.

Almost instantly, a shadow swoops past us, and I look up as a massive white dragon dives toward the ground. She lands hard, shaking the asphalt beneath us, but I don't so much as sway even as the policemen behind me are thrown off balance.

The regal dragon arches her beautiful neck, her piercing green eyes staring at me as she captures everyone's attention. For a destructive crazy woman, she's absolutely breathtaking to behold.

As I stare into her bright green eyes, I can't help but wonder if this is what Irena would look like if she ever shifts.

The dragon snarls, the sound almost sultry despite its threatening thunder. Ice seeps from her feet, radiating across the asphalt as if she can't even control it. She lowers her head, inviting me to speak with her privately, but we are far past the time for conversation.

"We have armies on their way," I tell her, taking a few steps forward, my shoulders squared as I face down one of the most powerful dragons in the world. "Two of them. You don't have much time."

She sneers like she doesn't believe me.

Joke's on her. Harper and Isaac are both on their way, and they'll be here in less than ten minutes—far faster than any human armies.

Magic burns along my body, the ribbons of white light cascading like the Northern Lights across to my skin. Even though I keep Kinsley's eye, I tilt my head as I address my men behind me. "You guys should go. Stop the soldiers and save anyone you can until Harper gets here."

I know they don't want to leave me, and I know they won't go far. But I can't focus on stopping Kinsley if I'm worried about everyone in the city who's in danger.

Begrudgingly, the men behind me shift, and I can feel the magic in the air as they let their dragons take over. They dart into the sky, their shadows cascading over us as they disperse—three masterful fighters off to stop her soldiers.

Kinsley growls, watching them take off and snaps at the air in front of me. Brilliant blue light builds in her throat as she summons a beam of ice, but I'm ready.

I'm *beyond* ready.

At the last second, she lifts her head, firing at the police line behind me instead of at me like I was expecting. But I don't let her touch them. I let loose a beam of white light, shattering the ice instantly. Mist falls across our faces as I block her blow, and several of the men behind me yell in panic.

"Will you get the hell out of here?!" I snap at the policemen behind me.

Half of them listen, and the thunder of their retreating footsteps barely drowns out their panicked screams.

Kinsley tilts her head, curious, and begins to pace in front of me.

It would seem I passed her first test—but it's unclear if that's really a good thing. I don't want this woman to know anything else about me.

A shadow soars over us, and moments later, a familiar black dragon lands behind Kinsley.

Natasha.

Shit. So, the Bane have officially joined the Vaer.

Just like that, all hell breaks loose—that one little moment of realization is all these two women gave me.

In unison, Natasha and Kinsley attack me—Kinsley with her ice, and Natasha with her fire. Gritting my teeth from the sheer force of what I have to do to block their blows, I let loose another beam of white light to intercept them both. They growl, leaning into their attacks, and I lean deeper into mine. My feet begin to slide backward as I struggle to keep their powerful magic at bay.

They're crazy, but they're strong as hell.

I reach deep into my gut, asking my dragon for all the help she can give me, and a second surge of strength bubbles through my body.

My magic is suddenly brighter. Hotter.

Stronger.

With a hot rush, my magic overpowers theirs. At the last second, Kinsley darts into the air and out of its path, but Natasha isn't fast enough. My magic hits her hard on the side, gouging her, and she screams as she's thrown into the nearby building. Blood cascades down her body, and one of her wings has a giant hole in it.

One I suspect will never heal. She'll fly, but not well. Her days of tight maneuvers and effortless control are gone.

She continues to scream in pain, lost in her agony, but Kinsley simply resumes pacing nearby.

She doesn't care that one of her allies was just hurt.

If anything, she just looks irritated.

Nearby, people scream, and I look over to find three women in business suits staring up at Kinsley as they walk out of a side entrance of a nearby building. They seem to have all frozen, like the moment they actually came face-to-face with a dragon, their bodies stopped working.

That's the thing about panic. Sometimes the adrenaline can root you in place when what you really need to do is run as fast as you can.

Kinsley sneers, summoning another blast of ice as she looks at them, and I figure she wants to turn them into ice sculptures.

Not if I can help it.

I fire a blast of my magic at her face, and she barely dodges it in time. She growls at me, and I once more have captured her full attention.

"Run!" I yell at the young women, and that seems to snap them out of their daze. They nod, racing toward the police line as several of the officers gesture for them to get to safety.

I need to get on the offense. I need to stop Kinsley, but protecting these humans is costing me. She's playing me, putting more and more people in danger just to keep me moving, just to keep me from getting a leg up on her.

But it's worth it.

After all, that's the only reason I'm even here.

To protect these people.

A wave of dragons overhead fires a slew of fire beams against the buildings nearby, and the scream of a jet interrupts them. The patter of gunfire screams through the air as Tucker takes out two. The dragons fall to the asphalt below several blocks over, and the rumbling thunder of their bodies hitting the ground shakes the earth.

My men are brilliant, but there's only five of us against an army.

I have to end this.

I race toward Kinsley, and as I reach her, she snaps at my face like she's trying to gobble me whole. I roll out of the way at the last second, summoning the blue blade of light into my hands as I gouge her neck. I aim for a main vein, but she twists at the last second and I miss. And instead of a devastating blow, I merely draw blood.

She screams in pain anyway and snaps at me again. I roll out of the way, summoning magic, and blast the white light at her face. Yet again, she's too fast. She darts out of the way like a snake, her claws digging into the asphalt and kicking up rubble as she smiles at me, summoning ice into her throat yet again as my white magic sails harmlessly into the sky.

With every blow and every step, I debate shifting.

Jace says it's inevitable, and I wonder if the secret is worth keeping anymore. But when I'm in my dragon form, I don't have as much power over my magic, and I could destroy everyone here. Even now, my magic surges, and I can't help but feel like Kinsley chose this moment on purpose because she didn't want to give me enough time to master my abilities.

I'll still kick her ass one way or another. I just need to be clever and figure out how.

Kinsley shoots a blast of ice at me, and I roll out of the way. If I shift, I want to make it count. I need to use the element of surprise against her to the best of my ability, and I need to pick the right moment.

This is not the right moment.

Kinsley's blast of ice hits a nearby building, and it sways a little from the force.

Natasha snarls nearby, the gaping wound on her side still bleeding heavily, and she darts off into the sky, blood dripping with every flap of her wings.

Damn it.

I can't help but wonder if she's going to try to steal the ore we set as bait in our trap, and I hope

Ashgrave can hold his own against her until we arrive.

If we arrive, that is.

None of us were counting on Kinsley when we set our trap, and I don't know how long this is going to take. If Natasha escapes with the bait that I set for her, I might never have another chance to catch her in the act—until it's too late.

Kinsley roars into the sky, and the sound makes my blood run cold. It's the sort of scream that summons something darker, something more powerful even than what I'm facing now, and I don't like that one bit.

Almost instantaneously, a dark cloud gathers on the horizon, and it takes me a moment to realize that those are dragons.

Soldiers.

Kinsley didn't just bring a few troops. She brought the whole damn *army*. I get the feeling that her goal for this battle is to leave this entire city in ruins—and absolutely everyone dead.

Possibly including me.

In retaliation, a jet, a red dragon, a blue dragon, and a black dragon with stunning blue magic burning along his skin gather in opposition to this brewing cloud of Kinsley's soldiers. Four against a horde.

So, that's what she was doing.

Distracting me.

Kinsley darts toward me, snapping at my face, and I barely roll out of the way before she bites my head off. Her distraction worked perhaps a little too well, and now all I can think about is saving my men.

She must think I can't get up there. She must think I feel helpless right now.

Poor fool.

She attacks, her blisteringly fast blows coming at my face like rapid-fire, and I'm barely able to duck out of the way each time.

She's a brilliant fighter, I have to hand her that.

But I'm better.

As her face gets too close, I summon my magic dagger and shove it deep into her cheek. It hits bone, and she screams in agony, reeling backward as she shakes her head. I summon my magic again, hoping the buildings around us are mostly empty at this point because the longer I fight, the less control I seem to have over my magic. I can feel it burning, pushing against me, desperate to break free and break loose.

It wants an outlet, and I can't be sure Kinsley will take the full brunt of my next blow.

She charges me again, and I brace myself to attack. But at the last moment, she darts to the side, and her tail hits my chest hard. I fly backward, rolling across the ground, the wind knocked out of me as she dives toward me, her dazzling white teeth all I can see.

Two explosions rock the ground. Fire rolls across her skin as she roars with pain and takes a few steps back, shaking her head as if she's dazed. She glares off to the side, and I look up to find Brett with a bazooka over one shoulder. He nods briefly to me and fires again, the third blast hitting her hard against the side.

Kinsley roars in frustration, and before I can so much as stand, she grabs me in her claws. She darts into the sky, taking us up in a straight line into the clouds as I wrestle in her grip.

Magic burns along my hand, sizzling as it eats away at her talons, everywhere I touch her, but she doesn't seem to notice or care. The scent of burning skin hits me hard, and it makes me realize just how little this woman cares about anything.

Even herself.

As we touch, our connection opens, and all I can

hear from her is the scream of a voice in her head. It burns through my mind, and I figure that's the scream of her pain. She's bottling it up, keeping it contained and quiet like Zurie always did.

Like I used to.

She hesitates in the air, and I look below me to see the skyscrapers like small sandcastles made of metal.

Fly, little dragon, she says through our connection. *After all, this is how I learned to do it.*

And with that, she drops me.

As I fall, my stomach soars into my throat, and there was a time where this would have scared me.

I've been waiting for the moment to shift, to show the world what I am and what I can do. Up until now, I wasn't sure if I was ready, if my dragon and I had enough connection and control to take the hell that will come for us the moment the world knows she exists.

But I am.

We are.

We're ready.

My body hums as I let my dragon take over, and in that moment of instinct and power, I roar into the sky as my wings catch the air. The sun glimmers across my scales as they dazzle the world like diamonds, showering the buildings below me with light.

As I roar, my white magic burns in my throat and tears through the clouds above me, and as the beam sails toward Kinsley, there's a beautiful moment where she looks both surprised and terrified.

Good.

She should be.

CHAPTER THIRTY-THREE

The first thing I do once I shift is soar toward Kinsley.

Toward her throat.

To rip it out.

The spell of her shock snaps as I reach her and dig my teeth into the base of her neck. I twist my head, gouging her deeper with every movement, and she screams in agony as her claws dig into my hide.

I sneer, snarling at her audacity to so much as touch me and dig my claws into her as my teeth clamp down ever tighter. She snaps at me, slashing my wings with her spiked tail, but I don't let her touch me.

She will never touch my wings.

We lose altitude as we tumble, our claws digging

into each other as my teeth grip her tighter. I want to blast my magic at her, and I'm trying to summon it even as we fall, but with every foot of altitude we lose, I lose a little more of my focus.

It's just too much to manage all at once.

The connection opens between us yet again, and once more, all I hear is the scream of her pain, of her agony.

And she deserves this.

She swipes me hard on the face, and I can't help but snarl with pain as my grip on her throat loosens. She wriggles free, trying to put distance between us, and I lose my grip on her throat entirely. As she tries to pull away, I dig my claws deep into her stomach, dragging them along her belly as she roars with pain and tries harder to shake free.

But she can't.

She's not fast enough.

A gaping wound that's eerily similar to the scar on Levi's stomach shines on her underbelly, the fresh blood dripping to the ground below, and I figure it serves her right for giving him his.

Now that we're in the air, I summon my magic, but I'm not sure I should use it. The more we drop in altitude, the closer we get to the buildings.

I need to get her back into the sky.

I stretch my wings out, snapping them as I fly up into the air again, and she follows me.

The fool.

She darts toward me, a blinding blur as her claws dig into my scales. I snarl, snapping at her face, trying to go for the jugular, but she wriggles just out of my grasp.

It's a brutal fight—claws slashing, blood flying, snarling as each of us tries to get the upper hand.

And as each of us fails.

I land hard on the roof of a nearby building, breathing heavily as I try to catch my breath and come up with a better plan. I'm astonished at how evenly matched we are, at least as long as I keep my magic at bay.

But if I let loose this close to a city, I could kill everything here.

I think she somehow knows that.

Kinsley recovers and dives toward me. I tense, snarling as I prepare to catch her. She hits me hard, and we tumble, our claws digging into each other yet again as I bite her hard on the neck. My teeth dig into her as our connection opens.

It would seem we're at an impasse, she says, her voice harsh in my head. *We'll meet again, little goddess. The longer you fight me, the worse it will be when I break you. I will kill everyone you love and destroy everything that's left.*

I growl as she tries to snap at me. This woman is astonishing. Truly. I'm amazed to think she believes she has the upper hand here or even any remote bargaining power at all.

Not if I kill you first, I tell her.

I clamp down harder on her neck, and she screams in pain. She summons ice into her throat and blasts it at me, hitting my face. It stings like a thousand bees stabbing me all at once, and I can't help but let go of her as I fall, disoriented. I shake my head, but for several moments, I can't see, and I dig my claws into the first thing I feel.

A building.

My claws tear through the glass, through the iron beams holding it upright as I slow my descent, and before long, I finally come to a stop with my claws digging into the nearest skyscraper. I shake my head, my vision finally returning and look upward to find two long gouges from my claws. They go at least ten stories up.

Oops.

I sneer, seething, trying to find Kinsley in the sky yet again, but she flies off.

Like hell.

I push off the building, catching myself as I race toward her, masterfully flying through the air as my dragon and I unite. She races toward the edge of the city, toward the parks that circle the metropolis.

She's retreating.

I chase her down, and she's only slightly faster. She looks over her shoulder at me, snarling in frustration, and I figure she thought she lost me.

Not if I can help it.

Kinsley soars through the buildings, weaving expertly back and forth as she tries to lose me, but I match her as best I can. We're getting farther and farther away from the city, and that means I might be able to use my magic.

I just have to get a clear shot.

Before I can take aim, the roar of a plane nearby catches my attention, and my heart pangs with dread.

In unison, she and I look over as a plane slowly angles away from the madness descending upon the city. It's far enough out that the pilot would have likely thought he was in the clear—until two dragons stormed through his path.

Now, however, it's too late to change course.

Kinsley is too close.

She darts toward it, summoning blue light into her throat, and I know exactly what she's doing.

She's giving me yet another ultimatum.

I roar, following after her, but I'm just a second too late.

As my claws dig into her back, ice shoots from her mouth and hits one of the engines. The plane instantly teeters, its nose diving toward the ground.

I snarl with the loss—with letting her have this.

I was just a second too slow.

She wriggles free, slashing at my face as she darts off again in the opposite direction, and yet again, I have to choose between Kinsley and the people she puts in harm's way. She roars into the sky, calling for a retreat as she flies off and casts one last look at me as she waits for me to decide what I'm going to do.

With a huff of frustration, white sparks shoot from my nose, and I dive toward the plane as it angles toward the ground.

I have to be careful. I don't want to hurt anyone, and if I hold the plane the wrong way, I could stab someone clear through the gut.

Can't kill the people I'm trying to save, after all.

I reach it, hovering overhead and slowly lowering myself toward it in the hopes I can make this work.

Because, honestly, this could all go up in very literal flames.

I reach my claws toward the plane, digging my talons into the bottom of the hull as I try to get a strong grip on it. Once I'm sure I'm not going to tear it apart, I stretch my wings and try to slow its descent.

Good lord, it's heavy.

I grit my teeth as I bat my wings against the air, trying to keep us both from crashing into the forest below. Bit by bit, I manage to slow the plane, and as I strain against the metal hull, I see a suitcase fly out.

Oops.

The trees are getting closer and closer, and I snarl with frustration as I try to keep the plane airborne just a few moments longer—just enough to keep us all from exploding once it hits the ground.

And, somehow, I manage, even though I feel like this plane is going to rip my damn arms off.

The plane stops fighting me, and as we reach the ground, I angle gently toward an open patch of grass. I roar with frustration and the strain of carrying a plane in my claws, pushing my enhanced dragon strength to the absolute brink as I beat my wings hard on the air and slowly lower it to the grass.

Holy shit.

I saved a *plane.*

My dragon and I practically glow with pride—and I give myself that one little moment of victory.

After all, Kinsley's still out there, so I'm not done.

The metal groans as I gently set the plane on the ground, but getting my talons out of the passenger jet is a delicate operation. I can't help but jostle the plane a bit as I wrestle my claws free, and each time I do, I hear a soft hum of timid screams from inside.

Oh, this is just *fantastic.*

When I wrench my last claw free, I sidestep the plane and glare into the sky to find Kinsley and her soldiers as nothing but dots on the horizon, too far away to catch.

I snarl in anger.

She got away.

A roar of voices catches my attention, and I look down, half expecting torches and pitchforks at my feet. After all, I shifted in a human zone. Even though I was trying to save them, I endangered people.

But I look down to find people cheering as they slide down the little yellow slides of the emergency exits.

One teenage girl runs toward me and wraps her

arms around my leg. The connection opens as her fingers brush my skin, and I can feel a surge of her relief and terror. Her adrenaline is pumping, and all she can think over and over again is *thank you, thank you, thank you.*

You're welcome, I say back.

She gasps, jumping in terror and surprise as she breaks the connection and takes several steps backward, looking at me with wide hazel eyes.

I chuckle. That was kind of cute.

Deep in my chest, my dragon curls with delight—a happy little warning that Jace is coming.

Sure enough, three dots race toward us from the city, and as they near, I recognize Jace, Drew, and Levi. Before long, they land, the ground rumbling underneath them as they sidestep humans and brush their heads against mine.

All at once, the connections between us open, and all I can feel is a rush of their gratitude and relief as we all take a moment to check on each other.

I'm fine, I say, chuckling.

You were brilliant, Drew says, growling affectionately.

Absolutely stunning, Jace agrees, nuzzling my head.

Thanks, but we're not done, I warn them, looking

after Kinsley. *We need to get back to the trap. Back there, Natasha—*

Levi snorts, a thin mist shooting through his nose as he shakes his head before he sets his wing against mine. *Enjoy the flowers while they bloom, Rory. It doesn't happen very often.*

Around us, the cheering gets louder as more and more people escape the downed plane, and I have to admit after a lifetime of people trying to kill me, this is pretty damn nice.

The scream of a jet catches my attention as Tucker flies by overhead, and for the briefest of moments, our eyes meet, and he nods affectionately.

But the fact is the fight isn't over.

At any moment, the trap could go off, and if Natasha thinks she's going to distract me that easily, she has another thing coming.

Namely, my fist—because I *really* want to punch that woman in the face.

CHAPTER THIRTY-FOUR

It doesn't take long for me to get my way.

Draped in a loose dress, I sit in the helicopter that Brett pilots as Levi, Jace, and Drew fly beside me. With Kinsley still at large, they all wanted to keep watch. Tucker continues to make rounds in his jet as it's significantly faster than the helicopter, flying ahead and scouting to the best of his ability and reporting back.

Meanwhile, I'm watching the beacon.

Motion sensors have gone off at our trap. It's sprung. And I know that Ashgrave is dueling whoever is there, and he's doing it solo.

He has my magic, sure, but that will only last him so long. It's comforting to know he can make another body, but I don't want to lose whoever he's currently fighting.

"Hurry the hell up, Brett!" I shout into the headset.

"What the hell do you think I'm doing, woman?" he snaps, gunning the controls.

We've come a long way from him pretending to have me bound and gagged in his backseat, that's for damn sure.

We near the site of the ore—a solitary warehouse built into a cliff not far from Ashgrave. It's one of Drew's isolated stockrooms, and he only bought it for two reasons.

One, this place is in the middle of nowhere. Isolated is an understatement, and the nearest *house* —much less *town*—is four hours away by air.

Two, this place was strategically designed to allow for only one entrance—and one exit. There's only one tunnel, and we have to enter in human form to reach the corridors inside. It's the perfect way to trap someone, and I'm not at all surprised my devious fire dragon owns a place like this.

As Brett gets ready to touch down, I hesitate by the door, ready to rip it open the moment we get close to the ground.

But I don't even have the patience to wait until the wheels are on the ground.

Before we even land, I throw the door open and jump to the rock below. The moment I hit the stone, I run, racing toward the opening that will take me down into the tunnels below the mountain.

As I near, I hear the blaring siren of our one and only Ashgrave.

"YOU DARE STEAL THE QUEEN'S HOARD?" he shouts, his voice echoing through the tunnel as I push through the busted gate. His voice is so loud it sends pebbles cascading over my head.

I shake my head at my dramatic castle. All he had to do was pin them. What bad guy is going to sit there and listen to a lecture?

"YOU ARE A FOOL TO HAVE STEPPED INTO OUR TRAP," he continues, giving just a little too much away for my liking. "YOU WILL GET YOUR RETRIBUTION."

As I round a corner, I hear the thunder of my men's footsteps behind me. Good, they're hot on my heels, and I won't face Natasha alone for long.

Ready to kick the Bane's ass, I step into a massive cavern—where we set our bait.

There, in the center of the room, is a pile of glimmering metal that looks more like a silver cloud than ore. It's soft and iridescent, and with every step I take, ribbons of rainbow light dance across its surface.

This is the ore the thief was trying to steal—the ore that might well be able to sap my magic from me.

Though I can hear Ashgrave, I can't see him, and I pause to look upward. To my surprise, the mechanical dragon is flying through the air with a woman held tightly in his claws. The fabric of her black dress flows as he jostles her every which way, blocking her face as she wrestles against him, which is too bad—I would love to see her expression now that we've caught her in the act.

"Bring her here," I demand.

"AT ONCE, MY QUEEN," Ashgrave says, barreling toward us.

He throws the woman on the ground, and she rolls, the black fabric of her cloak covering her face briefly as she slides to a stop at my feet.

"Did you really think it would be that easy?" I ask her. "That you could run away while I was distracted with Kinsley to—"

The woman fights with her black fabric of her dress, finally breaking through as she looks up at me.

Her piercing gaze interrupts me, and for a moment, I can barely breathe.

It's not Natasha at all.

It's Jade Nabal.

I suck in a deep breath of surprise, and I can't deny that I'm confused.

Jade watches me with a wary expression, her brows twisted as her palms press flat against the floor. Her gorgeous face is marred by a deep scar across her left eye.

Her shoulders droop as she looks up at me, and she doesn't try to stand. Instead, she hangs her head with shame.

"Explain yourself," I demand.

Her nose crinkles with disdain, but she just shakes her head and she looks like she's about to cry. "I want this all to stop, Rory. I really do."

She sobs briefly, and I'm not quite sure what to make of this. I was expecting Natasha to barrel in here trying to take what's mine. I wasn't expecting a crying girl who's barely eighteen to be trying to steal everything I love from me.

"Jade, tell me what's going on," I say, my tone harsher this time in case she's trying to tug on my heartstrings as a ploy.

"I don't want to do this again," she says. Her eyes

dip out of focus, like she's reliving something horrible.

She's not making any sense, damn it.

Help me out here, I ask my dragon, hoping she can pick up on something that I'm missing.

In that instant, I feel like I can look at Jade with new light. Something about her feels different. It feels vaguely like, well…

Like me.

My heart skips a beat, and I take a wary step backward as a shattering realization crashes through me.

"You were behind the first crystal," I say, glaring at her. "That scream I heard in the Knights' fortress when I destroyed it—that was you."

Jade doesn't answer. Instead, she swallows hard, looking up at me from the floor, and she simply nods.

"Oh, shit," Drew says, running his hand through his hair as he stares at the girl. "That means—"

The motion detectors by the entrance go off once. Twice. The pings become so rapid that they don't stop.

A *lot* of people are coming—through our only exit.

Jade looks at me with those tortured eyes. "You

should run. You should get as far from here as you can, and you should never look back."

I look down at her, and I can't deny that I feel a hint of pity. "I don't run, Jade."

As the shuffle of feet hitting the cavern ground echoes through the tunnel, I look over my shoulder to greet whoever is foolish enough to try to pin me.

Instantly, my men shift, and in the massive cavern, they have plenty of room to stretch their wings. Tucker and Brett, to their credit, cock their anti-dragon rifles and shove the butts of their guns into their shoulders, ready to fire at a moment's notice.

The first face I see around the bend in the entrance tunnel is none other than Aki Nabal, and he enters with a small army of soldiers behind him.

And just like that, I've become trapped in my own trap—that devious bastard.

"Finish what you started," Aki orders, glaring at his daughter. "Why can you *never* finish what you begin? Look at them." He gestures at me. "They're outnumbered. Yet again, I've had to come in and save your ass."

"Father, this is a mistake," she says, her voice catching as she shakes her head.

He scoffs in disgust. "Look at you, child. Absolutely pitiful. You never have the courage to act. You never have the courage to make a stand, and this is your one chance to change all of that." He hesitates, glaring at her. "To redeem yourself."

The words cut through me like daggers, and they weren't even *directed* at me. I can only imagine how much that must sting Jade to hear that from her own father.

From the man she's most likely admired all her life.

I look back at the girl on her hands and knees before me, and something in her expression shifts. It hardens, and in that moment, I know I've lost her.

"I'm sorry," she says quietly as she glares at me, the last hint of her tears dissolving.

"So am I," I say quietly, balling my hand into a fist as I prepare to end this.

In a move so blindingly fast I can't even see it, Jade shifts.

If she weren't trying to kill me, I'd be impressed.

With a seething roar, she attacks me. She digs her claws into my chest, the move lightning fast and slams me against the wall. Her talons pierce my shoulders as she snarls at me, a dragon in less than a second, her wings spread as she pins me to the side of the cavern.

In an instant, all hell breaks loose.

As she moves, I see my men trying to reach me, but each of them is outnumbered five-to-one. In a moment, the massive cavern is filled with dragons in the air, on the ground, and only three human forms remain.

Tucker, Brett, and Aki.

"MY QUEEN!" Ashgrave shouts, taking to the air as he soars toward me. "ALLOW ME TO ASSIST—"

"Help them!" I shout, gritting my teeth as I stave off Jade's claws. "Keep my men safe!"

"BUT MISTRESS—"

"Damn it, Ashgrave!" I interrupt.

He angles away, his body brimming with white light as he fires off a bolt at the nearest Nabal dragon —and I do believe that's the closest I've come to seeing my castle pissed.

Standing nearby, the Nabal Boss crosses his arms, unfazed by the war around him as snarls and the roars echo through the cavern. With his arms crossed, he merely watches his daughter.

He wants to make sure she delivers the final move.

I grimace as Jade's talons dig deeper into my shoulders, drawing blood. After the fight with Kinsley, I’m weaker, tired, exhausted, and hurt. I need a moment to heal, to recover.

But since when do I get that?

I'm a fighter, and even when I'm at my lowest, I fight back.

And this girl has asked for it.

I don't pause. I don't play. I don't dangle my shift over these people like I did with Kinsley. The world will know before I even leave this cavern that I'm a diamond dragon. The secret is long gone, and I don't need to protect it anymore.

So I shift.

Almost as quickly as she did, I let my dragon take over. My body hums and burns with magic as my dragon takes hold, and with a snarl, I shove her backward. Almost instantly, the gaping wounds in my shoulders heal as I dig my talons into the ground and roar. The sound echoes through the cavern, and everyone freezes, their heads turning toward me in shock.

My men use the moment to their advantage, and in a blistering second, three of Aki’s soldiers fall to the ground, dead.

That shatters the spell, and once again, chaos resumes behind Jade and Aki.

For a moment, Jade doesn't get up. She simply

lays there, staring at me with wide eyes, her chest heaving as she tries to get over her shock.

Beside her, her father stares at me as well, and I'm grateful I had this moment of surprise over them. I wasn't sure how quickly word would spread, and it seems they were too busy trying to take the ore to listen to the intelligence channels about me.

For once, something worked in my favor.

"This doesn't change anything," Aki says, shaking his head. It almost sounds like he's trying to convince himself. "Jade, all of this could be yours," he adds, pointing at me. "Get your ass up and finish this!"

Jade snarls, looking between me and her father. Even though she stands, even though she braces herself for the next attack, it's obvious.

She doesn't want to do this.

The Nabal heir launches at me, and even though she's only eighteen, she's an experienced fighter. The way she moves like a dancer, every step perfect and graceful. Every movement is made with utter precision. She races toward me, her wings balanced ever so slightly, and at the last second, she lifts her left wing to balance herself as she digs her right claw into the wall for added momentum.

If she weren't attacking me, I would be mesmerized by the beauty of it all.

She lands a devastating blow at the base of my neck, knocking me backward. I slide across the ground, digging a small rivet in the stony dirt from the force of her blow, and I can't lie.

I'm impressed.

Honestly, she's the kind of fighter I'd want on my side in a war. She's the kind of soldier that could take on a small battalion by herself. She's brutal, fast, and light on her feet.

She's damn good.

And I could probably kill her.

I have a choice to make. Something in me tells me killing her would be a mistake, something I would regret for the rest of my life. Even as she attacks me, teeth bared as she snarls, swiping her claws at my face, I simply duck. Dodge. I don't let her touch me, but I don’t go for the kill.

I need to buy myself some time.

I need to think.

As she and I face off, I see Brett fighting in my periphery. With three shots, he takes down one of Aki’s soldiers, rolling out of the way at the last second as the dragon hits the ground hard.

Brett proved himself, redeemed himself—

however slightly. And here, with all of us pinned in a corner, he fights at our side.

All he needed was a sense of purpose and a second chance.

Like him, there's still good left in Jade, and maybe I can help her find it.

I grit my teeth as I struggle with this decision I'm quickly coming to, as I wait to see if this is the right choice or if it's going to bite me—*hard*—in the ass.

It's hard to think of forgiving someone who tried to steal my magic. Who tried to kill my dragon. Who tried to take everything from me.

But as we fight, I see the wounded girl who just wants to impress her father.

It's obvious, to me. I can see it in the scar across her face. Behind her, her father urges her on, telling her how pitiful she is, how she never finishes anything. How she's weak.

His anger—his disappointment—that's the only thing pushing her forward. She's never known another life. She's never had an out.

Maybe I should give her one.

I switch to the offense, diving toward her and digging my claws into her hide. I twist violently, my claws hooked in her skin, and she can't help but succumb to the movement. I pin her against the wall, and she struggles beneath me. Even though she's a little faster than me, I'm far stronger.

As I pin her, a connection opens between us. All I feel for a moment is her panic. Her fear. Her doubt. Her raw emotions as they bubble beneath her skin, wild and untamed as she tries to repress them.

Come with me, I say as calmly as I can, given the chaos around me. *I will give you a home, and I will never ask you to be anyone but yourself.*

Jade catches my eye, and hers widen in disbelief. She goes still beneath me, twitching only slightly, as though it's just habit at this point. It's pretty obvious that she's looking for the trick. The trap.

To her, this must seem too good to be true.

She pauses, clearly torn between obeying her father and escaping the life he's forced her into.

I know firsthand how difficult it is to escape the person who raised you.

"You're such a disappointment," Aki says, his nose wrinkling with disdain.

As he glares at her, it takes me a moment to understand what he's saying. It seems like he's misinterpreting what's happening.

He thinks Jade is losing, and he thinks he has to save her.

"I always have to rescue you," he says, shaking his

head as he walks slowly toward us. "I'm getting tired of it. I'm getting tired of you failing me, and this right here," he adds, gesturing toward me, "this proves that you don't deserve the magic we're going to steal from this woman, even if you are the only one who knows how to make the crystal." He spits on the ground. "I'll just have to break the info out of you like I wring info out of everyone else." He hesitates, his hands balling into fists as he stares at her with disappointment. "You failed me, child."

In unison, Jade and I feel the pang of those words.

For me, I can almost hear Zurie's voice. For her—well, I can feel her heart shatter through our connection.

She looks at me with those wide eyes, and I see recognition there. I see a girl who understands my pain, and who knows I understand hers.

I just don't know if that's enough to end this—or if her love for her father will drive her back to him.

My attempt to forgive her could have been a huge mistake that costs me everything.

Time to find out.

Aki shifts, shaking out his body as he stretches his wings and snarls, his full focus now on me.

With my attention divided between the two of

them, Jade smacks her forehead hard against mine, and my world briefly spins. She wriggles out of my grip, rolling across the ground as she puts herself between me and her father. Her head darts between us, her claws digging into the ground, and I figure she's going to attack when he does.

I hate the thought of killing them both, but they're about to force my hand.

Aki snarls and launches at me, and I expect Jade to join him.

But she doesn't.

At the last second, she digs her claws into the ground and blasts him with a wave of ice so strong, so powerful, it casts a wave of light through the cavern. He roars in surprise, sending his own blast of ice to counter hers, and the two bursts of magic shatter each other. For a moment, snow fills the cavern, falling on us all as Jade and Aki stare each other down.

From this angle, I can catch only a hint of her expression, but everything I see looks terrified.

Like she can't believe what she just did.

She doesn't know it now, but this is her moment of triumph. Of truth.

Aki is furious, but I am so damn *proud*.

CHAPTER THIRTY-FIVE

The battle between Aki and Jade is furious and seething. He snarls, and she matches him blow-for-blow, roar-for-roar. Every now and then his tail smacks against me, and the connection opens briefly for just a second or two.

And every moment I hear his thoughts, he's telling her how awful she is.

How wrong she is.

How much she's going to regret this. How much he'll *make* her regret it.

And through it all, Jade holds her own.

He throws her against the wall, and the cavern trembles. I briefly wonder if it's going to fall, if it's going to collapse on us and cave in. But the structure miraculously holds.

For now.

Jade gets to her feet, snarling, and I brace myself to intervene. I don't want to interject at the wrong moment. After all, she's having a real moment here, but she's also starting to lose.

I can see it in the way she limps and the way she's favoring her right leg, thanks to the deep gash along her left side. Even though she snarls, I can see the fight starting to leave her eyes.

She's losing.

Part of me thinks this isn't my battle to finish, but I'm not going to let her die, and I'm not going to let Aki leave here with her.

Or me.

Aki swipes at Jade's face, and though she ducks the first two blows, the third hits her squarely in the throat. Four deep gouges scale down her neck, and she screams with pain as she falls to the ground, scrambling to get to her feet. Her eyes won't quite get into focus, and it's clear that was a far more devastating blow than it seemed.

Aki takes his time standing over her as she tries to get to her feet, and as he looks down at her, I catch a hint of disdain, of disgust. His throat glows with blinding blue magic as he looks down at her, and for a moment, all she can do is look up in shock. She goes still like she's frozen, and all she can do is watch as he goes to deal the final blow.

As he goes to kill her.

Like hell.

I dart toward him, and even though this is Jade's fight, I intend to finish it.

I slam him hard on the side, throwing off his aim, and his bolt of ice hits the ground, freezing a large section of the floor instantly.

The shimmering blue ice reminds me of Levi's memory, of watching Daisy frozen and then shattered, all in the span of a few seconds.

Aki was about to do that to his own daughter.

He slides along the ice, his talons digging into the sheer sheet and leaving long gouges in his wake as he regains his balance. He glares at me, snarling, and I growl. The cavern rumbles with my rage, the sound echoing through every inch of it.

And I have had enough.

I've had enough of Natasha. Of Kinsley. Of Aki. I've had enough of these Bosses who think I'm something to conquer, something to own, something to drain for their own benefit.

It's time they see what they're really up against.

I charge him, not bothering to wait for him to

act. I'm through waiting. Through wondering. Through with taking my time.

These assholes are going to bleed, and I'm going to be the one to cut them open.

I dig my talons into his side and bite down hard on his neck before he even has a chance to move, and he screams with pain. The sound echoes through the cavern, shaking it again, and with a violent twist of my head, I throw him halfway across the cavern. He crashes into two of his soldiers, taking them out, and they hit the wall, instantly going unconscious.

He stumbles to his feet and charges me again, barely giving himself enough time to process, and I don't stop either. I roar, snarling as I snap at his face, trying to rip open anything he's foolish enough to bring close to me, and yet again, I get hold of his neck. Once more, I twist my head violently, drawing blood, and the hot rusty liquid burns on my tongue. As the connection opens between us all, I can feel is his anger, his rage. He doesn't even have the time to think. All he can do is react, fight, defend.

But I won't let him.

When we first fought, Aki had the upper hand. He watched me, tested me, and looked for the weak points in my fighting. But now, I won't give him the pleasure. Now, in this moment, he's mine.

I twist my head violently and throw him against the wall, only letting go of my hold on his neck at the last moment, ripping open more of his skin.

Every time he comes for me, I'm going to leave him bleeding.

This time he's slower to get to his feet, and he glares at me, summoning the blue magic of his ice in his throat as he snarls.

That's cute.

I glare at him, spreading my wings like I've seen Jace and Drew do on occasion when they face a challenger. I lift my head, knowing the scars and blood that covers me offers a sharp contrast to the beautiful glimmering scales.

This is my silent command for surrender.

I'm demanding that he step down.

Since he's drawing his magic, I summon the white light into my mouth. My body hums with my energy, but it's a bluff I won't act on—not in this tight space, where it could kill us all.

He doesn't have to know that, though.

As we glare each other down, I see more and more of his warriors falling around us. Bodies litter the ground, and none of them are my soldiers, my men.

It's time to see how far his hatred goes and what he'll do in his lust for power.

He snarls, shaking his head, and the blue light in his throat instantly fades. With a surge of relief, I extinguish my own, but I don't back down.

I want to see him bow, even though I know he'll never do it.

Behind me, Jade rests against the wall, trying to stand but still injured from her fight with her father. He looks at her before his attention turns once again toward me, and he extends one wing in a silent truce.

It's not quite the surrender I wanted, but I'll at least hear what he has to say.

I extend my wing to his, and as our scales touch, the connection opens between us.

Tell her she's dead to me, he says.

Before I can so much as reply, he summons his ice into his throat and fires at the ceiling above us. The cavern trembles, shattering as the sunlight outside streams through the new opening above.

He bolts through the ceiling and into the sky, and his soldiers follow—those who are still alive anyway. They carry their wounded and dead with them, and in a matter of just a few moments, all of Aki's soldiers are gone.

I grit my teeth, wondering if I should follow, wondering if I should allow him to retreat or if I really have the means to end this.

There's so much I still don't know about my magic, so much I still need to control, and he is a boss. Killing him comes with repercussions.

When the last soldier is gone, Jade shifts to her human form behind me.

And she sobs.

It breaks my heart to watch her cry, to watch her shoulders heaving as she loses herself in her grief. That's what finally tears me from my thoughts of pursuing Aki. Her.

She needs comfort.

I coo softly, still in my dragon form, and wrap my wing around her. It's funny how small we look in our human forms compared to our dragon selves.

As I get closer, she wraps her arms around my leg and cries into my bloodstained scales, holding me tight. In that moment, our connection opens, and all I can feel is her terror. Her fear. Her grief.

And there, like a thin ribbon through it all, I also feel her relief that it's over.

It's okay, I tell her gently, nuzzling her forehead with my nose.

For a while, she doesn't answer, and I don't need her to. I look over my shoulder as Jace, Levi, and Drew shift down to their human forms. Tucker and Brett swing their rifles over their shoulders and watch the scene in front of them with a hint of confusion.

We expected to kill whoever was trying to steal my magic—not comfort them. I doubt they have any clue what the hell is going on, but I can't explain it yet.

"I need to get this ore out of here safely," Drew says nodding to the metal beside him.

I nod.

"Tucker, Brett, help me out," Drew orders, gesturing for them to come closer.

As Tucker and Brett oblige him, Jace and Levi hesitate, and I know they're looking for an excuse to leave as well. Sometimes it can be hard for others to see the grief of strangers, and I simply nod, silently letting them know it's okay.

"I didn't like what I was doing," Jade says softly, sniffling as her eyes gloss over. "But it wasn't until that video of you on the rooftop that I realized what I was doing was truly wrong. I thought you were some evil seductress who stole her magic from the gods, but when I listened to you talk about the Spectres…" she trails off, sniffing again. "I realized everything I was doing was being done to appease someone. Father made me feel like I had no choice." She looks up at me, her eyes wet. "I felt like I saw you for the first time, Rory. It hit so close to home for me, and I felt like if anyone in the world could understand what I was going through, it was you." She slowly shakes her head. "I couldn't bring myself to kill you."

I forgive you, I say calmly, brushing my nose against her forehead.

And I do.

I see repentance in her, feel it in her every breath, feel the guilt and shame that burns within her in having let this get so far.

"But why?" she asks, staring at me. "Why would you? I can't believe anyone would forgive what I've done."

I sigh. *I won't lie, Jade. I've never been big on forgiveness, but I know too well how you feel.*

I've done things I wish I could atone for, but I had no idea how. Now, perhaps, I can give others the second chance I always longed for.

I look once more at the skylight Aki tore into the

cavern, and I can't help but wonder when or if he'll realize the mistake he made here today had nothing at all to do with me.

It had everything to do with the daughter he failed.

CHAPTER THIRTY-SIX

Back in Ashgrave, I lead Jade down one of the many hallways that weave through the castle. This is the hall filled with bedrooms, one we've delegated for guests.

And in this case, long-term residents like Jade and Brett.

I hesitate at one of the doors and open it to peek inside and find the room Ashgrave prepared for her. Sunlight streams in through the open balcony doors on the opposite side of the suite, and the elegant bedroom is filled with delicate draperies and a four-post bed covered in silks.

Hell, I think this might be even a little nicer than my room.

I chuckle, pleasantly surprised with Ashgrave's

handiwork. I told him to make this room sparkle, as we would be having a very important guest stay here for the foreseeable future, and he certainly made me proud.

As Jade walks in behind me, she gasps quietly and sets her thin fingers over her lips. Her eyes scan the room, still wet at the corners, and I'm surprised that the dress I lent her fits her almost perfectly.

"I can't believe you're doing this," she says quietly, her gaze briefly landing on me as we walk together into her new room.

"Sometimes we just need a second chance," I say, shrugging, and the words hit home possibly more than she even realizes.

I set my hand on my chest, feeling as my dragon swirls within me, and I'm grateful for the second chance that saved me.

Now it's time to see if Jade takes hers.

"Rory," she says fishing a piece of paper out of her bra and fiddling with it. It's folded over a few times, and from here, I can't see what's written on it. "Can I tell you something?"

"Of course." I set my hands on my hips as I wait for her to speak.

"I have a confession," she says. "I want to tell you what I did. How I got that first crystal."

I nod, very much curious to hear this.

She licks her lips nervously and closes her eyes as she begins to speak. "I used my father's network to give Zurie the crystal, but I wanted it to seem as though it came at a great cost so that Zurie wouldn't get suspicious of what was happening. She wanted to destroy the magic, but Father wanted me to take it for myself."

Jade lets out a slow breath, shaking her head. "The crystal was supposed to drain your magic and give it to me, and as a result, my soul was tied to it. When it broke, it fractured a bit of me, of my magic. I'm scarred," she adds, gesturing briefly to the scar over her eye. "And this reminded Father of my failure every day. For a while, he just avoided me out of shame. Eventually, he cast me out altogether, telling me I could only come back when I'd redeemed myself."

"Once you'd finished what you started," I say, echoing Aki's comments in the cavern.

She sniffles and nods, handing me the page in her hands.

I take it, unfolding it to find a familiar piece of paper though it's covered in handwriting I don't recognize.

"Wait a minute," I say absently, narrowing my eyes as I study the page. "Is this—"

"It's a torn page from one of the Astor diaries," Jade says, nodding to it. "The one written by Brigid Astor."

For a moment, I just stare at it in shock, and in my heart, this confirms what I already suspected.

The other two diaries still exist.

"No one else ever saw this," Jade said, pointing to the page. "I never told my father where I got it or that I had a physical copy of it at all. He wanted it, but I knew that I needed some kind of leverage over him." She bites her lip, her gaze drifting toward the ground in shame.

Truth be told, I'm not sure what to say. It's strange to be in the room with someone whose magic so closely mirrors mine. It's not the same, but it's oddly similar, a fractured shattered version of what I have, and I wonder how that has affected her own ice magic.

Even more curious is how she could read the page at all. I suspect that, perhaps, the other Astor diaries aren't protected by an enchantment like Clara's is, but I'll have to wait to see for myself.

If I can find them, of course.

I set my hand on her shoulder. "You're safe, Jade."

For a moment, she sighs like her breath is trying to escape her in one heavy rush. Her shoulders droop, and a second later she looks up at me with wide and grateful eyes.

"I know you'll make me proud," I add, squeezing her shoulder slightly before I leave her to her room and her own space.

I walk down the hallway with the Astor diary page in my hands, and with every step, I'm more and more sure that yes, she absolutely will make me proud.

"Ashgrave," I say.

"YES, MY QUEEN?"

"Take me to the treasury please."

"AT ONCE."

A door opens from the stone in the wall ahead of me, and I jog in without questioning where I'm going. At this point, I trust my castle, and I follow the staircase downward until I reach a familiar doorframe and once more walk toward the massive doors of my treasury.

As I approach them, they open on their own, and I weave through the piles of gold, grabbing a coin while barely looking at the three suits of armor on my way past toward the small room in the back that Tucker first found.

Toward the pedestals that once held the Astor diaries.

The first Astor diary still remains on its pedestal, where I returned it once I was done. Now, I walk toward the second pedestal and set the page on top and set a single gold coin over it.

I won't lie, it's pretty badass to use real gold as a paperweight.

I look at the two pedestals with no diaries on them, and I'm more certain than ever that I need this information. Whatever is in those pages, it will make all the difference in the wars to come.

Because there will be wars—plural. That's what happens when people see power.

They want to take it for themselves.

And I will have to defend what's mine with blood, bone, and battle.

I head out into the main treasury room once again, but as I pass the other doorway that leads into the armory, I hesitate. I look over my shoulder as the rays of sunlight coming in from a nearby window glint across the metal barrel of several guns sitting on a table Tucker brought into the room.

I walk in, and to my surprise, I see three rows of new tables. It would seem that Tucker has been expanding his armory, most likely with the help of Drew and Jace combined.

He's probably not stealing them this time.

Probably.

I scan the nearby table and pick a standard handgun, nothing special but enough to get a job done. I grab a box of ammo, and I shove it in my pocket as I head back toward the door.

As I take the stairs, I wonder if this is a good move.

But I think it is.

"WHERE TO, MY QUEEN?" Ashgrave asks.

"Take me to Brett."

"RIGHT AWAY."

At the top of the stairwell, a door opens as I near, and I exit to the sound of knives hitting a dartboard. I chuckle under my breath. Brett's practicing again.

As I round the corner, I sure enough find him throwing knives at a large cork target on the other end of an empty room. With his back to me, he doesn't seem to notice me near him. In fact, the only other thing in the room is a small table beside him covered with throwing knives.

Without a word, I set the handgun on the table beside him, and only then does he see me. He flinches in surprise, dropping one of the knives and wisely not trying to catch it as it falls to the ground. He looks at me, his mouth slightly parted in surprise, but I don't say anything.

I don't need to.

In fact, I do what I never thought I would do to Brett Clarke.

I turn my back on him while he's armed, and I walk away.

"Thank you!" he shouts loudly after me, and yet again, I remain silent. All I do is leave and smirk in gratitude.

I won't lie. I'm proud of Brett and Jade both.

But I'm proud of my *men* the most.

CHAPTER THIRTY-SEVEN

As the day wears on, I simply close my eyes and lean against my balcony, enjoying the sun as it sets on the horizon. It's nice to have a moment of peace, a moment of quiet.

Behind me, Jace holds my shoulders and kisses the back of my head as we enjoy the silence together. I'm grateful for him, grateful for everything he is and everything he has pushed me to do and to be. I wouldn't be where I am without him, without his sway over my magic, without the way he pushes me to my limits, breaks them and helps me set new ones.

Jace Goodwin is a gift to me, and I'm grateful he's mine.

The door opens behind me, and I don't need to

look over my shoulder to recognize the voices of Drew and Levi as they enter, laughing about something I didn't catch.

I grin, closing my eyes as I lean back against Jace's hard chest. It's nice to see them getting along.

"There you are," Levi says, and I look around Jace as Levi and Drew join us on the balcony.

"You were looking for Jace, huh?" I ask, grinning.

Levi smirks. "You got me."

"I am quite pretty," Jace says, chuckling.

Drew laughs, clapping his friend on the back. "That's it, buddy. Stay modest."

"You're a hero, you know," Levi says, crossing his arms as he looks at me. "They're calling you 'the one who defeated Kinsley Vaer.'"

"Who's saying that?" I ask, quirking my eyebrow.

"Everyone," Drew says, rolling his eyes. "It's like we weren't even there, Rory."

I laugh. "You just need your recognition, huh, babe?"

"Guilty," he says, shrugging as he laughs.

"Well, it doesn't matter," I say, shrugging. "I didn't defeat her. I just delayed the big fight."

"Now who's being modest?" Jace pokes me hard in the side.

"I'm not," I say, chuckling.

That's just the way it is.

"You saved a lot of lives, Rory." Levi looks at me with pride. "At least be proud of that."

I smile warmly, and I'm not sure I would say it out loud, but I can accept that some people see me as a role model after all. It used to be me and my men against the world, but now there are others who need me too, and I have to live for them just as much as myself and my family.

"Hey, guys," Tucker shouts from down the hallway, his footsteps pounding on the ground as he gets nearer. "You've got to see this."

I look over my shoulder as he enters, holding up a plushie modeled after my dragon. For a moment, all I can do is stare at it in shock.

In unison, we all burst out laughing, and the spell is broken.

"Look, it even glimmers," Tucker says, turning it every which way as it softly glistens in the light.

"Oh my gods," I say, my face red and hot as I set my hand on my cheeks.

"I'm pretty sure that's copyright infringement," Drew says, shaking his head.

"Whatever," I say, dismissing the thought with the flick of my wrist. "I'm not going to stop them."

If people are selling plushies of me, that means

there's a demand for it, and the more people love me, the more good I can do.

"I have to say," Levi says with a nod toward the plushie, "that was some pretty impressive flying you did against Kinsley."

"Yeah, she might even get faster than you," Jace says, nudging the ice dragon next to him.

"I don't know about that," Levi says, laughing. "I mean come on guys, I have one use around here. Let me remain the fast and stealthy one." He looks at me and winks roguishly.

I grin, taking a few steps onto my balcony and hoisting myself onto the railing. "Why don't we find out?"

"Oh, Little Miss Cocky," Drew says, rolling up his sleeves. "And what do you propose we do?"

"I'll race you," I say, grinning at all of them. With that, I jump off the balcony and shift on the way down, the exhilarating rush of adrenaline burning through me as I shift into my dragon form. I effortlessly spread my wings long before I hit the ground and turn into the sky. As I look over my shoulder, my men fly after me, already shifted and racing to catch up.

"No fair," Tucker shouts, balling his hand into a fist as he stands on the balcony. "You guys got a head start." He darts back into the bedroom, and I know he's headed for his plane.

I chuckle, gold dust floating from my scales as my men slowly catch up.

I love them. I love this life.

And I absolutely *love* my dragon.

AUTHOR NOTES

Hey, babe!

This book was a thrilling ride that I did not want to end!

I couldn't write fast enough, getting out the heart-pounding action, reveling in the steamy love scene, and reacting with delight when Rory became the badass diamond dragon that the world needed to see. She's starting to accept her new role. Her place in this world. She's unique and destined to lead.

And right by her side (or on her shoulder) is Ashgrave, her evil butler. Ever vigilant and protective of his queen, even when she's away from the castle.

I mean, who *wouldn't* want to take him along?

Rory may be a reluctant queen, but when she's

faced with the damage and suffering Kinsley is causing, and a potential war that can kill thousands, she knows that she needs to step up and become a hero.

In *Reign of Dragons,* for the first time in her life, she defied her master.

In *Fate of Dragons,* she learned how to give up a bit of control. How to compromise.

In *Blood of Dragons,* she learned what it means to have family. To trust, to let down her guard to her inner circle, and grow as a person.

In *Age of Dragons,* Rory finally accepted who she is: a dragon, a warrior, and someone worthy of being loved.

In *Fall of Dragons,* Rory realizes she's not prey—she's a hunter, one who doesn't *need* the shadows to survive.

And in *Death of Dragons*, Rory steps up as a role model, learning to live not just for her close-knit family, but for others as well.

All while remaining her beautiful badass self, of course.

Once again, Tucker just melts my heart with his adorable charm and snarky quips. Our resident weapons expert finally gets a jet and is ready to fly with the dragons. Make no mistake, he's skilled with a plane and he uses it brilliantly to back up Rory when all hell breaks loose.

Drew loves Rory more than life itself, and it is touching to see her go out on a limb to try and keep him connected to his family, even when they're unworthy of him. She understands the importance of family ties, and she wants Drew to have a chance at it that she never got.

Jace is ready to be Rory's general. He knows that in order to defend her kingdom, he's going to need soldiers. He knows how to train Rory to fly and fight as a dragon and prepare her for what's to come.

And Levi, *swoon*! Even when he's silent next to Rory, the very look he gives her lets her know the depth of his passion and his fierce desire to protect her.

As for the universe of the Dragon Dojo Brotherhood? I loved how Rory met up with the Bosses without fear and outsmarted some of them. And there are other players edging their way onto the scene, but our badass babe refuses to be toyed with, manipulated, or captured. She bows to no one, and she puts her enemies on alert—mess with her and those under her protection, and she'll come for you.

They're finding out exactly who they're messing with.

Of course, I couldn't play in this world so much if you didn't love reading it. So, from the bottom of my heart, *thank you.* Thank you a million times over. If I ever get to meet you in person, I'm going to give you *such a big hug.*

You truly are such a gift to me!

I know you're probably chomping at the bit to learn what happens next. Now that Rory's uncovered Jade's attempt to create another crystal, will this be the turning point for the poor girl to redeem herself? And Milo—his fate looked grim in that revenge ring, but he humbled himself and the Fairfax Boss spared his life. Now, the question is if he's going to come back with an army, or if he'll go down another path and finally become his own man. We're still on the lookout for the other Astor Diaries, and the next orb to power up our evil butler.

Lucky Rory and her men are such brilliant fighters. They are stronger than ever as a close-knit family. Whatever lies ahead, they're ready.

Are you?

The next book will be available in six short weeks! That's right, babe, you can even order it *now.*

Make sure you **join the exclusive, fans-only Facebook group to get the latest release news & updates.**

Until next time, babe!

Keep on being your beautiful, badass self.

-Olivia

PS. Amazon won't tell you when the next Dragon Dojo Brotherhood book will come out, but there are several ways you can stay informed.

1) **Soar on over to the Facebook group, Olivia's secret club for cool ladies,** so we can hang out! I designed it *especially* for badass babes like you. Consider this as your invite! We talk about kickass heroines, gorgeous men, our favorite fantasy romances, and... did I mention pictures of *gorgeous men*?

2) **Follow me directly on Amazon**. To do this, **head to my profile** and click the Follow button beneath my picture. That will prompt Amazon to notify you when I release a new book. You'll just need to check your emails.

3) **You can join my mailing list by going to** https://wispvine.com/newsletter/olivia-ash-email-signup/. This lets me slide into your inbox and basically

means we become best friends. Yep, I'm pretty sure that's how it works.

Doing one of these or **all three** (for best results) is the best way to make sure you get an update every time a new volume of the *Dragon Dojo Brotherhood* series is released. Talk to you soon!

BOOKS BY OLIVIA ASH

Dragon Dojo Brotherhood

Reign of Dragons

Fate of Dragons

Blood of Dragons

Age of Dragons

Fall of Dragons

Death of Dragons

War of Dragons

Queen of Dragons

Myths of Dragons

Vessel of Dragons

Gods of Dragons

A Legend Among Dragons

Blackbriar Academy

The Trials of Blackbriar Academy

The Shadows of Blackbriar Academy

The Hex of Blackbriar Academy

The Blood Oath of Blackbriar Academy

The Battle of Blackbriar Academy

The Nighthelm Guardian Series

City of the Sleeping Gods

City of Fractured Souls

City of the Enchanted Queen

Demon Queen Saga

Princes of the Underworld

Wars of the Underworld

Sentinel Saga

By Dahlia Leigh and Olivia Ash

The Shadow Shifter

ABOUT THE AUTHOR

OLIVIA ASH

Olivia Ash spends her time dreaming up the perfect men to challenge, love, and protect her strong heroines (who actually don't need protecting at all). Her stories are meant to take you on a journey into the world of the characters and make you want to stay there.

Reviews are the best way to show Olivia that you care about her stories and want other people discover them. If you enjoyed this novel, please consider leaving a review at Amazon. Every review helps the author and she appreciates the time you take to write them.

Made in the USA
San Bernardino, CA
13 July 2020